# THE NEW JERUSALEM

*God Will Wipe Away Every Tear*

BORTOLAZZO
Publishing

## A Last Days Trilogy

# THE NEW JERUSALEM
*God Will Wipe Away Every Tear*

### PAUL BORTOLAZZO
~ Author of *'Til Eternity*

*The New Jerusalem*
© 2011 Paul Bortolazzo
**Published by Bortolazzo Publishing LLC**
P.O. Box 241915
Montgomery, Alabama 36124
bortjenny@juno.com
www.paulbortolazzo.com

All scripture quotations are taken from The New King James Version of the Bible (NKJV), copyright © 1992 by Thomas Nelson, Inc. Used by permission.

Cover design by Elizabeth E. Little  http://hyliian.deviantart.com
Interior design by The Author's Mentor™, Ellen C. Maze
www.ellencmaze.com

PRINTED IN THE UNITED STATES OF AMERICA

# THEN, I JOHN SAW THE HOLY CITY,

*New Jerusalem, coming down out of heaven from God, prepared as a bride adorned for her husband... 'Come, I will show you the bride, the Lamb's wife.' And he carried me away in the Spirit to a great and high mountain, and showed me the great city, the holy Jerusalem, descending out of heaven from God."*

*Revelation 21:2, 9b-10*

# DEDICATION

This story is dedicated to Christians who will persevere 'til the first day of Christ's reign over the nations. This day will begin when an angel casts the Devil into the bottomless pit for a thousand years. Then judgment will be committed to the twelve apostles seated upon their thrones. After this, Christians martyred by the Beast will be resurrected and receive their glorified bodies. Then everyone will see the Lamb of God descending with His bride inside the holy Jerusalem to a new earth. Surely, this will be a day to remember throughout all eternity!

# TABLE OF CONTENTS

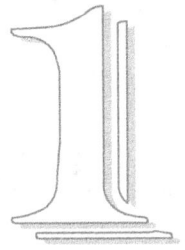

# THE WISE SHALL UNDERSTAND

"Many shall be purified, made white, and refined,
but the wicked shall do wickedly; and none of the wicked
shall understand, but the wise shall understand."
Daniel 12:10

The dampness of the early morning hour didn't seem to matter. Everyone was asleep but Greg Hudson. Standing watch by the mouth of the cave the former pastor was feeling sick to his stomach. God's final wrath could erupt at any moment. From behind he could hear her steps in the gritty dirt.

"Everything okay, Greg?"

"What are you doing up, Reenie?"

"Too much stuff to think about."

"Like what?"

"Like my mission. The Q Squad prayed about it. The Holy Spirit gave us a green light. But we never discussed what I'm supposed to do. I have no clue what God wants."

"I was waiting to talk to you about it. We really can't leave this cave before the first bowl is poured out. 1 It's going to get real ugly with those having the mark of the beast."

"How is that?"

"Remember the stings after the fifth trumpet?"

"The nightmares I had about them were horrible."

"The pain from the sores of the first bowl will be worse." 2

Shaking her head, she muttered back, "What a time to be living."

"Has anyone told you about the Vineyard?"

"Emma did. Isn't it the resister camp you created?"

"It was miraculous how the Holy Spirit led me to the Blue Ridge Mountains. Most of the kids we rescued were sent there. I've been praying for them. They may need our help."

"You think my mission is connected to the Vineyard?"

"Don't know for sure. Has the Holy Spirit shown you anything?"

"At first, I saw children crying for mercy. Now when I pray, I see a mysterious stranger in hiding. He's definitely waiting for someone. Someone he has never met."

"Is he waiting for you?"

Shrugging her shoulders she sat down beside him on a large rock.

"Greg, remember when Bret rushed me to the Gulf Shores Emergency Room?"

"Sure do, Death Angel is history; what a praise report!"

"I never told anybody but an angel visited me in my room."

"You mean at the ER?"

"I was pretty much out of it. It was standing at the end of my bed. This messenger was sent to explain my mission. I missed most of it."

"What a confirmation. You know, Reenie, rushing into this calling doesn't sound too appealing right now. The Holy Spirit will tell us when. We can't achieve what God desires through our own wisdom.

"Ain't it a trip understanding it all?"

Looking into the darkness of the Alabama hills, the former pastor knew what was coming. The sun would be up soon.

"Miracle Girl, my mother once told me the darkest hour is just before dawn. In a few weeks this Christ-rejecting world will be completely demolished. The closer we edge toward Armageddon, the darker God's wrath will become. We need to be discerning; blasphemers may try and pull us into their prison. Daniel warned us of this time of wrath. 'Many shall be purified, made white, and refined, but the wicked shall do wickedly; and none of the wicked shall understand, but the wise shall understand.'" 3

"But my vision of these children is so overwhelming!"

"Have you ever read how Moses dealt with the oppression by the Egyptians? At first, he thought he could deliver his people by himself. He even killed an Egyptian trying." 4

"God sent him to tend sheep for forty years! Talk about discouraging."

"Moses asked who am I that I should bring the children of Israel out of Egypt? He must have felt pretty unworthy. Even though his vision for his people was correct, God Almighty had to teach Moses many things. I AM WHO I AM would eventually send a mighty deliverer to Egypt." 5

"God wants me to be a deliverer? Yeah, uh huh, right."

"It's clear your mission is linked to what God has taught you these past two years. If you're willing, Reenie, God can make it happen."

"C'mon, Greg, why didn't the Holy Spirit pick you?"

"He has. Each member of the Q Squad has been called to protect you. We're all Watchmen; our role is just different than yours."

"So how can I know what God wants? This is too scary."

"Sometimes God wants us to make the decision to obey even before we know what His will is. Paul wrote, 'For we are His workmanship created in Christ Jesus for good works, which God prepared beforehand that we should walk in them.'" 6

"You mean God directs us in works He has already prepared?"

"Only He sees how your mission fits together."

"I guess the stakes are kinda high, huh?"

"The seventh trumpet has sounded. Those who survive God's final wrath, the seven bowls, will worship the Lord during His thousand year reign over the nations." 7

"To see Jesus strip Satan of his power yesterday was so cool." 8

"On Mount Zion for all to see," winked Greg. 9

"So how much time do we have left?"

He paused reflecting on the magnitude of his answer.

"Twenty-five days from now, during the supper of the great God, the Word of God will appear in heaven with His angelic armies. 10 Forty five days later; the Lamb of God will descend from heaven with His bride inside the Holy Jerusalem." 11

"This prophecy stuff can sort of play with your mind, can't it?"

"Miracle girl, on the first day of Christ's reign over the nations this foursquare city will hover over the Temple of the Lord."

"Is this the last event of His second coming?"

"Yep, the Lord will fill the Temple with His Shekinah glory." 12

"Wow, the Lamb is coming back with His spotless bride." 13

Gazing into the black Alabama hills, Greg gratefully replied, "His wife has made herself ready." 14

"So when will Jesus return to heaven and tie the knot?"

"As soon as He splits the Mount of Olives and hides His remnant." 15

"You mean any time now?"

# THE MOUNT OF OLIVES

"And in that day His feet will stand on the Mount of Olives, Which faces
Jerusalem on the east. And the Mount of Olives shall be split in two..."
Zechariah 14:4

The German Dove was out of store bought liquor. No one seemed to
care; the homemade beer and moonshine was good enough. The
mysterious leader in Jerusalem had just shocked the world again.
Standing atop the Mount of Olives, He raised His hands to pray. The
ensuing explosion rocked the ground beneath their feet as a cloud of
dust engulfed His remnant. In the darkness of the morning this
popular pub was jammed with customers seeking some sort of
feedback. Everyone could feel the tension at the end of the bar. While
cleaning glass mugs the bartender kept one eye on his shotgun
underneath the counter.

Pointing his finger in the doctor's face, the logger shouted,
"T'was nothing supernatural about it. Ain't no way in China this fake
is representing God."

"The Mount of Olives has just been spilt," chided the rotund
physician. "This leader and His followers are gone."

"Who gives a lick," sassed the bartender.

"Have you forgotten about the two Witnesses? They were left
hanging for over an hour."

"Doc, you should stick to practicing medicine," slurred the
drunken logger. "I've seen things this week no one would believe. You
hear me?"

"There's no debating it. Last Sunday the two Witnesses were dead. Somehow this leader breathed life into them on Wednesday. Now He has rescued His followers. It's a no brainer."

"What of it, Doc? Are you saying the plans the NWC has for our world are bogus? Like I said seeing is believing; I should know."

"Tell us what you saw?" bated one of his buddies.

"Aw, he's just showing off," scoffed another.

"Whatever he saw," taunted the cocky doctor, "it's gone by now."

They were pushing the right buttons. The spirit of Pride was desperately trying to control its subject. Sensing his agitation, the demon prompted the logger to step outside for a smoke. Slamming the front door behind him, it took everything within him to walk away. The drunk could easily hear their laughter from the jammed parking lot.

In the very back of the pub sat a stranger dressed in brown and green army fatigues. His stoic expression never changed as he finished off an ice cold beer. They were still laughing when he walked out.

The logger's trek down the small rocky hill was rough. A couple times he stumbled over some thick brush. Arriving at his truck, he vainly tried to light his cigar three times. He didn't notice the silhouette to his left.

"Need a light?"

Leaning forward he clumsily jabbed his cigar in his mouth.

"Must be hard trying to explain something no one believes in?"

"Yeah, it really blew my mind when I saw them."

"Saw who?"

Looking down, he rubbed some ashes from his cigar into the red clay with his boot.

"I don't know you, ah, you from Dahlonega?"

"Everyone calls me Lenard."

Blowing tiny circles of smoke, he bragged, "It was quite a crowd, must be sure-fire resisters, probably worth a heap for anyone turning them in."

"What are you waiting for?"

"I ain't interested."

"A lot of kids, huh?"

"Musta been a couple thousand. If the NWC finds them, you gotta figure there are others."

"So where is this camp?"

"Who wants to know?"

"Downright shame to see them executed for refusing to register."

"Naw, no way in Hades agents will ever bust this hideaway."

Watching for any witnesses, he reached underneath his jacket. Pointing the revolver in the logger's face he pulled back the trigger.

"Turn around and raise your hands."

"Hey, I was just running my mouth. I didn't mean nothing by it."

Pressing the barrel against the back of his neck he paused.

"I'm only going to ask you one time."

"I don't want no trouble. What'd ya wanna know?"

"Tell me the location of this resister camp."

"Well, uh, there ain't any roads..."

"Just give me the general vicinity."

"You ever hear of Black Rock Mountain?"

"Yeah, I know it."

"Are you a NWC bounty hunter?"

"If you care about the safety of your family, you best forget we ever had this conversation."

"I won't say nothing mister, I promise."

Ducking behind the logger's truck, the mysterious stranger disappeared.

They were waiting at a red light when the explosion from the Mount of Olives sent shivers through Jerusalem. The terror was hard to imagine. Aaron and Johanna Glazer found themselves sprinting through the swarming streets. Their destination was a small militia camp hidden deep within the Judean hills. These soldiers had not heard from their Commander in three days.

"It's Matthias alright," reported the lookout. "His daughter is with him. I don't see Miriam."

"This could be a trap by the NWC. Be ready to hide them."

The soldiers cheered as Aaron and Johanna strode through the camp side by side. Such loyalty had come with a high price. Matthias had always been there for his men, for their families, for his country. Even so, this recent explosion needed to be explained. Who was this mysterious leader who had come to Jerusalem? The soul searching among these Israeli freedom fighters was no secret. This bizarre parade of events began right after Joshua Kayin had the infamous two Witnesses killed. A few hours later, a man wearing a robe dipped in blood was seen praying with believers in the Jordanian wilderness. 1 Two days later, a multitude via the Highway of Holiness followed Him into Jerusalem. 2 The next day, the two Witnesses rose from the dead. 3 On Thursday; He led a remnant to the Temple Mount during the Feast of Tabernacles. 4 Now, on a cloudy Friday afternoon this mysterious leader somehow splits the Mount of Olives. 5

"Welcome back Commander Glazer," greeted his second in command. "We thought we had lost you."

He nervously saluted his officers. The relentless pain of war had strangely molded these men into a close-knit family; a fraternity willing to die for Israel. Tragically, they would also take a life. The spiritual warfare Miriam warned Aaron of was painfully underway. His heart was pounding nails. With so much blood already shed, he doubted God could ever change their hearts. Aaron hastily ordered his militia to be assembled.

"I'll see to it right away Commander."

"My daughter and I will be waiting in my office."

As they walked through the compound, Johanna caught a glimpse of several cuffed Jordanian mercenaries filing into a barbwire cell. Two of them looked no more than sixteen.

Once inside his office, Aaron rushed to his desk and pulled out a bottle of whiskey. He knew his men were talking. They could sense something wasn't right.

"Daddy what's up with that?"

"Honey, my nerves are shot. I need a drink."

"Not anymore! You're a new creature in Christ. Whiskey can't defeat these attacks from the enemy; only the Holy Spirit can. God Almighty has opened a door for you to witness eternal life through Yeshua. This is your calling to be a Watchman to our people. Your dreams for Israel, everything you have sacrificed, suffered for, will be measured by what you are about to share."

"I don't think I can do it," whispered the spirit of Lying in his ear.

"I don't think I can do it, Johanna."

"They won't listen to me," hissed the demon.

"They won't listen to me."

"It's too late, Yeshua is gone."

"Johanna, it's too late, Yeshua is gone."

Closing her eyes the American teenager boldly prayed, "Lord, we need Your discernment. May Your mighty presence enter this compound. By the power of Yeshua, I rebuke any demonic assignments coming against us. Father, You have given us a divine opportunity to share the gospel with over five hundred soldiers. No one can come to Yeshua unless drawn by You. 6 We ask for the salvation of every soldier. Let my Daddy understand the calling You have placed upon his life. May You give me a word powerful enough to open his spiritual eyes. "

"Johanna, I'm afraid this is way too much for me."

"Here is our answer." Opening her bible she read, "'I have set Watchmen on your walls, O Jerusalem; they shall never hold their peace day or night. You who make mention of the Lord, do not keep silent and give Him no rest till he establishes and till He makes Jerusalem a praise in the earth.'" 7

"Is this passage for me?"

"The Spirit of God just gave it to me. There's more. 'Indeed the Lord has proclaimed to the end of the world: "Say to the daughter of Zion, 'Surely your salvation is coming; Behold His reward is with Him, and His work before Him. And they shall call them The Holy People, The Redeemed of the Lord; and you shall be called Sought Out, A City Not Forsaken.'" 8

"What does this mean, honey?"

"Yeshua has redeemed His people. During His thousand year reign He will make Jerusalem a praise among the nations. Look how many times God prepared His people to hear the truth but His messengers refused to speak. The Holy Spirit will give you the words. I know your soldiers will respond. Be a Watchman, Daddy, for the glory of God."

"What makes you think I can convince them? I'm good at giving orders; not pleading for someone's salvation. What were we thinking when we left your mother? We were so naïve!"

"Only God can save a soul for eternity. Last night, during the Feast of Tabernacles, the Holy Spirit drew you to the Temple Mount. He used little Jeremiah to answer your questions. You saw the faith of this Israeli boy who lost everything dear to him; yet he remained faithful. Daddy, we can do no less. Salvation isn't by the insight of man; it's supernatural!"

"Come," echoed through his spirit.

Such love, such gentleness, as the radiant Christ nodded. The judgment seat of the saints was underway. 9 Scenes from the past were appearing in the minds of those being judged. During these flashbacks each person would give an account of what they did in the body. From the moment the Holy Spirit entered their soul, every opportunity, every sacrifice, every idle word, would be judged. Once the fire was applied, every work not of God would burn up. Only glistening jewels for His glory would endure His righteous judgment.

Miraculously, everyone in heaven could see this event flashing before the Bema Seat. A pastor from a small town in southeastern Alabama was praying for believers to prepare themselves to overcome the future persecution by the Beast. Kneeling on the floor of his study, he was weeping over their spiritual blindness. The Father wanted the body of Christ to acknowledge its complacency; its idolatry. God desired a human voice. A herald not intimidated by the fear of man; a Watchman remaining faithful no matter what the consequences. Jesus once warned believers, "'Not everyone who says to Me, 'Lord, Lord,' shall enter the kingdom of heaven, but he who does the will of My Father in heaven.'" 10

Mark Bishop was speechless as he looked into the loving eyes of his Lord and Savior. His witness against the powers of darkness was his Father's will. The persecution he suffered was nothing compared to the jewels left at His feet. The New Jerusalem was waiting.

Speaking into his spirit, the Son joyfully announced, "'Well done, My good and faithful servant... Come, you blessed of My Father, inherit the kingdom prepared from the foundation of the world.'" 11

Just south of the cave's entrance, Commander Doyle Mercer and SWAT team #1 watched from behind a massive rock formation. Equipped with night goggles, #2 was positioned to the west, #3 to the north. Each team understood their new directive. After Reenie Ann Tucker was apprehended, there were to be no witnesses.

"Someone just moved. Their lookout may have spotted us."

"Get them!" seethed Doyle.

Within seconds, nine commandos converged on the cave.

"I never saw Kurt or Emma," panted an out of breath Reenie.

"They must be with Jake," wheezed Greg. "Keep moving; the other tunnels are shorter. They'll meet us at our van."

Entering the cave, a disgusted Doyle barked, "Where are they?"

"If they have spotted us they could be hiding in these tunnels."

"How many were there?"

"Three, Sir. We don't know how long these tunnels are or where they end up. It's possible they could escape before we reach them. May I send two of my men to guard the exit road?"

"Negative! Get your butts down these tunnels. They can't be far."

# MAKE YOUR ELECTION SURE

"Therefore, brethren, be even more diligent to make your call and election sure, for if you do these things you will never stumble; for so an entrance will be supplied to you abundantly into the everlasting kingdom of our Lord and Savior Jesus Christ."
II Peter 1:10-11

The deafening applause from the heavenly host rang out as the final saint entered. She had always dreamed of this moment. There were no words as she crossed over the threshold into eternity. 1 Waiting inside the Holy City was the glorious bride to be. Rushing into their arms she worshipped the Lord. The judgment seat of Christ was over! 2

Hidden away in the Blue Ridge Mountains, the children's camp was buzzing with the news. In the past seventy-two hours, over nine hundred resisters were rescued. The leadership of the Vineyard had never taken such a risk. Its population would soon exceed five thousand. The day of the Lord was almost over. The recent splitting of the Mount of Olives only increased their anticipation.

"How ya doing, campers?" grinned the muscular staff member.

Cody Joe Parish was in charge of orientation for all children under sixteen. The twenty-one year old had just checked in almost two hundred kids. He was rescued a year ago just outside Charleston, South Carolina. The massive sting by agents over the coastal city achieved its objective. Christian families in hiding scattered under the strain of the relentless dragnet. Cody's mother and sister were arrested and executed for illegally bartering drinking water. Three weeks later, a Watchman spotted the ex-football star scrounging from a garbage bin outside a grocery store. Dressed in blue jeans, a black Gamecock football jersey, and a bright orange Parka; his dirty blonde hair covered his eyebrows. The once rugged running back looked weak, almost frail looking. After some coaxing, Cody accepted an offer to hide in a Christian camp in the mountains of northern Georgia.

"Praise God, you guys are doing great! Phase one of your orientation is over. This morning we will learn phase two. Now does anyone need any help on where to go?"

Several hands nervously slipped into the air.

"No problem; we've covered a lot of stuff. Tell you what, after breakfast anyone needing assistance can see me or our intake supervisor, Twanna Evers. Tee, where are you?"

Waving from the back of the crowd, Cody couldn't miss her beautiful smile. She was barely five feet tall and had to stand on her tiptoes just to be seen. The daughter of a black Baptist preacher, Twanna Paquita Evers made her initial escape from agents after the opening of the fifth seal. Holding her clipboard high above her head, she was ready to go to work.

Over their animated whispering, Cody announced, "Everyone listen up. Let's always remember how miraculously God got you here. He will never leave you nor forsake you. I know you all have a lot of questions about your future. Today, each of you will be assigned your own Bible study group. Be assured, the Holy Spirit will lead each of us as we prepare for the thousand year reign of Christ!"

Carefully weaving between kids, Tee stood by his side. Seeing their panicky faces, the young Watchman knew he couldn't wait any longer.

"Anyone have any questions."

To Cody's left, an anxious teenage girl raised her hand.

"When is the next judgment?"

"Any time now the plague of the first bowl will be poured out. Any person who worshiped Joshua Kayin, his image, or received his mark, will receive a foul sore."

The weeping was a given. Most of these campers had already lost family and friends to the deception of the Beast. Others were struggling with not knowing where their unregistered family members were. Cody and Twanna had conducted many orientations; but never one like this. The countdown to the supper of the great God was underway. 3

A boy from Marietta, Georgia yelled back, "So when is Jesus coming back?"

A hopeful Tee replied, "The Beast killed the two Witnesses last Saturday. We know from scripture the Abomination of Desolation will become desolate thirty days later at the battle of Armageddon. 4 This is when the Word of God will cast the Beast and his False Prophet into the lake of fire. We have to wait twenty-four more days."

"This earth is trashed! How can Jesus rule in this mess?"

"What about His bride?" another added. "Where will they be?"

As Cody fielded their questions, Twanna continued to pray. They knew what was at stake. Their calling from God was before them. Someone had to protect these little ones from the last seven plagues. 5

A sea of glass mingled with fire surrounded the Temple, saints victorious over the Beast were playing harps and singing.

"'...Great and marvelous are Your works, Lord God Almighty. Just and true are Your ways, O King of the saints. Who shall not fear You, O Lord, and glorify Your name? For You alone are holy. For all the nations shall come and worship before You, for Your judgments have been manifested.'" 6

Before the Father and the Lamb of God, the doors opened. Inside the Temple, amidst lightening and hail, was the Ark of His Covenant. 7 As a heavenly host watched in awe, seven angels emerged with golden bands girded across their chests. 8 They were dressed in pure bright linen.

Stepping forward one of the four living creatures gave each angel a shallow golden bowl. 9 Each was full of the wrath of God. Instantly the Temple was engulfed with smoke coming from the glory of God. Everyone understood. No one would be able to enter the Temple until all seven plagues from these angels were poured out upon the wicked. 10

# First Bowl: Loathsome Sores

"So the first went and poured out his bowl upon the earth, and a
foul and loathsome sore came upon the men who had the mark of
the beast and those who worshiped his image."
Revelation 16:2

A multitude of angels bowed. This solemn moment reflected their absolute reverence. The twenty-four elders were laid out in passionate prayer. Poised above the Temple of God were the four living creatures.

From the smoke inside the Temple, a loud voice announced, "'...Go and pour out the bowls of the wrath of God on the earth.'" 1

Immediately an angel emptied out the plague from the first bowl. Reaching earth this angelic messenger cried out, "Woe to those who worshipped the Beast, his image, or received his mark. Yea, foul and loathsome sores have gone forth in the fierceness of Almighty God." 2

Greg could see the panic in her eyes.

"Just ten more yards, Reenie. The exit is covered with brush. When we reach the van, remove the brush and join me as quick as you can."

"Are we leaving?"

"We'll pick up the boys and Emma on the way out."

"What if they don't make it?"

"Your mission is top priority!"

"We just can't leave them."

"Reenie, we've already gone over this."

The slender teenager reluctantly agreed as Greg slid head first through a dug out hole beside their van. After slipping through she jumped up and started dragging branches away from the exit.

"That's enough," whispered Greg.

Sliding through the hole his gun never left her back.

"Hold it, Tucker! Put your hands behind your head and get on your knees. Hudson, if you start the engine she gets two bullets. Now get out with your hands high."

"Do what he says, Reenie," Greg sadly muttered.

Opening his cell phone the Security Force Commander snapped, "Just shut up and listen. I've got Hudson and Tucker at the end of my tunnel. That's right; the others are your responsibility... I don't care who does it... After your assignment is over, have all three teams return to our command post... Yes, I'll meet you ahhhhhh!"

All he could do was squirm in the dirt as a purple sore spread up his face. The other shrieks echoing through the tunnels were daunting.

After grabbing Doyle's revolver Greg silently thanked the Lord.

"Get up, you're coming with us!"

The beleaguered agent offered no resistance. After handcuffing his wrists to the backseat armrest, the former pastor drove the van out of the mouth of the cave onto a steep narrow road.

"You'll never get away!" cursed Doyle.

"We'll be long gone before your men can backtrack through these tunnels. My only concern is the road out of here. Tell us, Commander, you wouldn't be stupid enough to use all your men for our capture?"

"As if it matters.... you're a marked man. My men won't stop until they see you dead!"

His left eye was already infected as yellow puss oozed from his purple sore. Leaning over he wiped his itchy sore on the backseat.

"His sore really stinks."

"Can you tape his mouth? We can't risk any unexpected noises."

Discreetly Reenie lifted a roll of tape from Doyle's belt.

"Okay, he won't be talking now. Any sign of the Q?"

"They can't be far. We either see them in the next minute or we're out of here."

Closing her eyes, the Miracle Girl urgently prayed, "Father, in the name of Your Son, Jesus, somehow alert Jake, Emma, and Kurt. We want Your perfect will; only Your perfect will."

The Chicago newsroom was shrouded in darkness. Channel 6 had just lost its power. Slouched behind the massive glass desk, Wes Mackish lit another cigarette. The oversized TV screen was blank; the cameras idle. For this veteran producer, it was a devastating defeat.

"Why God?" he boldly cursed. "The suffering from these sores is unimaginable! And for what?"

"Wes, we need to talk!"

"I'm over here by camera one."

It took a while for his disoriented assistant to ease down the stairs leading to the abandoned set. Wes was his hero. For every trial thrust at their station in the past seven years; his boss always had an answer. Time and again, this tireless producer would inspire his staff to keep the news going. No one could motivate like Wes Mackish, until now.

"Wes, we're still getting emails, what's going on?"

"Officially or unofficially," he bitterly replied.

"Are we going on the air tonight?"

"What do you think?"

"Even if we don't, Natalie still has an interview with the top dog from the NWC Emergency Alert System. Is she coming in?"

"Doubt it. She's out investigating some right wing Christian sect. I don't know where she is."

"Did you approve her assignment?"

"Can't you see what's happened? We're finished!"

"Wes, there are several stations still on the air. Some are broadcasting pictures of the sores. Have you been infected?"

"Not yet."

"My wife has. It's spreading up her arm. I told her I'd take the kids for a while. They're in my office. What do you want me to do?"

"Any updates?"

"These sores are hideous; a lot worse than last year's stings. My doctor believes the infection rate this time will be much higher because of the puss. The NWC says it's too early to make any assessment of how bad it will be."

"You mean too late. While everyone was debating whether the two Witnesses were dead, this so called miracle worker somehow splits the Mount of Olives and disappears with those following Him. Nate believes he might be the Messiah."

"You sure, boss? That's a bit much to swallow, even for Natalie."

"I always felt our world would be okay. When the super powers backed Kayin's crusade against terrorism everything turned around. Once the wars stopped, it wasn't long before the famines did too."

"For a while we had such peace and safety." 3

"So why can't we rid ourselves from these curses?"

"Wes, have you ever read the Book of Revelation?"

"When I was in college; it was way over my head."

"Do you remember the seven bowl judgments?"

"My priest believes the events in Revelation are symbolic of the fight between good and evil."

"Just minutes ago, the anchor from Channel 12 actually read Revelation 16:1-2 on the air. This passage says anyone who has the mark of the beast will receive a foul sore."

"Getting pretty brave, aren't they?"

"Not everyone is infected; seems the resisters are immune."

"Do you believe it?"

"Oh, you know how interpretations are. Anyone can make the scriptures say whatever they want. No one really knows what's happening. We just have to hold on and wait it out."

"That's just what I was thinking," winced the weary producer. "You never know; the world could get better almost overnight."

Hiding in a cave resting several feet above the narrow winding road, the frightened threesome sat perfectly still. The tire tracks in the moist dirt were fresh. It didn't take long for Jake to figure out what really happened.

"Do you think we should make a run for it?"

"No, Kurt, I'm afraid that's what they want."

"Who are you talking about?"

"Emma, you were the last one out. Did you get a look at them?"

"I heard their screams but never saw them....you thinking agents?"

"No way!" blurted her little brother. "Nobody is searching for resisters this late in the game?"

"Maybe they're friends of Death Angel?"

"Are you joking, Jake? What friends did Cassandra ever have? All she cared about was her satanic charade."

"Kurt, don't ever underestimate the power of revenge. Satan has gotten a lot of mileage out of that sin."

"But why would agents come after us way out here?"

The discerning Watchman calmly replied, "One moment they're practically on top of us; then they're gone. To me our getaway was a bit too easy."

"You mean they're after Miracle Girl? Could these agents be the dark figures you saw in your vision?"

"Yeah and this is just the beginning."

"Do you think Greg and Reenie got away in our van?"

"Only if it's bugged, agents use pretty sophisticated stuff. They could've picked up anything we said. If Greg and Reenie are heading for the Vineyard, they could be in for a big surprise when they arrive."

"C'mon, we have to warn them."

"Easy, Kurt, we need to pray for direction before we move out."

"This makes no sense. Why do they want Reenie so bad?"

"Emma, Cassandra warned there would be others. We aren't talking flesh and blood. If our Miracle Girl expects to quench the fiery darts from these demons she had better be wearing her shield of faith." 4

While Kurt watched, Emma and Jake retreated into the darkness of the cave to intercede. It wasn't long before their answer came.

"Praise God, I just received a word of knowledge." 5

"What is the Holy Spirit saying?" whispered Emma.

A grateful Jake replied, "Greg and Reenie got away."

Eyeing the target Kurt waved for them to come and see. A black SWAT truck was coasting down the narrow dirt road. The threesome watched as it faded out-of-site. They were giving up.

The abrupt knock on his office door startled the uneasy leader.

"Commander, your men are ready."

All eyes were on him as he reached the makeshift platform resting beneath the huge tent. These soldiers believed in the visionary Aaron Phinehas Glazer. Israel would soon be attacked by the largest army ever assembled. They were confident their leader would put everything in proper perspective. There was no turning back now.

To his left, wearing an Israeli army jacket, sat his confident daughter. Johanna's curly brown hair fell comfortably over her shoulders. She winked when their eyes met. He knew how much she loved him. God had used her to melt away the mask Satan had shaped in his life. This time, there could be no deception, no lying, and no game playing. While studying their faces he prayed for strength. He thought he was ready.

"His name is Jeremiah; he's ten years old. His entire family is dead. I met him at the base of Mount Moriah during the Feast of Tabernacles. Jeremiah had come to see a man. Not just any man. This young boy was searching for the Messiah. Of course, this scenario doesn't sound too extreme for a Jew living in Jerusalem in the latter days, now does it?"

Hushed sharing among his soldiers followed. Soon enemy tanks would be attacking their borders. Their Commander's speech was supposed to be a moving farewell; no regrets.

"It's strange how Jeremiah's perspective is so radically different than ours. I think I know why. When we were young, most of us lost loved ones at the hands of Muslim terrorists. Losing our innocence at such an early age can twist the way we look at life. Only God can discern the heartache of such pain. The older I got; the more cynical I became. It's a raw nerve most of us have never addressed. Yeshua said, 'Let the children come to Me, and do not forbid them; for of such is the kingdom of God. Assuredly, I say to you, whoever does not receive the kingdom of God as a little child will by no means enter in.'" 6

His second in command boldly inquired, "Matthias, what does this boy have to do with us?"

"It took a child of Abraham to show me the truth. He was looking for something beyond this world. Jeremiah was searching for a heavenly city; one not detected by our senses."

"Sir, how can dreaming about a city in heaven help us? Yesterday we captured several Jordanian soldiers. There is a possibility we can exchange them for some of our men. The Jordanian leadership will not negotiate with anyone but you."

Their infamous leader was wavering. During the Feast of Ingathering Aaron received the indwelling of the Holy Spirit. At first, he felt a powerful surge of forgiveness; followed by a soothing peace. A release from the painful scars of his past was in progress. Then a burden for his men gripped his heart. Another supernatural empowering was now vying for his attention.

"Listen up! I have something to share more important than surviving this conflict. As a group, we've experienced terror no human should ever witness. My sister was raped and killed by Syrian soldiers when I was nine years old. When I was twelve, my best friend was blown up by a Palestinian bomber. As a young man my father died in my arms after being gunned down by a Jordanian terrorist. We've all tasted the bitter cup of such pain. In a strange way it has brought us together like family. Someone had to defend our people from such horrendous assaults. It was Satan who pitted the sons of Ishmael against the sons of Isaac. 7 Only God knows the supposed justice of a war where innocent people die. I now know our thirst for blood, our desire for revenge, will never be satisfied. Not with a heart that refuses to forgive!"

"Why should we? Their Intifada will not stop until every Jew is dead. Surely, God weeps over the ongoing pain of His people?"

"Tell me," countered Aaron, "who are His people? Yeshua warned, 'And I say to you that many will come from the east and west, and sit down with Abraham, Isaac, and Jacob in the kingdom of heaven. But the sons of the kingdom will be cast out into outer darkness. There will be weeping and gnashing of teeth.'" 8

"Who are the sons cast out into outer darkness?"

Staring at the officers lining the wall to his left, Aaron read, "'Therefore whoever confesses Me before men, him I will also confess before My Father who is in heaven. But whoever denies Me before men, him I will also deny him before My Father who is in heaven.'" 9

Johanna slipped into an adjacent room as soon as she felt their evil presence. She knew these demons would not sit by idly. Falling on her knees she began praying in the Spirit for her father. She had never experienced such a deep groaning of intersession.

Over the loud murmuring Aaron motioned for quiet.

"Any Jew or Gentile can ask Yeshua for forgiveness of their sins. That's right; I have become a believer in the one true God, the Father, the Son, and the Holy Spirit. 10 Hear me out. Being a dedicated Jew will not guarantee you eternal life. The only way to enter the kingdom of heaven is by believing in Yeshua, the only begotten Son of God." 11

"How can you believe such a lie?" demanded an irate soldier.

"Not in my lifetime!" hollered another. "You can't make us listen to such nonsense!"

Matthias paused as officers scurried down the aisles ordering their men to be silent. Their jeering was filled with bitterness. To accept such propaganda was unthinkable. Not now; not with their beloved Israel hanging in the balance.

"What do you want me to say; surely not another Masada? Maybe we should nuke every country refusing to believe the way we do? Or take two lives for every one we lose?"

"Commander Glazer, you more than anyone know the cancer we're facing. How many more Jews must die before there is a lasting peace?"

"There won't be any real peace until the Prince of Peace restores the kingdom of Israel. 12 Before this is achieved two out of three from Israel will die during the day of the Lord."

"That's insane; we are His chosen people!"

"Zechariah prophesied of our day, 'And it shall come to pass in all the land, says the Lord, that two-thirds in it shall be cut off and die, but one-third shall be left in it: I will bring the one-third through the fire, will refine them as silver is refined, and test them as gold is tested.'" 13

"So what will happen to those who live?"

"The prophet predicted, 'They will call on My name, and I will answer them. I will say, 'This is my people'; and each one will say, The Lord is my God.'" 14

"Matthias, why promote such a death warrant for our people?"

"Do you really want the truth? Maybe a timetable when armies from the nations will merge as one? Or perhaps when Iran will launch their warheads against us?"

Their blatant approval to his sarcasm was shocking. How could he reach such resolute fighters; a group ready to die for their people?

In his mind he heard, "The truth shall set them free."

Without any hesitation Aaron confessed, "The assault from our enemies at Har-Magedon will come by the end of this month."

"Commander, will this war be worse than the Jehoshaphat invasion?"

"Jehoshaphat is vastly different than Har-Magedon. Whereas our enemies during the Jehoshaphat invasion attacked us in a valley, Har-Magedon will begin on the plains of Esdraelon, eventually covering our entire country. The timing is also different. The Jehoshaphat assault took place two years ago, just before The Feast of Trumpets. A week ago, Kayin had the two Witnesses executed on the Day of Atonement. Make no mistake; thirty days from their death our enemies will attack us on the great day of God Almighty. We all witnessed the judgment of the surrounding nations in the Valley of Jehoshaphat. 15 At Har-Magedon, the armies of the world will be destroyed!"

"Matthias, why have our allies deserted us?" pleaded a teenager. "In our last hour will we stand alone?"

"It was no coincidence our enemies were drawn into the Valley of Jehoshaphat just prior to Zikhron Teruah. Did not God deliver us? We were not alone then and we won't be at Har-Magedon."

"How can you dismiss the savage extermination of our people?" implored another officer. "Exactly how has God Almighty protected us since Joshua Kayin defiled our Temple?"

Stepping off the platform, he coolly replied, "From the day the NWC took control of Jerusalem, the God of Abraham, Isaac, and Jacob has supernaturally protected a remnant of believers from Israel. 16 During the Day of Atonement, Yeshua gathered the first fruits of His remnant from the Jordanian wilderness. 17 These believers are praying for the Messiah to make Zion a blessing among the nations. Earlier today, during the Feast of Tabernacles, He supernaturally spilt the Mount of Olives and His entire remnant escaped."

A witness of the eruption hollered back, "You don't know that! There was so much confusion; it's hard to know where they went. My Rabbi denounced everything He did as a total hoax. This man is just another false messiah."

"No matter how grim it gets in the next month, those who haven't worshipped Joshua Kayin can still receive salvation. Soon, demons will begin drawing the nations to Har-Magedon. [18] Their ultimate goal is to defeat the Word of God. Are you hearing me? After the plague of the seventh bowl is poured out, the Word of God will appear in heaven with His armies of angels. [19] At the supper of the great God every soldier following the Beast will be consumed with the breath of His mouth!"[20]

# IN THE LATTER DAYS

"Now I have come to make you understand what will happen to your people in the latter days, for the vision refers to many days yet to come."
Daniel 10:14

They just heard the news. The horrific sores from the first bowl were spreading fast. Even so, just feeling safe was still top priority for most campers. No more running or searching for food or worrying about whether the water was clean. It was the Holy Spirit who supernaturally drew them to this wonderful haven of safety. After a few days at the Vineyard most understood they would be taken care of.

It was exciting to watch as forty-nine children huddled together for their first Bible study. Each was given a green packet consisting of a pen, paper, a small Bible, end time charts, and detailed study notes. Cody's objective was to explain the timeline of events highlighted in The Revelation of Jesus Christ. The young Watchman would begin with the seven bowls, followed by the marriage of the Lamb, Armageddon, the restoration of earth and a new heaven, the millennial kingdom, the final deception of the nations, the casting of Satan into the lake of fire, and the White Throne judgment. Eternity will begin when the last enemy, physical death, is no more. This will happen when the Son gives the millennial kingdom back to His Father.

Failing to get their attention Cody glanced over at Twanna for some help. Pressing her forefinger to her lips, that's all it took.

"Does everyone have an outline of events? It's in the right flap of your packet. Anyone needing a Bible please raise your hand."

Their hopeful eyes spoke volumes. Each had sacrificed so much to make it this far. As Cody waited for the rustling of papers to fade,

Twanna received a word of knowledge.

Raising her hands high she boldly announced, "'He who has an ear, let him hear what the Spirit says to the churches. He who overcomes shall not be hurt by the second death.'" 1

Cody was not ashamed of his tears. It was such a joy for this young man to feel the presence of the Lord amidst so many overcomers. He knew only the Spirit could grant an understanding of the events demolishing the earth. Bowing his head he prayed for an anointing; especially for those who needed to be strengthened.

Twanna could also sense the spiritual warfare. Vineyard leadership knew only powerful intersession could stop the waves of demonic attacks coming against the minds of these children. Every camper had to grasp the urgency of the hour. Watchmen being used in rescue needed to be empowered by the prayers of others. Moving in the Father's will was imperative.

Stepping forward, Cody confidently announced, "Seven years ago, Joshua Kayin confirmed a covenant between Israel and surrounding Muslim nations. In exchange for peace, the Israeli leadership allowed the establishment of a permanent Palestinian State. This signaled the last seven years until the fulfillment of the mystery of God by our Jesus. After the opening of the first seal, Satan went out to conquer the saints through false teachers. The second seal prompted wars among the nations. Worldwide famines followed the third seal. These events, which lasted three and a half years, Jesus called the beginning of sorrows. In the middle of the seven years, Michael the restrainer cast the Devil out of heaven for the final time. This is when Satan came down with his wrath against the saints. After the opening of the fourth seal, the ruler of this world gave his power to a man many call the Beast. The Great Tribulation erupted when the Beast, Joshua Kayin, and his ten horns invaded an unsuspecting Jerusalem. 2 Given authority over the nations by Satan, the Beast introduced a worldwide financial agency called the New World Coalition. The second beast, Pope Michael, became the driving force behind NWC registration. The great tribulation of the saints during the fourth and fifth seals lasted nearly eighteen months. The opening of the next seal on the outside of the heavenly scroll was when the sun, moon, and stars, lost their light."

Chatter increased after hearing the sign of the day of the Lord.

A vibrant Twanna shouted out, "Who knows what happened the day the sun turned black and the moon red?"

Instantly hands shot up.

"In a twinkling of an eye my folks were taken!"

"Jesus shortened the Great Tribulation by gathering His elect." 3

"That's when all the fires started."

Cody respectfully waited for their testimonies to die down.

"Amen guys. On the same day overcomers were caught up to heaven, Jesus opened the seventh seal. Thirty minutes later, the first trumpet sounded and one third of the world's trees were set on fire."4

"So where are we now?"

"The seven years ended between the sixth and seventh trumpets."

"So the seventh trumpet is over?"

"It sounded yesterday during the Feast of Tabernacles. The world saw the Lamb of God take away Satan's authority over this earth." 5

Several campers were already sharing with the new converts. Tee gave Cody a quick glance to allow for more time. Both Watchmen knew how critical it was for peers to communicate the truth, especially the consequences leading up to the battle of Armageddon.

Another worried teen stood up with a question.

"Cody, when will the day of the Lord end?"

"The wrath of God will end when the seventh bowl is poured out. 6 After this, the Word of God will consume the Beast and his armies at Armageddon. We've got twenty-four days left."

"I don't think I can make it," he candidly confessed.

Waiting to get his eye contact, Twanna lovingly replied, "Right now our faith is being stretched. We must pray for the strength to believe His Word. Let's remember, with each new sunrise we are a day closer."

At times Aaron appeared evasive, almost inadequate, as he continued to field questions. His lack of knowledge of Bible prophecy was painting himself into a corner. Her smile was energizing as the weary Commander motioned for his daughter to join him. All eyes were on the tall brunette as she jogged toward the front.

"Listen up, my daughter has something to say."

Opening her Bible, Johanna read, "And it shall happen in that day that I will make Jerusalem a very heavy stone for all peoples; all who would heave it away will surely be cut in pieces, though all nations of the earth are gathered against it." 7

Aaron proudly nodded while thinking over his reply.

"The prophet Zechariah predicted this two-thousand-six-hundred years ago. For years we have witnessed the world's growing concern for the Palestinian people. The backing by the United Nations and the European Union of the so called Palestinian plight only helped isolate our people in fear. Now all nations are conspiring against us. It doesn't matter; in the end Israel shall stand victorious."

"How is this possible?" accused an officer. "You make no sense!"

In a loud voice Johanna shared, "'Then the Lord will go forth and fight against those nations, as He fights in the day of battle. And in that day His feet will stand on the Mount of Olives, which faces Jerusalem on the east. And the Mount of Olives shall be split in two, from east to west, making a very large valley...'" 8

"Matthias, how will the Lord fight against the nations?"

"God will show you if you ask Him. The Mount of Olives has been split. Only those who witnessed this miracle can explain the power which came from Yeshua. Those who believed in Him fled to Azal. My ex-wife, Miriam, is among this remnant."

"Why didn't you join her?" snapped a skeptical voice from his left.

"We stayed because of you," Johanna bravely replied. "There is still a window of opportunity for those who haven't worshipped Kayin."

"You don't get it; our Prime Minister gave away our souls when he gave away our land."

The determined teenager never flinched.

"'And this shall be the plague with which the Lord will strike all the people who fought against Jerusalem: Their flesh shall dissolve while they stand on their feet, their eyes shall dissolve in their sockets, and their tongues shall dissolve in their mouths.'" 9

"A remnant from Israel will never be lost!" shouted Aaron. "The covenant Abraham made with God is eternal. It's true; God used Gentile nations to discipline Israel for her unfaithfulness. Because of this many believe He deserted our people and our land. Don't be deceived, the Lord will vindicate the attacks against Zion. 'It shall be in that day that I will seek to destroy all the nations that come against Jerusalem.' 10 The armies attacking us will be destroyed. God Almighty has promised to intervene on the account of His remnant."

Hundreds jumped to their feet and cheered. Amidst their piercing ovation someone hollered back, "Sir, why such a painful conclusion?"

The courageous brunette raised her hand to speak.

"God has allowed us to be vulnerable in order to show His power to save. Only the Lord will be exalted during the day of the Lord. 11 Man can't stop what God has ordained. The judgment of blasphemers is almost over."

"Matthias, how can this Yeshua be the real Messiah? The Messiah will reveal Himself to everyone; not to just a few."

"Zechariah predicted, '...They will look on Me whom they pierced. Yes, they will mourn for Him as one mourns for his only son, and grieve for Him as one grieves for a firstborn.' 12

In earnest the soldier pleaded, "Who are you talking about?"

"I ask you, who did our forefathers pierce? It was Yeshua who willingly gave His life on a cross for the sins of mankind. He was the first to rise from the dead and never die. Remember when He marched into Jerusalem? The repentance of those hiding exploded. Seeing so many proclaim Him Lord during the Feast of Tabernacles was a miracle!"

"Tell us, where is He now? Has He run away? Maybe He is confused about His mission?" Isn't the Messiah supposed to defeat our enemies?"

Their muffled laughter was hard to watch. He had enough.

"None of you are required to be here. If you cannot respect me or my daughter, then we will leave. For those who have ears to hear what the Lord is offering, eternal life is awaiting you."

"Yeshua's mission is no mystery!" added Johanna. "His second coming will end on the first day of His thousand year reign over the nations. 13 'And the Lord shall be King over all the earth. In that day it shall be The Lord is one, and His name is one.'" 14

Slipping behind her father, Johanna silently interceded as he collected his final thoughts.

"Two thousand years ago, the Lamb of God was buried just before the Feast of Passover. The next day, during the Feast of Unleavened Bread, His body never decayed. On the third day, during the Feast of First Fruits, Yeshua rose from the dead. That evening He breathed on His disciples and they received the Holy Spirit. 15 Fifty days later the promise of the Father was given on Shavuot, the Feast of Weeks. Two years ago, during the Feast of Trumpets, the Son of Man gathered up those who believed. Last Saturday, Yeshua physically returned on the Day of Atonement for the salvation of Israel. 16 Five days later, the Lamb gathered His remnant to the Temple Mount during the Feast of Tabernacles. 17 Now He has split the Mount of Olives and hid His remnant in Azal." 18

"Try proving that!" taunted someone from the back.

"The Messiah has fulfilled the seven Feasts of the Lord. 19 The Holy One of Israel will soon return for a remnant depending on Him. Isaiah prophesied, '...It shall come to pass in that day that the remnant of Israel... will never again depend on him who defeated them, but will depend on the LORD, the Holy One of Israel, in truth.' 20

"When will He return?" his second in command skeptically posed.

"His Shekinah glory will fill the Temple during the Feast of Dedication! 21 Men, our time is short. I would like to pray with all who want to join the redeemed remnant of Israel. I invite you to come forward and believe in Yeshua as your Lord and Savior."

# LET THOSE WHO SUFFER

"If the righteous one is scarcely saved, where will the ungodly and the sinner appear? Therefore let those who suffer according to the will of God commit their souls to Him in doing good, as to a faithful Creator."
I Peter 4:18-19

After praying with his soldiers, Aaron noticed Johanna speaking to two prisoners through the barbed wire fence.

"I'm Rafa; this is my younger brother, Fadi. We're from Jordan."

"My name is Johanna. I'm a Christian from America."

"Why do you care about us?" scoffed Fadi.

"Johanna," added Rafa, "no one trusts your country anymore. Even though you've seen Israel's aggression against our people, many Americans still blaspheme Islam. The Qur'an promises a future judgment day. Blaspheming infidels will suffer torment."

"So what happens at death?"

Fadi patiently waited for the guard on duty to walk by.

"When a person dies, the angel of death removes their soul from their body. Everyone must go to the grave and wait for judgment day. The grave is either paradise or torment. If your good deeds outweigh your bad deeds you will be deemed righteous by Allah. The pain is intense for those who do evil."

"Are you going to paradise when you die?"

The young teenager couldn't help but smile.

"For sure! I am a shahid. When I die the first gush of my blood will be forgiven by Allah. I won't suffer any torment. Entering paradise I will be met by seventy-two dark eyed virgins."

"Rafa, what is your reward if you're martyred?"

"I get to choose my friends in paradise. Glancing away, she whispered, "Why are you here, Johanna? Are you a soldier?"

"No, I'm with my daddy. He used to be the Commander of this militia. He just resigned."

"Many of your leaders are giving up!" snickered Fadi.

"He has enrolled in another army."

Rafa proudly reflected, "Soon Allah will make all things right. There will be no more armies."

The resolute teenager was repeating what she had always been taught. Her search for the truth was just beginning.

"Didn't Muhammad teach Jesus would come back as the Messiah?"

"That's correct."

Opening her Bible, Joanna asked if she could read some scriptures. Despite her brother's reluctance, Rafa nodded.

"Jesus said, 'I have glorified You on earth, I have finished the work which You have given Me to do. And now, O Father, glorify Me together with Yourself, with the glory which I had with You before the world was.'" 1 Isn't this Jesus praying to His Father in heaven?"

"That's impossible!" snapped Fadi. "This is John speaking."

"Isn't this Jesus saying He was with His Father before the world was? 'Father, the hour has come. Glorify Your Son, that Your Son also may glorify You, as You have given Him authority over all flesh, that He should give eternal life to as many as You have given Him...' 2

"You believe Jesus is the Son of God, don't you?"

"With all my heart, Rafa. When I believed in Jesus as my Savior, I received the indwelling of the Holy Spirit. It's the Spirit of Christ who reveals the truth of Jesus' divinity. Let me read it to you. 'He was in the world, and the world was made through Him, and the world did not know Him. But as many as received Him, to them He gave the right to become children of God, to those who believe in His name: who were born, not of blood, nor of the will of the flesh, nor of the will of man, but of God. And the Word became flesh and dwelt among us, and we beheld His glory, the glory as of the only begotten of the Father, full of grace and truth.'" 3

"What does it mean the Word became flesh? Who is the Word?"

Johanna respectfully paused before reading, "'In the beginning was the Word, and the Word was with God, and the Word was God... And the Word became flesh and dwelt among us, and we beheld His glory, the glory as of the only begotten of the Father, full of grace and truth.' 4 The Word became a man to die for the sins of mankind. Jesus is the only begotten Son of the Father." 5

"God has no Son!" challenged an irate Fadi. "All who believe are children of God; just like Jesus."

"What about His death on the cross?"

"The Jews believe the Romans crucified Jesus. The Christians believe the Jews put Him to death. Even though this debate has gone on for centuries, the Prophet Muhammad taught this critical truth in the holy Qur'an. Jesus never died; He was caught up to heaven."

Suddenly the guard on duty shouted at the two prisoners to stop talking and move away from the fence.

Waving goodbye, the young Watchman whispered, "I'm praying for your release. Ask Jesus to help you; He is only a prayer away."

---

The farther they got away; the more despondent Reenie was becoming. Resting behind a closed down gas station, the former pastor was silently praying when her tears erupted.

"Greg, what's happening to me? After we prayed this morning I felt so encouraged. My doubts just disappeared. I wasn't scared anymore. Then, bam, it's like a ten-ton truck hit us! Now we don't even know where the boys and Emma are. Plus we get stuck with Mr. Wonderful."

He couldn't miss the pain in her sarcasm.

"How is Mr. Wonderful doing anyway?"

"Not good!" she gasped. "He's not breathing very well."

Reaching back, Greg pulled the tape off his mouth.

"Raise your voice, it goes right back on."

"No biggie. My men are trailing you. Soon a gun will be sticking in your ugly face."

"That's what you said about Death Angel."

"Tucker, you must've loved it when Cassandra got whacked. Did you kill her or did you make your little brother do it for you?"

"What about you, Doyle?" challenged Greg. "Why did you order Cassandra to kill Reenie in the first place?"

"Your Q Squad is history, Hudson! You accomplished nothing!"

"Half the world has died and you still don't get it?"

"What am I supposed to get, preacher? Enlighten me on why a loving God would torture innocent people who only wanted world peace? What is so wrong with the nations coming together under the leadership of one man? Is your God jealous? Maybe He's offended so many refused to bow down to His almighty decrees."

"The Revelation of Jesus Christ lays it out, Doyle. John wrote, 'But the rest of mankind, who were not killed by these plaques, did not repent by these plaques, did not repent of the works of their hands, that they should not worship demons, and idols of gold, silver, brass, stone, and wood, which can neither see nor hear nor walk.'" 6

"So now I'm a demon worshipper?"

"What was Cassandra, a girl scout?" fumed Reenie.

"Not all agents are alike, little lady," he coyly replied.

"God's wrath won't end until the seventh bowl is poured out."

"How close are we?

For a brief moment all she could do is turn around and stare at his wicked smile.

"You got a calendar?"

"Not on me. I thought you said Jesus returned last weekend? My pastor taught Jesus won't return until the end of the world."

"The times of the Gentiles ended the day Kayin killed the two Witnesses. 7 On that same day, the Messiah physically returned to fulfill the mystery of God, the salvation of Israel." 8

The agent didn't bother hiding his laughter.

"So why is God so concerned about the Jews? I'm afraid He's a bit late. Millions have died. And now your Messiah decides to show up and save some. What sort of nonsense is this?"

"God's love for Israel is a vital truth many Christians rejected." 9

"How do you figure?"

"God made a covenant with Abraham to bless the nations through his seed. Those believing in Yeshua as their Savior will receive eternal salvation."

His silence catching her off guard she awkwardly asked, "How's your sore?"

"It sucks, Reenie, what's it to you?"

"Believers don't have them."

"You're brain-dead!"

"Aren't you forgetting the fifth trumpet? Five months of torment for those having the mark, pretty ugly huh?"

"I know all sorts of Christians who were stung. Decent people who would help any way they can. Your prejudice against those who don't believe your way has destroyed our world."

Greg sighed. He had heard this infamous lie by the spirit of Antichrist many times.

"Doyle, the testing by Satan during the Great Tribulation actually produced a blameless bride. John wrote, 'And they overcame him by the blood of the Lamb...'" 10

"How so Hudson?"

"By the word of their testimony."

"Blah, blah, blah, I know you believe Satan used Joshua Kayin to deceive the world. Spare me; ya'll sound like programmed robots!"

---

Chugging up the dirt embankment was no easy task.

"Donnie, this hog and these roads aren't meant for each other."

Slowly his partner steered their Winnebago off the steep road.

"We can walk it from here, Jon. You see that cluster of maple trees up ahead? The path to the cave is just beyond them."

"How sure are you?"

"Hughes and I found the Santino's cave at night. I watched while he broke the news to Bret's mom. It's all coming back; trust me."

Parked near a small field of burned bushes they changed into rubber boots, black leather jackets and caps. Removing his shotgun from underneath the driver's seat, Jonathon Mendel loaded two shells and removed the safety.

"What's with the cannon?"

"Just a precaution, for real, you worried I'm going to break the sixth commandant?"

Donnell just rolled his eyes and whispered back, "Naw, I've just never felt comfortable hanging out at night with a white guy holding a loaded double barreled shotgun."

---

The three Watchmen were already feeling the dampness of the cave. Emma silently prayed as the boys talked about their next step.

"Jake, what if some agents stayed behind to pick us up?"

"If they're watching for us then we need to make our escape at night. The bottom line is Greg and Reenie need our help, especially if they're heading for the Vineyard."

"I know, I know."

"What's really bugging you, Kurt?"

"Well, being together was such a blessing from God. Now it

seems like we're moving backwards. Deep down I really want to do His will. 11 It just seems so hard when circumstances change so quickly. I wonder what our Miracle Girl is thinking right now?"

From a compact Bible his close friend read, "'Therefore having been justified by faith, we have peace with God through our Lord Jesus Christ, through whom also we have access by faith into this grace in which we stand, and rejoice in hope of the glory of God. And not only that, but we also glory in tribulations, knowing that tribulation produces perseverance; and perseverance, character; and character, hope. Now hope does not disappoint, because the love of God has been poured out in our hearts by the Holy Spirit who was given to us. For when we were still without strength, in due time Christ died for the ungodly.'" 12

"I'm feeling it, JJ," confessed the relieved redhead. "God is with us because this mission is His idea. It doesn't matter how weak we feel; He will guide us. Our love for Him is stronger than any fear coming against us."

"You ready to move out, little brother?"

"Anytime sis."

Bowing her head Emma prayed, "Father, we thank You so much for delivering us from these agents. Lord, may You continue to protect Greg and Reenie. Holy Spirit, we ask You to open a door for us to make it safely to the Vineyard. Our lives are in Your hands God, the Father, the Son, and the Holy Spirit."

Aaron was busy packing when she entered his office.

"Daddy, look at the soldiers who asked for salvation!"

"It's God! I could feel the Holy Spirit when you were speaking."

"Verses were just popping into my mind. The Father is drawing His people to His Son. There had to be more that were saved that didn't come forward."

"Your mother was right. It's not how you present it it's about the power unto salvation."

"Daddy, the soldiers behind the fence, where are they from?"

"They were caught were near our northern border crossing. The Jordanian Militia has requested a swap for those under eighteen."

"You mean Rafa and Fadi."

"Who are they?"

"Two teenage prisoners I shared with. The Lord wants us to help them."

"It's out of our hands. The soldiers are calling me a mashumed."

"Is that bad?"

"It's Hebrew for traitor. We must leave while we have the chance."

"Can we exchange Rafa and Fadi for your soldiers?"

"Crossing into Jordan is suicide. The salvation of our people is top priority. We have family and friends who still can be saved. I just received a memo concerning the arrest of Judah and Hanna Lentz."

"Are they okay?"

"They're still alive."

"What about Ruth?"

"This report is only about her parents. Maybe we can free them."

The frown on her face was so unexpected. Aaron couldn't discern the tug of war raging within his daughter. Her carnal nature was also resisting the prompting from the Holy Spirit.

"Daddy, it's kinda hard to explain what the Lord is showing me right now. Even if I tell you, I don't know if it will make any sense."

"Honey, you have no experience in such things. Just trust my judgment. The open door to rescue the Lentz's has to be from God."

Aaron was facing the same inner struggle. Both Watchmen passed their first test by faithfully witnessing to over five hundred Israeli soldiers. Their next assignment would require an even greater faith; a commitment fueled by supernatural love.

"Daddy, fifty days after Jesus rose from the dead, the apostle Peter taught the gospel of Jesus Christ on the day of Pentecost. He exhorted his people to be saved from their evil generation." [13]

"I remember, three thousand Jews believed in Jesus." [14]

"Several years later the Holy Spirit sent Peter to the Gentiles. [15] God was saying they could become members of the body of Christ too. 'If therefore God gave them (Gentiles) the same gift as He gave us (Jews) when we believed on the Lord Jesus Christ, who was I that could withstand God.'" [16]

"Wasn't Peter persecuted for preaching the gospel to the Gentiles?"

"So was another Jewish believer. Every city Paul visited; his own people either whipped or stoned him. This horrific persecution became a thorn in his flesh."

"Yes, Miriam taught me this. The apostle pleaded with God to take this thorn away. God had other plans. Paul was told he could be stronger for the Lord by being weak in himself."

"Amen Daddy! No matter how the Jews persecuted him he never gave up. Paul was ready to give his life for the Gentiles who wanted to be saved."

"C'mon, I know of an Israeli village west of Jerusalem. There are hundreds living there who haven't registered."

Rushing toward the door he glanced back. She wasn't moving.

"What's wrong, Johanna, we have to leave now!"

"I also know some who don't know Yeshua?"

"Like who?"

"Rafa, Fadi, their family, their relatives, even their friends."

"Not a chance. Jordanians are devout Muslims! A Jordanian terrorist murdered my father!"

"Daddy, I saw a vision similar to Peter's. The Holy Spirit is calling us to the Gentiles. If we obey I believe He will open the doors for us to witness to our own people."

"We just can't dismiss the word your mother gave us. We are called to be witnesses to Israel. What you're hearing isn't from God."

"I believe with all my heart the Holy Spirit is giving us an open door to witness to Muslims."

"Witness to the sworn enemies of Christians and Jews? You don't understand how their minds work. Your sympathy for these teenagers is clouding your judgment."

"Didn't Jesus command us to love our enemies? 17 Isaiah saw the Lord drawing Gentiles unto Himself in the latter days. What about our calling we received while on the Mount of Olives?"

"Yes, we are running in a race for souls."

"I never told you but many of those saved in my vision weren't Jewish. Daddy, the Lord has granted us an opportunity to witness to Jordanians. There are many who can still be saved by His grace."

Hiding near the mouth of the Santino's cave, the two Watchmen discussed their next move.

"I don't like it, Donnie, too many foot prints."

"Do you think it was a NWC bust?"

"This hideout isn't a secret anymore. Agents could be waiting for us inside. It's risky; no doubt."

"Are you getting anything from God?"

"Definitely," grinned Jon, "but you won't like it."

"I'd rather not know; just do it."

"Alright but be ready to run if any agents show up."

The blast echoing through the black hills sounded like a bomb.

Crouching down, Donnell was speechless.

"What was that, Jake?"

"Sounded like a shotgun, Emma. We ain't alone."

"Agent Doyle Mercer owns a shotgun," winced Kurt.

The two resisters took their time entering the cave.

"What do think, Donnie?"

"Whoever it was, they left in a hurry. C'mon let's go."

From a steep hill the Q could hear steps running down the dirt road. The sudden silence was eerie.

"Who's there? I'm Jonathan Mendel; this is Donnell Emery! We're from the Christian underground. Our assignment is to rescue a believer named Reenie Tucker. A SWAT team has been dispatched to execute her."

Jake shouted back, "How do we know you're Watchmen?"

"If you were hiding in Anthony Santino's cave then you may know his son, Bret. Donnell was with Bret when he was killed by a Special Forces agent. Besides, Jesus is Lord!"

The threesome didn't hesitate as they scampered down the hill.

"Thanks for coming; I'm Jake Jamison."

"I've heard of you. Wasn't Reenie hiding out with you?"

"For over a year, Donnell, this afternoon she escaped with Greg Hudson. This is Emma and Kurt Abbott. We're from the Q Squad."

"Wow, the Lord is still using the Q?"

"Oh yeah," beamed Kurt, "God isn't through with us yet."

# VENGEANCE IS MINE

*"'Vengeance is mine, I will repay,' says the Lord."*
*Romans 12:19*

The secluded red brick diner nestled between the sturdy pines had just opened for breakfast. Blue smoke was barely trickling out of its stout red metal chimney. Seated in worn rocking chairs on the front porch, two retirees were smoking corncob pipes. Dressed in faded overalls, they were in no hurry to do much of anything.

"I declare," stared one of the old timers. "You ever recollect seeing something like this?"

The shiny black limo was struggling making it up the narrow road leading to the parking lot of the diner.

Between puffs, his friend chuckled, "You reckon they're lost?"

Two bodyguards emerged from the limo. While one cautiously checked the grounds, the other raced up the wooden steps to the porch.

"Good morning gentlemen, anyone in there?"

"Just Maggie," each snorted at the same time.

After a search inside he returned to the black Lincoln. The other bodyguard was waiting. The driver carefully assisted his passenger out of the spacious backseat. Wearing a leather jacket over a tight red sweater, the damp red clay smeared the edges of her brown boots. Reaching the top of the porch, she playfully winked at the old timers before going in.

"Good morning," greeted an enthusiastic Maggie. "Make yourself comfortable. Want some coffee?"

"Thank you."

One bodyguard stood in front of the window facing her table; the other near the rear exit.

"Here's your coffee dearie. My, my, my, Natalie Roberts from Channel 6 out of Chicago! What brings you to Dahlonega?"

They could hear the engine accelerating. The old timer lowered his thick reading glasses for a better look. The souped-up Hummer easily cruised into the parking lot.

Wondering out loud he scratched his head and mumbled, "Why are these city folk hankering to eat at Maggie's?"

Each door opened at the same time. While one soldier circled around back, another hid behind some trees in the parking lot. The driver and his passenger briskly strode up the steps and entered the diner.

"What do you make of this?" hooted the old man.

Puffing on his pipe, his friend whispered, "Ain't our affair."

The popular reporter studied the soldier as he sat down. Delford Eiland was no stranger to the media. In the past three years, his private militia had grown into the thousands. His arrests were public record, bribery, money laundering, kidnapping, even attempted murder. Incredibly, the self-avowed prophet had never been convicted. Even so the reward for his arrest had grown considerably in the past few months.

"I appreciate you meeting with me."

Leaning forward, he looked eager.

"Anything for the cause…. I must ask, Ms. Roberts, why did you leave Jerusalem? You get your fill of Jews sucking us dry?"

"So Israel is responsible for the economic collapse of our world?"

"Over four million Jews are dead!" he cackled. "The smell must have been putrid."

"Delford, it appears your Christian militia is expanding. There are some wild accusations about the Prophetic Voice floating around. Two days ago, I received a tip about your little army. I've come to report on your beliefs as well as your future objectives."

"I'm a prophet of the Living God. The Lord has supernaturally given me revelation concerning the end of the age. For those who reject my exhortations; they do so at their own peril."

"Does your end time revelation include the United States?"

"Pastors in America have shamelessly preached their pharisaical lies. We are now reaping the rotten fruit sown from their pulpits."

"What type of lies?"

"Natalie, I believe in the one true God of the 1611 King James Bible. Not in some triune myth of three Gods in one."

"You mean the Father, the Son, and the Holy Spirit?"

"God moves in three offices not persons."

"I don't understand."

"Let's use a married teacher as an example. First, she is a wife to her husband, then a mother to her children, and finally a teacher to her students. She operates in a different office to each one."

"Haven't Christians throughout history believed..."

"The only way to understand the divine nature of God is to have it revealed by the Spirit. You don't know the Pharisees who created the trinity myth. They also teach Jesus was resurrected from the dead."

"But didn't He rise on the third day?"

"The Bible never speaks of a physical resurrection. Or the rapture lie either. As Jesus was spiritually raised, so will those who obey Him."

"Delford, does your fellowship believe in grace for salvation?"

"Jesus instructs sinners to be born again by water and Spirit. I see nothing about grace in His teaching."

"Why such secrecy, why not share your end time message openly? I notice you're unregistered. The resisters believe registering with NWC is the mark of the beast."

"Just another lie taught by fake Christians, anyone trusting in the traditions of man has the mark of the Beast!"

"Then who are the true followers of God?"

"Your answer is in the book of Genesis. The Word depicts Eve having sex with Satan. They conceived Cain. Which means the father of Cain was Satan. Cain's descendants are Kenites. They killed the Christ. Posing as scribes they also tried to corrupt the scriptures."

"So all non-white races are Kenites?"

"Kenites were created on the sixth day; whites on the eighth day."

"What about the 144,000 Jewish men following Jesus?"

"The Kenites trusting in this imposter are of the devil. In 722 B.C., ten tribes from Israel were taken away by the Assyrians. Eventually they traveled north populating Europe and North America. This is why God's chosen race is from America and Great Britain. In these last days, Kenites have purposely pitted nation against nation. They have fleeced our land. Their goal to destroy the white race in America is no secret."

"How do you intend to stop them?"

Leaning back in his chair, his hands clasped behind his head, his sneer reeked with hate.

"Have you ever heard of the great day of God Almighty?"

"I think it's somewhere in the bible?"

"Revelation 16:14-16. Armies of the world are preparing to annihilate Israel during the battle of Armageddon. The wrath of God will soon squash the Jews like parasites."

"Haven't Christians always had a love for Israel because of Jesus?"

"Not the ones I know."

"So how did you come to this conclusion?"

"From the Holy Spirit, His anointing opened my understanding to the pre-existence of man before the earth was formed."

"You lost me."

"Natalie, the history of mankind came in three earth ages. Genesis 1:1 teaches man pre-existed in soul bodies before the fall of Satan. Those who followed God became His elect. In the second earth age, Genesis 1:2, God remade the earth. During this age mankind will follow the Antichrist while the elect become overcomers. The third earth age begins with the Millennium and reaches throughout eternity. In this age the elect will live in spirit bodies."

"So how close are we to Armageddon?"

Without any emotion he replied, "At the doorstep."

"What's going to happen to the United States?"

"The Prophetic Voice has faithfully preached the truth of how Kenites have tried to control the destiny of our nation. Our goal is to protect the white race in America. But the liberal media has denounced us as religious bigots. They took away our first amendment rights by classifying our message as hate speech. It was the only way the government could prevent the truth from being spread."

"What truth?"

"For years I've warned of a future race war having the power to devastate America. I promise the Prophetic Voice will not sit by idly and allow the Jews to destroy our land. We are planning our own battle."

"What are you suggesting?"

"Jesus said of the Jews, "You are of your father the devil, and the desires of your father you want to do..."" 1

"Delford, why are you telling me this?"

"Anyone harboring Kenites will be dealt with judiciously."

"You must enjoy the notoriety you receive?"

"Our cause will be better served by your broadcast."

"Why haven't you registered? You're no better than the resisters."

Her bodyguard by the window looked uneasy as he unbuttoned his jacket and released the safety of his revolver.

"You mean the ones believing there was a Holocaust?"

"So Nazis' never used gas chambers to exterminate millions of Jews?"

"Their buildings couldn't handle so many Jews. The gas they used couldn't kill anyone. It was used to disinfect their clothes."

"The underground resistance teaches the Son of God has..."

"They're a cancer just like the Jews. They believe the leader of the Jewish mob that was atop Mount Zion is Jesus. They teach He will soon rule from Jerusalem for a thousand years."

"Yeah, I know, I saw Him."

"You saw nothing!"

"So you're the judge, or maybe your militia?"

Jumping to his feet, he cursed, "This interview is over. You're just another foul Kenite. For those who won't listen, they have no one to blame but themselves."

Clicking off her mini recorder the famous reporter shot a reassuring glance across the room to her tense bodyguard.

"Delford, what good is all this if you're wrong?"

"I pity you! You gave up a long time ago. Only the survivors of Armageddon will see the truth."

Reaching the front door she paused before looking back.

"Nobody knows that. But one thing is sure. If Jesus does return with His armies it will be the worst nightmare of all!"

As the agent slept, Greg Hudson pondered their chances of making it to the Vineyard. The Georgia State line was less than ten miles away.

"Reenie, is there anything you want to share with me?"

"Just thinking about the Q, the time we had around the fire was so anointed."

"Yeah, there is nothing like the presence of God. Are you excited about seeing Bret again?"

Blushing, she looked away and nodded.

"Bret Santino gave his life for me. At times I feel so unworthy. Satan has tried to gain a foothold in my spirit through guilt. What a liar. I can hardly wait to see Bret in his glorified body."

"Hallelujah! Those martyred by the Beast will reign with Christ on the first day of His thousand year reign over the nations" [2]

"Won't the Devil be bound on the same day?" [3]

"In the bottomless pit for a thousand years, this is why Satan wants the Beast to defeat the Word on the great day of God Almighty." [4]

"Aren't there thirty days from the end of the seventieth week of Daniel till Armageddon?" [5]

"You got it, Miracle Girl."

"So when is the fall of Babylon?"

"The blood of saints will be found in this spiritual counterfeit. [6] Through her fornication she bought and sold the souls of men." [7]

"Who're you talking about?"

"Rome is the seat of the Babylonian harlot. She will fall between the pouring out of the seventh bowl and Armageddon. God will remember Rome by giving her death, mourning, famine, and fire!" 8

Peeking in the rear view mirror the teenager looked distracted.

"What's bothering you, Reenie?

"I don't get the events after Armageddon? Can you fill me in?"

"Sure, according to Daniel, there will be forty-five days between Armageddon and the beginning of the Millennium. John saw five events taking place within this forty-five day restoration period."

"Luke Appleby once taught me Mount Zion will be restored."

"That's the first event after Armageddon. Isaiah prophesied, 'Now it shall come to pass in the latter days that the mountain of the Lord's house shall be established on the top of the mountains... And all nations shall flow to it. Many people shall come and say, "Come, and let us go up to the mountain of the LORD..."' 9

"But won't all the mountains be trashed by the seventh bowl?" 10

"Cities too, after the day of the Lord ends, Jerusalem will be restored to the highest point on earth." 11

"Then what happens?"

"A remnant will return to the land God promised Abraham. 12 'The remnant will return, the remnant of Jacob, to the Mighty God. For though your people, O Israel, be as the sand of the sea, a remnant of them will return; the destruction decreed shall overflow with righteousness. For the Lord GOD of hosts will make a determined end in the midst of all the land.'" 13

"Wow, Jews returning as believers in the Messiah." 14

"They're coming back to rely on the Holy One. 15 We will too!"

"What do you mean?"

"After the redeemed from Israel return to Zion, Gentile believers won't be far behind. 16 '... It shall be that I will gather all nations and tongues; and they shall come and see My glory...'" 17

"We're going to see our King in Jerusalem!"

"The fourth event within this forty-five day period is the rebuilding of the Temple. 18 The Temple we see now will be damaged during the bowl judgments. 19 It will be the Lord who rebuilds it."

"Where is that in scripture?"

"Let me read it. 'Behold, the Man whose name is the BRANCH. From His place He shall branch out, And He shall build the temple of the LORD; Yes, He shall build the temple of the LORD. He shall bear the glory, And shall sit and rule on His throne; So He shall be a priest on His throne, And the counsel of peace shall be between them both.'" [20]

"Amen, the Branch will rule from His throne within the Temple. This means Jesus will rebuild the Temple before His thousand year reign over the nations begins."

"Miracle Girl, John saw a new heaven and a new earth completed before His reign begins. Isaiah also prophesied, 'For behold, I create a new heavens and a new earth; and the former things shall not be remembered... But be glad and rejoice forever in what I create...'" [21]

"Greg, what does Isaiah mean by a new earth?"

"This Hebrew word 'new' means to restore something already existing. The destruction during the sounding of the trumpets and the pouring out of the bowls will be catastrophic. The earth will be renovated by God like the Garden of Eden."

The former pastor couldn't help reflecting back on the countless debates over end time events. So many were convinced how it would all transpire. In the end many willingly risked their salvation for what they erroneously believed in.

"So what happens right before Jesus reigns over the nations?"

"The Ancient of Days must anoint the Most Holy. The Son of Man will be granted dominion over an everlasting kingdom."

"Does this happen after Jesus rebuilds the Temple?"

"His return is highlighted by Daniel. 'I was watching in the night visions, And behold, One like the Son of Man, coming with the clouds of heaven. He came to the Ancient of Days, and they brought Him near before Him. Then to Him was given dominion and glory and a kingdom, that all peoples, nations, and languages should serve Him. His dominion is an everlasting dominion, which shall not pass away, and His kingdom the one which shall not be destroyed.'" [22]

"Isn't this the Son of Man coming in the clouds in Matthew 24:30?

"Take another look."

"Huh?"

"After the Temple is built, Daniel saw the Son of Man returning on the clouds to appear before the Ancient of Days. The Son is coming back to receive dominion over the throne of David from His Father. An angel prophesied, 'He will be great, and will be called the Son of the Highest; and the Lord God will give Him the throne of His father David.' 23

"Awesome….. a kingdom which will never pass away!"

"Now do you see how important our mission is?"

---

The inner circle was twice the size of those guarding the outer perimeter. Someone would have to be invisible to infiltrate the Vineyard. The two exit tunnels were almost ready. Only members of the staff understood the consequences of a NWC bust.

His Bible study group was praying when he slipped out of the cave. Hiking up the eastern boundary of the camp, he hid behind some pine trees before making the call on his cell phone.

"Eli here, I'm ready to report."

"Did everything go alright?"

"Lenard, your logger friend was right on. This camp is huge. Close to five thousand kids. They call it the Vineyard."

"Eli, this is Delford. How did you get through their security?"

"No problem, Sir. I was apprehended half way up the mountain by one of their sentries. I asked for help and he welcomed me with open arms... It's growing daily... They're teaching Armageddon is three weeks away... That's right; they believe the Word will kill all following Kayin."

"What weapons do they have?" inquired an uneasy Lenard.

"They use a couple of rifles for hunting. Trust me these resisters are harmless, just another cult worshiping a Jew savior."

"How many Kenites are they hiding?" fumed Delford.

"At least a thousand."

"Will they give them up?"

"No way, these resisters are tight."

"It's their choice. We'll add them to our list."

"Sir, most of these kids don't even know where their folks are."

"They all will be given an opportunity to join us."

"Hey, Eli?" yelled a surprised sentry.

Jamming his phone under his jacket, he turned around and waved.

"Why are you way out here?"

"The intersession was so intense; I needed a break."

"For sure," agreed the teenager. "Sorry, but you need to go back. Any movement this far out could attract airplane surveillance."

Re-entering the cave his prayer partners were sharing testimonies.

"You okay, Eli?"

"Glory to God, I just needed some alone time with the Lord."

The Glazers had just finished loading their jeep with food, water, and plastic containers of gasoline. The distain from his soldiers was obvious. Nothing could be more devastating than the desertion of the one called Matthias. Even so, Aaron agreed to swap two underage prisoners for three Israeli soldiers. Accelerating through the rear entrance of the camp, their ex-Commander never looked back.

"Fadi, what does your father do for a living?"

"Johanna, he is a Mujahideen; a servant of Allah."

"What is that, Daddy?"

"It's Arabic for holy warrior. Fadi, are you proud of your father?"

"His time is coming. Soon Allah will vindicate him. Praise be to Allah, the one true God."

"It's obvious Jews, Muslims, and Christians, each interpret the events of these latter days differently. Jews are praying for their Messiah to set up His kingdom on earth. Muslims are expecting Jesus to return as the Messiah. And Christians are preparing for the return of the Word of God at the battle of Armageddon."

"What more can Allah do for infidels to recognize the truth?"

"So how does one find the truth, Fadi?"

"Johanna, I've read the Qur'an five times."

"What have you learned?"

"The annihilation of Zionists will bless all nations."

"And when did you learn this revelation from Allah?"

"When I was seven," he smugly boasted.

Looking back at a troubled Rafa, she didn't have to ask.

"I was nine."

"Best I can do, Wes," confessed the light technician.

The worn out producer cursed, "Close enough."

"Remember, one more power surge and it's over anyway."

Chicago's Channel 6 was about to go live. The frenzied panic among the nations was out of control. With a world war looming in the Middle East, purple sores struck with no warning. Billons recoiled in agony after suffering another judgment from God. With their power to control fading, world leaders hastily enacted Marshall Law. Protecting citizens from roaming gangs and continual looting was now top priority.

"You got another call, Wes," yelled his assistant.

"Not now!"

"We transferred Natalie to your cell."

The usual up beat producer eagerly opened his phone.

"Nate, first just tell me where you are?"

"I'm in the Blue Ridge Mountains above Atlanta. I just interviewed a self-proclaimed prophet from the Prophetic Voice."

"Have you lost it, girl? You're the most respected News Anchor in America. We're trying to go live and you're hanging out with a racist cult leader. So what's your angle?"

"Wes, for me, the killing in the past two years was just too much. I'm burned out. For now, I simply want to save some lives. Delford Eiland is a dangerous man."

"Nate, World War III is about to break out in the Middle East and you're worried about a white supremacist group wasting a few Jews and Blacks. Just how do you propose to save lives?"

"One at a time," she moaned.

"Have you received a sore yet?"

"Yeah, my backside feels like jelly. What about you?"

"My right hand is worthless; can't even write."

"I would like to request some air time."

"You mean you're coming in?"

"I guess there's time. I'd like to expose the intentions of this cult."

"Nate, I need to know where you stand."

"On what?"

"NWC leadership is crumbling. They aren't enforcing any prior restrictions. We can broadcast anything we want. Several stations are quoting Revelation 16. Channel 12 announced these purple sores are the wrath of God. Some are predicting once the second bowl is poured out our oceans will be destroyed."

"What precautions is our Navy taking?"

"Not aware of any."

"That figures."

"But why would God want to destroy His own creation? Why won't He send His love?"

"He already did, Wes. He sent His Son to die for our sins."

---

Reenie couldn't miss his preoccupation.

"What's going down, Greg?"

"Now ain't this sweet, Reverend," mocked Doyle. "Your little resister still doesn't have a clue. You going to tell her or shall I?"

"Reenie, it's too dangerous for us to try and make it to the Vineyard. Agents could be shadowing us."

"Wow, a preacher who actually tells the truth."

Veering off the highway, he shot down a frontage road toward an abandoned town. After several turns he pulled into a run-down car wash. While closing the entrance door Greg could hear them arguing.

"Your threats mean nothing to me!" snapped Reenie.

"What future do you have by blindly following this religious fanatic?"

"How's your family doing, Doyle? You know I was once friends with your daughter?"

His head drooped; his eyes seemingly losing focus.

"Tell me; did Cammie ever graduate from Lakeview High? She was always so much fun. Just the life of the party until the mark of the beast was introduced. So, Chief, was it worth it?" You remember, the day you convinced Cammie to register when she didn't want to."

"She's old enough to make her own decisions."

"That's not what I heard. Kinda sad, your decision to follow the Devil, I was wondering who sucked the life out of your daughter."

"Hey, Hudson, you gotta hear this. Your teenage freak is trying to make me feel guilty."

"You didn't answer my question. How is Cammie doing?"

"None of your stinking business!"

"C'mon, how many executions have you actually watched?"

"Wake up, kid, they broke the law."

"Man's or God's?"

"Lighten up; I didn't pull the trigger on your precious boyfriend."

"Sure you did."

From outside her window, Greg whispered, "Stop it, Reenie."

"I'd love to know how many hits Doyle personally ordered."

"Listen to me."

"Save it, I don't need another lecture. This animal gave Death Angel her assignments."

Sliding out of her seat the bewildered brunette stepped away.

"Talk to me, Reenie."

"Sorry, Greg, I just went off. This isn't easy for me."

"You're right; Mercer is a cold blooded killer. He also ordered the execution of Anthony Delgado and his mother."

"So what can we do?"

"We can't do anything about the past. Vengeance doesn't help anything. God is the one who will repay. The only way to overcome evil is by doing good." 24

"I've changed my mind about my mission. There are lots of empty houses to crash in. I know I can wait it out till Armageddon."

Greg had prayed to avoid such mistakes. He knew this was a big one.

"Forgive me, Reenie, this is all my fault. The demons in Doyle can be very persuasive. I should have lost him the first chance I had."

"Aren't I a new creation? It's like the enemy knows the right buttons to push and I fall apart. All my flesh wants to do is fight back."

The ex-minister could certainly relate.

"Miracle Girl, it's called sanctification. Every believer is set apart by God for divine purposes. The victory over our sin nature can only come by relying on the Holy Spirit. Every Christian has a responsibility to mortify the desires of our sin nature." 25

"I just don't get the back and forth struggle."

"The more we yield to our flesh the stronger it becomes. This is what these deceiving spirits want. By refusing to entertain their lies we reckon ourselves dead to sin." 26

# FOR THEN I WILL RESTORE

"For then I will restore to the peoples a pure language that they all may
call on the name of the Lord, to serve Him with one accord."
Zephaniah 3:9

Maneuvering through the Alabama hills wasn't easy. A relieved Jon
Mendel thanked the Lord as the old Winnebago reached the highway.

"What now?"

"Jake, highway roadblocks are history. State borders are open
twenty four seven. Even scanning by agents depends on the city."

"What's happening to the NWC?"

"A loss of manpower," replied Donnell. "Kayin is sending as
many soldiers to Israel as he can. This is why Congress declared
Marshall Law. They can arrest anyone they want, anytime, anywhere.
What a madhouse since the purple sores broke out. Most are staying
indoors. National Guard troops are trying to limit the looting in the
big cities."

"How long have you two been in the underground resistance?"

"Two years for me, Kurt," answered a grateful Jon.

"Close enough," winked Donnell.

"So how has the agenda of the underground changed?"

Jon sighed before tipping back the bill of his hat.

"It depends. With Armageddon so close, some are struggling with
how to spend the remaining time. This is why Watchmen have
different agendas. For example, I know overcomers in Lake Mary,
Florida, solely protecting saints from the NWC. I also helped out a
team from Fort Myers the Lord is using in evangelism."

"Witnessing to whom?" Finding unregistered people is like

searching for a needle in a haystack."

"You'd be surprised, Jake. We're still getting reports of pockets of people who never worshiped the Beast or received his mark. The problem is the trust factor. No one trusts anybody."

"What about you guys? Who sent you to track Reenie?"

"I volunteered us, Kurt!" blurted his buddy.

Jon rolled his eyes as he headed toward Bethany.

"Donnie and I are specialists. We prefer high risk rescues. Reenie is high on their arrest list. It's a mystery why they want her so bad."

"High risk rescues! Pretty intense, huh, Donnell?"

His shoulders stiffened, his facial expression said it all.

"I was standing beside Bret Santino when he was assassinated. He never knew what hit him. He gave his life for Reenie."

"You helped Bret knowing Death Angel was targeting him?"

Staring out the passenger's window he didn't bother to reply.

"Guys, going over the past can be a real drainer. We need to stay focused on our mission."

"Which is, Jon?"

"To safely apprehend Reenie Ann Tucker."

"You mean you'll help us find our friends?" squealed Emma.

"Our God is faithful! Now where is this camp, Jake?"

"The Vineyard is on a small mountain near Dahlonega, Georgia. Our contact will meet us at a diner called Maggie's. He can lead us to the camp. Have you ever heard of Dahlonega?"

"Sure, it's a little town a couple hours north of Atlanta. It was once Cherokee country. Okay, I know a place in Bethany where we can pick up some gasoline."

"Who knows, Q squad," exhorted a hopeful Donnell, "maybe the underground has some new information on Reenie and Greg."

---

The car lanes leaving Israel were jammed. Vendors holding their goods walked back and forth shouting out prices. Teenage boys were aggressively bartering plastic bottles of water constantly.

"What do you think, Daddy?"

"It's hard to say, Johanna. It depends if the border guards are still scanning. What about it, Fadi, you registered or unregistered?"

"We're forbidden to register! It's the mark of an infidel."

Pulling off the road he cut the engine. For now he would wait.

"I don't get it, Daddy? Why are so many people fleeing Israel?"

"To avoid war," reflected Rafa. "Many call it Armageddon."

"Who told you this?"

"A Christian friend, she loved sharing about the last days."

"Where is she now?"

"She was executed for being an infidel."

"I knew my sister's friend. She was only guessing. Armageddon is a Christian myth. Only Allah can predict the future. It was her parents who turned her in."

"The Bible predicts when Armageddon will take place."

"How so, Johanna?"

"Rafa, before I answer your question let me read a scripture about our future. A prophet once wrote, 'Remember the former things of old, For I am God, and there is no other; I am God, and there is none like Me, Declaring the end from the beginning, And from ancient times things that are not yet done...'" 1

"Yes, Allah declares the beginning from the end."

"Fadi, does the Qur'an contain specific prophecies about the future?"

"Hardly any," interrupted a candid Rafa.

"Not true!"

"Easy, Fadi," cautioned Aaron, "we don't want any unwanted attention."

Glaring at his sister he shook his head in disgust.

"Johanna is saying it's impossible to foretell events unless it's from God. Armageddon is a future event predicted in the first century by a prophet named John."

"The prophet Muhammad predicted Jesus will return as the Messiah," stated a confident Rafa.

"So did the prophets of the Old Testament," replied a giddy Johanna. "Their prophecies concerning Jesus' first coming were fulfilled in the New Testament over five hundred years later."

"Can you share some?"

"Sure. The prophets predicted the Messiah would come from the tribe of Judah. 2 He would be born in Bethlehem. 3 He would be preceded by a messenger. 4 And finally, the Messiah would enter Jerusalem on a colt." 5

"Did these events really happen to Jesus?"

"To the letter. Old Testament prophets also said the Messiah would be betrayed by a friend. 6 He would be wounded and whipped by his enemies. 7 They would pierce his hands. 8 Even his clothes would be sold for thirty pieces of silver." 9

"I don't believe in such propaganda," scorned Fadi.

"One prophet prophesied the Messiah would be spit upon and beaten. 10 That He would be silent before His accusers."

"What is the name of this prophet?" asked a curious Rafa.

"Isaiah lived several centuries before Jesus. He predicted, 'He was oppressed and He was afflicted, yet He opened not His mouth; He was led as a lamb to the slaughter, And as a sheep before its shearers is silent, So He opened not His mouth.'" 11

"Could this be possible?"

"Rafa, in the first century, an apostle of Jesus named Matthew wrote, 'And while He was being accused by the chief priests and elders, He answered nothing. Then Pilate said to Him, "Do You not hear how many things they testify against You?" But He answered him not one word, so that the governor marveled greatly.'" 12

"Muhammad proved Jesus was never crucified!"

"Fadi, King David predicted the crucifixion of the Messiah hundreds of years before this torture was invented. He prophesied, '"For dogs have surrounded Me; The congregation of the wicked has enclosed Me. They pierced My hands and My feet; I can count all My bones. They look and stare at Me. They divide My garments among them, And for My clothing they cast lots.' 13 Isaiah also prophesied, 'Therefore I will divide Him a portion with the great, and He shall divide the spoil with the strong, because He poured out His soul unto death, and He was numbered with the transgressors, and He bore the sin of many, And made intercession for the transgressors.'" 14

"Reading from the bible proves nothing."

"Fadi, it's an historical fact Jesus was crucified between two thieves."

"How can you be so sure, Johanna?" asked Rafa.

"Matthew wrote, 'Then two robbers were crucified with Him, one on the right and another on the left.'" 15 It's astonishing to see how many prophecies were fulfilled concerning Jesus."

Glancing back, Aaron respectfully added, "Fadi, these men were spokesmen for God. Isaiah, Zechariah, and Micah, each wrote of God's sovereign plan for mankind and how it would unfold in history. It's easy to see how the events of the past and the events of the future are connected by the predictions from these prophets. They also warned of God Almighty's future judgment of sin."

"I'm not a sinner, are you?" challenged the naive Muslim.

"A sinner saved by grace. If we say we don't sin we call God a liar." 16

"If these prophecies are true, what can we do?"

"Rafa, Jesus criticized the religious leaders for failing to heed the prophecies which testified of Him as God's Son. They were not able to recognize who Jesus was because they refused to discern the signs of the times. In a few weeks history will repeat itself."

"These passages aren't about Israel," fumed Fadi.

Johanna was ready, she had done her homework.

"The prophet's name was Zephaniah. Around 520 B.C., he predicted the Hebrew language would be restored in the last days. He prophesied, 'For then I will restore to the peoples a pure language that they all may call on the name of the Lord, to serve Him with one accord.' 17 No other nation but Israel has ever lost its native language, only to recover it almost two thousand years later. Hebrew is once again the spoken language of my people."

"You actually believe this?" Rafa skeptically replied.

"In 1948, Israel became a nation in one day. 18 Jews from over seventy nations have now returned to the land God promised Abraham. Fifty years earlier a Jewish scholar received a burden to restore the ancient tongue of the prophets. Through the efforts of this one man, the modern Hebrew language was eventually restored."

"Why is this so important?"

"Rafa, having a common language brought unity to millions of Jews returning to their homeland. We call it Aliyah."

"What about Jordanians?"

Johanna peeked over at her praying father.

"Tell them, Daddy, the Holy Spirit will bear witness."

"Rafa, have you ever heard of Mount Seir?"

"Of course, it's a mountain in our country."

"Ezekiel spoke of this area concerning the last days. Go ahead, Johanna, read it."

"'Moreover the word of the Lord came to me, saying, "Son of man, set your face against Mount Seir and prophesy against it, and say to it, "Thus says the Lord God: "Behold, O Mount Seir, I am against you; I will stretch out My hand against you, And make you most desolate; I shall lay your cities waste, And you shall be desolate. Then you shall know that I am the Lord. Because you have had an ancient hatred, and have shed the blood of the children of Israel by the power of the sword at the time of their calamity, when their iniquity came to an end.'" 19

"But why is God so angry at my people?"

"It's not only Jordan, Rafa," Johanna gently replied. "King David foretold, 'Do not keep silent, O God. Do not hold Your peace... For behold, Your enemies make a tumult; And those who hate You have lifted up their head. They have taken crafty counsel against Your people, And consulted together against Your sheltered ones. They have said, "Come, and let us cut them off from being a nation, that the name of Israel may be remembered no more. For they have consulted together with one consent; they form a confederacy against You...'" 20

"Who is trying to cut off Israel from being a nation?"

"These nations represent Lebanon, Iran, Syria, Jordan..."

"What about the Muslims Israel has killed? A Palestinian State means nothing. The Jews despise us. Does Allah favor such hatred?"

"Rafa, the prophets predicted many Jews would return to their homeland in these last days. The remarkable arrival of so many Russian and Ethiopian Jews is the fulfillment of prophecy. The return of Jewish exiles to the Holy Land is without debate." 21

"You believe God has condemned my country. How does this help my people? Tell us, can your God change His mind?"

"Don't listen to them," chided Fadi. "Muhammad was a greater prophet than Isaiah or Zechariah, even Jesus. Such predictions mean nothing to our people."

"After the seventh bowl is poured out, every city on earth will fall. This includes Jerusalem." 22

"If this is true, then why aren't you warning your own people?"

"The Holy Spirit is leading us to witness the gospel to your people. Rafa, do you know anyone who has not registered?"

"Sure, Johanna, I know of several settlements only worshipping Allah."

---

The smoke swirling around his stone throne never let up. His demonic hosts were not able to stop the prophetic events leading up to the sounding of the seventh trumpet. Before the eyes of the world, during the Feast of Tabernacles, Satan relinquished his authority to the Lord. Even so, many demons were still targeting anyone who still could be saved. These fallen angels knew the Word of God would soon kill those who destroy the earth. 23

Amidst the thick haze only its falcon like face could be seen. The evil spirit reverently approached the massive stone throne. Its red eyes were focused on Kur, the herald of the underground.

"Lord of the dead, where have you come from?"

"I, Osiris, have come from the tombs. How can anyone comprehend the light without first experiencing the darkness? My judgment of the dead is forever more."

"Why have you come before our Master's throne?"

"I'm ready to perform anything Satan asks of me."

Kur knew how revered Osiris was. No other demon could emit such fear. Once commissioned, this courier of death would never give up until its victim drew their last breath.

"Destroy the girl you now see in the spirit."

Osiris bowed before vanishing through a wall of smoke.

Turning the corner the car wash was almost out of site.

Reenie awkwardly muttered, "What will happen to him?"

"After we lose this van, I'll inform the underground. They'll know what to do. His own agents will pick him up in a couple of hours."

"So we're being followed?"

"Probably."

The little town looked deserted. Most were just going through the motions. Such zombie expressions were less common in the big cities. Country folk weren't good at pretending. No one noticed as the van cruised down Main Street.

"Look," stared Reenie, "what a twilight zone!"

"Who would have ever thought," Greg soberly replied.

"Do you think Bethany is anything like this?"

"Not this bad. Most bought into the lie the judgments would stop after the Witnesses were executed. Nobody was prepared for this."

"How sick," she shrugged. "The mark of the beast sealed it."

Up ahead, some teenagers were milling around a red pickup truck.

"Here's our ticket," pointed Greg.

Pulling alongside the ex-pastor waved.

The boys continued to talk among themselves.

"Nice truck, wanna sell it?"

"How much you offering?"

"My van for your truck."

"You can't be serious?" chided the owner.

"I'm up for a change."

"C'mon, guys, it's time for a road trip."

After exchanging pink slips Greg stepped aside. His buddies quickly piled inside. Their laughter sounded hallow as they sped away.

Back on the highway, she could sense his uneasiness.

"Greg, what are our chances of reaching the Vineyard?"

"Our contact will know if we're being followed. If we are, we will have to split up. It's safer if you enter the Vineyard without me."

"But the Q is..."

"Reenie, your mission is about saving thousands for eternity. How can you measure something like that! My assignment is to protect you. We have to trust the Lord will take care of Emma and the boys."

# STANDING AT THE CROSSROADS

"You should not have stood at the crossroads to cut off those
among them who escaped; nor should you have delivered up those
among them who remained in the day of distress."
Obadiah 14

As the campers slept under a full moon; faithful sentries made their
appointed rounds. Her secret refuge was a blessing. Resting her
journal on her knees, a troubled Twanna Evers was writing. This was
her way of keeping her actions in line with the Word. Such prayerful
reflection was a lifeline amidst the greatest fear of her life.

From the ledge above her cave, he could barely make out her
prayers. With a full moon overhead he could see her raised hands.

"Holy Spirit You supernaturally plucked these campers from the
jaws of hell. I don't want to be a stumbling block. But I can't wait any
longer. Can I please leave the Vineyard?"

Her pleas weren't new. Under her contagious smile was a
tormented soul.

Little pebbles dribbling from the ledge jerked her head upward.
She could hear feet shifting in the gritty dirt.

"Who is there?"

"It's me, Tee."

She didn't move; she knew his familiar deep voice.

"Be careful coming down; it's not as easy as it looks."

Sliding down feet first he stopped between two large rocks.
Squeezing between them he landed on a clump of old pine needles.

"Bull's-eye!" he grinned. "Talk about a tight fit."

Seated a few feet away, wrapped in a red wool blanket, her blank
expression was not the norm. He finally got the message.

"Cody Joe Parish, you have the habit of dropping in on people at the strangest times. What are you doing here?"

"Must be the Holy Spirit, I felt such conviction walking by your empty sleeping bag. It's a miracle I found you; don't you think?"

When Twanna first arrived at the Vineyard, the fun loving football star was the first to befriend her. Cody introduced her to the staff, the campers, helped train her in camp induction, even volunteered to be her Bible study partner. Before long they were like brother and sister. His willingness to serve helped strengthen Twanna's faith. Even now, she was having a hard time getting angry at him.

"I guess you heard me praying. I come here to talk with the Lord. This is where I journal. It helps me keep my head straight."

"Tee, what's really bugging you?"

"There is a situation in my life needing closure."

His friend was always upbeat. Such anxiety was something new.

"Maybe I can help?"

"Sorry, bro, only God has this answer."

"When I pray for you I see a minister preaching. But no one is listening to him. Maybe you should share your situation with me. I'm a good listener. You ever notice how big my ears are?"

"For real?"

"Just remember, I'm not mister bible answer man."

The flashback in her mind never went away.....

"Daddy, our youth group is dwindling. My friends are disappearing."

"For heaven's sake, Twanna, I've just been elected Senior Pastor. I have a responsibility."

"To who?"

"To God Almighty. Girl, you need to pray. Our board will vote on it tomorrow night. That will settle it."

"Are you talking about mandatory ID registration?"

"This past week a doomsday evangelist has been scaring the heck out of our members. He's teaching the Great Tribulation has begun. He believes anyone registering is taking the mark of the beast." 1

"Is this preacher for real?"

"Oh, Stephen Corbin is nuts. Any fanatic can twist the scriptures. He thinks former President Kayin is somehow the Antichrist."

"Is this possible?"

"Of course not! The rapture comes before the Man of Sin is revealed. Satan is using such hysterics to deceive the weak-minded.

This is why I've decided to teach a new series on helping thy neighbor."

"Will we be registering soon?"

Taking her hands in his, he lovingly reflected, "Since your mother left us, I've tried to raise you the best I can. You know I will always protect you."

"I love you, Daddy."

"That's my girl. Besides, what makes you think taking an ID can affect our salvation? Nothing can ever separate us from His love."

No one knew how many died after the sounding of the sixth trumpet. The thriving farm town was no more. Bethany's beautiful landscaped streets were covered with trash. Gangs were getting high on paint, cold medicine, nail polish, anything to numb their pain.

Chugging down Cherry Street the Winnebago was on its last legs.

A puzzled Jon pointed, "Our contacts have vanished."

"Maybe they had to relocate," offered Donnell.

"What about checking in with your underground command post?"

"Jake, only those assigned are allowed in. Just enough to keep the information flowing. Most Watchmen are involved in rescue."

"Wow, a green light till Jesus kills the followers of the Beast."

"Just twenty days left."

A curious Kurt posed, "Jon, if you can't get in touch with the underground then how do you receive your next assignment?"

"Hearing from the Holy Spirit is the bottom line. We all know how quickly circumstances can change. There just aren't many constants left."

"Such as?" asked Emma.

"Word of knowledge, Word of wisdom. His sheep need to obey His voice. Kayin is paralyzed. Even so, his pet peeve is still resister camps. He hates them. They're like giant neon signs advertising rebellion against the NWC. His agenda isn't about keeping the masses in line anymore. He just wants his puppets to kill as many Christians and Jews as possible."

"So you're thinking agents purposely let Reenie escape?"

"Especially if they heard us mention the Vineyard. They'll just let Greg and Reenie lead them to the camp."

"Greg thinks the Vineyard is the biggest children's camp in the whole southeast. So what are we waiting for, Donnell?"

"Emma, it will take a ton of petrol to make it to the Blue Ridge Mountains, and what about a return trip? Or is this a one way ticket?"

"Don't you see?" insisted Jake. "This children's camp was in Reenie's vision. First we receive our calling to protect her. Then Satan sends his pawns. She and Greg escape. You guys arrive. It's all fitting together."

"You getting something, Jon boy?"

"Oh yeah Donnie! I'm talking a big time witness!"

"Where do you get your gas?"

"Kurt, the underground stores gasoline inside a closed restaurant on the Westside, no one can touch it except for emergencies."

"Hey, guys, our Miracle Girl is waiting on us."

"We're on it, Red!" beamed Donnell. "It's now or never!"

Her sobs meant much more than regret; Cody knew that much.

"Where is your father now, Tee?"

"I don't know. We separated to avoid the NWC. He told me to hide in these mountains. That's how I got here."

"So you want to go back to Charleston and find him?"

"We could do so much more than what we're doing right now."

"You think so? The kids just rescued have no clue what's coming."

"That's just it; look at how many more need our help."

"The Vineyard is beyond capacity. If we accept any more campers; we run the risk of being busted. You know the consequences."

"Yeah, it's just sometimes I feel like a babysitter."

"Tee, have you ever studied the functions of the body of Christ?"

"Lots of times, the Corinthian church was pretty messed up."

"They were having trouble figuring out how to work together. Paul wrote, 'For in fact the body is not one member but many. If the foot should say, "Because I am not a hand, I am not of the body," is it therefore not of the body? And if the ear should say, "Because I am not an eye, I am not of the body," is it therefore not of the body? If the whole body were an eye, where would be the hearing? If the whole body were hearing, where would be the smelling? But now God has set the members, each one of them, in the body just as He pleased.'" 2

"What's your point?"

"Paul is saying if one member suffers, we should all feel it. If one member is honored, we should all rejoice." 3

"So our assignment here is just as important as those in rescue?"

"This was a truth many believers got away from in these last days. By His grace, our Lord has shown us the power of unity within the body. Paul wrote, 'That there should be no schism in the body, but that the members should have the same care for one another.'" 4

"You know how much I love these kids. But I also love my daddy. How could my leaving cause division?"

"C'mon, you know where our camp is. You helped design our exit tunnels. You even know our rescue routes. If the NWC ever caught you, they could use you to find us."

Bowing his head, Cody could feel the spiritual warfare. He didn't want to report her. Somehow God would have to make it happen.

"Is there something else you're not telling me, Tee?"

With tears in her eyes she confessed, "I've been in church since I was three. I've taught Sunday school, led the children's choir, I was even the leader of our Youth group."

"Praise God, Tee, you're a blessing to so many."

"I wasn't saved, Cody. The Great Tribulation was torture!"

"What do you mean?"

"Two days after the coming of the Son of Man, I repented of my sins and asked Jesus to be my Lord and Savior. A week later I received a vision from the Holy Spirit. My calling is to disciple kids till the first day of the Millennium. Since arriving at the Vineyard you and I have seen so many rescued. Their trusting faces, their eagerness to learn, it's been awesome. Yet, now I'm getting a different direction."

"Like what?"

"It's almost like the Lord wants me to leave."

Cody and Twanna could hear the crunching of pine needles under her boots. The faithful guard was making her rounds beneath the tall pines covering the camp grounds. Just before the opening of the fifth seal her parents received the mark of the beast. After getting separated from her older brother, she was rescued on a cold rainy night by a Watchman from the Vineyard. The blonde teen from Columbus, Georgia was a shining example of an overcomer for Christ. Tragically, for many saints, such obedience required too high a price.

It took two more days before they made it across the border. Up ahead, Jordanian soldiers were dragging boys into a large truck.

"Fadi, what's happening?" gasped Johanna.

"It's our militia. They're enrolling for Jihad. Any boy over fourteen must enlist. No one can refuse."

"Aaron, you must turn back!" blurted a terrified Rafa.

Fadi's motioning to be quiet meant nothing to her.

"If they stop us, you'll be arrested. There is another way to my father's camp. Turn right at the next road."

Steering his jeep between two cars, Aaron made a quick right. Pulling off the road, he parked behind a bread shop.

"I'm not getting a good feeling about this, Daddy."

"We need to follow the instructions we agreed upon."

"How do we do that?"

"We wait, honey. The militia will soon move on."

In silence they watched mothers begging for bread. Their frantic cries to Allah were piercing. Such hopelessness was overwhelming.

"Oh, Daddy, what was I thinking? Most have already decided who they will follow."

"She's right," pressed Fadi. "Just release us; we won't report you."

"No one's going anywhere; not just yet."

From his jacket, Aaron laid the loaded revolver in his lap. His eyes never left the dirt road.

"Once the Jews are destroyed," bragged the young Jordanian, Allah will rule Palestine from Al-Masjid Al-Aqsa. We will reap the spoils of infidels; a people blinded from the truth. Allahu Akbar!"

Johanna dreaded looking into his angry brown eyes.

"Fadi, you have no idea of the devastation that's coming."

Pushing his hand away from her face, Rafa cried, "Stop it, Fadi, I want to hear what the Bible says about our country. Johanna, why do you speak such evil against our people?"

"When Esau separated from his brother Jacob, he settled in Edom. Throughout history, the people of this land have persecuted the children of Israel. The Old Testament prophet Obadiah foretold of the judgment of Edom during the day of the Lord."

"I want to hear what this prophet predicted."

Opening her Bible, Johanna read, "'But you should not have gazed on the day of your brother in the day of his captivity; nor should you have rejoiced over the children of Judah in the day of their destruction; nor should you have spoken proudly in the day of distress... You should not have stood at the crossroads to cut off those among them who escaped; nor should you have delivered up those among them who remained in the day of distress.'" 5

A shaken Rafa cried out, "Our people don't deserve judgment because of what happened thousands of years ago."

"They don't care who murders Palestinian children!" cursed Fadi. "Johanna, are you aware most Palestinians are Jordanian?"

She could sense their heaviness. Glancing toward her father, she silently prayed for some sort of direction.

"They deserve to hear it," encouraged Aaron.

Nodding her head, she read, "'For the day of the Lord upon all the nations is near... For as you drank on My holy mountain, so shall all the nations drink continually; Yes, they shall drink, and swallow, And they shall be as though they had never been.'" 6

"Trust me; Allah will soon crush the house of Jacob."

"'But on Mount Zion there shall be deliverance, and there shall be holiness; the house of Jacob shall possess their possessions. The house of Jacob shall be a fire, and the house of Joseph a flame; but the house of Esau shall be stubble; they shall kindle them and devour them, and no survivor shall remain of the house of Esau,' for the Lord has spoken.'" 7

"We shall see who survives!" threatened Fadi.

"Does your God condemn Zionists too?" asked a sarcastic Rafa.

"Don't believe them. Their prophecies say whatever they want."

"Jeremiah predicted the judgment of your land in the last days."

"I'll read it. 'Edom shall be astonishment; everyone who goes by it will be astonished and will hiss at all its plagues. As in the overthrow of Sodom and Gomorrah and their neighbors,' says the Lord, "No one shall remain there, nor shall a son of man dwell in it.'" 8

"Have you two ever heard of Sodom and Gomorrah?"

"There are no such cities!"

"Not anymore, Fadi," sighed Aaron. "Four thousand years ago, Sodom and Gomorrah was located near the Dead Sea. Lot settled in this region after separating from his uncle, Abraham. It was a rich land full of water and lush vegetation."

"What does this have to do with my people?"

"God judged these cities because of their rebellion. This land has been desolate ever since. Both are a picture of future judgment."

"So you approve of my people's destruction? What a hypocrite."

As his daughter silently interceded, the former freedom fighter confessed, "Fadi, there isn't time to share the regrets of my past. I have lived a lifetime of hate for Syrians, Egyptians, Iranians, and Jordanians. Bringing you across our border was not easy for me."

A confused Rafa pleaded, "Then why do it? What can you gain by driving into an armed camp full of your sworn enemies?"

"The salvation of their souls," whispered a hopeful Johanna.

## SECOND BOWL: DEATH IN THE SEA

*"Then the second angel poured out his bowl on the sea, and it became blood as of a dead man; and every living creature in the sea died."*
Revelation 16:3

After bowing before the Throne of God, an angel emptied the second bowl upon the earth. 1

---

The stunned cameraman couldn't believe what he was hearing.

"Really, Wes, she's coming in? What changed her mind?"

"Never forget, Natalie Rene Roberts has been a hard-hitting reporter from day one. Are your special takes ready?"

"All set. What a bloody mess."

Rushing down the hall from makeup, the most popular newscaster in America had a resolute look on her face.

"Wes, do you want to hear my opening statement?"

"No need; the pictures tell the story. Those evacuating the coasts are just feeding into the panic. Marshall Law isn't worth a dam. Are you up for this Nate? Once we begin, there's no backing away."

"Remember you owe me a Special Report."

Waiting for a final sound check he had so many questions.

"Nate, you were never interested in hate groups before; especially white supremacist cults. I checked out the Prophetic Voice. I can smell a hunch. You must have something on their leader."

"Delford Eiland is a loose cannon. He must be stopped!"

The green light was flashing. After two more adjustments, the pre-recorded tape introduced News with Natalie. The resolute Anchorwoman took a breath before looking into camera #1.

"Just minutes ago, every major ocean on earth spewed forth massive amounts of blood. This infection of marine life is in no way related to the purple sores many received last week. Congress is asking those living on the coasts of our great country to remain calm. All commercial and recreational boating has been temporarily suspended. In order for Marshall Law to function properly we must all..."

---

The leadership of the Vineyard consisted of different nationalities, ages, and sizes. Being picked to direct a Christian underground camp during the day of the Lord would become Ruben Rodriguez's greatest challenge in life. He was aware of the decisions he would eventually be forced to make. A former homicide detective from Atlanta, the middle age officer had seen a lot. The increase of teenage crime had skyrocketed in the past decade. There were many red flags contributing to the neglect of America's youth. Through it all, God was preparing this overcomer for a two year commitment in the Blue Ridge Mountains. Forced to train the youngest staff in the Southeast, this ex-cop knew Satan was planning an attack.

"Staff, before I address our campers with my decision, I need to share with you the consequences we're facing. Our camp is dangerously over capacity. This is why the underground is now diverting all new resisters to other camps."

Looking into their trusting eyes he silently thanked the Lord.

"We aren't alone. When Greg Hudson and I created the Vineyard we knew about the survivalist militias training in these mountains. The possibility of such groups drawing attention from the authorities is real. This is why the Holy Spirit is warning us about the size of our camp. As of today, I have no other choice but to call a Red Fox. From now on no one can leave our camp. Contact with anyone on the outside, whether by computer, phone, or letter, is forbidden."

Ruben had no intention of hiding the truth. He just never felt comfortable giving a report without having all the details.

"Are these religious survivalists?"

"Twanna, our biggest threat is from a white supremacist army called the Prophetic Voice. Delford Eiland is their leader."

"So they know about us?"

"Yes."

"So anyone Black or Jewish is putting this camp in danger?"

"Twanna, maintaining security for the Vineyard carries many risks. Satan has unsuccessfully attempted to destroy our camp several times. Before the Vineyard was a week old, a strain of flu infected most of our campers. Next, the enemy tried to scare our children with lies about their families. It wasn't long before deceiving spirits sowed jealously among our staff. That's where I come in. Armageddon is just weeks away. It's too late to allow our emotions to dictate what we will do for God. We must trust each other or the blood of these children will be on our hands. This ain't over until the Word of God returns with His angels."

The entire staff spontaneously stood and worshipped the Lord.

"I'm ready to address our campers. May the Spirit of Christ prepare them to receive the truth."

"There's a real uneasiness, Ruben," offered a concerned Cody. "Satan is turning up the heat."

"Guys, the way I see it, the bigger the diversion created by the enemy, the bigger opportunity to see the glory of God manifested. Twanna, are the prayer warriors in place?"

"Prayed up and ready to rumble."

Over two thousand children were assembled inside the cave adjacent to the mouth of the tunnel nicknamed Bethel. Everyone present had saved family members searching for them. Standing on a large rock he raised his hands to get their attention. Alert intercessors lined the damp walls of the massive cavern. They knew the cost if these children ever succumbed to mass panic. Camp security was at an all-time high. Even so, a man in his late 20's escorting two children just slipped in undetected. Resting on his hunches in the shadows, he clicked on his mini recorder.

"I'm Camp Commander Ruben Rodriguez. I've come here today to share a wonderful promise God has given each of us. This promise was given by the prophet Isaiah. He predicted, 'For behold, I create new heavens and a new earth...'" 2

"I don't get this?" teased a boy. "Why wreak it in the first place?"

Immediately staff members went to work. Loving but firm exhortations could be heard throughout the cave. There would be no more interruptions. The consequences were much too high. Ruben knew only the Comforter could reassure such fragile hearts.

"That's right; our Jesus will soon restore this earth like it was in the Garden of Eden. But before the Son of God performs this miracle there will be a battle. Three weeks from now, the Beast will lead armies from many nations in the invasion of Israel. The Bible calls it the great day of God Almighty, Armageddon. How many have studied this event?"

It was encouraging to see so many hands raised.

"When the Word appears followers of the Beast will be consumed with the breath of His mouth. Those believing in Jesus will be protected. This includes your family members who don't have the deceiver's mark."

No one knew how much these kids had suffered. Their struggle to survive was almost over. Amidst the cheers no one noticed the thin teenager standing to his feet. His shaggy brown hair was partly covering his blood shot eyes. Ruben could sense his resolve. The ex-cop lovingly paused and waited for his question.

"When will I get to see my folks again?"

"Son, the crooked mountains, the burning cities, the dead vegetation, the infected oceans, will be restored between Armageddon and the first day of Christ's thousand year reign over the nations. This is when surviving families will begin returning to Jerusalem." 3

"How do you know my folks will be there?"

He knew this boy was searching for somebody to trust in; someone willing to say everything would be okay.

"My brother in Christ, only Jesus knows where your folks are. We must all pray for the protection of our families; for those who believe and for those who still can be saved."

Near the back a girl shouted, "How will we get to Jerusalem?"

"And where will we be when Jesus restores the earth?"

Another teen threatened, "You can't keep me here against my will! I need to find my mom!"

The Commander couldn't wait any longer.

"I have an announcement. For many, it will sound harsh. Later today, when you meet in your prayer groups, you may ask your group leader any questions about my decision."

No one was talking. He could hear the sizzling of oil burning torches behind him. Even the moving of arms and legs stopped.

"For the security of our camp, I have ordered a total lockdown. The code name for such a procedure is called Red Fox. From now on we won't be able to accept any more campers. This means any members of your family rescued will be sent to other camps. Trust me; this is for your safety as well as your parents."

The damage was done. The news couldn't have been worse for those struggling with the lie they were deserted. Some didn't want to live any longer if they couldn't be with their family. Counselors quickly moved in to minister to the campers becoming hysterical.

The abrupt exodus was what Eli had hoped for. His recorder hidden in his jacket he had what he had come for.

---

The broken windows, the trash filled lawn, the broken redwood sign, Lakeview High School looked so out of place.

Jake, a former student, couldn't believe what he was seeing.

"Wow, guys, ole Lakeview took a big hit."

Glancing over at a preoccupied Kurt, the experienced Watchman wanted to help.

"What's up, Red?"

"Just more questions, Jon."

"Try me?"

"Like how will armies moving toward Israel arrive safely? The hailstones from the seventh bowl will weigh over a hundred pounds. All their troops can't hide? Won't they be annihilated?"

"Kurt, only through supernatural intervention can all the pieces of the latter days come together perfectly. The place, the players, the battle, it's all spelled out in His Word. After the sixth bowl is poured out, unclean spirits will use false signs to deceive. John described this in his vision. 'Then the sixth angel poured out his bowl on the great river Euphrates, and its water was dried up, so that the way of the kings from the east might be prepared. And I saw three unclean spirits like frogs coming out of the mouth of the dragon, out of the mouth of the beast, and out of the mouth of the false prophet. For they are spirits of demons, performing signs, which go out to the kings of the earth and of the whole world, to gather them to the battle of that great day of God Almighty.'" 4

"I once had a friend who was convinced the Antichrist is Satan. He believed Isaiah's description of Lucifer proves Satan is the leader who will make the earth tremble in the latter days." 5

"Not according to John the apostle. The Beast will be cast alive into the lake of fire when the Word of God appears in heaven during the supper of the great God. 6 After a thousand years, Satan will join him. ₇ Which means the Beast can't be Satan. Revelation 16:13 lists the dragon (Satan), the beast, and the false prophet, as different persons. It will be unclean spirits who will deceive the leaders of the nations."

"Aren't these the same leaders who saw Jesus take back authority from Satan at the seventh trumpet? How can the devil attack if God is now reigning?"

"Kurt, it's all in our Father's permissive will," reasoned a convinced Donnell. "After the fifth bowl, the Beast's kingdom will be history. Darkness will cover the nations trying to destroy Israel." ₈

"So the nations persecuting His anointed will suffer His wrath?"

"Everyone from the Beast's empire will gnaw at their tongues in total darkness. After the pouring out of the sixth bowl, ground troops will use a dried up Euphrates to reach Israel."

"Glory to God!" praised the naive redhead. "There were times I thought we would never see it."

A shaken Donnell muttered back, "When it's over maybe we will wish we never had!"

He could see the silhouette outside his tent. The intrusion didn't matter; the Commander couldn't sleep anyway. An agonizing burden for someone was gripping his heart.

"Ruben, I've got something I need to share with you."

"Come on in, Cody."

Raising the flap to his tent, the young Watchman sat down on the rug at the end of his cot. His arms resting on his legs, his hands tightly clasped, he waited. Easing into his rocking chair the former detective was good at reading faces.

"Talk to me, Cody, whatever you have to share God is greater."

"Twanna Evers has left camp."

"Are you sure? She could be a lot of places."

"Tee has missed two security checks. She left to find her father."

"Did she tell you this?"

"Every day we counsel campers who want to leave. After talking her through, I didn't think she'd do it. So I didn't report it."

"Where is she headed?"

"Her father lives on an island off Charleston, South Carolina."

"Have you heard the news? The second bowl has hit our oceans. Millions are evacuating our coastlines. The islands near Charleston are probably off limits by now."

"Which means we could be having more visitors?"

"The warfare is clearly heating up."

"But why now, when we are so close to the end?"

Stretching out on his portable cot, his hands resting under his head, Ruben was rehearsing future scenarios in his mind. This was his job. To foresee what was coming.

"Are you sure Twanna left because of her father?"

"What else could it be?"

"What about my report on the white supremacy cult, the Prophetic Voice? Maybe she left to protect our kids."

"Sorry, Ruben, I just didn't think she would do it."

"Well at least I know who I've been praying for."

"That's not all. Your lockdown announcement at dinner was a real curve for many of our campers. Our counselors are 24/7 trying to head off some serious melt downs."

He never flinched. This ex-cop had already defeated any doubts from the enemy on his decision.

"Sir, I thought Red Fox was a last resort; like a couple of days before Armageddon. Aren't there still a ton of believers needing our help? Tee is going for rescues; I'm sure of it."

"Cody, there are many factors to consider. It's not always black and white. From now on, all rescues by Vineyard Watchmen will be taken to other camps."

"Yeah, being led by the Holy Spirit is so critical."

"Our intercessors have received a witness of many families being reunited during the Millennium."

"Ruben, most of our campers know nothing about Christ's future reign over the nations."

"How sad; it's mentioned more than any other subject in the Bible."

"I had no clue. Could you share how the saints in heaven and the believers on earth function together during His thousand year reign?"

From underneath his cot Ruben grabbed his Bible. He loved to teach when feeling an anointing from the Holy Spirit. 9

"After Jesus returns in Revelation 19:11-21 John saw a thousand year period in Revelation 20:1-7. Millennium, which means thousand in the Greek, describes the time our Lord will rule over the nations. We are promised a new heaven and a new earth. The New Jerusalem will have a river of life flowing from the throne of God. 10 The leaves from the tree of life inside the Holy City will be used for the healing of the nations." 11

"So those surviving the day of the Lord will be living inside?"

"Actually, the glorified bride of Christ will be ruling from within the New Jerusalem. His wife, Old and New Testament believers, were gathered to heaven at the coming of the Son of Man." 12

"How does this work?"

"On the first day of His thousand year reign, the bride will descend to earth within the Holy Jerusalem. 13 The Lord will rule from the throne of God inside the Holy City. He will wipe away every tear. 14 There will be no more pain or dying, everything will be new." 15

"So what about believers like us?"

"After Armageddon, the earth will be restored like the Garden of Eden. The survivors from the Day of the Lord will live on a new earth."

"We are almost there."

"Daniel prophesied, 'And in the days of these kings the God of heaven will set up a kingdom which shall never be destroyed; and the kingdom shall not be left to other people; it shall break in pieces and consume all these kingdoms, and it shall stand forever.'" 16

"So God will first destroy the nations following the Beast?"

"Correct. Before the Son receives His millennial kingdom from His Father, He has to take back Satan's spiritual authority over the earth. Jesus did this during the Feast of Tabernacles, after the sounding of the seventh trumpet. The Word of God will take back physical control at the great day of God Almighty, Armageddon."

"At lunch I was introduced to several Messianic families. I have such a burden for the Jewish people. The NWC has killed so many."

"Son, the fullness of the Gentiles is over. The Deliverer has taken away Israel's sins. 17 Jesus has split the Mount of Olives. At this moment, a redeemed remnant from Israel is worshipping in Azal!"

"Yeah, so many are praying for the peace of Jerusalem." 18

"Amen, once Jesus rules over the nations from the Temple of the Lord there will be peace in Jerusalem." 19

"You're losing me, Ruben. How can Jesus rule from the Temple of the Lord and inside the Holy Jerusalem at the same time? The Holy City coming down doesn't have a Temple." 20

"Cody, the Temple will become the throne of God."

"I've never been taught this. Can you show me some verses?"

"Ok. Revelation 22:3 says, 'And there shall be no more curse, but the throne of God and of the Lamb shall be in it, and His servants shall serve Him.' 21 Ezekiel saw a physical throne filled with the glory of God." 22

"Now this is deep," teased the ex-football star.

"In Revelation 21, the nations will have no need of a sun or moon since the Lamb is its lamp. 23 The nations will walk by its light. Zechariah spoke of a unique day when there is no day or night. 24 He saw a restored Temple on Mount Zion bearing the glory of God. 25

"So the New Jerusalem and the Temple on Mount Zion are both called the throne of God having His glory?"

"Exactly, Revelation 22 has Christ reigning with His saints inside the New Jerusalem. Ezekiel saw the Son of Man ruling forever from a physical temple." 26

Shaking his head, the young man had no words.

"Check it out, Cody; Revelation 22 has a pure river of water proceeding from the throne of God. Zechariah saw living waters flowing from Jerusalem. A day our Lord shall be King over all the earth." 27

"How incredible!"

"Inside the Holy City leaves from the tree of life will bring healing to the nations. 28 Ezekiel also speaks of leaves being used as medicine. 29 In fact, both have believers' tears being wiped away." 30

"So those living on earth can enter the New Jerusalem?"

"Only those written in the Lamb's Book of Life." 31

"You mean we get to see the Lord?"

Leaning back, an amazed Ruben confessed, "After comparing scripture its clear the Temple our Lord will build on Mount Zion will become the throne inside the New Jerusalem for eternity!"

Spontaneously both Watchmen dropped to their knees in the dirt. Their petitioning would last until sun up. Within days the wrath of God will ravage the earth a final time. The cities will fall, mountains will crumble, and the oceans and lakes will emit the smell of death. Even angels on assignment will look on in horror.

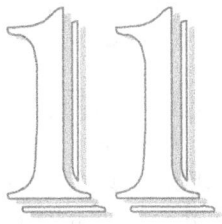

# LIKE THE GARDEN OF EDEN

"So they will say, 'This land that was laid waste has become like the Garden of Eden; the cities that were lying in ruins, desolate and destroyed, are now fortified and inhabited.'"
Ezekiel 36:35

Veering off the road, he let several cars pass by. His eyes focused on the rear view mirror, the old man turned his head lights off.

"What's up, Ben?"

"Well, Tee, missing one contact is understandable. Missing three in a row is too dangerous for my blood. We need to intercede. It appears the security perimeter of the Vineyard has been exposed."

"Ruben must have seen this coming."

"The intercessors did. That's why he locked down the camp."

"What security precautions is he taking? Our tunnels aren't ready. I pleaded with him not to take in so many kids."

"We're all trying to hear from the Lord. After I drop you off in Charleston, I'm heading for a rescue in North Carolina. After delivering them to a camp outside Ashville, I'll just ask the Holy Spirit what's next. It's the best way for me to hear from God."

"I left camp so I..."

"Tee, you don't have to give me a reason. You know words without action mean nothing. I saw how you loved our campers. Your background in engineering was critical in the construction of Bethel and Beulah. God will reward you for your faithfulness."

"But, I..."

"Let me finish, girl. When you first asked me to smuggle you out without authorization; I thought no way. I've never broken a camp rule; not once. Humanly speaking, allowing you to leave camp was out of the question. We can't afford the luxury of mistakes, especially with Armageddon being so close. But the more I prayed, I just couldn't deny what God was telling me to do."

"Which is?"

"Helping you is the greatest thing I'll ever do for the Lord."

"What exactly did the Lord show you?"

"My great, great grandfather was once the chief of a Cherokee tribe still living in these mountains. He was a respected leader among his people; a real jack of trades. What he loved to do the most was create dishware. He built his own stone kiln on Black Rock Mountain. You see, to make china strong you gotta burn it at least three times."

"Why so much heat?"

"To get the colors right, Grandpappy used to spend hours burning, sometimes even four times."

"How does this apply to me?"

"I don't know how to say this in a soft way, Tee."

"I can take it. I've been spending some quality time with Cody Parrish. You always know where you stand with that boy."

"A real piece of work; ain't he," chuckled the seventy-two year old Cherokee. "You two make a great team. Does he know you left?"

"He will by morning roll call. I wouldn't doubt if he's having a chat with Ruben right now. So what did God show you about me?"

"While praying I saw Cherokees being persecuted. To protect their children, these warriors surrendered near the trail of tears."

"What is the trail of tears?"

"It's a dark chapter in my people's history. Many chose to die so others could live. In my vision warriors were suffering under the heat of persecution. Then I saw a severely burned young woman. Like my grandfather's best china, she had been through the fire three times."

"Is she Cherokee?"

"She has beautiful brown eyes, a gorgeous smile, and a deep love for children."

"Ben, are you saying..."

"That's right. In my vision you were the one debating whether to go another time. Make no mistake, the persecution awaiting you could hurt big time. Tee, you need to count the cost. There is a reason why so many walked away from their calling in rescue." [1]

Twanna knew what she had to do. This was a rare opportunity to do her Father's will just before the great day of God Almighty.

Every window in the bar and grill was broken. From the outside barbecue pit the exhausted teenager stood watch. Dressed in baggy blue jeans and a faded Atlanta Falcons sweatshirt, Kurt couldn't believe the devastation. The empty faces, the rotten smell of dirty garbage, the looted businesses, it was the worst of nightmares.

Clicking on his flashlight a throng of cockroaches scurried across the dirty basement floor. Jon's hushed amen got their attention.

"Jake, Emma, you see these boxes? Each box has two red plastic containers. Each container holds four gallons of gas."

The check by the Holy Spirit was strong. Jogging upstairs Jon knew the boy needed some encouragement. The burning torch across the street gave off just enough light to see his downcast eyes.

"Pretty hard to take, huh, Kurt?"

"Yeah, just never figured it would get this bad. The apostle Peter wasn't playing when he predicted the earth would be burned up." 2

"Yet being here to see the miracle of a new earth is off the charts for me, how about you?"

"Didn't Ezekiel predict it will become like the Garden of Eden?"

Opening his Bible Jon read, 'The desolate land will be cultivated instead of lying desolate in the sight of all who pass through it. They will say, "This land that was laid waste has become like the Garden of Eden; the cities that were lying in ruins, desolate and destroyed, are now fortified and inhabited."' 3

"So everyone will know the Lord did this?"

"Here it is, 'Then the nations around you that remain will know that I the LORD have rebuilt what was destroyed and have replanted what was desolate. I the LORD have spoken, and I will do it.'" 4

"So the prophet is describing Christ's reign over the nations?" 5

"Yep, the new earth is the restoration of all things in Acts 3:21, the regeneration in Mathew 19:28, and the kingdom of Israel in Acts 1:7-11."

"Glory!" praised an animated Kurt, "the Lamb of God is coming back in a new heaven to a new earth!" 6

In the dreary stillness of downtown the resolute police officer was making his final round. He hit the accelerator as soon as he spotted movement in the closed down bar and grill.

"That's the last one," whispered Jake. "Let's get out of here, Em."

Parked in the back alley Donnell started the engine.

"What's the hold up? Where's Jon and Kurt?"

"Freeze! If you move I won't miss. Now get on your knees."

The frightened redhead didn't resist as he was handcuffed.

Sprinting through the pitch black parking lot Jon Mendel stumbled over several piles of trash. As soon he jumped inside, the RV sped away.

The small town nestled in the mountains showed no life. The trash filled streets, the ransacked shops; even the motels were abandoned. Their little red truck had gotten them this far.

"Look at this, Greg, Dahlonega is a ghost town."

"They must have run out of water. The only towns in these mountains making it are ones with a clean supply. The Vineyard gets its water from two wells the campers dug."

"How blind can you be? Even after the execution of thousands in camps created by Congress, most never saw what was coming." 7

"Reenie, in the 1940's American soldiers rescued thousands of Jews from death camps in Germany. Incredibly, many German citizens had no knowledge of such camps."

"Nothing has changed. Satan still wants to destroy the Jews."

"Praise God, Ezekiel supernaturally saw their homecoming in these last days. 'Surely I will take the children of Israel from among the nations, wherever they have gone, and will gather them from every side and bring them into their own land.'" 8

"Kurt taught this truth to me on our ride to the cave. Isn't this Ezekiel's vision of dry bones coming back to life?"

"Amen, Miracle Girl, 'Then I will sprinkle clean water on you, and you shall be clean; I will cleanse you from all your filthiness... I will give you a new heart and put a new spirit within you; I will take the heart of stone out of your flesh and give you a heart of flesh. I will put My Spirit within you and cause you to walk in My statutes, and you will keep My judgments and do them.'" 9

"I get it. This remnant returned in unbelief. When the 70th week ended, the Messiah took away their sins and gave them a new spirit."

"Did you know Ezekiel predicted the exact day the Jewish people would first return to their land?"

"C'mon, Greg, I really wanna hear this."

"The Lord told the prophet He would judge Israel for four hundred and thirty years for their refusal to repent. 10 This judgment began when the Jews were taken away to Babylon in 606 B.C. Seventy years later they were allowed to return to their land."

"Doesn't that leave 360 years of punishment?"

"That's right. Now in the Book of Leviticus, God promises to multiply Israel's judgment seven times if they refuse to repent." [11]

"So did Israel repent after being chastised in Babylon?"

"Nope. Now seven times 360 is 2,520 Hebrew years, when you convert it to solar years, it comes out to 2,483. The children of Israel had to suffer 2,483 more years before becoming a sovereign nation again."

"So when did the Jews return from Babylon?"

"In 536 B.C."

"So where do we end up after subtracting 2,483 years?"

"1948. On May 14th, 1948, Israel became a nation again."

"What a miracle from God!"

"Ezekiel isn't through yet. He also predicted the judgment of those who attack Israel. 'You shall fall upon the mountains of Israel, you and all your troops and the peoples who are with you; I will give you to birds of prey of every sort and to the beasts of the field to be devoured. So I will make My holy name known in the midst of My people Israel, and I will not let them profane My holy name anymore. Then the nations shall know that I am the Lord, the Holy One in Israel.'" [12]

Up ahead, a temporary roadblock caught his eye.

"What's wrong?" whispered Reenie.

"Agents."

"What are they doing way up here? Oh no, are they after us?"

Nonchalantly Greg turned right into a small strip mall. Parking between some broken down cars, he cut the engine.

"What now? What about our contact?"

"Even switching to this truck won't help us. Maggie's diner is two miles from here. We have to split up. A Watchman will meet you at Maggie's. He will escort you to the Vineyard. Ruben Rodriguez is in charge of the camp. Once inside, ask Ruben for Cody Parrish. They'll help you find the stranger in your vision."

"Please, Greg, I can't do this alone."

"The Holy Spirit will lead you."

"Then why don't I have a peace about this? I thought the Q Squad was supposed to work together. I hate this."

"Reenie, in the past two years you've achieved a lot by doing things you hated. Our Lord has prepared you for this mission. Doubt sees only the darkness; faith sees the light. You gotta understand we won't be getting any second chances to pull this off."

Pointing, Rafa shared, "You see the market ahead on your left? Across the street is a soccer field. You need to enter this area slowly."

"Commander, their jeep is almost here... Yes, it's been five days since they left Israel... Of course, as soon as they enter the compound...."

Aaron was thinking about his daughter. Sitting on the edge of her seat, she was quietly praying in the Spirit. She had risked everything to be in God's will. Now he was wishing it could have been different. From the time he was a teenager living near the West Bank, Aaron Glazer desperately sought after a destiny his father believed in. As family, friends, and fellow soldiers, were cut down; the legendary Matthias seemed to rise above it all. Many believed he was being divinely protected; while others revered his courage.

"Daddy, the Holy Spirit just gave a verse. It's about the race we are running in. You wanna hear it?"

"Sure do, honey."

"'Therefore we also, since we are surrounded by so great a cloud of witnesses, let us lay aside every weight, and the sin which so easily ensnares us, and let us run with endurance the race that is set before us, looking unto Jesus, the author and finisher of our faith, who for the joy that was set before Him endured the cross, despising the shame, and has sat down at the right hand of the throne of God. For consider Him who endured such hostility from sinners against Himself, lest you become weary and discouraged in your souls.'" 13

"You mean God just spoke this to you?"

"Yes, Rafa, it's called a word of knowledge."

"What is this race you're running in?"

"Just before Jesus split the Mount of Olives, my Daddy and I received a word from the Holy Spirit to run in a race to save souls. At first we thought it was just for our people. But after the Lord arranged our meeting with you and Fadi, we now feel it's for your people too."

"What type of word?"

"This passage describes the persecution Jesus received before he gave His life on the cross. As we run our race, we look to Jesus as our example. No matter what our Lord suffered, he was never discouraged. This is God's way of encouraging us, Rafa."

"You must turn back right now! My father has entered into a holy struggle to rid the world of Zionist Jews and immoral Christians. In his eyes you're infidels; enemies of Allah. He will show you no mercy. You will never leave alive."

"Rafa, think about what you just said. Who really is behind this so called holy Jihad?"

"Don't listen to him!" seethed Fadi.

She innocently concluded, "Our father is following the Qur'an like you're following the Bible."

"I once heard a Muslim leader call America the great Satan. He spoke of Americans as deceived infidels obsessed with pleasure, sex, and drugs. His hate for those who supported the rebuilding of the Temple next to the Al-Aqsa Mosque was obvious. He defied the Americans to force the Muslims out of their land like they did the Indians. He was so thankful to see so many Jews returning to Palestine. He boldly stated this would save his army the expense of tracking them down and killing them. So in reality, the demon behind this leader was attacking America because of her support of Israel. Why does Satan want to destroy Israel?"

"The world hates the Jews for many reasons."

"Fadi, the warfare over the souls of Muslims and Jews isn't about what the world believes. Demons are fueling the hate between us. You know atrocities we've committed against each other."

"Are you saying an evil spirit is behind Islam?"

"You reap what you sow, my friend. If you sow death, you will reap the consequences. If you can't see the difference between the love of Jesus and the hatred of Muhammad, you'll never be able to find the truth which can set your spirit free."

"Stop calling me your friend. You are no friend to me or my people. Your lies mean nothing. Do you actually think you have the power to convert Muslims into cross bearing Christians? Is this what you hope to accomplish by coming here?"

"Jesus is guiding us; He sees what we don't."

"Lord," Johanna reverently whispered, "we pray for the salvation of Rafa and Fadi. There must be thousands of Jordanians ready to receive salvation. Use us as instruments of Your love. 'Greater love has no one than this, than to lay down one's life for his friends.'" 14

The jeep eased through the narrow entrance of the armed camp. Immediately they were surrounded by M-16's.

"Raise your hands," ordered the sentry.

"We must trust God, Johanna," whispered Aaron.

As soon as their hands went up, Rafa and Fadi jumped out of the jeep. The surrounding soldiers were already thanking Allah for safely returning the children of their Commander.

"Blindfold them," ordered the officer in charge.

The blow from a rifle butt dropped him to his knees. Other soldiers quickly moved in. Johanna could hear their kicks.

"Daddddy!" screamed Johanna.

"Enough!" ordered the officer. "Take them away."

After hugging his son and daughter the proud Commander raised his hands and looked up.

"May Allah be praised! You have seen the inside of a Zionist terror camp and have lived to tell about it."

"When will the three Israeli soldiers be released?"

"You have done your duty. We'll talk later, Rafa."

"You already executed them, haven't you?"

"Glazer is a liar. You have no idea how many of our people he has murdered. What other propaganda has this Zionist fed you?"

"Father, they kept reading Bible verses trying to prove the future judgment of Muslim nations. They believe our people will be destroyed in three weeks."

"That's not fair, Fadi! The bowl judgments have ravaged every country. Aaron said all the cities will fall, even Jerusalem."

"You know nothing, Rafa! Do you deny these Zionists read passages of Jewish prophets predicting the destruction of our country? Johanna said only Jews will enter heaven."

"She never said that! She said whosoever comes to Jesus as a child will never be..."

"Silence! I forbid you to speak to Matthias or his daughter ever again. Not one word to anyone about your arrest, your imprisonment, even your trip across the border. Do you understand?"

"Father, I..."

"Rafa, there is no debate."

Both saluted before being escorted out.

It wasn't long before Aaron and Johanna were brought in and handcuffed to metal chairs. Pictures of revered suicide bombers covered the wall behind the commander's desk. Hand written portions of the Qur'an by children were proudly displayed. Across the room twenty-two flags of Arab nations were lined up. His most cherished art work was a drawing of the Al-Aqsa Mosque. Located atop Mount Moriah, it is the third most revered holy place in all of Islam. Below this drawing was a diagram of Israel. Palestine was scrawled across it in Jewish blood.

Stepping into his office, his stride looked confident. This Jordanian officer had often dreamed of this moment.

"Is this your daughter, Matthias?"

"Whom am I speaking to?"

"Remove their blindfolds."

The creases etched in his face were the result of what Arabs call the Jewish occupation. The short muscular officer looked familiar. Aaron could sense his agitation.

"I've delivered your children. May I see my soldiers?"

"This is unfortunate. They were shot trying to escape."

"Our agreement was made in good faith!"

"For thousands of years Arabs and Jews have fought over Palestine. A long time to fight over such a small piece of territory, don't you think?"

Aaron calmly looked into his eyes.

"At the time of Abraham, Mount Moriah wasn't a city. The Canaanites founded this village and named it Jerusalem. This is a Jebusite name. Years later, David's armies defeated the Jebusite's and captured Jerusalem. David then moved his capital from Hebron to a low hillside now called the Temple Mount. This is our claim to Jerusalem."

"Do you expect me to believe this?"

"In 135 A.D., a Roman emperor named Hadrian established a pagan colony in Jerusalem. He changed Jerusalem, the City of David, to Aelia Capitoliana. He also changed Israel to Palestine. Palestine was derived from the Philistines, an enemy of Israel."

"I suppose you can prove this?"

"The changing of Israel's name to Palestine has nothing to do with Moslem Palestinians. Islam wasn't created by Muhammad until the seventh century. Hadrian simply wanted to remove any Jewish influence in Israel and so do you."

"Such propaganda. You're drawing quite a picture for your daughter. Please continue."

"Your coalition of Arab States is five hundred times the size of my country. Since our independence in 1948, the Jewish people have been surrounded by two hundred million Arabs. Please, Commander, tell my daughter why you want our land?"

"I doubt she could handle it," he smugly replied.

"Islam is a major religion for thirty-five nations. Judaism is a major religion for only the nation of Israel."

"Why make this a religious issue?"

"Seven years ago, the Middle East Federation demanded a Palestinian state with its capital in east Jerusalem. This so called swap of land for peace was executed perfectly by Arab leadership."

"Matthias, the prophet Muhammad taught if our land is ever occupied by another it is our duty to recover it by Jihad. This gives my people the right to occupy Palestine. Of course, I can see why your people reject such a truth."

"Many of the Palestinian's living in Israel weren't even born there. They're Jordanians. For decades you've forced refugees from other nations to live in our country."

"I understand such reasoning..."

"I don't think you do," the American teen boldly interrupted.

"Miss Glazer, why did every member of the United Nations condemn the brutal occupation of our land by radical Zionists?"

"It's called Bible prophecy. King David prophesied over the nations trying to destroy Israel in these last days."

As she reached for her Bible on his desk, the Jordanian officer stood up and began to slowly pace back and forth.

"David wrote, 'For behold, Your enemies make a tumult; and those who hate You have lifted up their head. They have taken crafty counsel against Your people, and consulted together against Your sheltered ones. They have said, "Come, and let us cut them off from being a nation, that the name of Israel may be remembered no more. For they have consulted together with one consent; they form a confederacy against You: The tents of Edom..."' [15]

"Is this the type of indoctrination you used against my children? I assume you tried to convince them modern day Jordan is somewhere in this passage? Tell me, what other countries are mentioned?"

"Syria, Iraq, Iran, Egypt..."

"How convenient, Matthias," he angrily smirked. "You just insert whatever countries you want. The land of Palestine has always been special to my people."

A determined Johanna continued, "The apostle Paul also saw the division between the Arabs and Jews. He wrote, 'But, as he who was born according to the flesh then persecuted him who was born according to the Spirit, even so it is now.'" 16

"Why listen to someone from the past? I don't see these predictions in the Qur'an? It's not possible to have such prophecies."

"Ezekiel foretold of a valley of bones living again. 17 Miraculously, the children of Israel have returned to a city surrounded on three sides by mountains. In the middle, is a hill called Mount Moriah. This is where Abraham presented his son Isaac as a sacrifice. A sacrifice God stopped. A thousand years later, in this same spot, God the Father provided His own Son as an offering for the sins of mankind. It's called Golgotha."

The silence lasted a few moments as he thought about his reply.

"The Promised Land you're talking about was once owned by Muslims, just hard working families wanting a good life. But Zionists took away their dreams. Palestinian's were forced to live as ugly refugees until the Jerusalem Peace Accord was signed."

"You wanted the Palestinians to be seen as pawns! Your plan to destroy Israel is being executed with timely precision. The Old Testament prophets saw the consequences of such hatred."

"It's easy to see why you seek revenge, Matthias. For years you proclaimed Allah and the prophet Muhammad as instruments of war. Now you spew passages predicting the destruction of more innocent people. Could it be the God of Israel is the one seeking revenge?"

The Israeli freedom fighter closed his eyes. He had run out words.

"The Lord's patience has a limit," Johanna lovingly replied. "The Psalmist pleaded, 'How long, Lord? Will You be angry forever? Will Your jealousy burn like fire? Pour out Your wrath on the nations that do not know You, and on the kingdoms that do not call on Your name. For they have devoured Jacob...'" 18

"And what about the blood shed by Jews? Soon, Allah will annihilate your people. It's a shame neither of you will witness such a victory. Guards get them out of my sight."

# A LIGHT TO THE GENTILES

"...I will also give You as a light to the Gentiles, That You should be My salvation to the ends of the earth."
Isaiah 49:6

Sitting at a picnic table outside the entrance of Bethel the troubled Watchman was hardly touching his meal of soup and bread. He didn't know much about the camper taking a seat across from him.

"Hey, Cody, I want you to know I'm praying for Twanna."

"How did you hear, Eli?"

"It's top priority with Rueben. The intercessors are buzzing. It's too bad no one can go after her."

"She'll be fine. We got less than three weeks."

"So you know when the Word will return with His armies?"

Without looking up, he whispered back, "close to it."

"I'd like to hear it."

"Maybe another time."

"I always thought the Lord reveals His will to His prophets first?"

"He did to Daniel. The two Witnesses prophesied the second half of the 70th week (1260 days). 1 The 70th week ended between the sounding of the sixth and seventh trumpets, when Kayin had them killed. 2 According to Daniel, the Abomination of Desolation (Beast) will become desolate thirty days later (1290 days)." 3

"So when does the Beast die?"

"He will be cast alive into the lake of fire at the supper of the great God." 4

"Is this when Jesus supposedly sets up His kingdom?"

"His reign over the nations will begin forty-five days after the abomination (Beast) becomes desolate." 5

"So who will be serving the Lord on the earth?"

"Believing Jews and Gentiles; survivors from the day of the Lord." 6

The smug soldier could barely control his anger.

"Cody, the Jews rejected Jesus as their Messiah. They missed their time of visitation. The promises given to Israel now apply to the elect. I don't believe for a second Jesus came back to Jerusalem last week. If He did, then where is the bride of Christ?"

"The bride will return within the New Jerusalem on the first day of the Millennium. She will reside within the Holy City for eternity."

"That's not possible."

Pausing, the young convert respectfully replied, "I'm listening."

"Before I answer, let me ask you a question. Who taught you this end time scenario?"

"I suppose Ruben taught me the most."

"And who taught him?"

"Eli, are you accusing..."

"Hold up, I ain't against Rueben. All I'm saying is God anoints those who teach His Word. You're a good friend, Cody, not only to me, but too many here. What you teach can influence a lot of lives."

"I always ask the Holy Spirit to lead me."

"Exactly. Tell me, have you ever been taught by a real prophet?"

"Not that I know of."

"You see, God has already shown me the coming judgment of America. Those who reject the warnings of His prophets are doomed to follow the traditions of men."

"Have you met such a prophet?"

"Yes, I have. He carries a heavy anointing. You've always treated me right; this is why I'm sharing this truth with you. This prophet of the Living God also teaches a future Millennium. But the sequence of events he teaches are different than the events you just highlighted."

"What about this judgment of America?"

"Trust me, the separation of the saved from the unsaved will be because of what they believe, not because of a microchip under the skin. God is calling out a special people from the descendants of Abraham, Isaac, and Jacob. After His resurrection, Israel was called by a new name. Only those chosen will understand."

"Cody!" yelled a sentry, "Ruben is asking for you."

"Ok, I'll be right there. Thanks, Eli, I gotta go. By the way, what is the name of this prophet you studied under?"

Turning to leave, he whispered, "We'll talk later. Remember, this is between you and me."

From the rear window of the Winnebago, a relieved Donnell announced, "I don't see anybody. Let's boogie."

"But they've got my brother!" pleaded a frantic Emma.

Such situations were common for Jon Mendel and Donnell Emery. Being controlled by the urgency of the moment was never an option for them. To most, it looked unloving, even cruel. To an experienced Watchman, they were just obeying the Holy Spirit.

"Jon, where are we heading?" demanded a troubled Jake.

"We need to reach Dahlonega before Greg and Reenie meet their contact. They probably spilt up. Greg will go undercover while the contact takes Reenie into the camp. It's the safest play."

"What about my brother?"

"If we don't go now Reenie may be dead by the time we get there."

As the RV crept up the steep hill Emma burst into tears. Jake wanted to comfort her but didn't have the words. Reaching over he held her hand while silently interceding.

"Emma, I know this is a tough call for you."

"You got that right, Jon. Kurt would never abandon us. Never!"

"Yeah, it's the ole merry-go-round again."

"What are you saying?"

"Since His coming, how many times have we been in situations just going round and round until we learn our lesson?"

"Excuse me. Kurt is much more than your object lesson."

"Beating yourself up won't help either. There is a better way."

"Please, Donnell, no more sermonettes. Is it wrong for me to want to rescue my brother? The Q saved Reenie from the NWC. Why not Kurt? This makes no sense?"

In a softer tone he reasoned, "Did Jesus use common sense when He let Lazarus die? Or rubbing dirty mud in people's eyes for healing?"

"I guess not," she grudgingly confessed. "Even Peter refused to allow Jesus to wash his feet."

"Amen, Emma! Jesus told Peter, "...What I am doing you do not understand now, but you will know after this."" [7]

"So God will care for Kurt while we're about our Father's business?"

"It's called walking by faith. Look at the ministry of the twelve apostles. The great commission wasn't an attractive offer to their flesh. 8 Preaching this new gospel would not make them popular or rich. Most of the time they were severely persecuted."

"Old slew foot had no choice but attack," whispered Jake.

"Think of the lies Satan threw at them. Telling them how inadequate, how stupid, how foolish they were. There was no guarantee they would be successful. It must have been a real mind game."

"So, Donnell, how did the apostles defeat such lies?"

"They were captivated by their calling, Emma. Their relationship with Jesus swallowed up their ambitions, their desires, even their future dreams. Neither the approval or fear of man could deter them."

"Do you know what happened to some of them?"

"Peter and Andrew were crucified. James and Bartholomew were beat to death. Matthew and Thomas died of sword and spear wounds. Mark was dragged to death by horses. And I think the apostle who replaced Judas Iscariot, Matthias, was beheaded."

A hyped up Jake shared, "A relationship with the stone the builders rejected can carry a heavy price tag! 9 Just believing in something can be radically different than living it out. Emma, is our mission to protect Reenie still our top priority?"

"Nothing has changed."

"Which means God is still watching our boy! Trust me, Kurt ain't going nowhere without Jesus."

After a contrite Emma offered a prayer of thanks, everyone's eyes refocused on the road. Their next stop: Dahlonega, Georgia.

The guard looked nervous as she approached.

"I have permission to talk with the prisoners."

"Sorry, Rafa, no one can see Matthias. This order is from the Commander himself."

"I just want to speak with his daughter."

"Not without written permission."

"I can call my father if you want me to? He's in a very important meeting. He hates interruptions."

Glancing around, the uneasy guard whispered, "Five minutes."

After entering, she motioned to Johanna not to speak.

"Your father is alive. Earlier you said you've come to share the gospel. Will those believing in Jesus be protected from His wrath?"

"God will lead us. The hailstones after the seventh bowl is poured out will weigh over one hundred pounds. All believers must hide themselves underground."

"How many Gentiles will survive the day of the Lord?"

"It doesn't say. But Isaiah did prophesy the Jewish people will be a light to the Gentiles to the very ends of the earth." 10

"You must warn my people. There is an area an hour from here. None have embraced Kayin's lies."

"I've been praying. The Holy Spirit will make a way for us to escape."

Turning to leave, a skeptical Rafa mumbled back, "I pray so."

From a hill overlooking Dahlonega, the two teenagers dropped to their knees in the dirt and bowed their faces to the foul spirit.

"What is my name?" hissed the demon.

"You are Osiris, lord of the dead. It is written of you, I am yesterday I am today."

"Behold, my words live forevermore. Satan has opened a way for my return. I have come for the soul of Reenie Ann Tucker."

The boys boldly chanted, "Homage to Osiris, lord of eternity. We confess and believe. So shall it be!"

## BEFORE ABRAHAM WAS

"Then the Jews said to Him, 'You are not yet fifty years old, and have You
seen Abraham?' Jesus said to them, "Most assuredly, I say to you,
before Abraham was, I AM.'"
John 8:57-58

After being thrown to the floor, Aaron pleaded, "What have you done
with my Johanna?"

"Shut up and listen. Your soldiers are very resourceful. Earlier
this morning they kidnapped three of my officers. I have just received
a ransom note offering them for you and your daughter."

"They will never allow your men to live."

"Don't be so hasty, Matthias. You're valuable to us. I believe we
can get more for you. That is if I can get the information I want."

"The Matthias you knew is dead. I have nothing to say."

"Maybe the torture of your daughter might loosen your tongue?"

"It won't matter; nothing can change His wrath."

"Such a pity, acid can burn through her pretty skin in seconds."

"How can I make you understand? Soon, the blood of soldiers
will cover Israel. Everyone having Kayin's mark will die."

"Christians have been predicting this for centuries. Why now?"

"My daughter and I returned your children safely. Grant us our
freedom to share with your people who can still receive salvation."

From his leather chair the Commander smugly leaned back.

"You speak of salvation as if you are holding it like a glass of
water. It doesn't matter. All Muslims committing Kabir (great sins) will
go to hell but they will not always remain there."

"Will you go to paradise when you die?"

"There is no doubt in my mind."

"How do you know?"

"I pray five times a day. I recite the creed. I fast during Ramadan. I pay alms to the poor. And I have been to Mecca."

"So this guarantees your salvation in paradise?"

"Not necessarily. Salvation depends on the will of Allah. Every believer must pass over a narrow bridge resting above the flames. Those Allah deems righteous will be spared. They shall partake of paradise."

"And what happens to the others?"

"They shall suffer on judgment day."

"So you don't know for sure you're going to paradise?"

"Are you sure?"

"My salvation rests on the shed blood of Jesus. He bore my sins by being crucified on a cross. The Lamb of God became a sinless sacrifice for the sins of mankind."

"Allah had a plan for Jesus, the son of Mary, but it wasn't death on a cross. The Jews tried to trap our messenger but Allah rescued him. They crucified someone else in His place."

"Commander, Jesus told His disciples before he was crucified, "'Behold, we are going up to Jerusalem, and the Son of Man will be betrayed to the chief priests and to the scribes; and they will condemn Him to death, and deliver Him to the Gentiles to mock and to scourge and to crucify. And the third day He will rise again." 1

"I know Christians believe Jesus is the Son of God. So, where does it say God eats or sleeps? What nonsense is this?"

"What if a Muslim has doubts at the end of his life?"

"Enough of your worthless questions, there are no doubts when one dies. Good works mean nothing if there is unbelief."

Everything Aaron was sharing was being brushed aside. His head throbbing, he sat back struggling to stay focused. Closing his eyes he silently prayed for the Holy Spirit to soften the Commander's heart.

Instantly his rival looked distracted. In his mind was a picture from his childhood. The teacher was describing the wicked on judgment day. His classmates were studying a mural of faces trapped beneath yellowish flames. A sea of fire was swallowing those not faithful to Muhammad. In the back of the room, a boy was pleading for forgiveness.

"As a boy, Matthias, I remember my teacher comparing paradise with fire. There was never a day I didn't ask for forgiveness."

"I struggled with guilt too, especially when the killing began.

"As I grew older my desire for forgiveness left me."

"After I asked Jesus to be my Lord and Savior, I felt a tremendous release from my guilt. It was like weights falling off my shoulders."

"I know this feeling of guilt. I prayed it would go away when I visited Mecca. After returning home, it only got worse. Now I understand what will be, will be. It's the will of Allah."

"What about the patriarch Abraham?"

"Abraham was a Muslim; neither a Jew nor a Christian."

"How could he a Muslim? Abraham's relationship with God was entered into by a covenant of promise. The Law of Moses was given 430 years later. Abraham walked by faith. His relationship wasn't about keeping ceremonies or keeping the law perfectly."

"Abraham was deemed righteous because he was obedient to the vision God gave him."

"And what exactly did God Almighty tell Abraham?"

"You tell me," smirked the Commander.

"The Father gave him a future picture of His Son being crucified for the sins of the world."

"Allah is never called a father in the Qur'an."

"He came to His own, and His own did not receive Him. But as many as received Him, to them He gave the right to become children of God, to those who believe in His name.'" 2

"All believers are children of God; just like Jesus."

"May I share about Jesus' relationship with His Father? It's from the first century when religious leaders were confronting Him."

Curiously the officer nodded.

"'Jesus answered, "If I honor Myself, My honor is nothing. It is My Father who honors Me, of whom you say that He is your God. Yet you have not known Him, but I know Him. And if I say, 'I do not know Him,' I shall be a liar like you; but I do know Him and keep His word. Your father Abraham rejoiced to see My day, and he saw *it* and was glad." Then the Jews said to Him, "You are not yet fifty years old, and have You seen Abraham?" Jesus said to them, "Most assuredly, I say to you, before Abraham was, I AM." Then they took up stones to throw at Him; but Jesus hid Himself and went out of the temple, going through the midst of them, and so passed by.'" 3

For several seconds, the Jordanian Commander sat motionless, not saying a word.

"Why did Jesus call these Jews liars?"

"Jesus was saying He was with God before Abraham was born. By claiming to be I AM; He was making himself equal to God."

"So you believe everyone has a free will?"

"Jesus made this clear when He taught how one can have a relationship with His Father. '"At that day you will know that I am in My Father, and you in Me, and I in you. He who has My commandments and keeps them, it is he who loves Me. And he who loves Me will be loved by My Father, and I will love him and manifest Myself to him.'" 4

"With regards to salvation, the Qur'an makes no distinction between one's knowledge of Allah and His will. He guides before anyone has a choice. Allah is free to do as He pleases."

"Why would God guide people into unbelief and then condemn them to hell? The Lord doesn't create puppets. 'The Lord is not slack concerning His promise, as some count slackness, but is longsuffering toward us, not willing that any should perish but that all should come to repentance.' 5 Everyone has the free will to repent or not."

In his ear the spirit of Religion whispered, "What have you accomplished? None of your soldiers are saved. You sure do talk a lot about something that never happens."

"Matthias you lie! Muhammad teaches Al-Jabbar, The Tyrant, seals infidels against the good. Then on judgment day all infidels must face Al-Hasib, The Reckoner."

"You had your chance and you blew it," hissed Condemnation.

The former Israeli soldier stared not bothering to reply.

"Matthias, I pity you. But I will grant you one last question."

Edging forward in his chair Aaron issued a final challenge.

"If Muslims believe Jesus was a true prophet then why don't they believe what He prophesied?"

---

"Hey, Nate, it's your private number... He won't give his name... says it's about your report on the Prophetic Voice."

"This is Natalie Roberts. May I help you?"

"When I first saw you I knew you were a Kenite."

"Well, well, I must say, Delford, you really are predictable. I've been waiting for your call."

"You don't have any fear of God, do you?"

"Why should I. Obviously you don't."

"Thus sayth the Lord, '"Do not touch My anointed ones, and do My prophets no harm.'" 6

"Give it up, Delford. Your prophetic dream of America was just another excuse to hate those you despise. I'm more concerned for those you're targeting. You never told me how many Jews and Blacks your little army has killed so far? Why not broadcast the latest numbers? You once said fear is a suitable tool in controlling Kenites."

"Jesus foretold of me when He said, '...Assuredly, I say to you, no prophet is accepted in his own country.' 7 You know nothing about the holy nation I'm building. Your TV Special was filled with lies. You never had any intention of telling the truth. Your goal was to smear my reputation. The ironic twist is you've lost your power and you don't even know it. You used to be the top rated News Anchor in America. What value is your precious reporting now? The very judgments I predicted years ago are coming to pass. But you're so controlled by your left wing agenda you couldn't see the truth if you tripped over it."

"What left wing agenda?"

"It's your religion. Influencing the masses was a real power trip for you. When Kayin seized authority over the nations you didn't say a peep. After he dissolved the World Faith Movement you let it slide. When the Witnesses prophesied the seven trumpet judgments you called them insane. But their funeral didn't fit your political agenda, now did it?"

"So you believe Jesus resurrected the Witnesses?"

"I only follow what God Almighty gives me. Those believing in my message will be led by the Spirit."

"What do you see happening next?"

"Now that wasn't so hard to ask. You need to get yourself a 1611 King James Bible. The events in your future are written down."

"So who are the good and bad guys in your apocalyptic war?"

"The descendants of Abraham are saints of the Most High. The Lord is gathering a special people in this last day harvest."

"But you said no one would survive Armageddon?"

"His kingdom is everlasting. I've seen it in a vision."

"What about Israel?"

"She won't escape this time. These Kenites never worshipped the true God. Only the chosen will inherit the millennial kingdom."

"And where do these chosen people come from?"

"From the lost ten tribes of Israel in America and Great Britain."

"You mean the Assyrian's invasion of Israel in 722 B.C.?"

"I see you've studied it."

"A Bible professor taught me this during our interview on the Temple Mount. He said even though the northern kingdom was destroyed, a remnant was preserved."

"Fat chance!" snickered the racist.

"This teacher believes many fled to the southern kingdom of Judah; a fact confirmed by Jerusalem's swelling population by the end of the eighth century. Years later, many returned to the north and to Judah. He says the ten tribes of Israel were never lost."

"Just another private interpretation."

"He said James wrote about the twelve tribes of Israel. 8 Obviously, they weren't missing in the first century. Paul also mentioned the twelve tribes and their hope to attain the resurrection from the dead. So did John in The Revelation of Jesus Christ."

"Only those having ears to hear will understand."

"If the Middle East erupts in another war..."

"It's not our concern. We must prepare for judgment on our own shores. America needs to heed my admonition. You have the power to deliver this warning to millions of viewers."

From beneath her sleeping bag, he removed her notes on the last days. Nothing could have prepared him for this. He never heard her footsteps. Spinning around his cold eyes met hers.

"You're out of control, Fadi. Now give me back my notes."

"What if Father sees this propaganda? Gentiles and Jews worshipping together atop Mount Zion is a lie. This can be used against you. Let me destroy it. No one can question Allah."

"I make my own decisions. I have nothing more to say to you."

"You're so blind! Johanna Glazer is a liar. Your notes speak of a protected people traveling on a highway to holiness to Jerusalem. What nations are these people from?"

"Ancient Assyria was between the Euphrates and Tigris rivers." 9

Handing back her notes he refused to return her glance.

"Rafa, you can't mean Jordan?"

"It's possible. Let me read this prophecy by Ezekiel. 'Moreover I will make a covenant of peace with them, and it shall be an everlasting covenant with them; I will establish them and multiply them, and I will set My sanctuary in their midst forevermore. My tabernacle also shall be with them; indeed I will be their God, and they shall be My people. The nations also will know that I, the Lord, sanctify Israel, when My sanctuary is in their midst forevermore.'" 10

"How is this passage about Gentiles living in the last days?"

"The nations represent the Gentiles. God revealed Himself to the nations through Israel. He gave His Law to Moses for mankind to realize their sin before a Holy God." 11

"Why would Allah do such a thing?"

"The purpose of the Law was to convict man of his sinfulness. Second, it was to lead sinners to the Messiah. I'm talking about eternal salvation from the Father through His Son." 12

"Where does God ever speak of having a Son?"

"Johanna showed me this truth in the Book of Hebrews." 13

He wasn't listening; her brother already had his answer.

"The Father calls His Son, God. The throne of His Son is forever."

"Don't you care about our people anymore? Offering such a false hope has the power to destroy them."

"The Word will soon kill the followers of the Beast. Which means those who haven't worshipped Kayin can still be saved."

"Armies around the world have already made an alliance with Kayin. Soon they will annihilate Israel. The Jews have no chance."

"Old Testament prophets saw a different outcome of those fighting against Israel. Here it's in my notes. 'And this shall be the plague with which the Lord will strike all the people who fought against Jerusalem: Their flesh shall dissolve while they stand on their feet, their eyes shall dissolve in their sockets, and their tongues shall dissolve in their mouths.'" 14

"And what if He doesn't? Such speculation is so foolish."

Rafa wanted to help her people. Yet now knowing what was coming was sheer agony. Without any warning she burst into tears.

"C'mon, sis, let's trust in what we've always been taught."

"Why should we? Our world is over! The wrath of God will end when the Word of God appears at the great day of God Almighty. Don't you even care, Fadi?"

"No one will listen to you!"

"Aaron and Johanna have been called to be Watchmen to our people. They must be given the opportunity to preach the gospel."

"This is all happening way too fast. I'm also having doubts."

"Jesus said one must be born from above to enter the kingdom of heaven. Johanna believes anyone who believes in Jesus can be saved."

"Is this what you really want?"

"Yes, Fadi, this is what you and I have always wanted."

Grabbing his shoulder, she pulled him close for a hug.

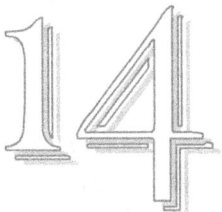

# PILGRIMS ON THE EARTH

"These all died in faith, not having received the promises, but having seen
them afar off were assured of them, embraced them and confessed that
they were strangers and pilgrims on the earth."
Hebrews 12:22

As Jon Mendel drove his Winnebago through the Blue Ridge
Mountains, the Q Squad couldn't get the desolate city of Atlanta out
of their minds. The fires, the public looting, the end was near.

"Just think, guys," reflected Donnell, "it won't be long before we
see the Word of God appearing with His bride at Armageddon."

"Greg taught us the armies in Revelation 19 are actually angels.

"Emma, this army is clothed in bright fine linens. This linen
represents the righteous acts of the saints." 1

"Angels can also be dressed in bright linen. Let me read it. 'And
out of the temple came the seven angels having the seven plagues,
clothed in pure bright linen, and having their chests girded with
golden bands.' 2 These angels will pour out the seven bowl
judgments."

The puzzled Watchman was trying to let it all sink in.

"What about Paul encouraging believers to establish their hearts
blameless in holiness at the coming of our Lord with all His saints.
Isn't this Jesus coming back with His bride at Armageddon?"

"In his first letter to the Thessalonians Paul highlighted the
coming of the Lord for His elect from the wrath to come in the first
five chapters, 1:10; 2:19; 3:13; 4:14-17; 5:23. I Thessalonians 3:13 isn't
about the Word of God appearing in heaven at the supper of the great
God. This is Jesus bringing the dead in Christ at His coming." 3

"So if the armies following the Word are angels, then when does the bride return for the marriage supper of the Lamb?"

"Jon, the only time the bride returns to earth is inside the Holy Jerusalem. This happens on the first day of Christ's thousand year reign over the nations."

"I thought the bride returns after the thousand years is up? Why would she descend on the first day of the Millennium?"

Opening his Bible the young Watchman read, "'And I heard a loud voice from heaven saying, "Behold, the tabernacle of God is with men, and He will dwell with them, and they shall be His people. God Himself will be with them and be their God."' 4

"What are you saying, Jake?"

"Guys, Jesus promised to reign with His bride for eternity. The Lamb of God will soon descend with her at the beginning of His reign over the nations; not at the end. If the bride remained in heaven while Christ ruled for a thousand years then that would contradict His promise."

"Ben, look at all these cars. They're all leaving."

"The putrid smell from the ocean must be beyond nauseating. The exodus from the coastal cities is a nightmare. Tee, reaching the island where your daddy lives won't be easy."

"Thanks for getting me this far, I'll catch another ride from here."

The old timer was feeling the pressure. He was painfully aware of the consequences facing this young Watchman. Even so, his urgency for rescue was still strong.

"I'll tag along for a little bit longer."

Exiting off the highway, he made an illegal turn onto a frontage road.

"Don't look back; I just saw some agents. From now on we'll only use neighborhood streets."

"Why are agents still scanning? Their registration system has collapsed. Kayin's directives are a joke. It makes no sense!"

"Tee, the nations are in turmoil. Most are blaspheming. Satan, the Beast, and his False Prophet, are trying to regain what they've lost." 5

"What about you, Ben, what have you lost?

"Nothing more than any other Overcomer." 6

"Cody shared your testimony with me. I'm so sorry."

"So the boy mentioned my two sons? Yeah, they just couldn't let go of the world. Right now, I don't know where they are."

"Followers of the Beast," she sadly replied.

"Tee, it's not like the Apostle Paul didn't warn us. '...And if anyone does not obey our word in this epistle, note that person and do not keep company with him, that he may be ashamed.'" 7

"So you broke fellowship with your sons?"

"Had no choice, sadly my pastor rebuked me for doing it. His lack of discernment was hard to accept. Remember the Muslim nations falling just before Kayin brokered the roadmap of peace with Israel? 8 The Beast was gathering his horns and most Christians didn't have a clue."

"Ben, are you having doubts about my discernment?"

"Just holding you accountable before it happens, if your father has the mark; there is nothing we can do. We'll have to leave him behind."

"Anything else?"

"Returning to the Vineyard isn't an option either. It's all about the Holy Spirit leading us till the Word kills the armies of the Beast."

---

"What is it this time?" he moaned.

"Commander, your daughter left our compound."

"Now why would my Rafa do such a foolish thing?"

"She helped Aaron Glazer's daughter escape."

Sitting underneath the bleachers of the soccer field both girls were grappling with the consequences they were facing.

"Rafa, my Daddy didn't make it out, did he?"

"I'm afraid not."

"Maybe we should go back?"

"We can never go back. Johanna what kinda things did Jesus teach about heaven?"

"Lots of things."

"Will the patriarch Abraham be there?"

"Yes, Yeshua spoke of believers who died before His resurrection. They were waiting in a place of comfort."

"Waiting for what?

"Abraham was waiting for a heavenly city whose builder and maker is God. 9 When Jesus rose from the dead He defeated death. He led captivity captive. All Old Testament believers in Abraham's bosom were taken to heaven by Jesus."

"So when did they receive their resurrection bodies?"

"The day the Son came in the glory of His Father. When God sounded His last trumpet, in the twinkling of an eye, the dead in Christ received their immortal resurrection bodies. Then all overcomers were changed and caught up."

"Johanna, what about unbelievers?"

"When an unsaved person dies their soul goes to Hades. After the thousand year reign of Christ ends all in Hades will be resurrected before the great white throne and be judged by Jesus."

"What type of judgment?"

"They'll all be cast into the lake of fire, the second death. The first death is physical. The second death is spiritual death for eternity."

"So if God destroys heaven and earth where will believers go?"

"This promise by Jesus is so awesome. Let me read it to you. '"Let not your heart be troubled; you believe in God, believe also in Me. In My Father's house are many mansions; if it were not so, I would have told you. I go to prepare a place for you. And if I go and prepare a place for you, I will come again and receive you to Myself; that where I am, there you may be also. And where I go you know, and the way you know.'" 10

"What do these mansions represent?"

"They're inside the New Jerusalem," praised Johanna. "The bride of Christ will live eternally inside this city."

"I've never heard of such a city."

"The New Jerusalem is only for those written in the Book of Life. This city has other names describing its beauty. It's called the tabernacle of God, Mount Zion, the city of the Living God, and the heavenly Jerusalem." 11

"Did Abraham believe in such a city?"

"He did. 'By faith Abraham obeyed when he was called to go out to the place which he would receive as an inheritance. And he went out, not knowing where he was going. By faith he dwelt in the land of promise as in a foreign country, dwelling in tents with Isaac and Jacob, the heirs with him of the same promise; for he waited for the city which has foundations, whose builder and maker is God.'" 12

"So Abraham was expecting a future city made by God?"

"For sure, God commended Old Testament believers for their faith in a heavenly city in which righteousness dwells. 'These all died in faith, not having received the promises, but having seen them afar off were assured of them, embraced them and confessed that they were strangers and pilgrims on the earth.'" 13

"So Abraham was a stranger on earth because he was looking for something better?"

"Yes Rafa, a heavenly city that never passes away!"

"How big is this city?"

"It's shaped like a square. 14 It may be bigger than earth. The names of the twelve tribes of Israel are written on the gates of the Holy City."

"Why will God honor Israel?"

"It's a memorial of the covenant God made with Abraham and his descendants. 15 Mary conceived Jesus after the Holy Spirit overshadowed her. Mary was a Jew which makes Jesus a Jew. "

"Johanna, your father told me the body of Christ is one. He said in the eyes of God, there is no difference between Jew and Gentile."

"That's true. Very soon a marriage between the Lamb of God and His bride will take place."

"Where and when will this marriage take place?"

"In heaven just before the Word of God appears at Armageddon."

"It's hard to share my feelings right now. The truths you so confidently share aren't part of my world. What should I do?"

Reaching over Johanna grasped her hand and softly replied, "Just keep asking the Holy Spirit to show you the truth."

---

Eli hastily grabbed his vibrating cell phone.

"Are you crazy, Lenard? You promised no more incoming calls."

"You're late. Is everything on schedule?"

"If the NWC connects us with this camp we all get busted."

"What's with you? You're getting mighty jumpy."

"We are in Red Fox. It's code for lockdown, no one in or out."

"Delford is tired of waiting; he wants your full report now!"

"These Kenites believe Jesus will kill everyone registered. They teach He will rule from Jerusalem for eternity. 16 They're brainwashing thousands of children. We just can't sit by and watch it happen."

"What do you suggest?"

"If exposed they plan to escape through two underground tunnels nicknamed Beulah and Bethel. Twanna Evers, a black Kenite, helped design them. After our militia was mentioned she left camp."

"She was afraid, huh?"

"Some think she did it to protect the campers. Others feel she went searching for her father. He's a pastor. Twanna has a close friend here named Cody Parish. He thinks an old Cherokee named Ben is driving her to her father's church in Charleston, South Carolina."

"Anything else?"

"Evers can give us detailed information on these tunnels. Getting her to talk would make our rescue a lot easier."

"Eli, this is Delford. Good job, soldier. I'm sending a team out within the hour. After we apprehend Evers and her father, I'll personally plan our offensive. Be thinking of a date."

# THEY HAVE NOT KNOWN THE FATHER

"...These things they will do to you because they have not known the
Father nor Me."
John 16:3

His release from the Jordanian compound came at a high price.
Walking through the crowded downtown, a bewildered Aaron Glazer
had no idea where his daughter was. He was beginning to doubt if he
would ever see her again.

He knew the Zionist was being followed. If he didn't act fast this
hated freedom fighter would never make it to the border alive.

Aaron wasn't familiar with the stranger signaling from inside the
small shop. The prompting by the Holy Spirit wasn't easy to accept.

"Lord, how can I trust a Jordanian I don't even know? I'm sorry
but how do I know this is from You?"

He felt nothing.

"If this person is from you then have him clap his hands."

Aaron's jaw dropped when the stranger started clapping his hands
above his head. Jogging across the street, they met behind the shop.

"Hurry, put this robe over your clothes. You're being followed."

"Who are you?"

Removing the shawl from his face, the teenager winked.

"Fadi, what are you doing here?"

"My father let you go because Rafa helped Johanna escape. After
you find your daughter he will execute you both."

"What's your plan?"

"The girls are waiting for us under the bleachers at the soccer
field. If we don't reach them soon they might have to hide somewhere
else. Just stay close to me. And keep your face covered."

Reaching the road, they hid in a small crowd begging for food.

"Fadi, I can't see how..."

"Aaron, either your God is with us or He isn't."

They looked down as their pursuers rushed by.

"Let's go, Fadi, what are we waiting for?"

"Once they realize they have lost you they may double back. We must wait a little longer. Other soldiers could also be watching."

"Why are you helping me? You must know the consequences."

"More than you will ever know," groaned the teenager.

"What will your father do if he finds Rafa?"

"My sister no longer has a father. She has renounced the teachings of Muhammad. She doesn't believe in the Qur'an anymore. The prophecies Johanna gave her really pierced her heart. She now believes Jesus is her Lord and Savior. "

"Do you feel the same, Fadi?"

"How can I?"

"But you risked everything by helping me?"

"I love my sister. If you don't help me, Rafa and Johanna will never make it out of Jordan alive. Besides, I have some questions."

"Like what?"

"Is your Lord still saving Gentiles?"

"He is. Isaiah prophesied, "'So it shall be in that day: the great trumpet will be blown; they will come, who are about to perish in the land of Assyria, and they who are outcasts in the land of Egypt, And shall worship the Lord in the holy mount at Jerusalem.' 1

"How funny is that? Rafa also shared this passage with me."

"Believers from Jordan will come to Jerusalem and worship the Lord. It's a promise from God."

"Deep down, I always wanted to believe you. I guess you really have come for the salvation of my people." 2

"Praise God, Fadi."

He could hear agents arguing in the corridor. He had lost track of time since his arrest. Sitting on the side of his bed his shaggy hair barely touched his shoulders. Resting his elbows on his knees, the plastic binding around his wrists was cutting his skin. The sound of a key unlocking his cell door got his attention.

"Hi, Kurt, my name is Lowery, how ya doing?"

"I'm kinda hungry, Mam'm."

"Call me, Sophie. Tell you what, you help me fill out this paperwork and you and I can have some lunch together. How does that sound?"

In his mind the Holy Spirit spoke, "'And these things they will do to you because they have not known the Father nor Me.'" 3

"My sister needs me, she's all alone. Why not just let me go?"

"Sure, I just need some names. Strange ya'll casing out a closed down restaurant? The arresting officer thinks you had some help."

Folding his arms across his chest he stared at the floor.

"So how old are you, Kurt?"

"Almost seventeen."

"And when was your original sign up date?"

"Talk about ancient history?" he chuckled.

"So you still think this is some sort of joke?"

"Agent Lowery, God's wrath is never a joke."

"Call me, Sophie."

"This earth doesn't have much time."

"So what's going to happen when Jesus returns?"

"I'll tell you if you untie me."

Reaching over she unlocked his plastic handcuffs.

From his pocket New Testament Kurt read, "'Then I saw an angel standing in the sun; and he cried with a loud voice, saying to all the birds that fly in the midst of heaven, "Come and gather together for the supper of the great God, that you may eat the flesh of kings, the flesh of captains, the flesh of mighty men, the flesh of horses and of those who sit on them, and the flesh of all people...'" 4

"So birds will eat the flesh of those God kills?"

"Not a pretty picture."

"Where do you get this gore from anyway?"

"The Revelation of Jesus Christ."

"Isn't this symbolic?"

"Not for those who die."

"No one really knows for sure."

"Satan will give you all the excuses you want."

"Afraid not; I don't even believe in Satan."

"'For those who live according to the flesh set their minds on the things of the flesh, but those who live according to the Spirit, the things of the Spirit. For to be carnally minded is death, but to be spiritually minded is life and peace.'" 5

"Can I be honest, Kurt?"

The weary redhead just shrugged before retying his dirty tennis shoes.

"You're just another burned out resister attacking with scripture. Jesus never judged anyone like that. He loved people where they were at. You sound a lot like the two Witnesses."

"That would be an honor."

"I seem to recall the two Witnesses predicting Jesus will appear at Armageddon. I thought no man knows the day or hour of His coming?"

"No one knew the exact day or hour of the Coming of the Son of Man. The gathering up of Christians initiated His second coming." 6

"What do you mean?"

"His coming includes more than the resurrection on the last day."

"So it was Jesus leading Jews to the Temple Mount last month?"

"You got it. The Lamb of God fulfilled the Feast of Tabernacles during the sounding of the seventh trumpet."

"So where is He now?"

"In heaven, after the seventh bowl is poured out, the Word will appear with His armies at the supper of the great God. 7 This is when the Beast, Kayin, and his false prophet, Pope Michael, will be cast alive into the lake of fire."

"Where is this in scripture?"

"Let me read it, 'Then the beast was captured, and with him the false prophet who worked signs in his presence, by which he deceived those who received the mark of the Beast and those who worshiped his image. These two were cast alive into the lake of fire...'" 8

"I thought you said birds will eat the flesh of those God kills?"

Easing back Kurt slowly replied, "That's the next verse, 'And the rest were killed with the sword which proceeded from the mouth of Him who sat on the horse. And all the birds were filled with their flesh.'" 9

"So His second coming ends here?"

"Not yet. His second coming will end when the Lamb of God descends with His bride on the first day of His reign over the nations." 10

The dreary basement was feeling more like a prison than a refuge. He wouldn't leave as long as he had water. The slightest noise outside the windows produced a crippling panic. Even his prayers were done in silence. Only one person knew of his hiding place. He was already regretting telling him. On a napkin was scrawled the events of the six seals. 11 Clenching his fists he pounded his dirty blanket.

Then the broken pastor read, "'Take heed, watch and pray; for you do not know when the time is. It is like a man going to a far country, who left his house and gave authority to his servants, and to each his work, and commanded the doorkeeper to watch. Watch therefore, for you do not know when the master of the house is coming—in the evening, at midnight, at the crowing of the rooster, or in the morning—lest, coming suddenly, he find you sleeping.'" 12

The sequence of events to watch for was always there. Casting the napkin aside, he felt like talking to God.

"The Blessed Hope came as a thief for those living in darkness. Lord, I was not only watching for the Beast and his mark, I wasn't even saved! What about my Twanna? There is still time for her to get saved. Maybe she can even become a Watchman for your glory." 13

The preoccupied minister never heard the door opening. Rushing down the stairs two soldiers pulled him up handcuffing his wrists.

From upstairs they heard, "Leave the ransom note on the table and tape his mouth. Ok, we're clear. Let's go."

He watched the young man jog up the steep embankment. A light powder of snow sprinkled the pine trees throughout the well hidden camp. The nearby river was partly frozen. He could hear campers chopping wood. It was late afternoon on Black Rock Mountain.

"Thanks for coming, Cody."

"Sure, Ruben, what's up?"

"I've just received some bad news. Seems Twanna Evers' father was hiding in the basement of his abandoned church in Charleston. One of our Watchmen picked up a lead on him just after Twanna left camp. Do you know anything about this?"

"How could I? Tee didn't know where he was hiding. She doesn't even know if he registered."

"Seems Reverend Evers is now a valuable commodity, he was kidnapped just before our Watchman arrived."

"How do you know this?

"They left a ransom note."

"Agents?"

"Naw, this was an inside job. My guess is soldiers from the Prophetic Voice. Since the fires of the first trumpet, thousands have joined. This white supremacy cult is led by a madman called Delford Eiland."

"What does he teach?"

"Typical heresies. Delford belittles anyone disagreeing with his deluded theology. He denies the physical resurrection of Jesus, the Trinity, the mark of the Beast, and the eternal lake of fire. He also brainwashes his followers with a heresy called serpent seed."

"Never heard of it."

"This heretic teaches Eve had sex with Satan and they conceived Cain. Descendants of Cain are non-Anglo Saxon people. Everyone not from the white race Eiland calls a Kenite."

"Why would anyone listen to such nonsense?"

"Such heresy is the fulfillment of prophecy. The Holy Spirit warned us there will be believers in the latter days departing from their faith in Jesus by heeding doctrines of demons. 14 The apostle Paul wrote, "For the time will come when they will not endure sound doctrine, but according to their own desires, because they have itching ears, they will heap up for themselves teachers; and they will turn their ears away from the truth, and be turned aside to fables." 15

"Why would they kidnap her father?"

"They want Twanna. The note says he won't be harmed if she surrenders. They must be seeking information about the Vineyard. This is big time trouble."

"Why would they harm us?"

"Eiland calls himself a doomsday prophet. He teaches judgment is coming upon America because of its blatant disobedience."

"So what? The day of the Lord is systemically destroying the earth and all those who follow Satan."

"Eiland sees himself as an extension of God's justice."

"Against who?"

"He's going to judge all who reject his end time message, especially Kenites, who he believes are Satan's offspring."

"How will he do that?"

"Who knows? For years he's been spewing out all types of threats."

"So what can I do?"

"How well do you know Ben?"

"He was the leader of my first Bible study group. Ben's a super teacher. You know he's Cherokee. His relatives live near here. He knows Black Rock Mountain like the back of his hand."

"Have you seen him lately?"

"Not since we went Red Fox."

"He left, Cody. He was the one who smuggled Twanna out."

"No way, Ben would never break our rules! This is so spooky. Look what had to go wrong for them to escape unnoticed."

"Aren't you from South Carolina?"

"I grew up in Charleston. My family moved to Columbia when I entered the University."

"Cody, it appears soldiers from the Prophetic Voice are targeting our outside Watchmen. My brother you know Charleston. Twanna and Ben trust you. This assignment has an edge to it."

"You want me to find them?"

"The Holy Spirit will lead you."

"And when I find them?"

"Under no circumstances can you return here."

"What about her father?"

"It's a long shot. Always remember; if Twanna ever gives herself up to Eiland, she's signing a death warrant for her father and herself."

"I understand."

"Will you pray about it?"

"I've already got a witness from the Holy Spirit."

"There is a Watchman living near Charleston. Check in with him first. I don't want you walking into a trap. This could save your life. No matter what goes down, we must be honest with each other. You can't afford to withhold any clues you find. The lives of thousands of children may depend on it."

"You can count on me, Ruben."

# FROM DARKNESS TO LIGHT

"I will deliver you from the Jewish people, as well as from the Gentiles, to whom I now send you, to open their eyes, in order to turn them from darkness to light, and from the power of Satan to God, that they may receive forgiveness of sins and an inheritance among those who are sanctified by faith in Me."
Acts 26:17-18

"He's here, Sir," reported the armed guard.

Seated in his brown leather chair the prophet looked pleased. The pictures were everything he had hoped for.

The tall soldier took a seat in front of his cluttered desk. Delford could see uneasiness in his eyes. Beads of perspiration were forming on his forehead. Unfastening his green army jacket, he tried to sit still.

"Lenard, these are pictures from Eli's cell phone. We're talking thousands of children. The NWC would have never found them."

"Did Eli mention how many woman and children?"

"Does it matter?"

"It will to those with family."

"Before we can assimilate..."

"You mean attack."

"You know their leadership will only listen to force."

"Delford, tell me how will attacking innocent people further the preservation of the white race?"

"These Kenites killed my sister. Soon the hand of God Almighty will extract His vengeance. We are simply instruments of His justice."

"These campers had nothing to do with her death. God's wrath is only getting worse."

"God has divinely ordained me as His prophetic voice. The

judgments in Revelation will fall on those rejecting my warnings. In my spirit I know we must cleanse this land of evil Kenites."

"You just can't kill them all."

"Our destiny, the destiny of our country, even the world, rests in those who act upon their convictions. God Almighty is using many groups like us. The Word of God is coming with vengeance."

Opening to the Book of Isaiah, the troubled soldier boldly read, 'For all those things My hand has made, and all those things exist," says the Lord. "But on this one will I look: On him who is poor and of a contrite spirit, and who trembles at My word.'" 1

"Lenard, how dare you lecture me! Without the Prophetic Voice, you'd be dead by now. After years of running, you thought you'd lost them. When the NWC picked up your trail again, you begged for help. You convinced me you bought into our vision. Now all I see is someone who doesn't have the courage to follow the truth."

"What about the kidnapping?"

"I won't hurt the preacher. If his daughter gives us the information on the tunnels, Lord willing, I'll let them go. Eli knows what he's doing. The timing of this operation is crucial. Once we commit, there is no stopping. Only God can foresee how many casualties there will be. Our success won't be measured by that. Now, are you with us or not?"

"What do you want me to do?"

"Praise God, Eli has just received information concerning the original leader of the Vineyard. Seems Pastor Greg Hudson is returning to the camp. He could be trouble. A resister named Reenie Tucker is with him. I don't want any interference from them."

"Isn't the Vineyard in Red Fox? No one is allowed in or out."

"Yes, yes, I know, you just make sure Hudson and Tucker never reach the Vineyard. Can you handle that?"

Downtown Charleston looked like a bomb had hit it.

"Gee, Ben, I never thought Americans would loot churches."

"Do you know the history of the land where the Vineyard is?"

"You mean Black Rock Mountain?"

"Tee, you've studied the cruelty of Africans on slave ships bound for America, but what about the history of the Cherokee nation? The trail of tears is evidence of how cruel the white man can be."

"I'm all ears."

"In the late 1820's gold was discovered near Dahlonega, Georgia. So Congress passed a bill calling for the removal of all Indians east of the Mississippi. This forced our Chiefs to bargain with the future of our people. The treaty they signed was the land for peace compromise."

"What did Congress promise?"

"The United States guaranteed safe passage to Oklahoma and Arkansas in exchange for ten million acres east of the Mississippi. You know Cherokees had their own government. Our people were farmers, merchants, and businessmen. It wasn't easy leaving and starting over. "

"Then why did they give up their land?"

"They had no choice. The massive roundup began in Georgia, eventually covering North Carolina, Tennessee, and Alabama. Thousands of Cherokees were forced to leave."

"How many made it?"

"The guaranteed safe passage turned out to be a forced march. Many died from bad food and rotten vegetables. Some walked the entire way with no shoes. At scheduled rest stops, the dead were buried. The Chief of my family's tribe was buried on the trail of tears near Nashville."

"How heartbreaking, Ben."

"His goal for our people was to live in peace. Often white children could be heard yelling, 'The only good Indian is a dead Indian.' He had hoped the treaty with the white man wasn't a death warrant."

"Are your people still living on Black Rock Mountain?"

"Does it matter? Most Americans could care less. But there was one foreigner who was very interested in this chapter of American history. He loved reading about the trail of tears. He wanted to know how one race could literally break the spirit of another. His name was Adolph Hitler."

Under the soccer field bleachers, she fell to her knees in the dirt and pleaded, "Where is he, Lord?"

"I'm sorry, Jo, if we stay any longer soldier patrols will pick us up. I know of a small village where we can hide."

"I'm a Watchman! I'm not leaving without my daddy."

"Where did you get the term 'Watchman' from?"

"Isaiah spoke of believers proclaiming the truth until our God reigns from Jerusalem. The prophet foretold, "I have set Watchmen on your walls, O Jerusalem; they shall never hold their peace day or night. You who make mention of the Lord, do not keep silent, and give Him no rest till He establishes and till He makes Jerusalem a praise in the earth." 2

"How will the Lord make Jerusalem a praise in the earth?"

"This is speaking of the reign of Jesus from Jerusalem."

"You must love this promise for your people?"

"Isaiah also prophesied, "For Zion's sake I will not hold My peace, and for Jerusalem's sake I will not rest, until her righteousness goes forth as brightness, and her salvation as a lamp that burns. The Gentiles shall see your righteousness, and all kings your glory. You shall be called by a new name, which the mouth of the Lord will name."' 3

"So do you only give this message with your father?"

"What do you mean?"

"You and I are a lot alike, Jo. We love our fathers, we love our people, and we're willing to sacrifice so the truth can be proclaimed to those who seek it."

"Rafa, your sacrifice..."

"Jo, I have no family anymore. I have given up everything dear to me so I can follow Jesus. I too want to run the race for souls."

"You already are."

"I ask you again, do you only share the gospel with your father? Doesn't it say Watchmen in the last days will not keep silent?"

Fighting back her tears, the slender American had no words.

"Acts 26:16-18 just popped into my mind. Do you know it?"

Opening her Bible she read, "'But rise and stand on your feet; for I have appeared to you for this purpose, to make you a minister and a witness both of the things which you have seen and of the things which I will yet reveal to you. I will deliver you from the Jewish people, as well as from the Gentiles, to whom I now send you, to open their eyes, in order to turn them from darkness to light, and from the power of Satan to God, that they may receive forgiveness of sins and an inheritance among those who are sanctified by faith in Me.'" 4

"What is the Holy Spirit saying?"

A determined Johanna replied, "God is speaking to us through

His Word. The Holy Spirit is sending us to preach the gospel to the Gentiles living in darkness."

"What about your father?"

"We have to trust our Lord will take care of him."

His Word. The Holy Spirit is sending us to preach the gospel to the

The front door of the deserted diner was unlocked. The only light were rays from the moon shining through the cracked windows. Stepping cautiously across the dirty dining room floor she felt drawn to a large picture on the far wall.

"This is too weird," she barely whispered to herself.

His deliberate steps down the wooden stairs startled her. His black coat reached the top of his spit shined black boots. Reaching the main floor, he slowly removed his gloves.

"I didn't think you'd come," he coldly reflected.

"The Lord is leading me. Why should I fear?"

"Listen to yourself. This isn't some game."

"You're not my contact. What have you done with him?"

"You never saw me. Now turn around and walk out that door."

"My name is..."

"Your name is Reenie Ann Tucker. You're nineteen years old, you have green eyes, auburn hair, and you're from Bethany, Alabama. You were attending Lakeview High when you refused to register. Somehow you made it to a resister camp near Birmingham. Your parents took the mark of the beast. Later your father committed suicide and your mother died from drinking Wormwood water."

"What's with the history lesson?"

"Oh yeah, and let's not forget your little brother. Travis was executed for killing a Special Forces agent nicknamed Death Angel."

Her tears meant nothing to him.

"What is your name and what do you want from me?"

"Are you searching for a resister camp called the Vineyard?"

"Where are your sores?"

"Don't have any."

"Are you a Christian?"

"Last time I checked."

"I don't know where the Vineyard is."

"Where is Pastor Greg Hudson?"

"Can't really say," she nervously confessed.

"Let me ask you something. Didn't Paul prophesy the Lawless One will be consumed with the breath of His mouth and destroyed with the brightness of His coming? This can only happen when Jesus casts the Beast and his false prophet into the lake of fire."

"You're close. This passage has a two-fold meaning. The days of Great Tribulation were cut short at His coming. 5 Kayin was paralyzed by the brightness of the Son coming in the glory of His Father. After the elect were caught up to heaven the day of the Lord began with fire. Only the Lord will be exalted during the day of the Lord. 6 After Jesus split the Mount of Olives and hid the redeemed from Israel; the sores from the first bowl were poured out. After the seventh bowl, the two beasts will be consumed by..."

"No, no, no the Jews rejected the Messiah. The Gentiles have been grafted into the olive tree. The promises of Israel are now for the body of Christ."

"I understand there is no Jew or Gentile in the body of Christ. Yet the church hasn't replaced the children of Israel in their covenant relationship with God."

"How can you prove that?" he chided.

"Their blindness to the gospel was never permanent."

"Who says?"

"Try Abraham, the covenant he cut with God made a way for a saved remnant in every generation.

"You're dreaming."

"You asked."

"Yes, for the truth; not your opinion."

"I'd love to hear the truth. Why are you so secret?"

Even with her heart racing, she could sense a divine peace settling upon her spirit.

"Reenie, you see that picture on the wall?"

"What of it?"

"It's a picture of the White House. Joshua and I were once friends."

"I don't understand."

"My name is Lenard Mayer. I was once a member of the White House Staff. Until I saw what was happening."

"So you know who Kayin really is?"

"The NWC has been after me since the famines of the third seal."

"I have to get to the Vineyard."

"They're harboring Blacks and Jews."

"Who cares? This is still a free country."

"There will be no questions, no mercy, these kids are in danger."

"Who are you talking about?"

"A renegade militia has infiltrated the Vineyard. When Eli gives the signal, these campers will never know what hit them."

"Does Greg know Eli?"

Shaking his head he scolded, "Reenie, this no time to be guessing. Have you seen the bloody tablecloth near the kitchen?"

"Can't miss the smell."

"Your contact is dead. So is the soldier sent by the Prophetic Voice. They must've shot each other. The blood bath has begun."

"Lenard, I don't know where Pastor Greg is. You're my only hope. Will you take me to the Vineyard?"

# Third Bowl: Rivers like Blood

"Then the third angel poured out his bowl on the rivers and springs
of water, and they became like blood."
Revelation 16:4

A holy hush in heaven preceded the third angel reaching earth. After
emptying its bowl rivers and lakes gushed forth blood. 1

The angel of the waters cried out, "'You are righteous, O Lord,
the One who is and who was and who is to be, because You judged
these things. For they have shed the blood of saints and prophets, and
You have given them blood to drink. For it is their just due.'" 2

From the altar another proclaimed, "'...Even so, Lord God
Almighty, true and righteous are Your judgments.'" 3

Sprawled across a plush Oriental rug in her dressing room she
cursed, "Why such suffering? No one deserves this!"

There was no response to the pounding on her door.

"Nate, this is Wes, are you there? We've got power for at least
another hour. The script is in place. You can read it from the
teleprompter. C'mon, all I want is a yes or no?"

His skeleton staff didn't look any better. While cameramen
rechecked their positions the soundman turned up the volume. Wes
Mackish gave the signal.

"This is a Channel 6 Emergency Update with Natalie Roberts.
Minutes ago, rivers and lakes throughout the world were infected
with..."

Johanna was praying when an anxious Rafa opened the door to the adjacent room. The Jordanian teenager could not deny the tugging on her heart by the Holy Spirit.

"I've told them all about you. Do not be fooled by the hurt on their faces. Most have come to listen. I don't think anyone will interrupt you. Just tell them what you told me. Okay?"

Walking hand in hand the girls entered the jammed room.

"My name is Johanna. I have a message of love for you. Jesus said, 'And as Moses lifted up the serpent in the wilderness, even so must the Son of Man be lifted up, that whoever believes in Him should not perish but have eternal life. For God so loved the world that He gave His only begotten Son, that whoever believes in Him should not perish but have everlasting life.'" [4]

Their murmuring stopped as soon as Rafa raised her hands.

"God's wrath is destroying this earth. The angel Gabriel gave Daniel a prophecy concerning Christ's first and second coming. Each involves Israel. When Jesus came the first time, His own people rejected him. John wrote, 'He came to His own, and His own did not receive Him.' [5] Because of this rejection salvation was offered to the Gentiles. 'But as many as received Him, to them He gave the right to become children of God, to those who believe in His name: who were born, not of blood, nor of the will of the flesh, nor of the will of man, but of God.'" [6]

All eyes were focused on the young American. Her concern for Muslims was easy to see.

"For almost two thousand years God Almighty has grafted Gentiles into the olive tree of life. He is no respecter of persons. Today, each of you will have an opportunity to receive eternal life."

A mother of two under conviction started to weep.

"Do you believe it was Jesus on Mount Moriah during the Feast of Tabernacles?"

"Yes, the Messiah saved a remnant from among His people. Soon He will come again and reign over a new earth."

"We are under the wrath of Allah!" cursed a man full of sores.

"Believers surviving His wrath will see a heavenly city descending upon a newly restored earth. From within this Holy City Jesus will rule over the nations with His glorified saints."

A confused teenage girl asked, "Isn't Allah reigning right now?"

Turning to Revelation 11 Johanna calmly read, "'...And there were loud voices in heaven, saying, "The kingdoms of this world have become the kingdoms of our Lord and of His Christ, and He shall reign forever and ever. And the twenty-four elders who sat before God on their thrones fell on their faces and worshiped God, saying: "We give You thanks, O Lord God Almighty, The One who is and who was and who is to come, Because You have taken Your great power and reigned.'" 7

"When did this happen?"

"After the sounding of the seventh trumpet during the Feast of Tabernacles, God Almighty is now reigning. This is why the nations are responding in anger. 8 Even so, Jesus is still saving souls."

After an hour of nonstop questions, a distraught Rafa impatiently interrupted.

"What more proof do you need?" demanded the ex-Muslim. "The same day Kayin killed the two Witnesses, the Messiah returned. He began by gathering the 144,000, the first fruits of His remnant. By the third day, Jesus returned to Jerusalem to save those who believed in Him. On the fourth day, He raised the two Witnesses from the dead. On the fifth day, He led a redeemed remnant to the top of Mount Zion. This was the fulfillment of the Feast of Tabernacles. The next day, the Lord spilt the Mount of Olives and hid them. Why can't you see this?"

---

Downtown Charleston was unrecognizable.

"Gee, Ben, what a mess. Our cities are being decimated." 9

"Babylon will soon bite the dust in one hour." 10

"You mean the mother of harlots who committed fornication with the kings of the earth? I thought Kayin dissolved the World Faith Movement just after he seized control of the nations?"

"In Revelation 18, an angel uses 'fallen' twice. John saw the fall of two Babylon's. The first was the World Faith Movement which consisted of all Christ rejecting religions."

"Didn't Pope Michael support this movement under the guise of achieving world peace?"

"He was a key player, Tee. He also helped destroy it."

"He did?"

"The False Prophet assisted Kayin in dissolving the Babylonian harlot after the nations accepted the NWC. 11 The city housing the mother of harlots will soon receive the full wrath of God!"

"You mean Rome? I thought Iraq was supposed to be Babylon?"

"Physical Babylon was cursed by God and will never rise again. This wasteland is outside Iraq. The harlot riding the scarlet beast is called Babylon the Great. This false religious system has persecuted the children of God for thousands of years. John saw her drunk with the blood of the saints and martyrs of Jesus."

"You know, Ben, it gave me the creeps when the Catholic Church used the mother Mary appearance to initiate the World Faith Movement. What really blew me away is how many saw nothing wrong with it. It didn't matter, Catholics, Muslims, Jews, Christians, Hindus, Buddhists, seemed like everyone was lining up."

"The harlot supporting the Beast was dissolved after Jesus opened the fourth seal. Rome will be destroyed by the seventh bowl."

"Yeah, the kings fornicating with her will weep over her." 12

Shaking his head he shared, 'Rejoice over her, O heaven, and you holy apostles and prophets, for God has avenged you on her.'" 13

"What about the famous prophets prophesying the Pope would be baptized in the Holy Spirit? Or the prophecy teachers declaring all Catholics are born again?"

"Tee, Jesus warned us of many deceptively coming in His name and deceiving many believers. I just never figured so many would depart from the faith by embracing such doctrines of demons."

Her father's church was a block away. Slowing down; Ben parked across the street. The side door to the sanctuary was ajar. Slipping by the baptismal they tiptoed down the steps into the torn up basement.

"Must have been quite a struggle, huh, Ben?"

"You mean someone wants us to think that."

Both flinched after a shadow passed by the basement window.

"We've got company," whispered Twanna.

The steps creaked as he edged down into the dimly lit basement.

"You there, Tee, it's Cody."

"Is anyone with you?"

"A Watchman spotted you two coming in. Where's Ben?"

"Right behind you."

Spinning around he threw a playful jab at the old Indian.

"Why are you here? Did you read my note I left on your bed?"

"I never saw it. Someone must have lifted it. I've got some bad news about your daddy."

Looking away she took a deep breath.

"Is he dead?"

"He's been kidnapped by a white supremacist group."

"Why?"

"The Prophetic Voice left a ransom note. They're after you, Tee."

"You mean the Vineyard," reasoned a solemn Ben.

"C'mon," insisted Cody, "let's get out of here."

Their pickup came off without a hitch. After dropping them off at an abandoned house, the driver of the black truck waved goodbye.

"Who is he?"

"Don't know, Tee. He says there's food and water upstairs in the guest bedroom closet."

Later, while munching on some stale beef jerky, Ben volunteered to stand watch by the second floor window. Twanna and Cody sat side by side with their backs up against the bedroom wall.

"Did you see the ransom note?"

"The underground destroyed it. This cult is asking for a straight swap; you for your father."

"Just tell me when and where?"

"This Saturday in Dahlonega, Georgia, the exchange will be at a small diner called Maggie's."

"What does Ruben think about this?"

"These are high stakes, Tee. If you surrender to this cult, they will kill you and your father. You can't negotiate with these racists."

"That's easy for you to say!" she snapped back.

The immediate silence was awkward.

"My people live near Dahlonega. If the Prophetic Voice has your father the Cherokees will find him."

"Ben, our rescue days are over. We know too much. And even if your tribe knows about this cult rescuing Tee's father is a whole different matter."

"If they're planning on attacking the Vineyard maybe we can somehow divert them?"

A stunned Cody pleaded, "Tee, we can't afford to get involved with such killers. My assignment from Ruben was clear. Find you and Ben and then hide out until the supper of the great God is over!"

## THE LAST DAY

"No one can come to Me unless the Father who sent Me draws him;
and I will raise him up at the last day."
John 6:44

Watching from a line of pine trees overlooking the secluded diner, there was no movement for the past hour. Nudging open the front door the decay made him gag. Across the dining room were streams of dried blood. Stepping into the kitchen he watched a scrawny black cat scamper out an open window over the sink. The dripping faucet meant there was still running water. Trails of ants were feasting on a clump of spilled maple syrup. Another blotch of blood stained the white tile floor. Two sets of eyes were watching from the parking lot.

"Jon, where will this Watchman meet us?"

"At a diner in Dahlonega called Maggie's."

"When do we meet him?"

"There is no set time, Jake. The Lord will lead us."

"What's his name?"

"Never gives it out, Emma. If Reenie and Greg passed through Dahlonega, he'll know. He will take you to the Vineyard."

"Donnell, why not call the underground."

"Anything traceable is out. From now on it's strictly word of mouth."

"Let's pray," exhorted Jon. "I'm getting a burden for someone."

Stepping back into the dining room he saw their faces in the main window. Their lips were moving but he couldn't hear them. It was like they were chanting something. Then the front door popped open.

"I'm unarmed. Do I know you?"

"You know someone we are looking for."

"Like who?"

"Reenie Ann Tucker."

The sickness in his stomach wasn't from nerves. The odor exuding from these skinny boys was disgusting.

"I left her in Alabama. I don't know where she is. I'm all alone."

"Osiris has come from the depth of darkness."

"What do you want with Reenie?"

"He wants her soul."

Greg now knew Reenie was on her way to the Vineyard. Backing away he bolted for the kitchen. Reaching the backdoor he was struck from behind. The boy holding the baseball bat started jumping up and down as his buddy summoned Osiris. The Watchman lay unconscious as the foul spirit manifested on the back steps of the diner.

"Neither you nor your friends have the power to stop me. When I find this girl I will feed her flesh to the ravens."

Glancing toward the boys the demon stared and hissed.

"Continue your search."

---

They could see Fadi was hiding a Jew. Anyone alerting the authorities would immediately be rewarded with water and food. Miraculously no one spoke up when asked by Jordanian soldiers. By the time they reached the bleachers the girls were gone

"Aaron, they're stopping all cars and trucks. We can walk it in an hour."

"What makes you think the girls are there?"

"Many people in this town haven't registered. Rafa has a special love for this area. She calls it, Eftah Al Bab, the open door."

"Fadi, in The Revelation of Jesus Christ, Jesus spoke of seven churches which represent Christians living in these last days. The overcomers from Philadelphia remained faithful under persecution."

"Can you read this passage to me?"

"'I know your works. See, I have set before you an open door, and no one can shut it; for you have a little strength, have kept My word, and have not denied My name.'" [1]

"Wow, is this actually in the Bible?"

"Jesus also rebuked believers who were lukewarm, 'I know your works, that you are neither cold nor hot. I could wish you were cold or hot. So then, because you are lukewarm, and neither cold nor hot, I will vomit you out of My mouth. Because you say, "I am rich, have become wealthy, and have need of nothing'—and do not know that you are wretched, miserable, poor, blind, and naked.'" 2

"So what caused these believers to become so blind?"

"They refused to renounce their sinful lifestyle. The lack of repentance was why so many lacked discernment."

"I'm not a sinner."

"You think so?"

"I have nothing to repent of. Do you?"

"Tell me, do you love your sister?"

"Actions speak louder than words. I sacrificed my future for my sister. I have no regrets."

"I loved my sister in the same way."

"Where is she now?"

"Syrian terrorists killed her. You wanted to know if I had anything to repent of. Forgiving those who took her life was at the top of my list."

"What list?"

"Fadi, walking with the Lord is new to me. Yes, I've studied the Bible but I've only been saved since Jesus split the Mount of Olives. Since then sins keep coming to mind I need to repent of. I'm not afraid to ask for forgiveness. The Bible says it better than I can. Can I read you a passage about man's sinfulness compared to God's holiness?"

"Go ahead."

"'If then you were raised with Christ, seek those things which are above, where Christ is, sitting at the right hand of God. Set your mind on things above, not on things on the earth. For you died, and your life is hidden with Christ in God. When Christ who is our life appears, then you also will appear with Him in glory. Therefore put to death your members which are on the earth: fornication, uncleanness, passion, evil desire, and covetousness, which is idolatry.'" 3

"I have no idols in my life."

"I had many," confessed the ex-freedom fighter.

"Name one?"

"Revenge fueled by bitterness. I was once a son of disobedience."

"You mean God has set you free from sinning?"

"No, Fadi, only Jesus is sinless. I'm talking about a relationship with Christ through the Holy Spirit. I forgive because Jesus has forgiven me."

Bowing his head, he openly confessed, "This love and forgiveness you're speaking of is what Rafa is seeking after. She was never satisfied with Islam. For her the Qur'an was just a religion of rules. She finally admitted she never felt the love of Allah."

"What about you?"

"I don't understand how Jesus can be human and divine at the same time? Can God die?"

"The Bible says, 'And the Word became flesh and dwelt among us, and we beheld His glory, the glory as of the only begotten of the Father, full of grace and truth.' 4 The only begotten means the Father's Son became human."

"When did Jesus ever say He was the Son of God?"

"Jesus asked a man who he had just healed of blindness, '"...Do you believe in the Son of God? He answered and said, "Who is He, Lord, that I may believe in Him?" And Jesus said to him, "You have both seen Him and it is He who is talking with you." Then he said, "Lord, I believe. And he worshipped Him."' 5

"This man actually worshipped Jesus as the Son of God?"

"This proves Jesus was both divine and human while on earth."

"I want to believe but I can't. There is something inside me that won't let me. If Muhammad and the Qur'an can't help me what makes you think Jesus and the Bible can?"

---

Their drive through the Blue Ridge Mountains was rough. Even after praying; the attacks kept coming. A discerning Jon finally spoke.

"How's your thought life, Emma?"

"My brother has always been there for me. I'm praying for Kurt's rescue. I'm hoping someone will have the courage to obey what the Spirit is telling them to do."

"Yeah, I can relate, my grandparents cried out for help but so many Christian's had a deaf ear."

Lashing back, she snapped, "What does your family have to do with my brother? You have no idea what he is suffering."

Slipping his arm around her shaking shoulders, Jake whispered, "C'mon, Em, let's hear him out."

As the RV motored down the road Jon Mendel recalled the tragic fate of his grandparents.

"It was a nightmare for those taking the journey. Everyone could hear the rattling metal wheels grinding to a halt. The doors to the filthy trains were slowly opened. Prisoners being jammed inside were assured by soldiers everything would be fine. Blood curdling screams rang out as the doors locked. Trapped in darkness for hours, with no food or water, their pleas for help went unanswered. The smell of dead bodies permeated the camp when they arrived."

"You're describing the Holocaust! Satan used Nazis not Christians!"

"If the church had taken a stand against anti-Semitism," sighed Donnell, "the Holocaust might never have happened."

"The evil Spanish Inquisition began in the fifteenth century. Over thirty thousand Jews were burned at the stake! Now you know why so many of my people were never introduced to their Messiah."

"Who you talking about, Jon?" asked Jake. "The killing of Jews and Muslims by Catholics was never part of the body of Christ."

"What about Martin Luther, you ever wonder why Adolph Hitler loved to read his books? The demonic transference of Luther's hate for the Jewish people spread worldwide. The wicked agenda of forced conversion was approved of way before the rise of Nazism."

"What is forced conversion?"

"Emma, many Jews were forced to abandon their heritage by being baptized into the Roman Catholic Church. Such manipulation actually drove many of my people into the arms of the Nazis. Instead of rejecting the past injustices the Germans built on them."

"Hitler was never a Christian. He was Catholic!"

"Jake, where did Hitler get the phrase, 'Kill a Jew and save a soul?'"

"What does the Holocaust have to do with us?"

"By the 1940's, many pastors were teaching the body of Christ is the Israel of God. Since Israel rejected their Messiah, all promises given to God's chosen people were now exclusively for the church."

"How is this teaching connected to the Holocaust?"

"In the eyes of many Christians there was no need for the Jewish people anymore. Israelites, who obtained the adoption, the glory, the covenants, the law, and the promises, were no longer His people. 6 This was never God's will."

"What does it matter now? Armageddon is almost here."

"This anti-Semitic spirit is still attacking. The blood of my grandparents is on the hands of those sowing such hate."

"So you guys really think this demon has something to do with

Reenie's vision and the Vineyard?"

Both Jon and Donnell nodded.

Bowing his head a wary Jake candidly confessed, "I just pray our Miracle Girl is listening to the Holy Spirit."

---

Parked on the side of the road Ben was interceding. It was like they were being supernaturally drawn into events they had no power over. He'd experienced the horror of losing family members; the same for Cody. The wise Cherokee was asking God whether infiltrating this dangerous identity group was really His will.

Waking up from a nap Cody yawned before stretching out.

"Why are we stopped, Ben, any trouble?"

"Been asking the Lord what to do, has the Holy Spirit shown you anything?"

"I just had the weirdest dream. I saw a white tornado. It was moving toward a crowd who could hear it but they couldn't see it. I was running up a hill toward them. I was screaming for them to hide in the nearby caves. But it didn't matter how fast I ran, I wasn't getting any closer."

"Did you get the interpretation?"

"The closer it got, the fiercer it became. It was destroying everything in its path. I begged the Lord to send it another way."

"The Cherokees have seen white tornados before but never in these mountains. A respected Chief once foretold of a white tornado coming in the last days and taking away the pain of my people."

"You mean the Son coming with His angels?"

"I suppose. But what you saw isn't about healing. I see fear in your eyes. There's more to your dream, isn't there?"

"Children were being tossed around like paper dolls. It didn't matter how many cried out for mercy. The tornado never let up."

"Anything else?"

"Strangely enough, I saw a girl standing inside the tornado. She has auburn hair, green eyes, slender, about twenty years old."

"Do you know her?"

"Nope, I think this dream may have a twofold meaning. The reason the Lord didn't answer my prayer to send the tornado away was because I was trying to do it my way. It was destroying everything I had planned. The wisdom of man can't stop it."

"What's the other meaning?"

"The destruction doesn't have to happen. This girl could be some sort of deliverer."

"You mean the people won't suffer if she does it God's way?"

"Popping her head up from the backseat, Twanna playfully asked, "Is she white or black?"

"Or maybe an Indian?" joked Ben.

"She's white, kinda looks southern."

"You think God is trying to warn us?"

"I don't know, Tee, it's Cody's dream. The consequences we're facing look pretty severe."

"Hold up, you mean my dream is somehow about the Vineyard?"

"Why is the Prophetic Voice offering a ransom?"

"Ruben thinks these racists are seeking information about our tunnels. Tee also knows all about our security precautions."

"But my Daddy..."

Cutting her off, the Indian offered the challenge.

"Guys, we are either walking into a deadly trap or the Lord is leading us to stop a massacre; near the trail of tears no less. This cult uses a perimeter much like the Vineyard's. If they haven't already seen us, they will once we reach Dahlonega. If anyone is having doubts about this rescue now's the time to speak up."

"I'm in," nodded an unwavering Twanna.

"This is so bizarre," reflected a suspicious Cody. "How can this girl stop the attack on the Vineyard? Why would God pick her? And what are our chances of getting caught?"

The wise Indian cautiously replied, "Sometimes, the closer you get in rescues the hotter it gets."

The sun would be up soon. His old truck was parked beside some charred spruce trees.

"I need some time to pray about it. I won't be long."

She waited until Cody disappeared into the woods.

"Ben, I feel like this rescue is way over my head. Have you ever felt this way?"

"Oh yeah, lots of times."

# EVERLASTING DESTRUCTION

"These shall be punished with everlasting destruction from the
presence of the Lord and from the glory of His power."
II Thessalonians 1:9

"See them; just behind the trees. They've found our wells."

"I told you protecting this many kids isn't possible. Most would
turn in our whole camp for one meal."

"You watch them," whispered the other sentry. "I'm going back
to camp. It's Ruben's call. He knows what's at stake."

The inner circle of the Vineyard staff was quietly interceding as
their Commander entered the entrance to the underground tunnel.

"Attention everyone, as you know, when the wrath from the third
bowl infected the river at the bottom of Black Rock Mountain many
people panicked. Some are moving up the mountain. An hour ago
two families found our wells."

A camp counselor anxiously interrupted, "Beulah's exit is just
fifty meters from our wells. What if they find it, Ruben?"

"The Vineyard has always had the protection of our Lord. As
your Commander I've sought the mind of Christ on every decision
I've made. Satan has attacked us in many different ways. It hasn't been
easy. Answers are not as black and white as they seem."

The staff ranged from fourteen to eighty-two. Most knew the
strengths and the weaknesses of Ruben Rodriguez. Being their leader
was not about being more holy than others. It wasn't even about
being closer to God. Obedience was the bottom line. This staff was
well trained in what to do if the Vineyard was compromised.

"I've been fasting for the past forty-eight hours. Our Lord sees
what we don't. We are in His loving hands. We must believe He will

protect us. Doubt from any of us can spread like an out of control fire. Don't be fooled, these children can spot unbelief a mile away."

"What do you want us to do, Ruben?"

"Twanna Evers has left camp which means the oversight of Beulah and Bethel will shift to foremen directing their construction. An evacuation isn't possible until both tunnels are declared safe."

"What if the NWC discovers us?"

"Let me be clear. A cave-in during an evacuation is unacceptable. We are almost ready. Right now our crews are shoring up the last twenty yards of Bethel."

The camp cook pleaded, "What about our supplies? As of today we are down to one meal a day. I thought a total evacuation was only an option if we had enough food?"

"We must trust the Lord. Tonight we will try a practice run."

A frightened counselor raised his hand to speak.

"The children are worn out. You know how worked up they can get with these drills."

"Okay, using group leaders will have to do."

"Will you lead us out, Ruben?"

"No, I'll be stationed at the mouth of Bethel. When I call Alpha, each squad leader will issue a head count. When I call Omega, the evacuation of the Vineyard will commence. Lord willing, I'll lead the last group out."

"Commander, how far can we go in defending ourselves and the children?"

"Where do we go now?"

"Does it matter?" snapped Rafa. "Their hearts are cold. They don't understand repentance."

"My people don't either," sighed Johanna. "Some things won't happen unless people pray. This is why Daniel was such a prayer warrior for those he loved."

"What do you mean?"

"It goes like this. I couldn't make you repent. That's between you and God. So my Daddy and I prayed against any lies holding you back from giving your heart to the Lord."

"May the Lord bless you," responded Rafa with a warm smile.

"When you were thinking about believing in Jesus as your Savior, was there any confusion coming against you?"

"Of course, the Qur'an warns against anyone believing Allah has a Son. According to Muhammad a painful fate awaits such blasphemers."

"How did God the Father reveal His Son to you?"

"He laid this passage from the Qur'an on my heart, 'O Mary verily God gives you good tidings of the Word from Himself; His name is Jesus Son of Mary exalted both in this world and world to come and one of those near the throne.'"

"Jesus is the Word made flesh," praised Johanna. 1

"Yep, the Word from Himself means Jesus is the Word of God. John wrote, 'In the beginning was the Word, and the Word was with God, and the Word was God.' 2 Suddenly my eyes were opened. And it's all because of your righteous prayers."

"Amen, Rafa, no one can come to the Son but by the Father."

"Then what are we doing wrong? My people are so blind. Not one person accepted the Lord back there. All they wanted to do was hurt us."

"Paul wrote, 'Bless those who persecute you; bless and do not curse. Rejoice with those who rejoice, and weep with those who weep.'" 3

"What is weep with those who weep? It's not my fault they refused the truth. You said we can't make them repent of their sin."

"When we intercede we need to identify with the pain of those we are praying for. This doesn't happen on its own."

"I thought the Lord can do anything?"

"Some things He will not do unless someone intercedes through heart-felt prayer. The prophet Daniel is an example of someone appropriating God's promises for His people."

"I also love my people very much. But what can I say to make them see the truth?"

"There are no magical words. We just give them the gospel. The Holy Spirit will bring the conviction."

"What about the prophecies concerning Jordan? How do I pray in light of what God has already predicted?"

"We can't surrender to fear. When Satan attacks we know God is working. Just like clockwork."

"So how do I know the Father's will?"

"Rafa, someday we will see Gentiles and Jews joining hands and proclaiming Jesus as Lord to the glory of God the Father."

---

"Hey, Sophie, one of our patrols just brought Doyle in. He's pretty ticked off. He wants to interrogate Kurt Abbott."

"Every time I talk with Kurt I'm getting closer."

"Sophie, you're new here. Chief makes all the calls. Some kids used to get a month to register. Now it only takes one refusal."

"Kurt is just a confused boy trying to find his sister. He's no threat to the NWC. Mercer has more important matters."

"Sophie, this little angel is a member of the Rescue Squad. Kurt Abbott and Greg Hudson once locked Chief in the trunk of his car. It was Hudson who left Doyle in a deserted carwash. When we found him he was so dehydrated he couldn't talk. It doesn't matter how old Kurt is. This punk better fess up or his life isn't worth a nickel."

The deep seated anger of the agents was festering. The euphoria over the execution of the two Witnesses was short lived. The loathsome sores from the first bowl punctured any hope mankind might have had. The lack of food and water was crippling. The execution of captured resisters was swift. The once full prison cells were almost empty.

Kurt's cellmate was barely fourteen. His pacing was annoying.

"What's bugging you, Parker?"

"I can't take this. It was a fluke they found me. Everyone I know is either dead or registered. What does it matter now?"

"Whoa, whoa, let's back up. Listen to me, Jesus' warnings not to be deceived matter big time. What we believe before Armageddon will determine how we will spend eternity!"

"I don't know who to trust anymore."

"Parker, how many times have we studied this? You know why it's important to get what's coming. It's to strengthen us."

"I know, I know, but my brain is so fried."

"Satan is a liar. What's the enemy been feeding you?"

"Will I go to the lake of fire if I take the mark of the beast?"

"In the Book of Revelation an angel clearly warns, '...If anyone worships the beast and his image, and receives his mark on his forehead or on his hand, he himself shall also drink of the wine of the wrath of God, which is poured out full strength into the cup of His indignation. He shall be tormented with fire and brimstone in the presence of the holy angels and in the presence of the Lamb.'" 4

"My Sunday school teacher taught me this fire isn't forever."

"The next verse says, 'And the smoke of their torment ascends forever and ever; and they have no rest day or night, who worship the beast and his image, and whoever receives the mark of his name.'" 5

"So you believe God wants to burn people in fire?"

"Parker, the lake of fire was created for the Devil and his angels who rebelled. 6 It was enlarged to accept man who also rejected God."

"Where does Jesus talk about fire? Give me one verse."

"Our Lord said, "If anyone does not abide in Me, he is cast out as a branch and is withered; and they gather them and throw them into the fire, and they are burned." 7

"Sounds symbolic to me."

"I wouldn't bet eternity on it. After the thousand year reign of Christ over the nations ends, everyone suffering in Hades will be resurrected before His white throne. Jesus will judge their works before casting them all into the lake of fire." 8

"You think they'll remember why they got there?"

"Does it matter?"

"Why would a loving God allow this?"

"You know why. We're in here because of our testimony of Jesus. The warfare we're facing is for keeps."

"I was taught the events in Revelation were in the first century."

"Are you blind? The followers of the Beast have infected sores. The oceans, rivers and lakes are contaminated. Once the fourth bowl is poured out many will be scorched by the sun. They're all blaspheming God!" 9

"I'm so sick of this world."

"Me too! C'mon now, Armageddon is just days away."

"Ok, what's your plan?"

"Let's keep it simple. Don't believe anything these agents say. We can never register! We remain faithful to our Jesus no matter what."

The relieved teenager whispered back, "Agreed."

All forty-one windows were dark except one. After parking in her circular white brick driveway he knew where to go. This was her dream home. A special haven carved out of hundreds of towering pine trees. Natalie Rene Roberts had hoped to marry and raise her kids here. Just ten minutes outside Chicago, this multi-million dollar getaway overlooking a beautiful lake was for her family and close friends. This was all made possible by her gift in broadcasting. Such success came with a price. She had sacrificed everything that could interfere. For a moment, the most popular News Anchor in America could practically have anything she wanted. At least it seemed that way until the day the heavens went black. 10

There was no response at the side entrance. He carefully invited himself in. The pre-recorded nightly news could be heard coming from her eighty inch TV mounted on the wall in her immaculate study. Walking down the hallway he reminisced of better days.

"Thanks for coming, Wes."

"I never turn down an invite."

"Want some coffee?"

"Where did you get it?"

"I have a secret stash in my basement."

From her bar she poured her friend a hot cup of hazelnut coffee.

"Are you all alone, Nate?"

"Still got a maid and a cook coming in. Have you seen my lake?"

"Lake Michigan was enough for me."

"There are four more bowls," she dryly replied.

"You mean the judgments from the Book of Revelation?"

"The next bowl will scorch men with heat."

"Is your family ok?"

"My uncle from Jersey just called. He used to be so happy. Nothing ever got him down. Now he just stays in bed all day."

"How are you coping?"

"I can't get Delford's voice out of my head. I hate the scary nightmares I've been having since his last phone call."

"Are you planning another trip to the Blue Ridge Mountains?"

"Thinking about it."

"Why? Your Special Report on the Prophetic Voice was excellent. What can you accomplish by another visit? Eiland isn't someone to fool with."

Sipping her coffee, she reflected, "His apocalyptic survivalism is an attractive alternative to the crumbling NWC. His doctrine isn't attracting soldiers. It's his hate for other races. He has to be stopped."

"Is this racist baiting you?"

"Delford believes whites are God's chosen people. All other races are from Satan."

"Who gives a rip? You're just wasting your time."

"Many identity groups believe America is the Promised Land. A final war against the Kenites will usher in a white race utopia. Did you know no one from the Prophetic Voice has registered?"

He paused while searching for the right words.

"I would like for you to come stay with my family. At least until we see what happens in the Middle East."

"Want some more coffee?"

"You're really going to do this?"

"Many will suffer if Eiland somehow pulls off this race war. Maybe I can prevent it."

"Like how? Don't underestimate your TV Special. You may have persuaded thousands to leave such cults."

Her frown was puzzling to the experienced producer.

"Wes, if this is the end I don't want to be stuck in a dark TV studio. Remember my interview in Jerusalem after the two Witnesses came back to life?"

"Some of the best reporting you've ever done."

"When I interviewed Delford I only saw hate. The glimpse I got of Yeshua was totally different. The depth of love coming from His eyes is difficult to explain. At first, like so many others, I denied it. Now I'm thinking it was supernatural."

# THE SALVATION OF OUR GOD

"The Lord has made bare His holy arm. In the eyes of all the nations; and all the ends of the earth shall see, the salvation of our God."
Isaiah 52:10

Lenard's house was a mile from Maggie's. His brown jacket, faded blue jeans and red running shoes looked so out of place. Slipping into the front seat of his SUV Reenie hardly recognized him.

"What's with the disguise?" she teased.

He didn't reply. His black SUV was jammed with packaged food, water, sleeping bags, and six containers of gasoline. Several boxes of ammunition and high grade explosives caught her eye. Pulling back onto the road, he checked to see how much gas he had left.

"The headquarters of the Prophetic Voice is not far from here. I was sent by Delford Eiland to stop you and Greg Hudson from ever reaching the Vineyard. Escaping through their security net will take a miracle. Reenie, what instructions did Greg give you?"

"I was to find the trail of tears if I missed my contact."

"Well, the trail of tears begins near Black Rock Mountain."

"Our Lord is faithful. How long is our drive?"

"A couple of miles, do you have any idea where Greg might be?"

"I have no clue."

"The third bowl has been poured out."

"Figures, the river we just passed was streaked with blood."

He was thinking, never taking his eyes off the road. She noticed the gun underneath his brown jacket.

"I once had a friend that used a Glock like yours."

"Where is he now?"

"Bret was martyred for his testimony of Jesus."

"Reenie, so how will your friend be part of the first resurrection?"

"Pastor Greg taught us the first resurrection will take place over a period of time covering several events. Jesus was the first fruits of the first resurrection; the first to rise from the dead and never die. 1 After the sixth seal, the Son of Man came and His angels gathered the dead in Christ immediately followed by overcomers out of the great tribulation. 2 They each received their resurrection bodies in a twinkling of an eye. 3 On the first day of Christ's thousand year reign those martyred by the Beast will be resurrected. 4 Finally, all believers on earth remaining faithful during the Millennium will receive their glorified bodies before the Son returns His rule back to His Father. 5 Each is part of the first resurrection."

He respectfully nodded. Lenard Mayer was now convinced the end time vision he saw as a ten year old was for real. He was supernaturally being drawn into events involving the day of the Lord. Until now, his only protection was from a survivalist militia hidden in the Blue Ridge Mountains. But they were as lost as he was. This ex-cult member was searching for the truth. He was wary at first but now he was sure of it. The green eyed teenager sitting beside him was the same girl he saw in his vision. Originally sent to eliminate her, he would now try and save her life.

---

The boys could hear her high heels echoing down the lonely corridor. She despised Doyle's tactics. This wasn't why she joined the Bethany Security Force. She was close to quitting.

"What's up, Sophie?"

"Someone wants to talk to you and Parker."

Kurt could sense her urgency. Her strained face, her rigid walk, even the agent patrolling the hallway looked sad.

"Guess whose back in town?"

"Hopefully no one I know."

"An agent found Doyle Mercer in a small town near the Georgia border. He was handcuffed inside a closed down car wash. He would have died if the underground resistance hadn't called in a tip."

"Who did this to him?"

"Seems your friends Hudson and Tucker kidnapped him from the cave you were hiding in."

"They got away!" yelped a giddy Kurt.

"You didn't hear it from me," cautioned the uneasy agent.

Their walk down the eerie corridor took forever.

"Chief, we're ready. Each boy is in adjoining rooms. How do you want to use agent Lowery? She knows these kids pretty good."

"Since I've been back, I've heard her name at least a dozen times. Yet as far as I can see she hasn't done squat. Has Kurt Abbott given her the names of any Watchmen?"

"No sir."

"Any clues on the whereabouts of the underground?"

"No sir."

"Maybe the location of the Vineyard?"

"Sir, Sophie believes the best way to obtain..."

"Get out of my way!"

Brushing past the guard, Doyle Mercer was out of control. The execution of the Rescue Squad was becoming his obsession.

Outside both rooms the resolute agent was waiting.

"Good afternoon, Chief Mercer, I'm Sophie Lowery."

"I know who are you are. As of now you're dismissed from these two cases. I will personally oversee their interrogation."

"I've spent some quality time with these boys. May I assist you?"

"Agent Lowery can you or can you not obey a direct order?"

"Sir, Kurt and Parker pose no threat to anyone."

"I ask for more agents and they send me a left wing psychologist. What have you accomplished with these underage resisters?"

"I'm against the death penalty for children. It's not a deterrent."

"And how did you come to this brilliant conclusion?"

"The killing of underage resisters is cruel and unusual punishment."

"I have no time for such psychobabble. We don't make the rules. When you signed on did you swear to uphold the laws of the NWC?"

"Yes sir."

"We have a polluted water supply, a shortage of food and gasoline, looting in our cities and you're crying over these two punks?"

"Sir, I will have to report you if you exert any undue influence..."

"You're fired! Turn in your badge and gun. By the time I'm through with these kids you better be gone."

The overhead light was making him sweat. On the wall was a picture of an execution of a sixteen year old girl. He was at a loss on how to pray. The boy never saw the agent enter the room.

"Hello, Parker, I'm Doyle Mercer. You have been read your rights under the NWC. So tell me, what's your story?"

"My parents told me never to register."

"You're breaking the law, son. You know the consequences."

The lying spirit speaking through this agent knew what to say.

"If you register some of your friends are here to take you home."

It had been two days since his last drink of water. The wobbly redhead couldn't remember feeling so restless; so disoriented. His dizziness from dehydration was common place.

"How ya doing, Kurt?" greeted the tall agent.

"Do I know you?"

"Name's Abernathy, your friend Reenie Tucker knows me. I knew her father and brother. Did you ever meet Travis?"

"I know him."

"Did you meet him before or after he killed a Special Forces agent?"

"Cassandra was the killer."

"So Travis did your dirty work and your hands are clean? What a surprise; another loving Christian justifying murder. It doesn't much matter since Travis was executed, now does it?"

"Why are you telling me this?"

"Such a shame, it all could have been avoided. Travis just refused to cooperate with us."

"Do you want to know where Greg and Reenie are hiding?"

"That would be your best move."

"I have no idea."

"What about the location of the Vineyard camp?"

"Never been there."

"You know who's in the next room? Your buddy Parker is crying like a baby. Chief Mercer is breaking him down. You remember Doyle? He was the agent you stuffed inside the trunk of a squad car. You must have thought it was pretty funny at the time."

"It will be a massacre when the Word of God appears."

"Mighty big talk for a traitor, tell me, why did you desert your sister the night you were arrested?"

"Can't remember."

"Doyle is jotting down Parker's confession right now. It was much more than we ever expected."

"Nothing you say means anything to me."

His assistant arrived as Doyle stepped out into the hall.

"Chief, I don't understand? I thought Agent Lowry was supposed to oversee the interrogation of all underage resisters?"

"This kid is a goldmine. Parker has friends at the Vineyard. I'd give anything to capture the resister camp Greg Hudson created."

"Excuse me, Chief; doesn't the nationwide rationing of water make the arrest of resisters a mute issue? What if you do bust this camp; what would we do with so many children?"

"Are there any SWAT teams available?"

"They're all working in Birmingham, Montgomery or Mobile."

"Okay, Abernathy and I need a couple days."

"Chief, we are barely maintaining..."

"You're in charge until we get back. My objective is to expose one of the largest resister camps in America."

"How can this help us?"

"This could break the back of the Christian underground!"

"What about these boys?"

"They're coming with us. Parker knows the way to the Vineyard."

"Then why take Abbott?"

"He's our insurance policy. The first time Parker lies to us; I'll waste his punk friend."

---

Everything the two beasts had meticulously built was unraveling. Sitting in his dimly lit office, his oozing sore was turning a deep purple. The false prophet knew the voice over his intercom. This paid activist was as callous as they come. Like so many others who failed, he still believed for a better future.

"That's right, his vision hasn't changed. Trust me; after this invasion Israel will be eliminated...Just tell them Kayin has already picked the time...You heard me...Engagement must begin by..."

---

The sheer joy from their tears was reward enough. An exhausted Rafa took Johanna's hand.

"C'mon, I know of a room where we can rest."

"How can we stop now?"

"Your new nickname is relentless," laughed Rafa. "My people will continue asking questions until you say no. Besides, being an interpreter is ten times harder than sharing. Honestly, Jo, I'm losing my voice. I just need a five minute break."

Sporting grateful smiles they scurried up the narrow steps. Stretching out on a dirty sofa Johanna lifted her hands and praised the Lord for saving souls. Her new friend sat in the corner of the room silently reading her Bible.

"Rafa, what does your name mean in Arabic?"

Looking up, she sheepishly replied, "It means mercy."

"God is so merciful! The Father is drawing your people to His Son. There must be two hundred converts downstairs. It's happening just like in my vision. Gentiles are getting saved and are running with Jesus. They can sense our love for them. Our prayers are being answered supernaturally."

In a perplexed tone, she confessed, "Jo, the Holy Spirit just gave me another scripture."

"Praise the Lord. Let's hear it."

"'How beautiful upon the mountains are the feet of him who brings good news, Who proclaims peace, Who brings glad tidings of good things, Who proclaims salvation, Who says to Zion, "Your God reigns." Your Watchmen shall lift up their voices, with their voices they shall sing together; For they shall see eye to eye when the Lord brings back Zion. Break forth into joy, sing together, You waste places of Jerusalem. For the Lord has comforted His people, He has redeemed Jerusalem. The Lord has made bare His holy arm in the eyes of all the nations; and all the ends of the earth shall see the salvation of our God.'" 6

"Wow, it's a confirmation of what just happened. As Watchmen, we are proclaiming salvation to your people. Our God reigns."

"Jo, this passage is speaking of Jerusalem being redeemed. The world will look on the salvation of those who live in Zion."

"All the nations shall see the salvation of our Lord. Jew or Gentile, it doesn't matter, the body of Christ is one. We are simply called to be obedient. He will take care of the rest."

"Are we being obedient?"

"Look at the fruit. Your people are trusting in the Son of the Living God. What's gotten into you?"

"Tell me about Watchmen witnessing in Israel? Wasn't it hard for you and your father to come to Jordan?"

"God made a way."

"Yet Aaron wants to share with people who despise Jews?"

"My daddy is a walking miracle. He's probably trying to find us."
"Maybe the Lord led him back to Jerusalem?"
"It's possible."
"Isn't he a Watchman for those in Zion?"
"What's bothering you, Rafa?"
"When we first arrived here I saw the change for the first time."
"Saw what?"
"All of a sudden thousands are desperately trying to cross over into Israel. Jo, they're searching for the Messiah. Isaiah wrote, 'Who has believed our report? And to whom has the arm of the Lord been revealed?'" 7

"Are you suggesting we leave your country? Why now when the need for salvation is so great. We've identified with the pain of your people. We just can't leave them."

"Have you forgotten so easily? Soon, darkness during the fifth bowl will cover the nations. Didn't you tell me to pray for understanding concerning future Bible prophecy?"

"What is the Holy Spirit saying?"

"While praying, I saw in my mind a picture of the Lord standing at the right hand of His Father. His face was bright like the sun, His hair was like snow, and His feet were like pillars of fire. He was looking toward earth."

"What was He looking at?"
"Jerusalem!"

# THE BLOOD OF THE SAINTS

"For they have shed the blood of saints and prophets, And You have
given them blood to drink. For it is their just due."
Revelation 16:6

"What's the verdict, Ben?"

"Too many eyes in Dahlonega, it's safer to hide with my people."

"So Cherokees really are living in these mountains?"

"Cody, a scout is only twenty feet away."

"Where?"

"Tee, you wouldn't believe me if I told you."

No one spoke for a while.

"Have any of your people registered?"

"Yes, those purchasing supplies."

"Have you witnessed to the ones who haven't?"

"Never had a chance, I was banished after rejecting their pagan
rituals."

"Does your tribe know where my daddy is?"

"If the Prophetic Voice has him; the Cherokees will know."

"Have your people seen their campsite?"

"You mean campsites. They have several. Our scouts don't even
know the one Eiland uses. They're heavily guarded. It won't be easy
getting in or out. Several soldiers from this cult have made threats
against our tribe. One wrong move and someone will suffer."

Reaching over Cody held her hand.

"Was there anything else, Ben?"

"I just got some bad news from a scout. There was a shootout at
Maggie's. A soldier from the Prophetic Voice and our contact are
dead."

Reenie was dreading another delay. Parked behind an abandoned fruit stand Lenard pulled the bill of his hat over his eyes and sat back in his seat. Even so, she could still sense his inner struggle.

"How long this time?" she sighed.

"Whatever it takes."

"You know I've been thinking. You seem to know a lot about the Vineyard. It's almost like you've been there."

"In a way I have. A soldier from the Prophetic Voice is already inside the camp. He sent pictures to Delford from his cell phone."

"Who is it?"

"The less you know the better."

"Why such secrecy?"

"Knowing too much could cost you your life.

"My life isn't the issue."

"Let's have it, Reenie, what exactly are you concerned about?"

"The fulfillment of my Father's will."

"So how does one find God's will?"

"The day of the Lord is almost over. The mission God has given me is to save souls for His millennial reign."

"Tell me more."

"It involves children."

"How would you know that?"

"I was hoping you'd tell me?"

"Huh?"

"Somehow you're involved. The day I accepted this assignment from the Lord I was hiding in a cave with the Q Squad. Later I saw your face in a vision."

"Most Christians I know don't believe in visions from God."

"It's their loss. The Holy Spirit showed me your face. He led me to these mountains to find you. You're the stranger in my vision."

"So has God showed you what we're supposed to do?"

"Not yet."

"Now isn't this sweet," he snickered. "I'm trying to avert a full fledge race war and I get stuck with a Christian girl scout on a secret mission from God."

"The Holy Spirit will show you, Lenard, if you let Him."

"What makes you so sure?"

"Satan's attacks are real. Somehow the devil has crippled you from hearing from the Lord. He is a liar; the father of lies."

"So you think I'm a threat to Satan's kingdom?"

"You once were. Why was the NWC after you?

"Don't you understand; I want nothing to do with this!"

"Did you know Kayin before he became President?"

Somehow this innocent teenager had touched the nerve the Holy Spirit was convicting. This was one confession he never talked about.

"Joshua was always the life of the party. After college, he didn't know what he wanted to do. He decided on politics. His rise to the Presidency shocked everyone."

"It must have been tough for you to see him change?"

"His agenda to bring democracy to Muslim nations was a smokescreen. Telling this to my friends at the White House didn't win me any favors. When I tried to convince them the President was the Antichrist no one would listen."

"So this is why you're hiding in these mountains. You somehow knew Satan convinced Kayin to turn against Israel."

"Literal Bible prophecy for all to see."

"Why haven't you received any sores from the first bowl?"

"Delford despises the NWC. None of his soldiers or their families have worshipped the Beast, his image, or taken his mark."

"You mean woman and children are part of the Prophetic Voice?"

"A couple thousand, several camps are used to avoid detection. If one is infiltrated they just move their families to another."

As they filed into the massive cave he knew their painted faces, their dress, even their posture was a sign. Sitting around a blazing fire surrounded by white rocks a wooden pipe was passed by hand. Ben was purposely skipped over. He was an uninvited guest. He was no longer part of their privileged ritual. Their Chief spoke first.

"Our Counsel is present. Running Bear, why have you come back into our lives?"

"I have come to ask for your help."

"You had no need of us when you left last year. What has changed?"

"I have come on the behalf of another family. A white militia living in these mountains, called the Prophetic Voice, has kidnapped a father and his daughter."

"Is this a Cherokee family?"

"Black-American, Pastor Evers and his daughter, Twanna, are from Charleston, South Carolina."

"We are aware of this militia. Their camps are all around us. Our scouts have seen them execute men, women and children."

The youngest member of the Council asked to speak.

"Chief Ostenaco, their soldiers are heavily armed. We'll only endanger the lives of our people if we get involved. How can the rescue of two strangers be worth that?"

Their grunts of approval around the fire were a familiar gesture to Ben. He was once a respected member of this Cherokee Council. Their disgust toward him now was obvious. The old Chief was thinking. He was formulating his reply. The Council's decision would be final. Ben knew there would be no second chance.

"Running Bear, my heart is heavy. This earth is heaving in pain. It appears there is no way to stop the hate people have for one another. This is why my focus is now the safety of our tribe. There has been too much Cherokee blood already shed in these mountains. I cannot partner in any more killing. There is nothing you can say to convince me to jeopardize the lives of my people."

Breaking protocol, Ben stood to his feet.

"Chief Ostenaco, is this not the land of our ancestors? Is the shed blood of Cherokees taken in vain? When the arm of the white man drove our people from this soil, what were the words of our Chiefs?"

"You're living in the past, Running Bear." interrupted a young Council member. "Why bring up such sorrows? How can this help our people now?"

"Lessons from the past can help us see the difference between what is right and wrong."

"Isn't it true your friends are not from here?"

"Council, please hear me out. In the 1770's, the Cherokees moved into these mountains by capturing five hundred Catawba warriors. They were sold at a slave market in Charleston. These Indians were sent to work in the Caribbean. Our Chiefs rejoiced at the removal of such a dangerous enemy. What our leaders failed to recognize was the increasing threat of the white man."

"We all understand the cost of such a mistake," added another.

"What about the Prophetic Voice? Every Council member has personally witnessed the hate fueling this cult."

"Their leader is called Delford Eiland. His dream is a totally white America. He believes his people are descendants from the lost ten tribes of Israel. Do you believe this Running Bear?"

"No, Chief Ostenaco, this is not the truth."

"Are your friends Christians like you?"

The old man simply nodded.

"Is this all you have to say?"

"What good is our legacy if we allow the white man to attack the helpless on the very land our ancestors shed their blood? Isn't their blood crying out to us? Or shall we again close our eyes to the truth?"

"You believe Jesus Christ is the only truth!" rebuked an angry head scout. "It is Running Bear who has rejected his people. Tell the Council; are your friends connected with the deaths at Maggie's? The soldier underestimated his rival."

"This is just the beginning," groaned Ben.

"Running Bear, what is your God telling you to do?"

"My calling involves the rescue of unregistered children. I'm a Watchman for the Lord."

"It seems we are also involved in rescue," Chief Ostenaco cautiously replied. "Our young people found him unconscious in Maggie's kitchen. He too calls himself a Watchman."

"What is his name?"

"We don't know," mumbled the weary Chief. "He's been in and out of consciousness."

Sitting back down, a puzzled Ben made one last plea.

"The soldiers from the Prophetic Voice are being brainwashed by deceiving spirits. They will kill anyone not white. I'm asking for you to help me find Twanna and her father. This young lady helped construct the escape tunnels inside the Vineyard camp. This is why the leader of this cult wants her. His army is planning an attack on the Vineyard."

"Don't these soldiers also believe in Jesus Christ?"

"It's not what it appears. They worship a different Jesus."

"Why is your God so angry?"

"The wrath we're experiencing is the result of sinful man rejecting the love of a Holy God. The Christian in the diner was simply defending himself against the kingdom of darkness." 1

"What is the next judgment?"

"Within days heat from the sun will scorch mankind."

"How can the rescue of this girl prevent this militia from attacking your Christian camp?"

"I don't know if it will," Ben bravely replied. "But what is preventing us from at least trying?"

---

The Winnebago left deep tracks in the steep hill connected to Maggie's parking lot. All eyes were on the front porch.

"Anyone see anything?" whispered Jon.

"Just smoke," coughed Emma. "The people camping out in these woods are multiplying like rabbits."

"They can run but they can't hide," reflected Donnell. "For centuries the harlot shed the blood of saints and prophets. Now 'the One who is, who was, and who is to be', has sent His wrath." 2

"Soon," added a solemn Jake, "the Lord will scorch the followers of the Beast. Must be some great places to hide around here, huh?"

"Trust me, our contact knows these mountains. This is why he volunteered for this area. It's time, Jon."

"Okay, Donnie. Jake, you're the driver. Emma you're on point. Once we enter the diner if we don't signal back in one minute, you take a ride down the hill, a quarter of a mile. You wait on the Holy Spirit. If you are to leave us; He will give you the release."

"Are you sure about this?" asked an anxious Emma.

"If we do split up go east five miles. Get off the road and hide the RV. We will meet you there in two hours. Didn't you say Greg gave Reenie some sort of a warning signal?"

"Yeah, the whole Q Squad knows it."

"Alright, let's do this for the glory of God."

Slowly making their way up the porch steps, Donnell whispered, "Not the shotgun again?"

"You're first. And remember; my peashooter is right behind you."

"That's what I was afraid of," he kidded back.

The creaking front door brought no response. Donnell quickly slid behind the main counter while Jon crouched behind a table lying on its side. Signaling for a diversion with his eyes his partner nodded. Grabbing an empty flower vase Donnell heaved it across the room. As it shattered, Jon broke for the kitchen.

"You hear that, Jake?"

"Just keep praying, Em, they can handle this."

Coasting down the road Jake veered between two large pine trees.

"Jon!"

"C'mon, it's clear."

Reaching the kitchen, he cringed.

"What's with all this blood?"

"There's another blotch in the dining room."

Stepping out on the back porch they both bent down.

"Donnie, why is this blood so smeared on these steps?"

"Talk to me."

"The struggle must have started in the kitchen. The one who was bleeding was dragged down these steps."

"Look at the backyard! There are no footprints or blood."

"Whoever removed the body didn't want to leave a trail."

"What now?"

"I pray Greg and Reenie got away. We now know whoever is tracking them won't hesitate to take a life."

Something caught Jake's attention as he stepped out of the RV.

Walking down the hill they both liked what they saw.

"Praise God, Donnie, they obeyed our orders. I'd say they are Watchmen, wouldn't you?"

Reaching their Winnebago, Donnell gave Emma a fist pump before offering to drive.

"Any sign of our contact?"

"Not anymore, Emma," Jon sadly replied.

"Hey, Jake, you find something?"

"Donnie, I just found Reenie's leather belt on the side of the road. She must've thrown it out while driving by. It's her signal for us to follow."

# FOURTH BOWL: SCORCHED WITH FIRE

*"Then the fourth angel poured out his bowl on the sun and power was given to him to scorch men with fire."*
*Revelation 16:8*

With all eyes upon the Father and His Son, an angel bowed before pouring out the fourth bowl upon the sun. With the fury of an angry God this angel shot forth massive rays of heat.

Another flying overhead issued the horrific decree.

"'And men were scorched with great heat, and they blasphemed the name of God who has power over these plagues; and they did not repent and give Him glory.'" 1

---

Cody Parrish was praying while Ben met with the Cherokee Council. Then it happened. Threats from the enemy followed. The former football star had never been so scared.

"Lord, how could they kidnap Tee without a sound? I was gone for less than a minute. Ben wanted me to stay with her but I wouldn't listen, and for what? We didn't even make it to Maggie's. Lord, I was sent to find and protect Tee and I wind up practically handing her over. I ask for Your forgiveness. Can You help us rescue her and her daddy?"

The little boy couldn't resist. Poking his head inside the mouth of the cave he waved.

"Hi, I'm Little Turkey."

"Nice to meet you, I'm Cody."

"Are you a Watchman? I know a Watchman. He is really brave."

"Yes, Running Bear is a warrior for the Lord."

"Shining Path is much younger than Ben. He's going to fly a kite with me when he gets better."

"Little Turkey, is Shining Path a Cherokee?"

"No, he's a stranger to our tribe. I gave him his name. I know one day he will leave us."

"Do you know his real name, Little Turkey?"

"My mother cleaned his wound. He doesn't remember what happened. Sometimes his words made no sense."

"Did he say he was a Watchman?"

"Just like you and Ben. He rescues kids. He believes God sits on a throne in heaven. Shining Path says Jesus sits next to Him. Ain't that something?"

"Can you take me to see him?"

Grabbing his hand he pulled Cody to his feet. The small cave was separated from the others. No one was around when they arrived.

"Look at the sun!" screamed the boy, "Can't you feel the heat?"

"Little Turkey, go and tell your people to hide in the caves. Hurry, everyone must stay in the caves until the sun goes down."

As the young Cherokee ran down the hill, Cody entered the cave. The wounded Watchman was asleep under two blankets.

Bending down the young man softly whispered, "You're safe, Greg. I'm going to take care of you. Just hold on."

---

"C'mon, Wes!" shouted the cameraman, "I've got a great shot."

"We don't go on the air until I give the signal."

"But the sun is almost gone."

"Not until the suffering stops."

"What do we tell our viewers? What happens if it gets worse tomorrow morning?"

"We'll know once the sun rises in New Zealand. Is Natalie ready?"

"Sorry, Wes, she's a no show. Dawn is in the saddle."

"Everyone ready...5...4...3...2...1..."

"This is Special Report. I'm Dawn Mitchell filling in for Natalie Roberts. Earlier this afternoon a catastrophic eruption from the sun punctured our earth's ozone layer. Millions have sustained burns as the heat index continues to rise. A National Emergency Alert has been issued. Under no circumstances should anyone expose themselves to the sun while we are under this emergency alert. I repeat; exposure from the sun is scorching people from every nation!"

"How are they taking it?"

Fighting back his tears, Ben moaned, "You mean the children who were burned?"

Wiping his sweaty forehead, Cody mumbled back, "This is heartbreaking. What is your Chief saying?"

"He wants the Council to meet again."

"You mean you're going to get to share again?"

"Not me. They want to hear from you and Greg."

"Why us?"

"They have their reasons. Will you meet with them?"

"Sure. How is Greg?"

"Still pretty weak, you see the gash on the back of his head? Whoever hit him could care less if he lived! That's for sure."

Racing out of the cave an excited Little Turkey had good news.

"Running Bear, Shining Path is asking for you."

A curious crowd of Cherokees watched as the three Watchmen greeted each other in one big hug.

"Praise the Lord, Greg, my people rescued you."

He reached out and touched Ben's arm without speaking.

"Hi, Pastor, it's Cody Parrish from the Vineyard."

"Thanks for your help," he mumbled back.

"Should we come back later when you're feeling better?"

"Ben, a girl named Reenie Tucker is on her way to the Vineyard. She must be found."

"Is the Prophetic Voice after her too? They kidnapped Twanna Evers and her daddy."

He tried but his words just wouldn't come.

"Can you help us?" begged Cody. "The Prophetic Voice is planning an attack on the Vineyard. Ruben had to call a Red Fox. The two tunnels are almost ready to use."

"Evacuate the camp?" gasped Greg.

"What other choice do they have?"

"Do you remember the members of the Q Squad?"

"Yes, were you able to find them?"

"The Lord has called them to protect Reenie."

"From who?"

"God has called Reenie. She is to..."

"Excuse us, Greg, we'll be right back."

Exiting the cave the young man took a deep breath of cold air before sharing.

"Ben, I know this sounds harsh but Ruben gave me strict orders."

"Circumstances have changed. Our chances of rescuing Twanna are slim. The Council believes Greg's recovery is a miracle. No one gave him any chance of living."

"What are you saying?"

"I'm effective on rescues where the believers are waiting on me. I'm too old for pursuit. Will you go after Reenie?"

"Greg's description of her is interesting. Do you think she could be the girl in my dream?"

"You mean the deliverer from the white tornado?"

"I guess it's possible. What's your plan?"

"You find Reenie; I'll take care of Greg. My people have agreed to rescue Twanna and her father. I was the one who took her away from the camp; I'll be the one to protect her."

# I SAY TO YOU ARISE

"'But that you may know that the Son of Man has power on earth to forgive sins'--He said to the paralytic, 'I say to you, arise, take up your bed, and go to your house.'"
Mark 2:10-11

In the early morning darkness, huddled in a huge crowd near the border, the two girls were fervently praying. After hearing the broadcast the long lines scattered. Families with children rushed for cover.

"You hear, Jo?" shouted Rafa over the panic. "Americans are being scorched with fire. We must find a safe hiding place!"

As the sun rose over the Middle East the vast majority held their breath. For now, the extreme heat was gone.

---

"Sir, Eli is on the line, he wants out."

"He wants what? Give me the phone!"

The overnight hysteria of billions being burned changed everything. Eiland's future utopia of a white nation was fading. His promise of protection was sounding hallow. The exodus was growing. The racist leader was searching for an angle; something to use to maintain control over his soldiers and their families.

"Eli, this is Delford. What's happening?"

"Ruben is preparing the campers for an all-out evacuation. You should make your move on the Vineyard soon."

"Where are the exits to their tunnels?"

"Hasn't Evers told you yet?"

"Not yet."

"I've given you what you want. My job is over. I'm outta here."

"We need you inside the camp when we attack."

"How much longer?"

"I'm moving up the date."

"We can only go outside at night. During the day we're jammed in these caves. These kids are crazy. I'm getting claustrophobic."

"What do you want me to do; hold your hand?"

"Ruben has sent an ex-jock named Cody Parish to find Twanna Evers. He could be trouble."

"Fat chance, I've got her locked up in Zion."

"Lenard, look at these people. There are campsites everywhere."

"They're searching for fresh water."

"Have they all registered?"

"You'd be surprised at how many refused. It's a miracle so many are still alive. Reenie, do you really think God gives visions?"

"He does to me."

"What if I told you I saw pictures as a young boy?"

"Depends on what kind of pictures?"

"My first vision was of children. They were crying out for help. It was like they were trapped in dark tunnels. No one was listening."

"Anything else?"

"You won't believe me."

"Why not?"

"My family and friends didn't. My pastor thought it was a joke."

Her lapse in concentration was annoying.

"Hey, let's stop and witness, how about it?"

"It's too dangerous. We should keep moving. We can't afford to lose our transportation."

"Look at all these families. Don't you even care?"

"You don't think I care? Have you any idea the consequences for disobeying Eiland?"

"Is this the guy who wants me dead?"

"By now he wants us both dead. You've got to learn to pick your fights, Reenie."

"I'm tired of fighting. I simply want to lead someone out of darkness and into salvation in Jesus. Driving by and just praying isn't doing much for me right now."

Jerking right, his black SUV coasted to a stop between two campfires.

His glassy stare seemed phony to her.

"What are you waiting for?"

"You mean here?"

"These families look just as lost as the others. You have an hour."

---

"They're waiting to hear. The scorching heat has them searching for the truth."

"How many are unregistered?"

"Most of them."

A prayed up Aaron Glazer walked into the jammed gymnasium. It was a mixed crowd; mostly teenagers. Some had come to hear the truth about God, others only to disrupt.

A nervous Fadi translated as Aaron explained the death, burial, and resurrection. At first you could hear a pin drop. But as the conviction grew so did the uneasiness of those having the number of the Beast. The battle between light and darkness could erupt at any moment. His gospel presentation took less than ten minutes.

"That's all I have to say. Are there any questions about Jesus?"

A curious teenager raised his hand to speak.

"So after we die, what does Jesus promise us?"

"'For God so loved the world that He gave His only begotten Son, that whoever believes in Him should not perish but have everlasting life.'" 1

"What does 'only begotten' mean?"

"The Word was with the Father before creation. He took the form of a baby when the Holy Spirit overshadowed Mary. Immanuel, means God with us."

"Who is this Immanuel?"

"Jesus willingly gave His life on the cross as a holy sacrifice for your sins and mine. This is why He is also called the Lamb of God."

"So every sin I've committed will be forgiven?"

"Like it never happened, let's remember; only the Son has the power to forgive you of your sins."

"Only God can forgive sin!" insisted an irate old man.

"Amen! Jesus told the paralytic your sins are forgiven." 2

"Blasphemy!" he shouted back.

"The scribes said the same when Jesus forgave the paralytic." 3

"Sins are forgiven by the intercession of Muhammad in the hereafter," challenged a cleric. "Only Al-Ghaffar accepts repentance."

"Where did this paralytic find such faith?" asked a young girl.

Aaron answered, "'For by grace you have been saved through faith, and that not of yourselves; it is the gift of God.'" 4

"No one has the free will to accept or reject salvation!" yelled the incensed teacher. "You're speaking against the Qur'an."

Raising his hand, Fadi respectfully requested their attention.

"I have always believed Allah predetermines everything. My good works must outweigh my bad ones. But after spending time with Aaron, I now see naja (salvation) as a relationship! It's different than earning merits. For my sister, Jesus is the bridge to eternal life. Anyone can cross over; it's the will of God none should perish."

Taking a step back the shocked young man had to catch his breath. The raised hands covered most of the gym. Aaron wasted little time as he led Jordanian men, women, and children, who hadn't worshipped the Beast or taken his mark in a salvation prayer. His elated interpreter never missed a word.

## THE SECOND DEATH

"But the cowardly, unbelieving, abominable, murderers, sexually
immoral, sorcerers, idolaters, and all liars shall have their part in the lake
which burns with fire and brimstone, which is the second death."
Revelation 21:8

"Donnell, if your RV was yellow I'd nickname her the banana slug.

"Jake, you best not forget her soft beds and great shower. That is
when we have water."

"Jon, look at all these lost people! Most can't last much longer."

"Emma, all seven bowls will be poured out in just twenty-five
days. You gotta admit Zephaniah's description is super terrifying.
'Therefore wait for Me,' says the Lord, 'Until the day I rise up for
plunder; My determination is to gather the nations. To My assembly of
kingdoms, To pour on them My indignation, All My fierce anger; All
the earth shall be devoured with the fire of My jealousy.'" 1

Their silence was obvious. How could anyone comprehend such
fury from a Holy God? Slowing down behind a bottleneck of cars, Jon
released the safety to his shotgun.

"What's our play, Jon?"

"Jake, it could be an accident. Or some may be stopping to
barter. A lot of people are out of gas."

"What about agents?

"Doubt they're scanning up here. To be safe let's pull off and
wait."

"Look," pointed Donnell, "there is a parking space between the
red truck and that black SUV."

Watching ex-Muslims praising the Lord was such a joy to the former Israeli freedom fighter. To experience such jubilant celebrations of salvation was well worth the sacrifice.

"Isn't this awesome, Fadi?"

"I'm worried Aaron. You know we're being watched."

"By who?"

"By Muslim clerics, converting Muslims to Christianity is still against the law. As soon as they raised their hands to receive Jesus we were reported to the authorities."

"Then why are we still here?"

"The clerics have requested a private meeting. They are supposedly guaranteeing our safety. I don't trust them."

"Why not?"

The young Jordanian was struggling. It was like hurdles were deliberately being set in front of him. Each hurdle represented something he had always believed in.

"In my life, I've only seen a handful of Muslims convert to Christianity. To watch hundreds weeping with joy for Jesus is such a miracle. When they responded to the gospel, the clerics went crazy. They could barely control themselves. This has to be the devil."

"Fadi, legalism is no match for a relationship with a loving God."

"What can you say to these clerics? They aren't after the truth. They don't care about my people. They only love their religious rules."

Aaron felt his bewilderment. To believe in something for many years only to find out it was a counterfeit was not easy to overcome.

"My brother, it's worth it if only one gets saved. This heat is like the parting of the Red Sea. We can see the ones who still can be saved."

Entering the secret entrance to the mosque, they could hear the screams of those burned by the sun. The dark winding passage led to a room lined with horrified Muslims. All eyes were upon the reviled Matthias. He knew the young teenager was being stretched. Grasping Fadi's right shoulder, his gentle squeeze was a sign of encouragement. Both understood the penalty for openly sharing the gospel is death.

The head cleric spoke first.

"We have observed your emotional proselytizing. Isn't it strange a Jew should attempt to convert a Muslim to Christianity?"

"God is no respecter of persons," Aaron calmly replied.

"You're taking advantage of our people because of their pain. Jesus is just one of many prophets. No prophet is greater than Muhammad. The emotions produced by your tricks will quickly pass."

"Then why have you invited us here today?" challenged Fadi.

"You speak only when addressed. Somehow the legendary Matthias has deceived the son of one of our greatest soldiers."

"Fadi is my interpreter. He can leave any time he wants."

"Your declaration of salvation in Jesus means nothing."

"The Word not only created this world but is the giver of eternal salvation. The incarnation was a labor of love to mankind."

"Such lies!" shouted another.

"The joy of those receiving the Spirit of Christ speaks otherwise. I've not come here today to debate with you the divinity of Jesus. The wrath of God is being poured out as we speak. The next bowl will bring darkness to those living under the authority of the Beast. There is still hope for those who haven't taken Kayin's mark or worshiped him. Salvation is in no other name but Jesus." [2]

"We believe in Jesus, the son of Mary."

"Do you believe He died on a cross for the sins of mankind?"

"No, He was taken alive to heaven by Allah."

"Then why did Jesus say, '...Destroy this temple, and in three days I will raise it up.'" [3]

"You promised our people eternal life. The Qur'an teaches both hell and paradise will pass away. Everlasting life is a myth."

"Then why did Jesus say, '"And as Moses lifted up the serpent in the wilderness, even so must the Son of Man be lifted up, that whoever believes in Him should not perish but have eternal life.'" [4]

"Where did Jesus ever claim to be God?"

"Jesus said, '"For where two or three are gathered together in My name, I am there in the midst of them." [5]

A head cleric shouted back, 'Hear, O Israel: The Lord our God, the Lord is one.'" [6]

"My friends, the Hebrew word for 'one' in this passage is achid. Achid means united one. The Godhead consists of the Father, His Son, and the Holy Spirit. [7] Another Hebrew word, yachid, means only one. It is God himself who declares that He is achid (united one)!" [8]

The agent supervising the children's cell block was punching out.

"You forget something, Sophie?"

"I need to say goodbye to my boys."

"No can do, Lowry."

"You owe me, bro."

"Not enough to break the rules."

"Just five minutes."

His glance over his shoulder lasted several seconds.

"My keys better be in my desk drawer when I get back."

The tall blonde had been down this corridor many times.

"What's doing, Sophie?"

"I'm getting you and Parker out of here."

"No way, if Mercer catches us we'll be executed."

"Kurt, remember the first time we met. At first, you had nothing to say because I had the mark. Later you talked about your sister Emma and your calling to be Watchman."

"My sister has a greater mission than finding me."

"Why didn't she try and rescue you?"

"God knows."

"So why help us?" whispered a puzzled Parker.

"You boys are a real inspiration to me. Your inner strength to live out your convictions is a valuable asset nowadays."

"Our faith is not for sale."

"Everything else is, Kurt. Both my husbands gave their lives trying to make this world a better place."

"When was that?"

"My first husband was killed five years ago in a ground war offensive. My second died fighting fires a year later. "

"We're so sorry, Sophie."

"As these plagues spread, the oppressive agenda of the NWC only grew worse. Your testimonies taught me the truth."

An impatient Parker gasped, "What truth?"

"God is judging the wickedness of mankind."

Kurt motioned to his friend to just listen.

"The execution of Christians has nothing to do with maintaining security. It's more about hate and ignorance. The contempt for Christians throughout the world started at the top. Joshua Kayin's psychological profile explains a lot. He definitely hates Jews and Christians. So much so he even tried to become a divine oracle over Judaism and Christianity. After losing my second husband, I knew then Kayin's roadmap to peace was a lie. It began when our rights as citizens were taken away."

"Didn't the President promise to protect us?"

"Parker, the laws he pushed through Congress wasn't about stopping terrorism. The implementation of worldwide registration wasn't either. Kayin's goal all along was to eradicate Christians!"

After a quick glance down the corridor, Kurt could sense something wasn't right.

"Sophie, what's really going down?"

"Doyle and agent Abernathy want to bust the Vineyard."

"Every camper will die if they do."

"But we're so close!" winced a frightened Parker.

"Mercer is an out of control killer. Someone has to stop him from reaching the Vineyard. Couldn't this be part of the mission God gave you, Kurt? If it is, I want to help."

"Does your car have a full tank of gas?"

"Yes, plus four more gallons in my trunk."

"Ok, our first stop is a town in the mountains north of Atlanta."

Their walk down the corridor fetched a few cat calls. Once outside she locked the backdoor and threw the key away. Racing through the pitch black parking lot they safely reached her car.

"No way!" gasped Parker. "Someone slashed your tires."

From behind her car the glare from his flashlight was blinding.

"Planning a little trip, Sophie?"

"Just let us go, Doyle."

"I really want to know your smoking gun in this charade?"

"I was going to ask you the same question."

"Abe, lock the boys in my car."

"You're losing it, Doyle."

"Your days of interfering are over. Turn around and put your hands behind your back."

After handcuffing her wrists he opened the trunk door of her car and shoved her inside. She could hear his footsteps as he walked away.

---

Up ahead, about twenty meters from the parked Winnebago, was a crowd huddled around a roaring fire.

"How strange," wondered Jon, "Why are so many out in this cold air? They must be searching for hiding places before the sunrises."

"Anyone up for some witnessing?" posed an excited Jake. "This could be a divine appointment."

"My man, if you find anyone unregistered, witness to them in private. We can't lose our focus on what God has called us to."

"I understand, Jon, how about it, Emma?"

"I'm still praying for Kurt."

"Well, I ain't going alone. What do you say, Donnell?"

"I love fishing for the Lord. You never know what you're going to catch. Let's go."

The crowd around the fire was three deep. The stranger near the back was just about to lose his cool. Donnell couldn't resist asking.

"What's happening?"

"Just someone yakking about Jesus, she's predicting He's coming back soon. Hey, sweetie, tell us something we haven't heard."

"Are you a real resister?" mocked a teenager.

"I'm a Christian who loves Jesus."

"Me too," declared a deceived mother having the mark. "After the nations invade Israel Jesus will return at Armageddon."

"So you must think America is Babylon?" challenged a trucker.

"Why would a loving God allow such suffering?"

"No one knows when Jesus is coming back?"

Their questions just kept coming.

"She's taking a beating, Jake. You wanna help her?"

After seeing her green eyes he praised the Lord.

"Donnell, weren't you with Bret Santino when he was shot?"

"Yes, right beside him."

"Did you ever see Reenie Tucker?"

"No, never got the chance."

"Now you have. She's the one sitting between the two truckers."

Both Watchmen quickly scanned the campsite for any agents.

"Excuse me, little lady; if you're such a wonderful Christian shouldn't you know more about the Bible than us?"

"Well, uh, there are lots of things I don't understand."

"How come, honey?" taunted the drunken trucker. "Doesn't God reveal to you the future?"

"Jesus is coming back on a white horse."

"Earlier you said it was Satan riding a white horse during the first seal. Is Jesus coming back on the same horse?"

"Well, I guess..."

"You guess?" he hooted. "Isn't it a bit late to be guessing about the end of the world?"

It seemed like a dream when she spotted him.

"Jake, is it really you?"

"It's me in the flesh, Miracle Girl! How're ya doing?"

"She's doing a bang up job if you ask me," hollered the other drunk. "We aren't done with her yet so just butt out."

"You are now."

The shocked crowd stepped away as the two truckers faced the young Watchmen. One laughed as the other casually removed a long knife from his jacket.

Slurring his words he cursed, "So, hot shot, you a resister too?"

"We don't want any trouble. My friend and we need to be going."

"You ain't going anywhere."

As the trucker extended his knife Jake stepped in front of Reenie.

"Now listen real good, punk. We all wanna see you and your little girlfriend deny Jesus. Now get on your knees..."

From behind the trees a voice shouted out "Hold up!"

"You best not be talking to me!" threatened the trucker.

Stepping out into the light of the fire, Jon raised his shotgun.

"Your fun is over. Nobody move or the one with the knife gets the first barrel."

Donnell honked the horn after backing the RV up to the campsite. Jake and Reenie took off running.

"Is there anyone here who hasn't registered?"

The only response was the crackling fire.

Reenie could hardly wait until Jon returned.

"Guys, I found the stranger in my vision."

"Where is he?"

"He's here, Emma, waiting for me in his black SUV."

"Sorry, Reenie, he drove away a few minutes ago."

"No way!" she sobbed. "Why would Lenard leave me now?"

# THE LAMB'S BOOK OF LIFE

"But there shall by no means enter it anything that defiles, or causes
an abomination or a lie, but only those who are written in the Lamb's
Book of Life."
Revelation 21:27

The sadness of those huddled around scattered campfires was heartbreaking. Turning off the road he parked underneath some sixty foot birch trees. Rays from the moon were shining through the limbs. His thoughts racing; he methodically loaded and reloaded his revolver.

"Lord, why did I run away? It was like a compulsion controlling me. The fact is I really want to do Your will."

In his mind he heard, "Are you sure?"

He wasn't listening. Hurts from his past were having their way. Rambling on about his childhood he had a long list of grievances. The most painful memory was an exhortation from his father.

"Lenard, you're a member of the White House Staff. If you continue in this madness you'll lose everything you've achieved."

"Dad, last week Joshua visited Egypt, Libya, and Ethiopia. 1 This week he is dialoging with several more Muslim nations."

"Isn't it wonderful? Becoming a friend with Muslim leaders is a brilliant plan. He's really the only world leader willing to defeat terrorism through world peace."

"Kayin is gathering his ten horns (nations). Once Satan grants him authority he will invade an unsuspecting Jerusalem with armies from these horns and seize control of all nations. 2 Someone must expose his evil agenda!"

"You're out of your mind! Does this have anything to do with the vision you had as a child? If it does, I want no part of it. Just leave your mother and me out of it."

Lenard saw the pictures Eli sent through his cell phone; their inquisitive eyes, their anxious smiles, children seeking after the Lamb of God. He too wanted to be part of a new earth and a new heaven where peace rules and Satan is banished. 3

"Yes, Lord, I know," he thoughtfully replied. "'But there shall by no means enter it anything that defiles, or causes an abomination or a lie, but only those who are written in the Lamb's Book of Life.'" 4

Lenard Mayer received his first vision from God when he was a young boy. It was his father's stern rebuff that helped him bury it deep within his soul. Even so, the frightened children, the teenage girl, the city of many colors, the vision never left, it didn't matter how many times it resurfaced in his mind. At this moment, the calling placed upon his life by God was still up for grabs. His only response was to disappear. He thought if he could just hide maybe it would all go away.

The False Prophet could hear the Beast ranting in his office. He had no idea how many had been burned. News agencies were graphically reporting the indescribable panic. The attacks were random; the sun would erupt at any moment.

"Yes, Lord Kayin, you called for me?"

The sun was out of sight ending another day of horror. His touch of a button drew back the drapes from his picturesque window. He loved watching the lights of the ancient city resting on seven hills.

"Michael, you have the pulse of most religious leaders. What are they saying about these plagues?"

"Their reactions are as wide as they are varied."

"Who would inflict such sores on the faces of children? Why infect the water supply of six billion people? Is God purposely burning all who have shown alliance to my vision? Isn't this what everyone is asking? If I really had the power of God backing me why haven't I stopped these plagues?"

"Yes, from the euphoria of the Witnesses' funeral to the utter despair we are seeing now has been devastating."

"How are people coping?"

"Most are blaspheming. I just received a report of a rally of four hundred thousand raising their burned arms before cursing God."

"Do you know what time it is?"

"His wrath from the fifth bowl is near. 5 This is why leaders from the Middle East Federation have come. They're waiting on you."

"What should I tell them? Everything we hold dear will soon be shrouded in darkness."

"Most still believe in your vision."

"It's our only hope. Israel has always been the apple of God's eye. When the armies of the nations destroy the Jews, then and only then will God cease these cursed plaques!"

---

Those severely burned could barely walk. The crying of children never ceased. The despair of those believing in Islam was growing. Pulling her shawl beneath her eyes couldn't disguise her tears.

"Jo, I never thought I'd see the day when my people would openly curse Muhammad. They feel so deceived."

"It will only get worse. Can you make some more inquires? Maybe your father has some connections here?"

After a reassuring hug, Rafa disappeared into a group of Palestinian soldiers patrolling the streets. Moments later she hastily returned.

"Jo, we must cross over now. My father is offering a reward for you and your father. I was afraid this would happen. This must be why the Holy Spirit is prompting us to return to Jerusalem."

"Glory to God, my daddy got away."

A determined Rafa took Johanna's hand as they headed toward the Palestinian/Israeli border. Inwardly she was praising the Lord for Aaron's escape. At the same time she was dreading the possibility of never seeing her father again.

---

"Delford, our Dahlonega sentry was the first to spot her....She is interviewing families camping out...He has her in his sights right now...She's alone...Yes, we'll bring her in."

All one could see from the air were the tops of trees. A high voltage wire encircled the disguised camp. Armed guards paced the perimeter. Hiking up a hill beneath Zion he was surrounded by his entourage. Delford Eiland was making an unscheduled visit.

"Sir, she is blindfolded. She has no idea where she is."

Entering her dark cell was a rush for the frustrated leader. Apprehending her was never part of his plan. He knew it was only a matter of time before her snooping around would bring unwanted attention. Reluctantly he was forced to bring her inside his world.

"So you just couldn't stay away?" taunted Delford.

Sitting with her back against the cold wall she didn't reply.

"Tell me, Natalie, what didn't you understand about our first visit? How odd, you always made yourself out to be such a savior of causes and now you can't even help yourself."

"Where am I?"

"Zion is my headquarters. You were trespassing. No one knows where you are. Which means no one is coming for you."

"You promised me another interview."

"Now why would I do that? Your Special Report spread enough lies. Truthfully, you wouldn't have come back unless there was something in it for you. I'm at a loss what it could be."

"Tell me your agenda for the white race?"

"If I do it will cost you your life!"

"Some believe Jesus will return soon. Are you and your band of cutthroats ready to meet Him?"

"I have no time for such nonsense. Before you get your final story, I want you to meet someone. Take her away. They deserve each other."

The adjoining cell smelled of fresh blood. The lonely figure sprawled in the far corner looked dazed. Her facial expression never changed as the celebrity was escorted in. The bolting of the locks against the metal door was a clear reminder of where they were.

Crouching down the reporter tried to remain calm.

"I'm Natalie Roberts. Why are you a prisoner?"

"What do you want from me?"

"I'm an investigative journalist. Eiland is planning a race war. I've come to try and..."

"For the record, Ms. Roberts, do you have any Jewish friends?"

"Does it matter?"

"Didn't you cover the massacre during Jerusalem invasion? 6 And if you rode the fence then, why are you so concerned now about a few Blacks being wasted?"

"Innocent lives are in danger is a good enough reason."

"And who's going to enforce the laws of the great United States of America? Excuse me, I mean no disrespect to the celebrated Natalie Rene Roberts. I'm sure some of your rich friends could make some calls and get us out of this hell hole."

Natalie didn't know how to break through such bitterness. In the stillness of their cell they could hear soldiers doing training exercises.

"My name is Twanna Evers. This cult kidnapped me and my father. We are from Charleston, South Carolina."

"Where is your father now?"

"Don't know. When I told them the location of the twin tunnels, they took him away."

"What tunnels?"

"There is a children's camp called the Vineyard. Two tunnels were dug out as escape exits."

"Is this a resister camp? I've never heard of a camp specially outfitted for children? Whose idea was this?"

"A preacher called Greg Hudson. Our Watchmen kept rescuing children who were hiding from the NWC. No one ever thought the camp population would reach five thousand."

"But why attack innocent children?"

"Eiland foresees an all-white America. His assault is about the rescue of white children. To him it's the separation of the wheat from the tares."

"When will they attack the Vineyard?"

"Probably when the Beast's armies invade Armageddon. Eiland sees it as one big race war against the Kenites."

"You haven't been burned. Are you a resister?"

She could only hold back her disgust for a moment.

"I'm a Christian, Natalie. Jesus is my Lord and Savior. You never should have come; you've just made things worse."

## FIFTH BOWL: THE THRONE OF THE BEAST

"Then the fifth angel poured out his bowl on the throne of the beast,
and his kingdom became full of darkness; and they gnawed their tongues
because of the pain."
Revelation 16:10

"Running Bear, I have a message for you."

What is it Little Turkey?"

"Shining Path is leaving us."

Ben rambled down the hill the best he could. He was already feeling guilty. He could see the Watchman walking out into the cold night air.

"Can I help, Greg?"

"I can make it, Ben, thanks."

"You need to hear me out before you leave. Believe me there are just too many loose ends."

The pastor didn't need to be convinced. His retreat back into the cave was out of respect for his brother in Christ.

"Greg, what really happened to you at Maggie's diner?"

"Two teenage boys are after Reenie. Said something about being sent by a demon called Osiris, must be Satanists. I've got to find her first."

"Remember Twanna Evers? You and Ruben picked her to head up the construction of Bethel and Beulah. The Lord led me to help her leave the Vineyard. Her father is a pastor..."

It took over an hour. Ben didn't want to leave out any details.

"Where are we now?"

"The heat from the fourth bowl is over. The fifth bowl, darkness covering the Beast's kingdom, is next up."

"How many days left till Armageddon?"

"As of tomorrow, seven days."

"How is Ruben holding up?"

"It's been tough. Just the possibility of being attacked forced a total lock down. Some of our staff left."

"Is acquiring Twanna still possible?"

"Our scouts know the camp where she is being held. It's Eiland's favorite, he calls it Zion. There could be casualties if we try."

"So who sent Cody to find Twanna?"

"It was Ruben's call."

"Has Cody received any training in search and rescue?"

"Afraid not, I sent him to find Reenie."

"Wow, Ben, keeping track of all the players is not easy. So what are our chances of rescuing Twanna and her father?"

"It's a stretch," the old man sadly confessed.

<br>

Jon Mendel already had a release from the Holy Spirit. He was waiting on Reenie for the confirmation. Losing the stranger from her vision was a definite setback. The time had come for a new plan of action. Slowing down, he parked the Winnebago behind a burned down log cabin. The only sounds inside the RV were Reenie's heart-felt prayers. When Jon's eyes met his, the young Watchman nodded.

"It's time, Miracle Girl."

"What do you mean, Jake?"

"You need to tell us everything you know. When was the last time you saw Greg? Has anyone seen you since you split up? Who have you talked with? Were you ever followed? Jon and Donnell are trained in rescue. If you want their help you can't hold anything back."

"Where's Kurt?"

"He was arrested when we were in Bethany."

"Emma, why didn't you try to...?"

"Cause we made a commitment to protect you. Kurt knows how to follow God. Now just start from the beginning."

Wiping away her tears; Reenie explained how she escaped with Greg, why they split up, her meeting with Lenard, and the planned attack by the Prophetic Voice on the Vineyard. Her decision to go with Lenard to warn the campers seemed so right.

"Reenie, how do you know this Lenard is for real? What if he is hooked up with this cult and is using you to deceive these campers. Who knows, they might even be blackmailing him!"

"Jon, all I know is what he told me. And what I saw in my vision. I don't care about his intentions; he's involved with my mission. We need to find him before Eiland's soldiers do."

"But why would Lenard leave?" questioned Donnell. "You think he split to protect Reenie?"

Rolling her eyes she muttered back, "This is so evil."

"So you want to prevent this cult from attacking the Vineyard?"

"After hearing Lenard's vision, yeah I do. But there's more, Jon. Now when I pray, I see a three legged stool."

"Maybe there're three parts to your mission. The first leg could be the deliverance of the campers. I have to admit when I pray I see frightened soldiers running for cover. This could be the second leg."

"Oh get real!" blurted Reenie. "How can we help the very cult trying to destroy the Vineyard?"

"Has the Lord shown you anything else?"

"While praying I saw a frightened mother and her baby. They are huddled in fear with other families. But no one is hearing their pleas for help."

"Could this be the third leg of your mission?" asked Donnell.

"I wish I knew."

"Where is Lenard from?"

"His last name is Mayer. He was once on the White House Staff."

"So this dude knows Kayin is the Man of Sin?"

His throne on earth was in jeopardy. 1 In a moment in time the angel holding the fifth bowl poured out its plague. All his followers could do was gnaw their tongues in pain as darkness swept over the kingdom of the Beast. There would be no repentance; just a gushing forth of blasphemy against a Holy God in heaven. 2

Moving from town to town was risky. The small tent given to them came in handy. Wearing Muslim clothing helped them become even more invisible.

"More are arriving, Aaron, what shall I tell them?"

"Fadi, the most effective witness is a new creation in Christ. The Lord wants to use the Jordanians that were saved yesterday. For Muslims to hear the gospel being openly proclaimed is a powerful weapon."

"Several have been arrested."

"Our Lord will be with them."

"How can you be so sure?"

"You worried about Rafa?"

"She can be pretty reckless."

"My daughter is no lightweight," kidded Aaron.

"I've been studying some of your notes. Jeremiah was quite a prophet. He wrote, 'O Lord, "I know the way of man is not in himself; It is not in man who walks to direct his own steps. O Lord, correct me, but with justice; not in Your anger, lest You bring me to nothing.'" 3

"My favorite proverb says, "'A man's steps are of the Lord; How then can a man understand his own way?'" 4

"So you believe we are in this tent, in this specific town, at this particular time, because God directed it?"

"I also entrust our girls into the loving arms of our Savior."

"You've got great faith, Aaron. By your own admission you've only been saved since the Feast of Tabernacles. 5 Yet you have a way with my people I've never seen before. They somehow sense God's anointing on your words."

"Praise Him for His mercy," the ex-soldier humbly confessed.

"Let me finish the passage I just read you. 'Pour out Your fury on the Gentiles, who do not know You...on the families who do not call on Your name; For they have eaten up Jacob...'" 6

His silence was a dead giveaway. The teenager was trying to find the right words.

"Over two thousand years ago, Old Testament prophets predicted which Islamic nations would attack Israel at this time. Now I know why my father hates. His hate always bothered Rafa."

"Did it bother you?"

"Not at all, all I ever wanted was the approval of my father. Obeying him was my ambition. As a boy my father taught me to hate Jews and Christians. For the first time I now see how the Qur'an builds walls, not bridges. You and Johanna were sent to break down these walls. I can't deny the love I've experienced. Islam doesn't have such love."

"I hear ya, forgiving your enemies can be tough. Satan still attacks me in this area. Do you love your father?"

"Very much."

"I loved my father too."

"Where is he now?"

"He was killed by a terrorist when I was a young man."

"Do you still seek revenge?"

"There are times when the Devil fills my mind with thoughts of vengeance. These mind games can only be defeated through prayer. My ex-wife calls it spiritual warfare."

Suddenly darkness overshadowed the top of their tent.

"Look, they're scratching their sores and gnawing their tongues!" [7]

"The fifth bowl has been poured out. Soon armies from the nations will be converging on Israel."

"Aaron, there is nothing left for us here. I want to become a Watchman to your people." [8]

"Fadi, our success as Watchmen is connected to His timing. As for the salvation of your people, I still don't have a release to leave. Not yet."

# Being in the Form of God

"Let this mind be in you which was also in Christ Jesus, who, being in the form of God, did not consider it robbery to be equal with God."
Philippians 2:5-6

"Hi, Wes, it's Joel Friedman from Jerusalem."

So, Joel, how's it looking from your perspective?"

"The sun has returned to normal. The ozone is still holding up."

"What about the darkness covering the Middle East?"

"The enemies of Israel are being targeted. It's today's headline."

"Hear anything from Kayin?"

"He's in Rome. Kayin has no comment on anything about Israel."

"Isn't Rome covered in darkness?"

"Yeah, I hear it's pretty surreal."

"How are your people coping?"

"I've never witnessed such fear. The thousands of Jordanians and Egyptians crossing over our border didn't help either. 1 This only ignited more tension between Palestinian and Israeli soldiers."

"Sorry, about Nate leaving you hanging."

"It was for the best. She isn't the same reporter anymore. The emotional fervor from the Messiah cult played her for a fool. She actually believes Jesus is their leader."

"Nate told me all about it."

"Where is she now?"

"No one knows."

"Dam, another Anchor calling it quits."

"I wouldn't count her out just yet."

"How do you figure?"

"Nate had a personal interview with a white supremacy leader in northern Georgia. Whatever this racist said really lit a fire in her. After she came back, a lot of the emotional baggage she was carrying was gone. Her recent Special Report was excellent!"

---

Cody's first attempts to witness were a waste of time.

"What are you doing?" whispered the spirit of Doubt. "Wasn't your assignment to protect Twanna? Now you run away pretending to search for Reenie. You're not fooling God. Don't Ben and Greg need your help? So far you've accomplished nothing."

The campfire up ahead looked inviting. He needed to at least try. The demonic bombardment suddenly vanished. After parking his car next to several Harleys he walked over.

At first, those holding their hands over the fire said nothing. It was a suspicious looking Hell's Angel that spoke first.

"Was this green eyed brunette traveling with anybody?"

"Don't know. Her first name is Reenie."

"Is that your car?"

"What if it is?"

"Well the kid that just siphoned your gas is long gone."

Sitting on a large log by the fire, Cody didn't even bother to look. An old man stirring a hot pot of stew couldn't help but laugh.

"How much for some food?"

"Two bowls of stew and three cups of coffee for your jacket. That's final; I don't haggle."

The warmth of the fire felt soothing. Standing up he removed his favorite red parka. He had another in his car. As he sipped on his first cup of coffee the old man handed him his first bowl of beef and beans. Those sitting around the fire studied him as he ate. Sporting no sores or burns on his body, they knew he was different.

"Is this Reenie a resister?" mocked the biker.

Cody simply nodded before taking another sip of coffee.

"So you believe Jesus is coming to judge the world, is that it?"

"That's it."

"You must think God is causing this darkness?"

"The next bowl will dry up the Euphrates River."

"Now why would God do something that stupid?"

"The leaders of your world are being deceived. 2 Their armies are gathering for the great day of God Almighty." 3

"What do you mean 'your' world?"

"Jesus said, '"If you were of the world, the world would love its own. Yet because you are not of the world, but I chose you out of the world, therefore the world hates you." 4

"Listen up guys, this punk can tell us how we can escape hell.'"

"Thanks for the meal."

"C'mon, the cat got your tongue."

"There is no escape for anyone taking the mark of the Beast. 5 For those of you who don't Jesus says..."

Lunging forward the biker grabbed him by his throat.

"That's enough! I know why the world hates religious fundies like you. And it's not because you speak the truth. Kayin was right when he exposed those teaching Jesus is only way to heaven. Say, who wants to be the first to set this fanatic straight?"

They could all hear movement from the dark shadows.

"No one is going to do anything!" boomed a loud voice.

"Ok, big mouth, come out where I can see you."

Emerging from the trees both agents drew their guns.

"Let's go, son, you're under arrest."

After cuffing his suspect, Abe poured himself two cups of coffee. Doyle waited until they were out of site.

"You can all make it easy on yourself. None of you saw anything tonight. And thanks for the coffee."

Chained to the backseat of their van, the Watchman whispered encouragement to the two boys who were tied up and gagged.

"What's your name and where are you from?"

"Cody Parrish. Columbia, South Carolina."

"So what's your interest in Reenie Ann Tucker?"

"She's a friend of a friend."

"You mean Pastor Greg Hudson?"

"I have nothing more to say."

"I'm Doyle Mercer; this is agent Abernathy. We are searching for a resister camp called the Vineyard. You help us find this camp and you can go free. Food, water, car, everything you need to get home."

"Not interested."

"Do you know who's tracking Tucker?"

"Nope."

"Well, she better be praying. Yesterday two teenagers with baseball bats killed two girls looking just like her."

---

"Get going, Jo!" screamed Rafa. "These soldiers have orders from my father. They will be here any moment. You don't have a choice."

"We're racing together, Rafa. We need each other."

"The cries of your people must be answered. Fulfill your calling as a Watchman. I will never forget you my sister."

Her argument with the border guards was heated. Once Rafa stepped away, the guards allowed Johanna to cross over. After passing through Israeli security she couldn't resist looking back. She felt faint as two Palestinian soldiers seized her friend and dragged her away.

---

The dark room had no windows. When he entered, his eyes were cold; his countenance distant. He had no reason to hide the betrayal he was feeling. His daughter had prayed for so much more.

"Rafa, what has gotten into you?"

"The Spirit of God," she nervously replied.

"Why have you sided with the enemy? Are you aware of the consequences? What lies could this Jewish infidel possibly tell you to make you turn away from your faith?"

"Father, when you die do you expect to go to heaven?"

"What did you say?"

"How do you know God will accept you?"

"You deserted your country, your family, even your faith. As a soldier helping the enemy, you're now considered a coward. Even your own brother has become a traitor. What can you possibly gain by such treasonous actions?"

"When John baptized Jesus in the Jordan River, he saw the Holy Spirit descend upon Jesus like a dove. A voice from heaven announced, '...This is My beloved Son, in whom I am well pleased.' 6 Later, John called Jesus the Lamb of God." 7

"John came as a witness to the Word from God. Jesus was conceived by the command of Allah. Allah has no son."

"Wasn't Adam also created by the command of Allah?"

"So what?"

"So why wasn't Adam called the Word? Only Jesus is called the Word in the Bible and the Qur'an."

"You're so confused. The dove resting upon Jesus wasn't the Holy Spirit. It was the angel Gabriel."

"I was always taught Jesus received revelation directly from God. There is no mention of angels assisting Him in gaining revelation from God."

"What is the point of such worthless semantics? Rafa, you are a total embarrassment to me. Obviously something has changed you."

"You're so right."

"So being brainwashed against your family is from Allah?"

"Jesus has given us a promise."

"What sort of promise?"

"Jesus is the Alpha and Omega; the Beginning and the End. He promises to be our God. All things promised us we will inherit." 8

"Quote me one verse in the Bible that says Jesus is God?"

"Try Revelation 21:7."

"The Qur'an has an answer for every one of your questions. I can't believe the truth doesn't mean anything to you anymore?"

"Is Fadi alright?"

"Aaron Glazer has taken him to Israel against his will."

"What makes you think Fadi wants to return?"

"Your contempt is appalling."

"So what are you going to do with me?"

"Absolutely nothing! The mask you're wearing will soon be stripped away. Allah will punish you for your disobedience."

"Father, you can still be saved for eternity by believing in Jesus. The forgiveness taught in the New Testament is not in the Qur'an. My sins have been washed away by the blood of Jesus."

"Is this all you have to say to me?"

"It's the most important thing I could ever say to you. Jesus is only a prayer away."

"You've made your choice; now I must make mine. You're not my daughter anymore. You died the moment you chose to become an infidel. Now go away and never come back!"

Closing his office door behind her he never acknowledged her frantic pleas. The Commander silently thanked Allah for the courage to stand for the truth.

His pacing was not the norm; Ruben knew he had to confront him. The crunching of pine needles outside his tent got his attention.

"Thank you for coming, Eli."

"No problem, what's up?"

"Seems we have a traitor in our camp, he has been communicating with a white supremacy cult."

"Why?"

"Have you been missing this?"

Tossing him his cell phone Ruben looked pale.

"Thanks, where did you find it?"

"A sentry found it vibrating under your bunk. He answered the call. Eli, I need some answers. I'm responsible for these kids."

"Hey, when a fire starts the just as well as the unjust suffer. Choices have consequences."

"There's a critical difference. These campers choose life; you're choosing death. You can still help us if you want."

"Why would I? You have deliberately brainwashed thousands of white children. We have no choice. The Prophetic Voice is God's arm of mercy. We must rescue these kids before judgment falls."

"When is Eiland planning his attack?"

"You can't resist his army. Evacuation through these tunnels is no answer. You should save your butt and get out while you can."

"Eli, you can be spiritually saved by repenting of your hate. Jesus has the grace to wipe away all your sins. This is why you are here."

"You don't know who is saved. You're just a self-righteous hypocrite blinded by the traditions of men. You foul Kenite; your seed is of the devil. Soon all who reject the truth will be destroyed."

"Let's talk about your soul, 'And I say to you, My friends, do not be afraid of those who kill the body, and after that have no more that they can do. But I will show you whom you should fear: Fear Him who, after He has killed, has power to cast into hell; yes, I say to you, fear Him.'" 9

"I don't fear anything."

"Somehow Satan has gotten a stronghold in your life. This is why you fear man more than God. It was Delford who sent you to do his bidding. He has the same fear you do. Jesus exhorts us not to fear man. At the great white throne, all unbelievers will be resurrected out of Hades before being cast into the lake of fire for eternity."

"So you actually believe a loving God plans to roast those He created in His image? How blind is that?"

"The Word is coming. Those denying Him will be cast into everlasting fire originally prepared for the Devil and his angels." 10

"The scriptures say we shall know believers by their fruit. Your manipulation can't hurt me. This proves you don't have God's seal!"

# THE WILL OF MY FATHER

"Not everyone who says to Me, 'Lord, Lord,' shall enter the kingdom
of heaven, but he who does the will of My Father in heaven."
Matthew 7:21

Aaron was praying with great intensity. Even so, he was beginning to
fear the worst. Fadi's meeting was taking way too long. Finally the
despondent teenager emerged from the abandoned factory.

"What did they say?"

"They don't trust you."

"What about you?"

"You think they'll listen to a former Muslim sharing about a
Jewish Savior coming in judgment?"

The word from the Holy Spirit was crystal clear.

"Fadi, I once asked you the meaning of your first name but we
got interrupted."

"Fadi means redeemer."

The former pastor nodded after hearing the confirmation.

"This is from the Lord. We can't walk away; not this time."

"How can you be sure?"

"The darkness covering most of the Middle East is a judgment
from God. Many of your people are seeing this. The prophets speak
of the glory of the Lord rising above the darkness. Not only Jews
believing in Jesus will return to Zion but Gentiles too."

"They won't believe me! It's just a fairytale to them. Christianity
means nothing. The promises of Islam have brainwashed them."

"Then you give them God's promise to restore the earth. You
know the sequence of events by heart. Just make sure you read them
the verses. The power to convict is in His Word."

This was not what this new convert wanted to hear.

Grasping his shoulders, Aaron pleaded, "Trust Him. The message you're bringing is from a loving God redeeming lost souls. Just be faithful to what the Holy Spirit gives you. You can do no less."

As the Jordanian teenager re-entered the factory, a surge of faith touched Aaron's heart. The Spirit of Christ was going before the boy. Even so, the spirits of unbelief and religion were ready to attack.

"Look, the infidel has returned," ridiculed a cleric in his forties.

"I have a message from an Old Testament prophet."

"Muhammad was the greatest prophet."

"How do you know Muhammad was a true prophet of God?"

"You should be ashamed asking such an ignorant question. Just the miracles he performed are proof enough."

"Then why doesn't the Qur'an mention such miracles?"

"Why disgrace the prophet?"

"The Qur'an states all prophets are related to Isaac or Jacob."

"It is written."

"Muhammad came from Ishmael."

"Leave us while you are still able."

"The message I have for you comes from the prophet Isaiah. He foretold, 'For your light has come. And the glory of the Lord is risen upon you. For behold, the darkness shall cover the earth, and deep darkness the people; But the Lord will arise over you, and His glory will be seen upon you. The Gentiles shall come to your light, and kings to the brightness of your rising.'" 1

"Is this the darkness covering the nations surrounding Israel?"

"It's God's wrath from the fifth bowl."

"They're not listening," hissed the Spirit of Doubt. "You're just wasting time. There are others who need to hear the truth."

Their contempt felt like a suffocating cloud as he studied their faces. Sharing the gospel seemed so futile.

"Aaron is in trouble," whispered the Spirit of Lying. "He needs your help; you'd better go now."

Turning to leave Fadi silently prayed for their salvation.

"Why do you give up so easily?" taunted a teenager his age. "Maybe your God isn't so powerful after all."

Stopping in his tracks, Fadi boldly replied, "The restoration of all things began with the salvation of Israel. Gentiles will also be saved."

"How do you know this?"

"The Messiah will perform everything the prophets predicted. This includes a new earth and a new heaven."

"Can't you see this boy is a liar!" rebuked another.

"The Revelation of Jesus Christ highlights the wrath of God Almighty coming upon a Christ rejecting world. Since Jesus split the Mount of Olives, we have experienced the first five bowls. After the sixth bowl is poured out, the armies of the world will converge on the Middle East. The final bowl will be the most destructive of all. Hailstones from heaven will destroy our cities. Mount Moriah will be leveled. The Temple, Al-Haram Ash-Sharif, and the Dome of the Rock, will all be destroyed. But this isn't the end. The prophets describe a restored earth with the nations flowing to Jerusalem." [2]

"What nations?" scoffed an ex-soldier, "We're the walking dead."

"Isaiah predicted a future time when nations would not war against each other!" Opening his Bible he read, "'He shall judge between the nations, and rebuke many people; They shall beat their swords into plowshares, and their spears into pruning hooks; Nation shall not lift up sword against nation, neither shall they learn war anymore.'" [3]

"How do you know this will happen?"

"Micah prophesied, 'Now it shall come to pass in the latter days that the mountain of the Lord's house shall be established on the top of the mountains, and shall be exalted above the hills; and peoples shall flow to it. Many nations shall come and say, "Come, and let us go up to the mountain of the Lord..."'" [4]

"Why will Mount Moriah be the highest mountain? You're quoting prophets predicting the return of Jews to their temple!"

"Gentiles will also see the glory of God, 'For I know their works and their thoughts. It shall be that I will gather all nations and tongues; and they shall come and see My glory.'" [5]

"So what happens after everyone is gathered?"

"The Lord will rule from His throne in Jerusalem." [6]

"We don't believe in such prophets. Their empty predictions mean nothing to us."

The young Watchman had his answer.

"It's your choice! You have heard enough to believe. I only share with those who have ears to hear."

A devastated mother begged, "Don't you care about your own people?" Grasping her daughter she wept, "What can your God do for my little girl?"

Reaching over Fadi gently touched her badly burned arm. In a loud voice he called upon the mighty power in Jesus' name! All eyes were watching as the girl raised her arm high.

"Look Mama," she screeched, "the redness is gone. I don't feel any pain. I'm healed! I'm healed!" [7]

Dropping to her knees her grateful mother began praising the Lord. A line quickly formed. Salvation had come to the descendants of Ishmael. Before long there wasn't a dry eye in the factory.

"I must leave you now."

"Fadi, what do we do now?"

"In a couple of days hailstones weighing over one hundred pounds will demolish this earth. For your protection you must hide underground. The Holy Spirit will guide you."

"How can we thank you?"

"All thanks go to the Father, the Son, and the Holy Spirit. Before I leave I would like to share a song about the Lamb of God. It was sung by the saints that got the victory over the Beast."

"Is such a song in the Bible?"

"Yes, I'll read it, 'Great and marvelous are Your works, Lord God Almighty. Just and true are Your ways, O King of the saints. Who shall not fear You, O Lord, and glorify Your name? For You alone are holy. For all nations shall come and worship before You, For Your judgments have been manifested.'" [8]

"Where and when did the saints sing this song?"

"On a sea of glass after Jesus split the Mount of Olives."

"But they're in heaven and we are still here!" cried an old man.

The determined Jordanian raised his hands getting their full attention.

"The saints are also singing about us. We are the believers from the nations who will worship the Lord during the Millennium. Let's remember, we too overcame the Beast!"

This redeemed crowd spontaneously burst into grateful cheers as he reached the factory exit. The teenager openly wept as he waved a final goodbye.

"Mama, why does Fadi have to leave us?"

Looking into her daughter's eyes, she lovingly replied, "Fadi must give the gospel to others. He is a Watchman for our Lord."

After finishing off lunch in the abandoned house a curious Jake had a question about the final judgment of the unsaved.

"Jon, what do you know about the future lake of fire?"

"Bro, most pastors stayed away from anything having to do with eternal punishment. The Holy Spirit led me to do my own study."

"Is it true Hades is not the lake of fire?"

"They're two different places. Hades will be cast into the lake of fire after the great white throne judgment." 9

"Can you give us a quick teaching on it?"

"Sure, turn to Revelation 20:11-15. John saw a great white throne after the thousand year reign of Christ. It's between earth and heaven. Now we know the Father has committed all judgment to His Son." 10

"Which means Jesus is sitting on the great white throne."

"Amen, Reenie. Our Lord will judge those not written in the Book of Life."

"So there are no believers at this judgment?"

"Correct. The wicked in Hades will be resurrected before the great white throne. Jesus will judge them before casting them into the lake of fire. Like I said Hades or hell is not the lake of fire."

"So how is this resurrection different than the first resurrection?"

"Reenie, the first resurrection unto eternal life has four phases. Jesus was the first to be gloriously resurrected and never die again. Later, at His coming the elect received their resurrection bodies." 11

"Oh yeah, the resurrection of the dead in Christ followed by believers alive during the Great Tribulation! Angels cut short this persecution by the Beast by gathering overcomers from every nation!"

"That's right. After His coming Jesus sat on His heavenly throne and separated the sheep from the goats."

"Did this happen at the judgment seat of Christ?"

"Yes, Miracle Girl. Jesus gave us several other parables representing His coming followed by the judgment seat."

"Can you name a few?" asked a curious Jake.

"In Matthew 24:45-51, Jesus warned of a faithful servant becoming unfaithful when the Son of Man comes back. In Matthew 25:1-13, there are ten virgins. In Matthew 25:14-30, there are three servants with talents. And of course, in Matthew 13:37-50, the Son of Man sent out angels to gather both the wheat and the tares out of His kingdom."

"So the wheat and tares were gathered to heaven at His coming?"

"Those receiving glorified bodies will enter the New Jerusalem."

"So what happened to the virgins who didn't have any oil?"

"They weren't allowed to enter into the wedding of the Lamb."

"Are you sure, Jon?" Jake barely mumbled back.

"All believers at the judgment seat were rewarded because their works were built upon the foundation of Jesus. 12 This was one aspect of this judgment. There were others that denied their Lord. They were cast into outer darkness of weeping and gnashing of teeth." 13

"You mean Hades?" reflected Jake.

"According to Jesus, those hearing the voice of the Son of God, that did evil, will be resurrected unto condemnation." 14

"Whoa, Jon, this is the first time I've ever heard this teaching on the parables of Matthew 24 and 25. Yet it makes so much sense."

"How so?"

"Well, there is only one coming of the Son of Man with His holy angels for His elect. Believers will be judged for their works following His coming. Don't you see, guys, Jesus won't separate the sheep from the goats on earth. After the resurrection at the sixth seal the Son of Man is in heaven not on earth!

"Hallelujah!" praised Donnell. "So when is the third and fourth phase of the first resurrection?"

"I know the third," offered a grateful Reenie. "On the first day of the millennium all martyrs will be raised. They will reign with Christ for a thousand years."

"So when do we get our resurrection bodies? C'mon, Jon, don't leave us hanging."

"Donnie, the final phase involves all believers living on earth during the Millennium. They will eventually receive their resurrection bodies and live eternally inside the New Jerusalem."

Their hands and ankles chained, Natalie Roberts and Twanna Evers were escorted into his office. Both knew their lives were in danger. One was gripped with fear; the other a peace from God.

All was not well within the Prophetic Voice. His bloodshot eyes and nervous twitch was a dead giveaway. Tilting his head back the racist leader was searching for a scapegoat.

"So have you two been comparing notes? I'm curious what you've come up with?"

The shrewd reporter knew his self-importance was his biggest weakness. Eiland wanted something. By appealing to his pride she was hoping to trip him up.

"Delford have any of your soldiers ever worshipped Kayin?" 15

"Not one, Natalie!" he smugly acknowledged. "You still don't know who he is? Kayin is Satan in the flesh!"

"I thought Satan was a fallen angel?"

"Isaiah saw Lucifer as a man that made the earth tremble." 16

"Can't God stop Satan from doing this?"

"It's His perfect will. In the first age, souls resisting Lucifer were called the elect. After his fall from heaven, Lucifer was re-named Satan. God then re-made the world. In this age, everyone will receive the mark except the elect. The third age is called the Millennium. During the Millennium, the elect will live on earth in spirit bodies."

"Seems like you got this end time scenario pretty wired," laughed Twanna. "When do you get your spiritual body?"

"You'll never know," hissed the demon from his lips.

"So if God is going to set up his kingdom on earth then why would He attack the Vineyard?"

"To save hostages, Natalie."

"There are no hostages!" screamed Twanna. "These children were taken to this camp for protection."

"Did you say taken?" he seethed. "Eli believes your Kenite leader, Ruben Rodriguez, has a hidden agenda."

"How do you know, Eli?"

"Such lack of discernment is not from God."

"Delford, what are you really after? Are your soldiers having doubts? This gibberish has nothing to do with Twanna."

"You're right, Natalie. Once she told us the location of the tunnels her destiny was sealed."

"You killed my father, didn't you?"

The smile on his face was like a knife to her heart.

"Wake up, Eiland!" she shrieked. "The darkness spreading across America is the wrath of God. Your followers are putting the pieces together and you can't stand that."

Collapsing just a couple feet from the small stream of water, his dehydrated body went limp. Hours passed before three teenagers found him almost unconscious.

"C'mon, he's all alone," whispered one of the boys.

"I got dubs on his boots," claimed his friend.

"No, we barter them."

With one boy on lookout, his two buddies removed his boots and jacket and stuffed them in an old duffel bag.

"What about the gold cross around his neck?"

"Leave it; it ain't worth nothing."

With one hand covering his mouth the lookout didn't even try to move. He could hear the trigger of a gun being pulled back.

"Hello, boys, how's business?"

"Hey, mister, we just found him. No harm, no foul."

"Just let him die, is that it?"

"It ain't our fault. Look how far gone he is."

"Are you boys unregistered?"

"Registered."

"How did you make it up here?"

"We just followed the stream."

"Where are your parents?"

One shrugged, while the other just looked away.

"Okay, you can go. And don't forget to leave the bag."

"Thanks, mister, sorry about your friend."

The trees against the hill protected them from the wind. It wasn't long before he regained consciousness. Wrapped in a dirty blanket the groggy soldier didn't know what to say when he saw him.

"You're fortunate to be alive, Eli."

"Thanks for the help, Lenard."

"Did Ruben kick you out of the Vineyard or have you had your fill of Eiland's propaganda?"

"If you're running they'll find you."

"Your yellow streak was never really appealing to me. Aren't you tired of being afraid?"

"Look who's talking? When you joined the Prophetic Voice your hands were shaking so badly you couldn't even hold a cup of coffee."

"Being hunted like an animal is no fun. You have no idea how it messes with your mind."

"So you just gave in to Satan?"

"I'm out of the loop. I'm going solo."

"What's happened?"

"Eiland is facing big time defections."

"Why now?" a depressed Eli muttered to himself.

Lenard looked away. It was heartbreaking to watch a tyrant prey on the dreams of those wanting to be part of something meaningful.

"Eli, for me it was about protection. I was never into Eiland's white supremacy delusion."

"You sure fooled me."

"Delford fooled thousands through his demonic manipulation. He did it by intimidating the weak through hate and fear. He is demon possessed like Joshua Kayin. Both are doing the Devil's bidding."

"You have no right to judge God's anointed."

"The Bible does it quite nicely, 'But he who hates his brother is in darkness and walks in darkness, and does not know where he is going, because the darkness has blinded his eyes.'" [17]

"So Delford is now in darkness? Is this your new revelation?"

"What type of animal murders children?"

"The Kenites are clever how they twist scriptures. Who is my brother in the Lord? A real Jew from the ten tribes of Israel is either from Great Britain or America. Our real brothers are those..."

"Stop it, you're being used. Delford will suck everything out of you if you let him. 'Who is a liar but he who denies that Jesus is the Christ? He is antichrist who denies the Father and the Son. Whoever denies the Son does not have the Father either; he who acknowledges the Son has the Father also. Therefore let that abide in you which you heard from the beginning. If what you heard from the beginning abides in you, you also will abide in the Son and in the Father.'" [18]

"What do you want from me?"

"Jesus promises eternal life for those abiding in His teaching."

"All of a sudden you're sounding mighty religious."

"It's a long story. I met the girl in my vision."

"You mean the vision you had as a kid?"

"She is a Watchman. Her name is Reenie Ann Tucker."

"Whatever."

There was no conviction. Their talk seemed pointless.

"Eli, John wrote, 'Dear children, do not let anyone lead you astray. He who does what is right is righteous, just as he is righteous. He who does what is sinful is of the devil, because the devil has been sinning from the beginning. The reason the Son of God appeared was to destroy the devil's work.'" [19]

"Delford's plan to rescue is a gift from above."

"These children have been rescued. Most would be marked by now if Watchmen hadn't risked their lives saving them."

"I know all about your so-called Watchmen."

"When the Word of God returns don't you want to be on the right side? I not only want to follow Jesus but I want to be His instrument in destroying the work of the enemy."

"No man will ever be able destroy the Prophetic Voice. There may be some doubters of Delford's vision but the vast majority will give their lives before renouncing his teaching."

"I'm not alone."

"Oh, yeah, you and Tucker make two."

"Reenie has friends. The Holy Spirit is drawing more Watchmen to the Vineyard. You know Ruben and his staff. If we trust in the Lord the Holy Spirit will guide us. Come join us."

Miraculously Lenard could sense a change.

"They blindfolded me just before we exited Bethel. I don't know how far they took me from the tunnel. I'll help you find it. That's all I can do. My reputation with the Vineyard staff is history."

The hopeful Watchman helped his weary friend up.

"What direction?"

"Did you remember a waterfall just over a small embankment?"

"Yeah, it's about a hundred yards upstream."

"I heard it when they released me. Let's begin there."

"Are you sure? If Delford finds out it could mean the end."

"Let's ask God."

"Excuse me?"

"You heard me. I'm tired of being controlled by others. I want to repent of this cult garbage and believe in Jesus Christ as my Lord and Savior."

# A REMNANT

*"Even so then, at this present time there is a remnant according to the election of grace."*
Romans 11:5

Their urgency was at an all-time high. No one was moving.

"Saints, I've come tonight with a burden from the Lord. The dilemma we're facing doesn't scare God or catch Him off guard. Our Lord has the power to bring victory even when we can't see it."

Ruben Rodriguez knew God's will for the Vineyard. These caverns were specifically outfitted for the last days. He also knew his staff would willingly face martyrdom in order to save these children.

"The darkness over the nations has ceased. Kayin is hiding in Rome. The Euphrates will dry up once the sixth bowl is poured out. Demons will convince many armies to invade Israel."

"Ruben, so there is no judgment involved with the sixth bowl?"

"Yes, it appears the armies following the Beast will invade Israel without any interference."

"What about the hailstones of the seventh bowl?"

"Some of you have never met Greg Hudson. He chose this mountain for protection against the seventh bowl."

"So what is the Holy Spirit showing you?"

No one likes giving bad news. The former cop promised himself to never allow Satan to bully him into lying to his staff.

"Remember the day I warned you of a white supremacy militia called the Prophetic Voice? Tragically, Satan has been fueling their wickedness. They've been watching us. Those who know Eli will be shocked to hear he was their plant. He gathered information about our camp. Everything from security to our evacuation plans. This is why I called this meeting. The Holy Spirit has exposed their evil plot. Eli refused to help us so I had him removed through the Bethel exit."

"You mean they want to attack us?"

"Any day now, let's begin preparing for close quarters. Beulah and Bethel can only be used for evacuation; never for shelter against God's wrath. Any tunnel cave-in would be disastrous. Being caught outside after the seventh bowl is not an option. Everyone must be inside a cave before one hailstone hits Black Rock Mountain."

"What caves are you talking about?"

"Our sentries are already tagging caves above both exits strong enough to withstand a direct hit. During the evacuation we will escape in groups of fifty. I will lead the last group out."

Walking the lonely streets of Jerusalem, Johanna Glazer couldn't help thinking about her mother. Their last visit on the Mount of Olives was feeling more like a dream.

"Oh, mama, everything has turned out so differently."

Sitting on a street bench, Johanna read, "'Brethren, my heart's desire and prayer to God for Israel is that they may be saved. For I bear them witness that they have a zeal for God, but not according to knowledge. For they being ignorant of God's righteousness, and seeking to establish their own righteousness, have not submitted to the righteousness of God...Even so then, at this present time there is a remnant according to the election of grace.'" 1

Miriam's tears were heartfelt. With intercessors surrounding her, she knelt and prayed, "Lord, the mystery of God has been accomplished. 2 You are still gathering believers from among the nations according to Your grace. May You speak to my Johanna. In Your name, I rebuke any demonic assignments sent her way by the evil one. For those still in unbelief, their eternity is hanging in the balance. Somehow Johanna must see this. May You give her eyes of faith so she can see the final harvest. 'How then shall they call on Him in whom they have not believed? And how shall they believe in Him of whom they have not heard? And how shall they hear without a preacher?'" 3

Johanna felt a chill down her back. She could almost hear her mother's prayers. Somewhere in Azal, a redeemed remnant was interceding. Her tears were for her people.

The old man shuffling down the street picked up the pace. His heart felt energized when their eyes met.

"Hello, do we know each other?"

"Are you Aaron Glazer's daughter?"

"I am."

"Have you lost your way? Where did you first see the Lord? Go back; someone is waiting for you."

"Yes, I remember the street. But who is waiting?"

Having delivered his message the old man walked away.

The remnant roared. Joanna was moving. She knew the way to go.

---

The respect Greg and Ben had for each other had been forged through the fire of persecution. Even so, they could sense the strain of each other. They were waiting for a leading from the Holy Spirit.

"Ben, I've never heard much about your family tree."

"Ever hear of the trail of tears?"

"Bits and pieces, when I chose Black Rock Mountain as the site for the Vineyard I found out this was the starting point for the trail of tears. Wasn't this a forced march in the 1830's?"

"My great grandmother told me stories about it."

"President Jackson promised the Indians a land of their own."

"The white man gave his word until he wanted more land. The tribes taken away were the Seminoles, Creeks, Choctaws, Chickasaws, and Cherokees. Most were forced to relocate in Oklahoma, which means 'red people'. President Jackson boldly testified no state could progress culturally as long as Indians lived inside their borders."

"So the President knew what he was proposing?"

"Jackson believed the extinction of Indians was a necessary evil. The Removal Act of 1830 was the beginning of the end."

---

Night shift was almost over. Their short coffee break stretched into twenty. By the time they got back to their posts the power line encircling Zion had been cut.

"Our juice is gone!" gasped the northern sentry.

"Begin a perimeter check!" ordered his superior.

"The Cherokees resisted the most," Ben sadly reflected. "They were the last tribe taken. My family can be traced back to a Cherokee Chief called Running Bear. My tribe graciously gave me his name. You know, the Cherokees were once a proud nation of people. They had houses, laws, even a constitution. When missionaries translated the Bible into the Cherokee language many of my people got saved. Running Bear was the first to learn how to talk on paper. Eventually, over sixteen thousand Cherokees were evicted from these mountains.

"So why was this land so valuable to the white man?"

"In 1829, a miner discovered gold near Dahlonega. The treaty my people agreed to was declared void. On May 28th, 1830, Congress approved the Indian Removal Act. Eventually over one hundred thousand Native Americans were relocated west of the Mississippi river. Many saw their houses seized before their death march even began."

"I heard Indians were taught never to cry."

Ben shook his head in disgust.

"That's just another lie. In the movies when the white man wins it's called a victory, but when the Indians win it's called a massacre. Trust me, there were many tears shed as thousands were buried along the way. Some Indians originally called it, 'The Trail Where They Cried'. By 1838, the Cherokees were forced into encampments in Tennessee. They were held there before their removal out West. Chief Running Bear was brought to Fort Cass. His detachment left by gunpoint. He never made it. The Chief died of small pox in Paducah, Kentucky."

"Ben, do any of your living relatives believe in Christ?"

"No, today I'm the only one saved."

"Sir, Zion is under attack on our northern perimeter."

"Attack!" scoffed the officer. "Who would dare attack us?"

The blows from behind left them both unconscious.

The sound of an owl hooting pieced the air.

"Did you hear that?" whispered another soldier.

"Get your hands up!" ordered the scout.

"I don't know you but you just made the biggest mistake of your life. We have other camps in these mountains. You're a dead man."

The Cherokee pointing the soldier's semi-automatic rifle smiled.

---

Twanna and Natalie were moving as soon as their cell door opened. The scout was just a teenager.

"You must trust me if you want to stay alive. Don't speak, no noise with your feet, and never lose sight of me."

Every sentry on the north side was bound and gagged. Disappearing into the night the Cherokees had what they came for.

---

Their fire was smoldering. Both knew time was running out.

"Ben, it's no surprise why God has brought you back to your tribe just days before Armageddon. You are a Watchman to your people."

"That would be a blessing, Greg."

From the mouth of the cave, she whispered, "You're already a witness to me old man."

"Teeee!"

Slipping inside the reporter was right behind her.

"Your scouts rescued us from Zion."

Squinting his eyes, "Twanna, is this really Natalie Roberts?"

"Channel 6 her-self, Greg. Nate came for a story."

"More like a war," she wryly replied.

"How is your father, Tee?"

"A martyr for Jesus, Ben."

"I praise God you're still with us."

"Eiland is ready to attack. Where's Cody?"

"The Lord has him on another assignment."

"Has it got to do with the Vineyard?"

"Big time."

"Greg, someone has to warn Ruben."

---

"Where are we going?"

"Shame about the Vineyard," chided Doyle. "You can't tell me God wanted it to go down this way. Of course, if you cooperate maybe you can save some lives."

"I can't help you," yawned Cody.

"You know, son, preparing for something which can affect your future is a good thing, is it not? You have an opportunity to prevent a tragedy. We have no interest in your camp. We have just received a tip Reenie Tucker and Greg Hudson are headed there. You help us catch them and I promise you no one at the Vineyard will be arrested."

"What has this girl done anyway?"

"She assisted her brother in the murder of a Special Forces agent. C'mon, real Christians don't kill people. Tucker must be searching for someone to protect her. Why risk thousands of lives for this killer?"

"Do you really care about these children?" pressured Abernathy. "Try thinking of their safety before you make your decision."

"So if you get Reenie, you promise to leave the Vineyard alone?"

"In a heartbeat."

"What about these boys?"

"Parker and Kurt go free if you give us Tucker."

"But I've never met her."

"Just take us to the leader of the Vineyard."

"Okay, I'll take you. Now release these boys."

"That depends how close the Vineyard is?"

"You'll never find it without my help."

"I'll let one go; take it or leave it."

Regretfully, the young Watchman nodded his head.

"Abe, untie Abbott. I'm sick of looking at him."

The redhead took off running toward a cluster of trees.

"Let's begin with the leader of the Vineyard?"

"His name is Ruben Rodriguez. Do you know him?"

Glancing back with an evil smile, Doyle nodded.

"Oh yeah, Ruben and I go way back."

# THE FEAST OF DEDICATION

*"Now it was the Feast of Dedication in Jerusalem...And Jesus*
*walked in the temple..."*
*John 10:22*

Fadi was amazed as the army jeep drove away. Their trip from the Jordanian border to the Temple Mount was a divine appointment. Aaron was praising the Lord.

"Who were they and why did they help us?"

"Soldiers I served with. So when was the last time you saw...?"

"I've never seen Al-Haram Ash-Sharif."

No one seemed to care as a Jew and an Arab, saved by the blood of Jesus, walked side by side up the Temple Mount. It was a vivid picture of the Father's will in the last days.

"The Temple looks so abandoned," reflected the sad teenager.

"Almost forty-three months since Kayin defiled it."

"Wow, this is where Jesus will rule from."

"Jerusalem will soon be split in three places. After Armageddon, the Lord will rebuild the Temple. 1 Zechariah, Isaiah, and Ezekiel predicted the Shekinah glory will return. Some believe it will be on Hanukkah." 2

"What does Hanukkah represent?"

"Hanukkah means dedication. This holiday was established after the writing of the Old Testament. In 168 B.C., a leader named Epiphanies ordered his army to attack Jerusalem. His goal was to force the Greek language, culture, and religion, upon the Jewish people. He wanted to control the masses by uniting all religions into one."

"Sounds like what Kayin and Pope Michael tried."

"Their mission was a blueprint of Epiphanies' terror. You see Israel is a bridge between Africa, Asia, and Europe. It's always been the critical piece of land needed to control the Middle East. This is why the Lord has promised to dry up the Euphrates's during the sixth bowl judgment. The dry riverbed will be used by armies to make it safely for the great day of God Almighty."

"You mean Armageddon?"

"Yes, the supper of the great God. Forty-five days later, the thousand year reign of Christ will begin on the Feast of Dedication."

The teenager's thoughts were wandering.

"You okay?"

"Thinking of Rafa and Johanna, you think they'll make it alive?"

Changing the subject Aaron tried to encourage his new friend.

"Hey, did you know those written in the Lamb's Book of Life will have the opportunity to enter the gates of the New Jerusalem?" 3

"We get to see Jesus ruling from His glorious throne?"

"Yep, the resurrected martyrs and saints will be with Him."

"Anyone else?"

"The apostles will be ruling from their thrones. Jesus promised, "Assuredly I say to you, that in the regeneration, when the Son of Man sits on the throne of His glory, you who have followed Me will also sit on twelve thrones, judging the twelve tribes of Israel.'" 4

"What about my people? You know, the Gentiles?"

The Watchman smiled; he knew this verse by heart.

"'And everyone who has left houses or brothers or sisters or father or mother or wife or children or lands, for My name's sake, shall receive a hundredfold, and inherit eternal life.'" 5

---

A weary Lenard could sense something wasn't right. Their rest near the waterfall was taking too long. Eli was hiding something.

"What's our next move?"

"Getting here was the easy part. You gotta remember, any one of these caves could lead you nowhere. They did a good job of camouflaging Bethel's exit."

"You can provide information Ruben has no way of knowing. It could mean the difference if Delford attacks. Think of the children."

Keeping a watchful eye, he sheepishly posed, "What makes you think I'm not?"

"I need to say this, Eli. Deep down you never really wanted this assignment. Delford sensed your fear. This is why he picked you. Demons gained a stronghold in his life when he was young. Through the years he gradually surrendered to these deceiving spirits. Everyone following Eiland's lies is being seduced."

"Not me!"

"When you saw how real these Christians are the struggle for your loyalty began. You must have had some doubts. Maybe it was during one of their Bible studies. Perhaps you became friends with a staff member. Personally, I think it was the faces of the children. Maybe the ones who lost their parents, are your folks still alive?"

"Don't go there, Lenard."

"I had to repent of my connection with this cult too. Even though I didn't believe Eiland; I was still part of his racist agenda. Instead of trusting God to protect me I turned to man."

"So when did you reach this enlightenment?"

"Reenie helped me see the truth about myself."

"Is this the same girl trying to find the Vineyard?"

"Yeah, the same camp I saw in my vision."

"Then why did you run away from her? If this is a God thing then why are you making it so hard? I'm not afraid to die, are you?"

"I was the first to tell my friends at the White House who Joshua Kayin really was. After I got away some were arrested. Seeing it go down on TV was hard."

"Why are you wavering now?"

"I admit Satan got to me when I left Reenie. I've asked for forgiveness. God has granted me another opportunity."

An hour later, after searching the openings of four more caves, Eli motioned for Lenard to look downstream.

"What's up?"

"You see the trees on the right? They're rare in these mountains. I remember stepping on needles from these trees just before the guards from the Vineyard released me."

"You mean Bethel's exit is near here?"

"If I'm not mistaken, the exit is right over there."

Lenard followed his eyes to a small ravine.

"You might have to do some digging. No more than a foot. It's a security precaution."

"Why not join me, Eli? The Lord will be with us."

"I've done enough damage. My return would only divide.

Remember, the fulfillment of your vision is in God's hands."

As the RV slowed the driver softly began praising the Lord.

"Have something for us, Jon?"

"Jake, you see the stream between those spruce trees? This is the beginning of the trail of tears."

"So this is Black Rock Mountain?"

"You guys made it, Reenie!" hollered a relived Donnell.

Lasting only a few moments there was an edge to their silence.

"Q Squad, this is where Donnie and I say goodbye."

"No way, not now!" insisted Jake.

"Just follow this stream up the mountain. A Vineyard sentry will bring you into the camp."

"What about Reenie's mission?" beseeched Emma.

"Have you forgotten I'm Jewish and Donnell is Black? Lenard Mayer is convinced a race war is imminent. We have no desire to add fuel to a fire. The Holy Spirit will lead you."

Pulling out his mini calendar from his jacket Jake announced, "Right now we are at 1286 days. Just four days left. Are you planning any more rescues?"

"Always up for one more," laughed Donnell.

"We can't thank you enough," confessed a choked up Reenie.

"It's all Jesus!" praised Jon.

After a big group hug it only took a few seconds for the old Winnebago to disappear.

Their eyes never left the threesome. Trailing at a safe distance the two boys hardly made a sound. For Osiris, the lord of the dead, the stalking was as exciting as the kill.

The two soldiers knew they were being watched. Yet helping their commander find his daughter was a risk they just had to take.

"C'mon, Fadi, this is way too dangerous. We gotta get out of here. Most have registered. Those who refused were forced to go AWOL."

"Did your soldiers say anything?"

"One spotted Johanna near the Wailing Wall a few hours ago."

"Was Rafa with her?"
"I'm sorry, she was alone."

---

"Ruben, this is big time trouble. There are hundreds living on this mountain. Most are armed. It won't be long before someone penetrates our inner perimeter."

He was actually surprised they had lasted this long.

"We will review each intrusion on a case by case evaluation. Alert our sentries. It's their call if fired upon. Is there anything else?"

"Three teenagers are following the stream."

"Where are they?"

"In the area we released Eli."

"We can't afford to let them expose our camp. You'll have to bring them in before they reach our wells."

---

Turning the corner she remembered the stone cobbled street where she first saw the Messiah. So much had changed in three weeks. Weaving around a crowd of people bartering for clean water an excited Johanna reached her destination. Standing on the sidewalk she frantically scanned both sides of the street.

"Lord, I don't get this? The old man said someone would be waiting for me. What now?"

Some children crossing the street were begging for food. Johanna wished she had something to give them. Her stomach was growling too. She hadn't eaten in three days.

The tallest child hesitated. Motioning toward Johanna she removed her shawl from her face.

"Is it true you live near Disneyworld?"

A stunned Johanna was speechless.

"Ruth, is it really you?"

# SIXTH BOWL: KINGS FROM THE EAST

"Then the sixth angel poured out his bowl on the great river
Euphrates, and its water was dried up, so that the way of the kings from
the east might be prepared."
Revelations 16:12

Walking through the huge campsite they waved to the inquisitive
children. The sentries escorting them looked nervous. His senior staff
was waiting under lit torches just inside Beulah. After everyone
introduced themselves all eyes were on a troubled Ruben Rodriguez.

"Jake, Emma, Reenie, we praise God you made it here safely. It
took courage for you to find us. Have you seen, Greg Hudson?"

"I was the last one to see him. We separated in Dahlonega. He
decided the best way to protect me was to follow at a distance."

"So Greg is following you?"

"I doubt if he is now."

"Reenie, can you share your mission with us?"

The one they affectionately call the Miracle Girl methodically laid
it out, the agents' assault upon the Q, her getaway with Greg, her
vision of children under attack, and finally the description of the tall
stranger.

"I'm curious about this stranger?"

"His name is Lenard Mayer. He's in his fifties. Has blond hair and
blue eyes. He was once a member of the White House Staff. I met
him at Maggie's when I found out my contact was dead. He was trying
to warn you of a future attack from the Prophetic Voice."

"How did he obtain such information?"

"Lenard joined the Prophetic Voice in exchange for protection
from the NWC. He became a member of Eiland's inner circle. Their

planned attack of the Vineyard was too much like the vision he had as a boy. So he left. We both believe our visions are the same."

"Where is he now?"

"I don't know. He left when Jake found me. I guess he didn't feel safe getting others involved. Lenard is convinced the Vineyard will be attacked before Armageddon. We must act before it is too late."

"What do you suggest?"

"This is a big risk for Eiland. Let's offer him food to call it off."

"No, he can't be trusted!"

"But his soldiers are so brainwashed. Once it begins they will show no mercy. In my vision this massacre doesn't have to happen. If you could just talk with Lenard, he could make you understand."

"We already have," smiled the commander.

Poking his face inside the mouth of the tunnel he winked.

"Morning, Reenie."

"Lenard, we made it!"

"Yeah," he smiled, "just like in our vision."

---

The angel stood beside the Euphrates. Looking heavenward it knew the will of the Father. The sixth bowl emptied out quickly. The enormous river was subsiding. 1 Within the hour this dried up riverbed will be overflowing with soldiers coming from the East.

---

He was just a shell of what he used to be. Crouched behind his desk the bewildered producer felt content sipping stale coffee. The urgent knocking on his open door meant nothing to him.

"You nailed it, Wes!" yelled his assistant. "No one knows who did it, could be Muslim terrorists. Some say..."

"Try giving it to me in plain English."

"The Euphrates River is drying up like an old prune."

"So where's the water going?"

"Talk to Joel Friedman. He's got it on tape."

"Please answer my question."

"Wes, you predicted Israel would be attacked this year. Let's jump on this story. Soldiers are using it to surround Israel."

"No one is damming up the Euphrates."

"I'm not following you."

"Natalie was right about these bowl judgments. You hear about her ransom note? A white supremacy cult snagged her."

"How much are they asking for?"

"Their leader probably needs food and water for his people. So what does our girl do? She waltzes into his camp like a bright neon sign saying grab me. Nate knows we can't help her."

"I'm sorry, boss, you two go back a long way. Wasn't her first break in broadcasting because of you?"

"She would've made it to the top without my help. By the way, what's the feature for tonight's show?"

"Kayin is assembling the largest army ever..."

In mock laughter, the popular editor bellowed, "God Almighty is moving us around like pawns on a chessboard. We lost our power to broadcast an hour ago. I'm going home to my family; so should you."

---

Nestled under the small bridge the make shift cardboard shelter could sleep two. Crouched inside both girls were praying.

"Lord, seeing Johanna again is a miracle. I glorify You with all my heart. May the Holy Spirit lead us as we work together as a team."

Raising her hands the tall brunette bowed her head.

"Father, You are still drawing souls to Your Son. You can speak a word no man can. 2 You can arrange circumstances in the blink of an eye. No matter what we have to sacrifice help us not to fear. We only desire Your perfect will." 3

So many things were on her mind.

"Johanna, obeying the Holy Spirit can be painful at times, can't it?

Her question seemed so out of place.

"Ruth, remember my good friend, Jake Jamison?"

"Yes, he resisted with you against the NWC."

"Jake wants God's will; it doesn't matter how much it hurts. It was actually your folks who taught me obedience is better than sacrifice."

"But we weren't even saved when we met after the fifth trumpet. At first, my parents were kinda jealous. 4 We knew other Christians who loved our people, kept the feasts, studied the Torah, and even believed in the promises given to Abraham. Then God sent you and you taught us when Yeshua would physically return on Yom Kippur. 5

Five days later, during the Feast of Tabernacles, He gathered His remnant atop Mount Zion. You convinced my parents a remnant from Israel would be spiritually saved for all eternity." 6

"Ruth, you're a reflection of their example. You learned by watching their actions; observing how their convictions were tested. You have lived out precious truths which cost them a lot to learn. They even sacrificed themselves so we could get away."

"So my parent's sacrifice wasn't wasted?"

"Ruth, we're standing on their shoulders. Their sacrifice for us wasn't a burden for them; it was a joy."

"Are you sure?"

"Have you heard anything?"

The next hour seemed like minutes. Each testified how God used them in rescue. Their divine appointments were far more precious than things. Most understood the end was near. For overcomers this wasn't the time to hold back.

"So your vision about my parents came true, Ruth. God used you to bring us together."

"How exciting! Have you heard about the Euphrates?"

"Yes, armies from around the world must be using it by now. Were you ever burned?"

"Never! The Lord protected me. But I'm not so sure about the next bowl? Do you think this bridge is strong enough to withstand the hailstones from the seventh bowl?"

"Not a chance. Everything will be leveled. If we hope to survive we've got to find a hiding place underground."

"What about your Daddy's militia compound? Don't they use underground bunkers?"

"Out of the mouth of babes," praised Johanna. "I remember at least two abandoned bunkers in the Judean hills we could hide in. It could be dangerous. My father revealed military information to the Jordanians in order to save lives. Both sides consider him a traitor."

Sliding over to a dirty pile of clothes, a determined Ruth grabbed her favorite sweater and leather jacket. After rechecking her backpack she announced she was ready to go.

"Ruth, I'm still up for one more rescue before our Lord returns."

"Really, where are they hiding?"

"Don't know."

"Are they in trouble?"

"Probably."

"Are these friends of yours?"

"More like family," grinned Johanna.

With her mouth wide open Ruth reached over for a huge hug.

"Is the Lord really leading you to help me find my parents?"

———

"You have no clue who did it...What direction did they escape...How is it possible not one soldier was hurt...What is happening to your unit...I want to move up our attack date...The Vineyard consists mainly of unarmed children...Then why are you afraid...?"

Slamming the phone down, Delford Eiland couldn't believe what he was hearing. The buzzer from under his office desk was timely. The soldier looked uneasy as he walked in and sat down.

"So what does Eli want now?"

"He left the Vineyard. It was the last item on his check list."

"This isn't how I planned it. I want no more screw ups. Does everyone realize what is expected? This assignment encapsulates everything we stand for. How are our supplies?"

"We have enough food for two more days."

"What about Roberts' ransom note?"

"They never replied."

"We have our answer. There will be no witnesses. Those who can't stomach the blood have twenty-four hours to get out."

"Where can they go? Most have cut their ties with the outside world."

"Everyone knew what they were getting into when they joined. The burden I'm getting from the Lord is powerful. Assemble the troops; they need to hear this from me personally. "

From just inside his office door, another soldier reported, "Sir, Eli is here to see you."

The brash soldier appeared confident as he strolled in.

"Eli, you weren't to leave the Vineyard until we arrived?"

"Lenard exposed my identity. He betrayed our family."

"He's more of a fool than I thought."

"They blindfolded me and took me out of one of their tunnels. I guess they thought I would never survive. Some kids found me. They helped me regain my strength."

"Evers spilled her guts in Zion the first time we beat her father.

We know all about Beulah and Bethel. Moving in and sealing off both exits will be a piece of cake."

"Funny, I didn't see any prisoners at Zion?"

"It was a real screw up. Someone invaded Zion the other night and helped Evers and Natalie Roberts escape."

"You mean the famous news anchor from Chicago?"

"Yeah, she was nosing around Zion so I had to bring her in. No doubt whoever rescued her will be paid a pretty penny. Do you think Evers could lead Roberts back to the Vineyard?"

"Naw, she would never take such a risk."

"So what is Rodriguez planning?"

"He's in a quandary. The tunnels aren't ready. Besides, there are just too many kids. If he does evacuate where will they hide them?"

"This is how you know we are in God's will."

"What do you mean, Sir?"

"When I first learned about the Vineyard the Spirit showed me a passage in Deuteronomy. The next day I received a prophetic word. Our intercessors got the same word a week later. Everything is falling into place. I call it confirming circumstances. Clearly, God is going before us. I believe it's time we make our move."

# THREE UNCLEAN SPIRITS

*"And I saw three unclean spirits like frogs coming out of the mouth of the dragon, out of the mouth of the beast, and out of the mouth of the false prophet."*
Revelation 16:13

Subconsciously, Greg and Twanna were preparing for the worst. Rushing toward his RV Ben looked tired.

"I just talked with the Council. Eiland has ordered an attack on the Vineyard. Thirty families have already defected. You better hurry, you must warn Ruben."

"Are you coming with us?"

"Tee, you came to these mountains out of love for your father. You walked through the fire with the Lord by your side. Your sacrifice has rekindled my love for my people."

"Don't forget you walked with me."

"We call you the Black Dove. You had the power to fly away from trouble yet you remain. Even now you're returning to the fire."

"What's ahead for you, Ben?"

"Natalie, there is a cave in the side of this mountain where the Cherokees have hidden food and water. Chief Ostenaco has invited every family to attend. The Lord has given me an opportunity to share the gospel with the entire tribe."

"Our Lord is faithful!" praised Twanna.

"I'll never forget you guys."

Shaking hands his new friend Greg lovingly predicted, "Running Bear, our rescues are never in vain. For you, God has saved the biggest rescue for the very end. 1 The final chapter of your tribe will be written in the Lamb's Book of Life." 2

Cautiously entering the beautiful garden, the limbs of the tree were weighed down with fruit. The symbolism was evident. This tree was personally picked by the dragon.

"So," howled Satan, "have you seen the Euphrates River?"

The Beast and his False Prophet nodded meekly.

"Are you aware the Euphrates once passed below the Garden of Eden? 3 Most never knew the tree of good and evil was originally atop Mount Moriah!"

Circling his two pawns the father of lies wasn't happy.

"I can sense the One from Above is playing with your minds. Trust me; the judgment from the sixth bowl won't hurt a soul. The Euphrates has dried up. The stage is set. Zion is the apple of His eye. The time to attack is now."

The dragon bayed as two unclean spirits crawled out of the mouths of the two beasts. The regurgitation of the frog-like spirit from the devil's mouth was even more repulsive.

"I command you to bring forth the armies of this earth to Armageddon for the great day of God Almighty!"

"The Word of God will be defeated!" bragged the Beast.

"It shall come to pass as we envision!" confirmed his prophet.

The experienced soldier didn't need to be told. He knew the difference between training exercises and real war. The heightened alert, the massing of troops along Israel's border, the heavy artillery being rechecked, someone had given the order.

Fadi could see the pain on Aaron's face as more soldiers marched by. Their sheer contempt was hard to accept. The Jordanian teenager could relate. The prophesied demise of his people never went away. Since becoming a believer, everything he had trusted in, fought for, held close to his heart, was being exposed. He too was an outcast.

"What's happening to me, Aaron? Why do I feel so lonely?"

"It's all coming to an end, my brother. The prophet Daniel foretold, 'Many shall be purified, made white, and refined, but the wicked shall do wickedly; and none of the wicked shall understand, but the wise shall understand.'" 4

"What is the Holy Spirit saying to you?"

"Look at them. They see but they don't understand. This is the work of demons. I remember seeing a puppet show when I was a child. I asked my mother how the puppets moved. She said there were tiny strings attached to them controlled by people. I refused to believe her. I finally understood after she took me backstage."

"So Armageddon is Satan's final puppet show?"

"God allows each soul free will. His wrath against the wicked will end at the supper of the great God. Later, on the first day of Christ's reign over the nations Satan will be bound in the bottomless pit. His last stand will come a thousand years later. 5 This is why the Devil will be released." 6

"But why let him out again?"

"The Lord promises to restore this earth after Armageddon. During the millennial reign of Christ, Satan will be bound. Fadi, our greatest scientists taught man is merely a product of his environment. A better environment is supposed to counteract the problem of sin. But even after living a thousand years in a Garden of Eden atmosphere mankind will still reject God's love because of their sinful desires. Their deception will be the result of their own carnal choosing."

"I don't get this? Jesus will be ruling from Jerusalem! Won't they be able to see Him?"

"Only the saved will be able to enter into the New Jerusalem. After the thousand years is up Satan will be allowed to deceive the nations. He will gather them like the sand of the sea."

"Is this before Satan is cast into the lake of fire?"

"Yes, God will first devour by fire those who follow the Devil." 7

"Aaron, how exactly does the Holy Spirit give you these verses? This morning a passage just popped into my mind. How can I know this is from God and not my own imagination?"

"You need to test it. Let's hear it?"

"'...The Watchman said, "The morning comes, and also the night. If you will inquire...return. Come back."'" 8

"Awesome! What's the first thing you thought after receiving it?"

Turning away the young man blurted out, "I felt like returning home. No matter what I do; this desire refuses to go away."

"Fadi, I will always cherish the time watching the Lord transform your life. It's been such a special blessing. God is giving you another chance to witness to your father. Don't worry. The Lord will protect Rafa and Johanna. Your calling is to be a faithful Watchman."

"Are we splitting up? I don't know if I can face my people again?"

"You have nothing to be ashamed of. Your love has touched the feet of your enemies. Jesus wants us to love those persecuting us."

"This is so strange. All my life I hated Jews. The painful trials my father had only made my anger grow stronger. I wanted to hate. But when I believed in Jesus it left. I can now forgive because Jesus has forgiven me. Changing is all about His love, isn't it, Aaron?"

The staff's discussion lasted all night. There was still no consensus. A light snow was falling on the trees outside the entrances of both caves. Reenie and Lenard were gathering wood. He could only laugh after she mischievously threw a snowball just over his head.

"So are you getting any new revelations?"

The faces in their vision now had names. It was slowly becoming a torment of what could happen.

"Lenny, if all Christians have the Holy Spirit then why all the arguing?"

He didn't have an answer.

"Reenie, I thought our visions were identical?"

"Pretty close."

"But you told Ruben the Lord expanded your vision. You said the attack on the children doesn't have to happen?"

"I saw children running up a ravine. As they reached the top it split in two like a giant fork. There were two ways to go."

"I never saw a fork. When did you first receive your mission?"

"Does it matter?" she defensively replied.

Her eyes weren't right. He could sense her agitation.

"It could."

"This Eli must be a smooth operator?"

"He's had enough."

"So what is this Eiland dude really like?"

"His specialty is preying upon weakness. He saw Eli's potential way before he gained control of him."

"You mean the potential to deceive?"

"Yes, he personally groomed Eli for this assignment."

"Did he also handpick you?"

"He tried."

The wrinkles under her eyes looked permanent. He knew she had been through a lot. It was times like this he wished he could just walk away. Tragically many already had. 9

"Lenny, one more time, you tell me your vision; I'll tell you mine."

He loved her youthful innocence.

"I think I was ten years old. The Sunday morning service had just concluded. I was on my knees praying at an old wooden altar. It didn't seem supernatural at the time. In my mind I saw pictures of children playing together. Then it began. Many started dropping to the ground. I couldn't hear anything but somehow I knew they were screaming. I could feel their pain. They needed help. I cried out to the Lord to send me. It didn't matter how much I prayed the fear on their faces never left."

"Who did you share this with?"

"Only my mother would listen. We used to talk about it, especially when I was in high school. I told her about you being in my vision."

"Are you sure it was me?"

"When I saw you at Maggie's it took my breath away."

Pulling her hair up, she teased, "How's this look? I was planning this doo for my senior prom?"

She immediately thought of Bret and how he could always find ways to make her laugh.

"In my vision the children are following us."

"For how long?"

"We leave them before my vision ends."

"Why?"

Shrugging his shoulders, he replied, "Your turn."

Looking away she remembered it like it was yesterday.

"After the sixth trumpet sounded a close friend named Bret rushed me to the Gulf Shores Emergency Room. I somehow lost consciousness. Satan tried to take my life by sending a Special Forces agent to execute me. At the same time agents arrived to arrest me. So what does our Lord do? He sends an angel to my bedside. This messenger explained my mission. It's all about saving lives the enemy is targeting. The kicker is those closest to me will have to suffer. All I know is if I hadn't obeyed the angel and escaped out the window of my room I wouldn't be here today."

"I can relate. My friends at the White House who helped me escape paid a heavy price. Most never understood the warfare involved."

"Yeah, I thank the Lord for the Q Squad. Greg, Jake, Emma and Kurt all helped me piece it together just hours before Jesus split the Mount of Olives."

"His perfect timing, huh?"

"A moment to remember, the Lord even laid Bret's favorite passage on my heart, 'To them God willed to make known what are the riches of the glory of this mystery among the Gentiles: which is Christ in you, the hope of glory. Him we preach, warning every man and teaching every man in all wisdom, that we may present every man perfect in Christ Jesus. To this end I also labor, striving according to His working which works in me mightily.'" 10

"The hope of glory! So when does our mission end?"

"Just before the Word appears at the supper of the great God, Armageddon."

"So what is God telling you to do right now?"

"Ruben wants to try..."

"Forget about him. What about the fork you saw?"

"I saw it just after I met you. The focus of our mission became clear when I realized how many lives could be saved for eternity. I believe the Lord will provide a way of escape for the children if we obey Him. This is the opposite of your vision. Your vision is torture because you believe there is no way to prevent it."

"So you think we can stop the attack on the Vineyard?"

"Why do we suddenly disappear in your vision? It must be because we leave for Eiland's camp. This is why the Lord had you scope out this cult. Isn't it obvious?"

"Not to me."

"You know all about Zion. No one else can avert what Satan is planning for these children. I thought you said you wanted to know what God was showing me."

"That's what I've been praying for."

"And....?"

"Now I know why God picked you for this mission."

## THE TIMES OF RESTORATION

*"And that He may send Jesus Christ, who was preached to you before, whom heaven must receive until the times of restoration of all things."*
Acts 3:20

"Are you sure?" questioned an anxious Ruben.

"It was Cody. We talked for a moment before two agents moved in. They may be blackmailing him. He looked scared. Maybe he's just lost it."

"Did they say anything about Twanna?"

"No, they want to know if Reenie is in our camp. They want to exchange Cody for her. They'll kill him if we don't surrender her."

"Who are they?"

"The one in charge calls himself Doyle Mercer."

The sentry couldn't miss his wince.

"Do you know this Mercer?"

"We were once partners on the Atlanta police force. Doyle was a good detective until he nearly beat a teenager to death. No one knows what set him off. After I turned him in he was thrown off the force. He's a scary man. Doyle means what he says."

"What now, Ruben?"

"Let's talk with Reenie. We'll make the exchange if she's willing. Sounds cruel but this could buy us more time. Bring her in."

Minutes later the young man returned out of breath.

"Reenie and Lenard are gone. No sign of Jake or Emma either."

"I know where they're going."

"Do you want me to go after them?"

"Not enough time. Greg was always right about the end. He once told me, 'When the attack of the enemy looks so massive, just remember, the darkest hour is just before dawn.'"

Their frantic pleas were heartbreaking. Millions were desperately trusting in the pagan deity of Islam to deliver them. Instead the wrath from the God of Abraham, Isaac, and Jacob was demolishing the earth. Tragically the vast majority in the world never was able to come to the knowledge of the truth. 1

The Jordanian base was within shouting distance. Aaron's heartfelt goodbye had energized the teenager in a profound way. His friends milling around the corner street were shocked to see him.

"Well, well, the traitor is coming home," laughed one of the boys. "Fadi, you and your ugly sister have really made your father proud."

"Have any of you seen, Rafa?"

"Her burial service was yesterday. Heard the rumor you've become a Christian too."

"Why do you want to know?"

"I just want to hear you say it."

"Yes, Jesus is my Savior. Rafa and I have been forgiven of our sins and have received the indwelling of the Holy Spirit. While this world suffers God's wrath we have been blessed with His love."

"You sound like a cursed infidel!"

From behind another boy spat on his shoes.

The new convert could hear their laughter as he walked away. The flashback in his mind was word for word.

"Fadi, I will commit to pray for you until the first day of the Christ's thousand year reign over the nations. This is also the beginning of the Feast of Dedication. Let's try and find each other."

"You're not only my brother in Christ but you've become my spiritual father. I thank God for you, Aaron Glazer."

"And you're the son I always wanted. Remember, your friends might attack you if they get an opportunity. You need to be extra careful."

"Aaron, I have no desire to be a martyr. If my return means the salvation of my father; may God's will be done. As for my friends they were never an idol in my life. Whatever is lost because of my testimony means nothing to me. I'm a new creation in Christ."

"Just be discerning my brother. Their reaction to the day of the Lord will result in the most horrific blasphemy ever witnessed."

The soccer field was up ahead. So much had changed. The silence under the bleachers somehow seemed eerie. It was like the wrath of God was speeding up time. Pictures of what could have been kept coming in his mind. His head down, he could barely hear her voice.

"Fadi, Fadi," she yelled before breaking into a sprint.

Their joyful embrace felt so good.

"How long have you been here?"

"Jordanian soldiers arrested me at the border just after Jo passed over into Israel. Later, father interrogated me. It was a nightmare. Satan has a real foothold in his spirit."

"Rafa, I've come back to witness to him."

"Something evil is eating him up inside."

"Remember the conviction we felt when we first heard Johanna's testimony? I know the Lord can do the same for father."

"Are you sure?"

"God doesn't desire anyone should perish.

"Did you hear about my funeral service?"

"Yeah, Satan must have loved that."

"So what's your plan?"

"There's got to be a key to unlock his bitterness. God sees it. If we seek the mind of Christ we can see it too."

"How's Aaron?"

"We saw thousands of our people saved. I left him in Jerusalem. His love for the lost is so contagious. What about Johanna?"

"Her new nickname is relentless! There was just one divine appointment after another. At times I had to beg for a break. To see so many believing in the resurrection of Jesus was so miraculous."

"Glory to God, Rafa, we're running the race so others can receive an imperishable crown!"

Greg drove while Twanna quietly prayed in the Spirit. Black Rock Mountain was just minutes away. The animated reporter sat erect in the backseat firing one question after another.

"Greg, why were the Witnesses raised the day before the Feast of Tabernacles, you said something about a fourth day?"

"Natalie, Jesus saved a believing remnant from Israel by the third day. The next day Jesus raised the two Witnesses from the dead. I wouldn't underestimate this miracle the whole world was watching."

"So God will restore this earth after He burns it up?"

"The prophets saw it."

"Name one?"

"The apostle Peter called it the restoration of all things, 'Repent therefore and be converted, that your sins may be blotted out, so that times of refreshing may come from the presence of the Lord, and that He may send Jesus Christ, who was preached to you before, whom heaven must receive until the times of restoration of all things, which God has spoken by the mouth of all His holy prophets since the world began.'" 2

"So God was controlling all these events?"

"All the way until He rules from Jerusalem!" beamed Twanna.

Leaning back against the headrest the reporter looked so confused.

"You mean the physical return of the Messiah, the redeemed remnant following Him to Jerusalem, the two Witnesses coming alive, the splitting of the Mount of Olives; these all were predicted by prophets thousands of years ago?"

"The timing of these events is in His Word."

"Greg, can the Devil prevent God's will?"

"The Lord has raised up many Watchmen. These men, women, and children, refused to remain silent. The message of the last day was sent forth by the anointing of God. No demon can stop it!"

"Are you referring to the second coming of Christ?"

Her desperation was painful to listen to. Pausing he just nodded.

"In my senior year in high school a close girlfriend of mine became a Christian. The overnight change in her was amazing. She told me how Jesus forgave her of her sins."

"Did it make any sense?"

"Not at the time. A voice kept telling me her faith was a crutch."

"And now?"

"Oh, I've seen a lot of crazy scenarios in my time as a broadcaster. But nothing like the past two years. The deception by Kayin had Satan's fingerprints all over it."

"In the end it was for those who had ears to hear."

Bowing her head, the once confident journalist was still trying to figure out the end time events she saw and how they fit together.

"Greg, could you explain second coming to me? I'd really like to understand His coming before this all ends."

As Twanna interceded the former pastor laid out the events.

"His second coming began after Jesus opened the sixth seal on the heavenly scroll in heaven. This was the night the sun, moon, and stars, lost their light. The days of the Great Tribulation by the Beast, Satan's wrath against the saints, was cut short when angels gathered His elect."

"You mean the night the fires began?"

"Yes, the first trumpet sounded thirty minutes after Jesus opened the seventh seal of the heavenly scroll. Five more trumpets were blown which completed the 70th week of Daniel. The Messiah returned the same day the Beast killed the two Witnesses."

"Is this when Jesus physically returned a second time?"

"That's right. The Holy One returned to earth on the Day of Atonement between the sixth and seventh trumpets. His return is highlighted in Revelation 10:1-7. This was the fulfillment of an Old Testament prophecy concerning the return of the Messiah for the salvation of Israel. The angel Gabriel revealed to Daniel the Messiah would return and forgive Israel of her sins after the 70th week is over."

"What about Jesus returning at Armageddon?"

"This is a different event. The Word of God will appear in heaven, not on earth, during the supper of the great God."

"When will this take place?"

"After hailstones from the seventh bowl are poured out."

"So when does His second coming end?"

"When the Lamb of God descends to a new earth inside the Holy Jerusalem, this event concludes His second coming."

"Then why didn't..."

"It's called free will, Natalie. God never created programmed robots in His image. Everyone had a choice to love God."

At first her silence felt awkward. Yet her heart was wide open.

"God even used children as Watchmen, didn't He?"

"During the future marriage supper of the Lamb, those He used will be honored. This will include all the children that were martyred."

"So how will Armageddon affect America?"

Slowing down Greg looked distracted. Twanna finally spoke.

"Armageddon is the last event of the day of the Lord. All having the mark of the Beast will be killed by the rider of the white horse."

"So who will clean up the dead bodies?"

"Excuse me. I suggest you..."

"It's okay, Tee," interrupted Greg, "I'll answer it. Natalie, even though Jesus promises to restore the earth He is going to purposely leave behind explicit remains from the judgment of man. Ezekiel foresaw dead bodies unburied after seven months. [3] Several countries will still be burning. It will be a sobering reminder of God's justice."

"But thou shall not kill!" snapped the astute reporter. "How can God violate one of His own commandments?"

Twanna knew what had to be done. Too many lives were at stake. She was praying for Greg to make the call. Stopping on the shoulder of the road he cut the engine.

"Natalie, we know you came here because you love children. Your return to Dahlonega saved Tee's life. We thank you for your sacrifice. Black Rock Mountain is a mile away. We have to let you out now. No one having the mark is ever allowed inside the camp."

"I understand your rules but I can help. If Delford orders the attack you can use me as a bargaining chip. He knows my value. I've talked with him. I know how his mind works. Let me come with you."

His hesitation seemed odd. The founder of the Vineyard was questioning the very rule he once implemented. After receiving a reassuring nod from Twanna he restarted the engine.

At first Johanna didn't recognize the ransacked law office.

"Agents arrested my parents across the street. The resistance told me all about it."

"How did you find them?"

"Let me show you."

They walked almost four blocks before stopping at an empty garage. Circling around back they entered a side door.

"It's safe, Jo, they have helped me before."

"Who has?"

Stepping down into the basement they could hear their muffled voices.

"It's the Lentz girl again. She shouldn't be here."

"Ruth, do you know what time it is?" griped the other soldier. "You should be underground by now."

"Then why are you still here?"

"We won't be for long. One more exchange and we are heading for the Judean hills. That's where you should be."

"This is my friend Johanna. She knows my..."

"We have no news on your parents. Now you must go. And make sure no one sees you leaving."

From a dark corner a deep voice asked, "Ruth, do you believe in the judgments in The Revelation of Jesus Christ?"

"Yes, right now God's wrath is destroying this earth."

"What happens when His wrath ends?"

"The Holy Jerusalem will descend."

"Why believe in such fairy tales? This city is symbolic. That's all."

"John saw a lot more than that."

"So, little one, when we will see this city?"

"After heaven and earth are burned up during the day of the Lord, then a new heaven will hover over a new earth."

"What for?"

"The bride will live inside the Holy City for eternity."

"These are symbols not literal truths."

"How do you know the difference?" challenged Johanna.

"When it makes sense, a city coming from heaven is ridiculous!"

"Then why did John use such physical details?"

"Do you deny he used figurative language?"

"At times he did. Yet his literal description of the Holy Jerusalem was on purpose so the reader could understand."

"Give me one example this city is physical and not symbolic?"

"I'll give you three. John described a foursquare city fifteen hundred miles long. The names of the twelve apostles will be written on the foundations of this city and the names of the twelve tribes of Israel on the twelve pearl gates."

"Why would God do something so insane?" mocked the hostage.

"God Almighty did it to show His unbreakable covenant with Abraham and His chosen people."

"What did you say?"

"You heard me."

"How can you be so blind? Over four million Jews have died. As we speak armies are surrounding Palestine. In a couple of days Jews will be just a memory. Who are you anyway?"

"I'm a Jew who loves God! A Jew believing Israel will never be destroyed by her enemies! A Jew believing Yeshua is the Messiah! That's right; I'm a Jew waiting for the creation of a new heaven and a new earth by the King of Kings and Lord of Lords!"

"You have no idea..."

"Lay off the girls, Abdullah! They're not part of the agreement."

"Then get rid of them."

"Tell us what you believe, Abdullah?"

"Does it matter, Ruth?"

"It will determine where you will spend eternity."

"If you remove my blindfold then I will share with you the coming of Al Mahdi, the guided one. The holy prophet Muhammad spoke of his return before judgment day. May Allah be praised."

Both Ruth and Johanna were silently praying as one of the soldiers reluctantly got up and removed his blindfold.

"Five minutes, Abdullah, that's about all I can take."

"Muhammad prophesied believers would be severely persecuted by infidels in these last days. In the past decade, the oppression of Muslims has spread around the world. It's no secret the Prime Minister of Israel convinced the American President to hunt down and kill so called radical Muslim terrorists. This only unified us against our oppressors. Soon Al Mahdi will spread justice for all. He will lead us in a prayer from Mecca."

Johanna couldn't help but ask, "Do you believe Jesus was a Jew?"

"No, the son of Mary was a Muslim."

"But Mary was from the tribe of Judah..."

"Al Mahdi will rise from the family of the Prophet Muhammad; descendants from Fatima. A voice from heaven will announce his mission. He will offer refuge for those seduced by polytheism."

"How will you know when Al Mahdi arrives?"

"Yawm al-Qiyamah, the destruction of all things, is near."

"In a few days the greatest earthquake ever will be unleashed." [4]

"Stop such utter folly!" he cursed under his breath. "May your own words be your judge."

"Why are you here? Where is your family?"

"Ruth, Zionists murdered my wife and children. The only reason I'm alive is because I'm being held as a hostage."

"That's enough, Abdullah!" insisted one of the soldiers. "Please girls you have to go now."

Looking the Muslim terrorist squarely in the eyes, Ruth calmly shared, "My parents are Judah and Hanna Lentz. They were arrested by the NWC for not registering. The last time I saw them..."

"Don't you even know?" he snickered. "I'm the hostage they're offering for your parents."

"I'm sorry, Ruth, no one can know about this exchange."

"And what about your friend's family?" sneered the hostage.

"My father is a Watchman for the Lord. He is sharing the gospel with anyone having ears to hear, whether Jew or Muslim."

"What is his name?"

"Aaron Glazer."

"You lie. Matthias is dead. Besides, he was never a Christian."

"Time is up," announced the other soldier.

"I'm making a change!" demanded the rejuvenated hostage.

"You're in no position to offer..."

"Listen to me! These girls must accompany me or no swap!"

## AN APPOINTED TIME

*"For the vision is yet for an appointed time; But at the end it will speak, and it will not lie. Though it tarries, wait for it; because it will surely come..."*
*Habakkuk 2:3*

The lone gunshot echoed through the ravine where they were hiding. Even those stationed inside the tunnels could hear it. The sentry reporting in could barely speak.

"Ruben, they refused to wait. Cody is with the Lord."

"How could this have happened?"

"Mercer is now asking for Greg Hudson. If we don't turn him over they're going to kill a boy named Parker."

"Doyle must know we don't have Greg. It's me he wants."

"What good is it giving your-self up? You know how evil he is. He'll never stop killing!"

"I was the one who sent Cody to find Twanna. Deep down, I knew he was in way over his head. I sent him to his death and now the camp is in danger. Get me a rifle."

"What for?"

"Someone should have done this a long time ago. I'm going to put this animal away."

"Let's wait until dark, Ruben, maybe we can rush them."

"And watch Parker die? This is my call. Doyle has to be stopped."

In stunned silence no one even blinked as the threesome entered.

"Maybe we can help."

Instantly they were engulfed with ecstatic staff members.

He sensed Ruben's guilt. Cody Parrish was also dear to his heart.

"Good to see ya, Greg. Twanna, we praise the Lord for bringing you back. Is your father...?"

"He remained faithful, Ruben. A soldier from the Prophetic Voice killed him. In the end he was an overcomer. He didn't fear those who could just kill his body." 1

"Our Lord is faithful," encouraged Greg. "You're facing a two front attack. Doyle Mercer on one side and the Prophetic Voice on the other. Sounds like the devil."

"Are Bethel and Beulah operational?"

"Yes, Twanna, we are prepared to evacuate."

"Do you have any idea when this cult will attack?"

"Originally we thought the same day the armies of the Beast invade Armageddon. But it could happen any time now."

The loud whispering among his staff was so out of place. It was easy to see why.

"Now this is quite a surprise; News Anchor Natalie Roberts from Channel 6. Staff, I need five minutes."

Sitting on benches around the fire Ruben poured each guest a cup of hot coffee.

"Ms. Roberts, I have no idea how you got involved in this conflict. Do you realize this is a spiritual battle over souls?"

"Greg and Twanna filled me in. I've interviewed Delford Eiland. He believes his own propaganda. His army is coming."

"We've split up our campers. We have one hundred groups of fifty ready to move out."

"You're going to run for it?" pressed an anxious Twanna.

"Right now it's our best move."

"Have you heard from the Q Squad?"

"Greg, Lenard Mayer took one of our trucks and left our camp. Reenie is with him. Jake and Emma are also gone."

"You mean the stranger in Reenie's vision?"

"Yep, he used to be with the Prophetic Voice. He knows Eli, who was sent by Eiland to infiltrate our camp. Greg, the players in this scenario are a little too cozy for my comfort."

"Jake and Emma are committed to protecting Reenie. This is why they're shadowing her. Her mission involves Delford. Lenard must be taking her back to Zion. My guess is to somehow stop this attack."

"I want to go with you," pleaded Rafa.

"Our father is a man of principle. His judgment on you is final. My only chance is to face him alone."

"He contradicted every scripture I gave him. I've never felt such evil. He not only approves of this spirit; he craves it. This demon is the one feeding his bitterness. Father almost lost it when I mentioned you. He called you a coward."

"We helped the enemy escape. Think of the shame on our family. It's the ultimate disgrace."

"I'm praying for the Lord to reveal it."

"Reveal what?"

"Father's contempt for Zionist leaders is no secret. When Aaron showed up in his office something snapped inside him. I'm asking the Holy Spirit to reveal this stronghold Satan has over him."

"I'm going. You wait here. If I am not back in two hours you need to hide beneath the hills outside the city. Do you agree?"

Knowing this might be their final hug she held him tight.

Exiting from underneath the bleachers he humbly prayed for discernment.

———————

Pacing the hallway of his private underground bunker Joshua Kayin was feeling the pressure.

"It says He will rule with a rod of iron?" 2

"Just symbolism," insisted his false prophet. "These words don't apply to our time. Think of how many ways this passage has been misinterpreted."

"How is our deployment progressing?"

"As of today you have gathered the largest army ever assembled. In the end not one Jew will be left standing."

"Is my jet ready? I need to be inside the Temple on Mount Moriah when my armies blanket Armageddon."

———————

Arriving, Fadi was amazed to see such fear. The compound had been swept clean. It was like they knew they weren't coming back.

His office door was wide open. Sitting at his desk he looked dazed. The Commander could see his son in the hallway.

"Father, may I speak with you?"

"Why?"

Stepping inside he boldly replied, "It's about your future."

"The death of every Zionist I know is my future. This includes Aaron Glazer and all who assist him."

"Aaron's life was once about death. He now chooses eternal life."

"Tell me how this killer is now your hero? Did he ever mention his father, Isaac Glazer? There is no way of knowing how many Jordanians this highly decorated Israeli officer killed. There is no doubt the son believed the lies his father taught him."

"And what did you teach me?"

"To believe in the one true God, Allah! Your denial of the prophet Muhammad is proof you were never really my son."

"I now know the difference between Muhammad and Jesus. When Muhammad was dying he prayed for the death of Christians and Jews. When Jesus was dying He asked His Father to forgive His accusers."

"What do you know about forgiveness?"

"For someone to forgive is a powerful act. One can choose to forgive in a moment of time. Or it can take an hour, a day, maybe a week. For some it may take months to forgive. The most tragic are those clinging to their bitterness for years. Sometimes it's harder to forgive ourselves for the sins we have committed against others."

"I'm a Muslim; not a sinner."

"If this is true then please explain the curse which has plagued our family since the days of my great-great-grandfather? A sin passed down from generation to generation."

"You know nothing."

"I'm talking about a stronghold that has brought bondage to us in so many ways. Something transferred from a father to his son."

"And what is this sin of our family?"

"Killing, the killing of innocent people can be traced through our family tree."

"You mean the purging of Zionists? Our resistance to their evil occupation has kept our people alive. How is this sin? "

"I used to believe you. Deep down Rafa never did. Your excuses to kill were just lies from Satan."

"I'm curious why such evil accusations now?"

"Look at the fruit of such death!"

"Obviously, an apostate has no love for Allah or his people. Maybe now you believe all Muslims deserve to be wiped out by the Jews. Is this the vile propaganda Matthias is feeding you?"

At first, the word of knowledge was more of a distraction than a help. Even so, Fadi finally posed the question.

"Somehow Aaron's life is attached to yours. I want to know why?"

"What about converting me? Your sister failed. Don't you care about my soul burning in the lake of fire?"

"Before Rafa and I..."

"Never mention her name again."

"Becoming a believer in Jesus is much more than acknowledging Him as the Father's only Son. Jesus is the Alpha and Omega, the First and the Last. You must ask Him for the forgiveness of your sins. No one can be born again by the Spirit of God unless they're willing to repent and live a holy life. One must be truthful..."

"Let me be truthful!" he seethed. "The NWC has decimated the Sunday people. Soon we will annihilate the Saturday people. Tell me, traitor, when have I ever kept the truth from you?"

"Father, I've always wanted to ask you about the scar behind your right ear? Where did you get it?"

"From a Zionist who ordered..."

"And whatever happened to him?"

"I shot him."

"Do you remember his name?"

His smile reeked of hate. Nevertheless, the teenager wasn't leaving without an answer.

"I remember the shooting like it was yesterday. He never saw it coming. You know why?"

From the doorway Rafa boldly replied, "It was because you were huddled in darkness. You shot down an unsuspecting Isaac Glazer in cold blood. You used his death to propel your military career."

"I told you to never to come back."

"Is this true?" asked her stunned brother.

"Isaac Glazer was a dog I put out of his misery. At this very moment we are tracking his son. Hopefully, Aaron Glazer will suffer the same fate. Now leave me."

Standing in the doorway Fadi held his sister's hand.

"Your worthless war means nothing to God. And don't be fooled by the protection your troops will have after the seventh bowl is poured out. Once the hailstorms stop the Word of God will come and birds will feed themselves with the flesh from your armies. 3 If only you had eyes to see and ears to hear the truth. Goodbye Father."

Their lonely walk toward the border between Jordan and Israel felt like slow motion. Somehow, someway, this brother and sister desperately wanted to make a difference.

She couldn't believe what he was suggesting.

"Fadi, you want to warn them? But Aaron could be anywhere, the same for Jo. The pouring out of the seventh bowl is so close. They have to be underground by now."

Downstream the lifeless body of Cody Parrish lay face down between two rocks. As both agents scanned the hilly terrain a terrified Parker silently prayed for a miracle.

"I don't like it, Doyle," blurted a panicky Abernathy. "What makes you think they won't fire on us? I heard about some Christians from Talladega who refused to register. The day three agents arrived these rednecks never hesitated. They shot two of them."

"What about the other agent?"

"They painted his face red before hanging him from a tree."

Doyle knew the resisters within the Vineyard were a different breed. He was already regretting having to kill the young man. He kinda liked him. But time was running out.

"The leader of this camp and I go way back. To babysit these children ole Ruben must have become a full-fledged resister. Don't sweat it. This cop will recognize my calling card."

"Why should we get involved? They may not have Tucker or the preacher. If this race war erupts we could be dodging a lot of bullets. This army from the Prophetic Voice is capable of doing a lot of damage. C'mon, let's release Parker and go home."

"Go home to what? Your family was wiped out during the second trumpet, mine by the sixth. Bethany has been picked clean by looters. Those alive are just going through the motions."

"Going out in a blaze of glory, huh? Your bitterness isn't about people. It's God you hate. Bottom line these resisters simply love Jesus. This is what drives you crazy."

"Abe, I'd hold my tongue if I were you."

"We all saw the joy on your face when Reenie's brother was executed. The payback was obvious. Your personal vendetta against Travis made me puke. This is why most of your agents resigned."

"So what made you stay?"

"Reenie's father was my friend. I was the one who arrested her. If you catch her I know you'll kill her. It was worth a try."

"So you've come to rescue sweet little Reenie Ann Tucker? Maybe you're hoping this can atone for your sins?"

Drawing his gun from his shoulder holster he pointed it at his commander. Shaking his head he calmly pulled back the trigger.

"It's over! Your petty revenge stops here."

The gunshot to his neck echoed down the mountain. Greg and Twanna froze. The stream was streaked with blood from the dead body. Pressing the hot barrel to Parker's head the desperate agent waited. Running up the ravine Greg raised his hands.

"You win, Mercer, I'm giving up!"

"Ain't that easy, Preacher. Two have died because of your delay."

"Listen to what you're saying."

"Where is Ruben hiding Tucker?"

"Let the boy go and we will make the exchange."

"This poker hand cost me more than I figured."

"You're all alone. It won't cost you anything to fold!"

"What ever happened to your Q Squad? It's a shame my SWAT team wasn't able to complete their task."

From his blind side he heard, "Down-right shame if you ask me."

"Another surprise," smirked Doyle.

"Get out of here, Kurt!"

"Now, Reverend, let's hear what the spunky redhead has to say. I freed him a ways back. Never dreamed he could make it this far."

"I'm not alone. Check out the pile of rocks just ahead of you."

"Why?"

"A shotgun is pointed right at your chest."

The experienced agent somehow knew this wasn't a bluff. This is why he invited agent Abernathy to tag alone. He was caught in the one scenario he wanted to avoid.

"Doyle, do you really want to die?"

"Not exactly my first choice preacher man."

"Then lay down your weapon and raise your hands."

"Do I know your friend, Kurt?" the tense agent spat out.

"Jon Mendel here, I'm warning you not to move! I won't miss at this short range. Now let the boy go."

Parker took off in a sprint as soon as his handcuffs dropped to the ground. An animated Twanna was waving at him from the Bethel exit.

"What's next, Doyle?"

"Haven't decided yet."

The bullet knocked his shotgun out of his hand. By the time the agent could react Kurt was pointing both barrels in his face.

"Nice shot, Jon."

"It wasn't me, bro."

As the pastor made it over the ridge, a giddy Kurt hollered, "Awesome, Greg, your sniper really threaded the needle."

"What sniper? Did any of you see him?"

The remaining soldiers guarding Zion were restless. No one knew the black Kenite bravely hiking into their campsite.

"He's alone, Delford. We haven't sighted anyone following him."

"What's his angle?"

"He'll only talk with you."

"What a fool."

"He says he has valuable information on the Vineyard camp."

From inside his cave he was regretting his decision. As soon as he saw his eyes he sensed peace. The lanky Black American appeared confident. This racist leader couldn't help but think he was a decoy.

"I'm Delford Eiland."

"Donnell Emery."

"Is this the name of your ancestors or your slave name?"

"Does it matter?"

"For those following my teachings it does."

"Obedience to Jesus Christ is what counts."

"I have no desire to talk with you. What do you want?"

"The Vineyard staff knows all about your plan."

"All Ruben has to do is surrender."

"Both sides will suffer casualties if your soldiers attack."

"You think the resisters on Black Rock Mountain want to fight my soldiers? So be it. I promise their blood will flow through the ravine where they're hiding. Why are you really here? Are you kin to Twanna Evers or maybe you've come for Natalie Roberts?"

"I've come for you. Your entire camp is surrounded. Most of your guards have been captured. Those who haven't deserted will be meeting you and me at a clearing just below this cave."

"I'm not going anywhere."

"I'll give you one more chance."

"How dare you threaten me? Guards take this animal out of my sight and shoot him. Do you hear me?"

"No one is listening. It's just you, me, and God. It's miraculous how the Lord has brought judgment upon your teaching. Even so, Jesus is willing to give you one last opportunity to believe in Him as your Savior."

The disoriented leader never made it past the entrance. The soldiers bound and gagged outside his cave was a mystery.

Spinning around, he cursed, "Who do you represent?"

"Your execution of Reverend Evers didn't sit well with those living in these mountains. It served as a painful reminder. Actually their injustices came first."

"Who are you babbling about?"

From behind, pointing a loaded colt 45, the old Indian gratefully nodded at Donnell.

"Most call us the forgotten ones. To racists like you the Cherokee people are invisible. Your vision of white supremacy gives you the excuse to hate!"

"You can't stop God's will!" shrieked Eiland. "How many nations are ruled by Indians? None. And how many nations ruled by Africans are prosperous? None. Those from the seed of Cain are cursed. Your people are the vultures standing watch at the doors of Hades. As a prophet sent by God I broke the code of silence."

"What code?" a perplexed Ben asked.

"Only white Anglo Saxon's can receive salvation from the Lord!"

# SEVENTH BOWL: IT IS DONE

"Then the seventh angel poured out his bowl into the air, and a loud
voice came out of the temple of heaven, from the throne, saying, 'It is
done.'"
Revelation 16:17

Hamas commandos spotted their hostage emerging from a crowd of
shoppers. Two girls were walking beside him. Judah and Hanna Lentz
were waiting at a prearranged spot a block away.

"You love your parents, Ruth?"

"Yes very much, Abdullah."

"I loved mine too. My daughter was close to your age."

"What's going to happen to you?"

"I'll be executed within the hour."

"Are you sure?"

"I've revealed too much. I was hoping having Aaron Glazer's
daughter might change their minds. It won't."

"Abdullah, it doesn't matter what they do to your physical body.
Only Jesus can save your soul. You can be born again right now."

Looking down he was humbly searching for the right words.

"Johanna, how can I be saved?"

"Just repeat after me."

With no hesitation Johanna grasped his right hand while Ruth laid
her hands upon his trembling shoulders. Her simple prayer brought
forth tears of repentance streaming down his cheeks. Both girls were
praising the Lord as his countenance supernaturally changed before
their eyes.

"I can't explain the love I'm feeling! Jesus really has forgiven me!"

He could also feel their evil stares toward the tall brunette.

"Johanna, you need to leave us right now!"

The teenager miraculously received a witness from the Holy Spirit. She had learned obedience was better than sacrifice.

"Ruth, I love you and your folks so much."

Hugging her around the waist Ruth didn't want to let go.

She could only wave as her best friend disappeared into a crowd.

Everyone knew this wasn't a drill. The Alpha command was underway. The twin tunnels were jammed with children.

"We're ready, Ruben. Our head count is in. There are fifty-three groups in Bethel and forty-nine in Beulah."

"Okay. Twanna will signal the direction to go when a group arrives at either exit. Each group leader is responsible for securing a hiding place. I'll lead the last group of campers out of Bethel and Greg will lead out of Beulah. Remember, Twanna, our campers need time to take cover if fired upon."

"Ruben, our final Watchman is inside. Eiland's army is just minutes away from our camp entrance."

"May the Lord be with us all, I thank Him for every one of you. No matter what happens may we be faithful."

Their loving praises were a reflection of their gratitude of what the Father had already accomplished.

His Omega command echoed through the twin tunnels. Within seconds the outside ravine was clogged with frightened children.

The great multitude surrounding the temple in heaven braced themselves as the seventh angel poured out his bowl into the air. 1

A massive earthquake instantly rocked the earth. 2 Fires streaking through cities ravaged with deadly accuracy. A traumatized mankind sought refuge from the great day of God Almighty.

From the throne of God the saints heard, "It is done!"

The old Indian could see lightning in the distance. The ground under their feet was already shifting. The women and children inside the mammoth cave were horrified.

"Listen up everyone. Very soon, the Rider of the white horse will kill every follower of the Beast! 3 Those of you who haven't worshipped Kayin or taken his mark can still be saved."

"What about our husbands?"

"There is no more Prophetic Voice. Delford Eiland has been exposed. Your husbands will also have an opportunity to believe in Jesus. This is why you have been gathered here for this special moment. The only thing holding you back is your sin."

"What can we do?" begged a teenage girl.

"...If you confess with your mouth the Lord Jesus and believe in your heart that God has raised Him from the dead, you will be saved. For with the heart one believes unto righteousness, and with the mouth confession is made unto salvation.' For the Scripture says, 'Whoever believes on Him will not be put to shame.'" 4

"Why would God accept us now?" cried another.

"Jesus told this story to His disciples. It's about His love toward His creation. There was a landowner who sent laborers into his vineyard. Some worked all day in the hot sun, while others were hired for just one hour. At the end of the day each worker was paid the same amount. Those who worked all day complained. Then Jesus said, "'Take what is yours and go your way. I wish to give to this last man the same as to you. Is it not lawful for me to do what I wish with my own things? Or is your eye evil because I am good?' So the last will be first, and the first last. For many are called, but few chosen.'" 5

"What did Jesus mean by this?"

"He is referring to those who follow Him for just a short time. Each of us is just as saved as someone serving Him all their life."

The hailstone struck with such force it could be heard for miles. Those on watch quickly withdrew deep within their caves.

"Donnell, Donnell!" summoned a Cherokee scout. "Come see, your Miracle Girl has arrived. Just like the Holy Spirit said."

Rushing up the embankment Reenie fell into his arms. Amidst the cheers from the newly converted Cherokees the other members from the Rescue Squad followed close behind.

Catching their breath a bent over Emma and Jake waved.

"Are you Lenard Mayer?"

"Praise God, Donnell! I've heard lots of good things about you."

"It's the Lord you all made it here safely. Eiland ordered the attack earlier today. The Cherokees captured Zion just after his army left for the Vineyard. Ben has been witnessing to his tribe as well as to the families of the soldiers. It's a miracle. Thousands have been saved."

"Where is Delford now?"

"Follow me."

Walking into the shadows of the damp cave Lenard could hear his heavy breathing. As soon as he removed the rag from his mouth the self-proclaimed prophet spit at him.

"Why are you here? I suppose the fighting was too much for you. You never did have much of a stomach for blood."

"Eli didn't either. He prayed with me to receive Jesus."

"If you can bear it, it took me less than an hour to gain control of him, so much for being born again. Eli's leading the attack on the Vineyard as we speak."

"You know I think it's time we re-program Eli."

"Fat chance, the hailstones have begun! We wouldn't make it a mile on these back roads. Who are you kidding? You're not man enough to try something so stupid."

"Reenie can decide for us."

"You can't mean the girl in your vision? Just admit it you missed your date with destiny."

Joining Lenard in a circle were Reenie, Donnell, Jake, and Emma.

"Is he talking? How many will his soldiers bring back to Zion?"

Turning over on his side Delford howled with laughter.

"Lenard, you don't even have the guts to tell her!"

"Reenie, there won't be any hostages."

"But Eli said..."

"All we can do is pray."

"Lenny, only Eiland can call off this attack. Which means our only chance is to transport the anointed one back to the Vineyard."

"What did I you tell you, Delford?"

"Even if you force me Eli won't buy it."

"What do you say, Lenny?"

"No joke, girl, even a partial hit by one of these hailstones and it's over. For now they're coming in flurries. After each barrage there is a let up. We could make it by finding shelter along the way."

Greg sat alone at the Beulah entrance. He didn't like the feel of the high powered rifle in his hands. From inside the tunnel he could hear her footsteps in the dirt. He wasn't surprised.

"Are you alright, Nate?"

"Tired of babysitting can you use some company?"

With hailstones striking in the distance, Greg earnestly interceded, "Lord, we need you now more than ever."

"What about the children? What if they get caught out in the open?"

"The group leaders know what to do. How's Doyle doing?"

"Still whining, you know he still hasn't figured it out."

"When did you get it, Nate?"

"On my way here from Chicago; the burning of billions was the clincher. It had to be God's judgment."

"Where were you burned?"

"My back feels like red hot jelly."

Scampering across the picnic area, the young Watchman dove into the Beulah entrance.

"Are you crazy, Jon?" rebuked the shocked reporter.

After catching his breath, he shared, "Greg, they've just divided into two groups on the hill below us. The last furry is keeping them at bay for now."

"Such madness," he moaned. "Our twin tunnels weren't created to hide campers. The first direct hit on this mountain and Beulah and Bethel could be history."

"They ain't getting one child!"

Taking a defensive position behind a large rock at the mouth of the tunnel Jon removed four boxes of shells from his backpack.

Knelling between the two Watchmen, Natalie clicked off the safety of her rifle.

"Where did they assign, Kurt?"

Shaking his head, an amazed Jon replied, "Nate, he signed up for counseling. He's sharing with kids who want to give up."

"Why are you guys so surprised?"

An appreciative Greg confessed, "In the past two years the boy has really grown up in the Lord. Kurt admits he was pretty much of a taker all of his life. Now as a believer he's become a giver."

It had been hours since anyone knocked on his office door. His favorite cigar smoke was still lingering in the air. As usual his desk was overflowing with stories underlined in yellow ink. Wes Mackish had always believed broadcasting could further a specific cause more than anything else. His entire life was dedicated to shaping public perception. Wes had made a lot of enemies along the way. But on this dreary afternoon his mind wasn't on those who could slander his reputation. Certainly many tried to topple this respected reporter. Yet in the end it wouldn't be his enemies who would bring about his downfall.

His cold body wound up underneath his desk. Pink pills were scattered across the dirty floor. Just after reading his suicide note out loud he went to sleep for the final time. There was no one there to hear his last words. Oddly enough he wasn't thinking about his reputation, his broadcasting awards, even his family. For some reason the safety of his protégé was his last wish. Natalie Roberts was still on assignment.

*Dear Natalie, minutes ago massive hailstones destroyed our TV towers. At this moment, thousands of fires have taken our Chicago hostage. I can even see the flames reflecting off my office windows. You were right about how it's going to end. So let's focus on our beginning. It's easy to recall the first day you reported to work. Your enthusiasm, your charisma, your joy of living, it was such a high for us in broadcasting. Your innocence was a breath of fresh air. So many tried to grasp it but ultimately failed. That's what made you so special. Even now you're somewhere in the Blue Ridge Mountains trying to protect children. I know you'll make a difference; you always have. It was quite a shock for me to find you so disillusioned after your flight home from Jerusalem. Joel told me you let the events of the past month overwhelm you. Now I understand how much courage that took. The armies of the world are converging on Israel. Their borders have been sealed off. The Jewish people are trapped. You won't believe this but advancing troops are almost completely intact. Something is protecting them from the falling hailstones. Wow, there really is going to be an Armageddon. When you tried to convince me Jesus returned to earth I thought you had lost it. I still have so many questions. I guess when I wake up from these pills I will finally get some answers. Wherever you are I hope you're safe. I've never felt so alone, so helpless. So long Nate.*

*Your friend, Wes*

# That Great City Babylon

*"...That great city Babylon...in one hour your judgment has come."*
*Revelation 18:10*

The ancient city lay in ruins. The glory of an angel was illuminating earth. Only he had the authority to speak it. 1

"'...Babylon the great is fallen, is fallen...has become a dwelling place of demons...For all the nations have drunk of the wine of the wrath of her fornication, the kings of the earth have committed fornication with her, and the merchants of the earth have become rich through the abundance of her luxury.'" 2

Another heavenly voice rang out, "'...Come out of her, my people, lest you share in her sins, and lest you receive of her plagues. For her sins have reached to heaven, and God has remembered her iniquities. Render to her just as she rendered to you, and repay her double according to her works; in the cup which she has mixed, mix double for her. In the measure that she glorified herself and lived luxuriously, in the same measure give her torment and sorrow; for she says in her heart, "I sit as queen, and am no widow, and will not see sorrow. Therefore her plagues will come in one day—death and mourning and famine. And she will be utterly burned with fire, for strong is the Lord God who judges her. The kings of the earth who committed fornication and lived luxuriously with her will weep and lament for her, when they see the smoke of her burning, standing at a distance for fear of her torment, saying, "Alas, alas, that great city Babylon, that mighty city. For in one hour your judgment has come."'" 3

Before declaring final judgment another mighty angel easily picked up a massive millstone and cast it into the sea.

"'Thus with violence the great city Babylon shall be thrown down, and shall not be found anymore...The light of a lamp shall not shine in you anymore, and the voice of bridegroom and bride shall not be heard in you anymore. For your merchants were the great men of the earth, for by your sorcery all the nations were deceived. And in her was found the blood of prophets and saints, and of all who were slain on the earth.'" 4

The righteous judgment ringing forth from the lips of this great multitude in heaven was not for human ears.

"'...Alleluia. Salvation and glory and honor and power belong to the Lord our God. For true and righteous are His judgments, because He has judged the great harlot who corrupted the earth with her fornication; and He has avenged on her the blood of His servants shed by her.'" 5

---

"Praise Jesus!" shouted a grateful Lenard, "we made it!"

A giddy Jake slapped him on the back while Emma loved the super high five she received from a relieved Reenie.

Scenes from his vision were falling into place. It was hard to accept. Only one camouflaged truck remained. The tracks from the other trucks pointed in the same direction.

His arms tied around the trunk of a tree, Delford cursed, "Before you begin your hallelujah party let's see how many Kenites have died?"

"Who has the tape to shut him up?"

From a hill overlooking the soldiers' temporary headquarters he could barely control his anger.

"We missed them. Troops from the Prophetic Voice have left for the Vineyard. It appears Delford's control over Eli is for real."

For a determined Reenie it was black and white.

"Lenny, you have carried this burden since you were nine. There is no way we can sit this one out. These children need someone to care. This is our Father's will for our lives. C'mon, we can't quit now."

The desertions erupted after the first hailstone imbedded itself on the back side of Black Rock Mountain. In just minutes sixteen soldiers were killed by successive hits.

"What is Eli thinking?" cursed a soldier. "We're stuck out here like sitting ducks while he makes up his mind about these worthless Kenites. If Delford was here this mess would be over by now."

From his truck, Eli called out for their attention.

"Let's do this for the glory of God. My unit will capture the entrances to both tunnels. Unit 2 will cut off the exits. Move out."

The silence blanketing the huge campground felt strange. Leading his soldiers toward the tunnels he received a vivid flashback in his mind. The little boy was drawn up like a ball inside his bedroom closet. He would use his hands to cover his ears until the shouting stopped. If his mother lost their fight she would beat him with a metal hanger. His father favored a thick leather strap. As the years went by Eli preferred the darkness. Locked away in his dark sanctuary he felt protected. No one could make fun of the bruises on his body. He didn't have to hide his feelings of guilt. His spirit guide never failed to visit him. Over and over the demon would indoctrinate its victim. Layers upon layers of lies built a foundation built upon fear. He would carry these scars for a lifetime; with no chance of healing in sight.

Jon's shotgun blast above their heads sent soldiers scurrying for cover. Eli instantly ordered his men to hold their fire.

"Identify yourself?"

"Greg Hudson."

"Listen up, preacher. There's no way to stop us. You need to step aside. Now come out with your hands up."

"No can do. So why did Delford send you in his place? Let me guess, he's calling the shots from Zion. He's a deceiver, Eli, obsessed with a demonic agenda. He doesn't care about you or his soldiers."

"God called him at seventeen. His teachings have brought hope to thousands. Eiland is a forerunner of what is to come."

"You mean a forerunner of death! Delford was taught his racist propaganda from deceiving spirits. Did you ever ask what happened to him after he received his calling?"

"He saw a vision of the great day of God Almighty. Armies will soon destroy the evil empire Jews built around our world. Birds will eat their flesh. Delford is a prophet most never appreciated."

"You're mixing lies with the truth. We are experiencing the seventh bowl right now. Armageddon is near. At the supper of the great God birds will eat the flesh of armies following the Beast."

The pounding of the mountain was escalating. Those outside had a panoramic view of hailstones ravaging the landscape.

"You know Lenard's vision!" hollered Greg. "You're acting it out. Lenard and Reenie have gone to speak with Delford. This attack of children doesn't have to be."

"Did Lenard tell you this? Not bad for a deserter. Their vision is a fabrication. I have no doubt Delford Eiland hears from God."

The flashback in his mind was a girl who had just arrived at the Vineyard. The sad ten-year-old was eating alone; purposely avoiding her Bible study group.

"Hi, my name is Eli, what's yours?"

"April."

"Why are you eating your lunch alone?"

"I just lost my family."

"Gee, April, look around. We are all your family."

"But I don't know anyone here."

"You ask God, He will show you. I just know He will."

A week later April ran up for a big hug.

"You're right, Uncle Eli, God can speak to us. He told me to trust Him with my future. Then I saw a picture in my mind. A dark cloud was coming but you refused to run away. You're my hero."

Raising his revolver Eli closed his eyes and pulled the trigger. The barrage of gunfire prompted a massive retreat within the tunnels. Before his soldiers could move in a hailstone struck the campsite. The entrance to Beulah was instantly buried under an avalanche of dirt.

From the Bethel exit Ruben shouted, "How bad?"

Everyone heard the cave-in. The shots through the ravine scattered many into heavy brush. The groups had to move faster.

"The children are terrified!" screamed Twanna.

"How many casualties?"

"Just warning shots so far."

The sniper moved from behind a rock formation just above the Beulah exit. Suddenly a soldier enjoying the attack tumbled down the steep embankment into the ravine. Crack, crack, two more soldiers slumped to the ground.

As his unit moved up the steep embankment across from the twin exits, Eli yelled out, "What's happening?"

"They're using a sniper. Three of our men are dead. We can't pinpoint his location. Give the command and we'll blow them away."

"Not yet! Explosives are our last resort."

"But our directive is no survivors!"

"Cease firing. Prepare to deliver a cocktail on my command. No more shooting until we kill the sniper."

The silence was only interrupted by weeping children. Several hundred lay helplessly exposed in the ravine across from the tunnel exits. For now the lone sniper was waiting.

Slipping between the frightened children trapped in Beulah was like a nightmare. Jon and Greg could hardly breathe by the time they reached the exit.

"What's up, Twanna?"

"Right now, Ruben has a red light on Bethel."

"What about Beulah?"

"Greg, we've still got twenty one groups to get out. A minute ago a shooter from the Vineyard returned fire. This is when the shooting stopped."

"What's their next move?"

"Jon, if you were Eli what would you do?"

"I'd nail the shooter."

Running through the empty campsite the Q squad could see the entrances to both tunnels up ahead.

"Beulah is buried!" a devastated Reenie cringed.

"Bethel looks clear but there's no way to know for sure," reflected Jake. "Going around will take longer, Lenny, but it's safer."

Everyone could hear the cries of the children echoing through the ravine.

"Jake and Emma you follow the trail leading to the wells. Reenie and I will take Delford through Bethel. It's the fastest way to find Ruben."

"Too risky, bro, we can't lose Eiland. Let Emma and me go."

Lenard was dreading their next move. Reenie was definitely on edge. Looking into her exhausted eyes he somehow knew her answer.

"Miracle Girl, what is the Spirit of Christ telling you?"

"Jake and Emma have always protected me. I trust their judgment. You and I can take the trail. C'mon, Lenny, may the Lord use us all."

Huddled inside the Bethel exit an intercessor suggested, "Ruben, our campers can't last much longer. Surrender is our only choice."

"Never!"

"Don't you see they must be waiting on our sniper?"

Ruben knew the voice calling from across the ravine.

"I hear you, Eli, what do you want?"

"Enough blood has been shed. You give the command to surrender and your staff will respond. You can make this happen."

"You're an enemy of God, Eli. He gave you time to repent but you refused. You have the power to stop this insanity right now yet you defiantly persist."

Crouched behind some trees they could hear every word. Removing the safety of his revolver Lenard stared at his hostage.

"What's it going to be, Delford? It's your call?"

Stepping out in plain view, an impatient Reenie hollered, "Eli, I have just returned from Zion. I have a message from Delford."

"That's impossible!" he shouted back.

Her hands held high, she pleaded, "Only you can be the judge."

Not waiting for a reply the skinny teenager scurried down the hill into the ravine. As soon as she crossed over the stream two soldiers took her jacket and shoes.

"Ruben, I'll give her five minutes. If any of my men are shot at, if any of you even move, we will begin taking lives."

"Agreed," he replied reluctantly.

"Where's Lenard Mayer?"

"I warn you, Eli," he threatened, "don't harm her."

"I see you Lenard. Now where's Hudson? Before I talk with Tucker I want to hear from the preacher?"

From the Beulah exit, Greg called out, "I'm over here. The Lord sees your heart and I know..."

"None of you ever knew me!" he seethed. "I despise your hollow words. You shoot your mouths off like you have a secret weapon. Do you hear me?"

As the seconds ticked by no one seemed to notice the dark rain cloud hovering over Black Rock Mountain.

He was in no mood for games. Removing the tape from Delford's mouth, Lenard whispered, "You give us away and it's over for you. Now I need some information."

The prophet's smile was clearly demonic. He was accustomed to being in control but this was turning out better than he ever expected. His pride couldn't resist bragging about it.

"Don't you get it? Why the five minute time limit? Think soldier, why is Eli stalling for more time?"

"He could be repositioning his men to attack our exits."

"No, no, no, there're way too many children for that. The answer is in the faces of my soldiers. What do you see?"

"Guilt, shame, it's really pathetic. What could be more evil than killing innocent children?"

"Where's your discernment? These soldiers aren't killers. They're just everyday folk seeking a cause to believe in. You know, anti-government, anti-gun control, anti-gay marriage, and anti-abortion. It's just a crap shoot."

"So why did they choose your cause?"

"They were drawn by my passion. It didn't hurt most of them suffered from reverse discrimination. The Kenites have infiltrated our society like a cancer. Once a body is poisoned it eventually expires. Open your eyes. Our water is polluted. Our cities are on fire. Mankind is infected with sores. I saw this coming. My soldiers did too. Why would anybody reject pharisaical Christianity? That's easy; to foster something worth living for."

"And the killing of Jewish, Black, and Hispanic children somehow furthers your cause?"

"How do you prevent a cancer from growing?"

"Why is Eli stalling? Is Reenie in trouble?"

"Is she the only one you're worried about? Eli is following my orders to the letter. My soldiers need more time to wire their explosives. It won't be long before this mountain becomes a gigantic ball of fire. Thus sayth the Lord, the arm of God Almighty will judge all coming against His anointed!"

# THE MARRIAGE OF THE LAMB

"Let us be glad and rejoice and give Him glory, for the marriage of
the Lamb has come, and His wife has made herself ready."
Revelation 19:7

Greg wasn't comfortable waiting any longer. Yet trying to reach Eli
would be suicide. Reenie's bold move was the sacrifice he had come
to expect from her. It was still a long shot for Eli to call off the attack.

Jake and Emma asked the Lord's protection just before sprinting
toward the Beulah exit.

"Hey, Greg!" gasped an out of breath Jake.

"Praise God you two made it! Talk to me."

"Lenard and Reenie have Delford."

"Reenie is meeting with Eli right now. Delford is Lenard's trump
card. Our Miracle Girl needs wisdom. She is calling Eli's bluff right
now. The problem is if she backs him into a corner he could bust like
a hot water bottle."

Inside the Holy Jerusalem a multitude of voices joyfully
proclaimed, "'...Alleluia. For the Lord God Omnipotent reigns. Let us
be glad and rejoice and give Him glory, for the marriage of the Lamb
has come, and His wife has made herself ready.'" 1

The clean fine linen worn by the bride represents the righteous
acts of the saints. 2 All of heaven heard the next announcement.
Blessed are those called to the marriage supper of the Lamb! 3

As Eli paced, Reenie silently used the name of Jesus to rebuke any demons empowering his solders.

"I must admit it took guts for you and Lenard to come back."

"The Lord made it possible. You're leading your men into a slaughter. Anyone attacking these children will suffer God's wrath."

"If not me someone else would have to do it."

"Do what? You're no killer. I can see it in your eyes."

"I'm nothing. The Lord's hand of justice is upon me. This was a truth Lenard never could grasp. No one can change God's perfect will. In the end His righteous judgment will never spare these Kenites."

"Delford is demon possessed! Satan is blinding you to this truth."

"Careful, girl, speaking against God's anointed is blasphemy."

"Only you can put a stop to this charade. This was the Lord's plan from the beginning."

"It's too late. These soldiers have their orders."

"Why play Delford's evil game? There is no way you can allow the pain of your past to affect the lives of these innocent children."

"So you did visit Zion. Somehow you thought you could convince Delford to reject his convictions. Many tried but none succeeded."

"There was a far greater purpose for visiting Zion; something greater than the martyrdom of these children who love Jesus. Those martyred today will receive resurrection bodies." 4

"You don't know that!"

"I know more than you think. I know the horrors of the evil one. The nightmares, the paranoia, the crippling fears; they're all part of the package. Jezebel entered me when I was five. The other demons in me were under her command. When she was cast out they left."

"How long did Jezebel control you?"

"Thirteen years. What about your spirit guide?"

"Anton has been with me since I was seven. He persuaded me to join the Prophetic Voice. Delford also takes his orders from Anton. I denied it at first. Then God revealed it to me."

"When did this happen?"

"After I was kicked out of the Vineyard, dehydration was killing me then Lenard found me. I prayed with him to receive Christ. It was like scales falling from my eyes."

"Anton is a liar. He's not in you anymore!"

"He will never leave me."

"Jezebel tried this same lame trick on me. Anton's threats are operating outside your spirit. He's bluffing."

"It's too late for me."

"Have you ever tested to see? By the power in the name of Jesus I command Anton to manifest itself."

Closing his eyes the soldier recoiled in fear.

"Anton is coming after you."

"Bring him on! I have something to tell him. 'Greater is He that is in me that he that is in the world.'" 5

---

Silently praying Lenard was in no hurry.

"It's a shame to see so many die."

"Sure would be," he calmly replied.

"If you intervene now Eli might make some concessions."

"I don't dance with the Devil."

"You have no choice!" cackled the racist. "Their blood is on your hands if you refuse to help."

"You think so?"

"Have you ever seen a mushroom of fire? The judgment of God Almighty will erupt just like I envisioned."

"I remember; I was once your right hand man. Or should I say stooge."

With perspiration dripping from his forehead, the cult leader confessed, "You're just signing our death warrant."

"The real issue facing us is not physical death. If this fireball does fry us where will your spirit go and where will mine go? You once said you enjoyed seeing Kenites suffer, especially the ones begging for mercy."

"You're confused."

"Seeing soldiers die for your vision is a real rush, huh?"

"Don't you care if we die?" he pleaded. "What type of Christian are you?"

Jumping up and down Eli gratefully looked up to God.

"He's gone, he's gone, Anton is just playing mind games. I'm free from his control. I can just feel the peace of God. The Holy Spirit is speaking to me!"

"Amen my brother in Christ! C'mon, we don't have much time."

"Reenie, these soldiers are devout followers of Delford. Several have already been shot by a Vineyard sniper. What can I say to convince them to lay down their arms?"

"It's not about us. We just have to take the first step. Then God will make a way."

# ARMAGEDDON

"And they gathered them together to the place called in Hebrew,
Armageddon...And I saw the beast, the kings of the earth, and their armies,
gathered together to make war against Him who sat on the horse and
against His army."
Revelation 16:16, 19:19

"What are you waiting for? Once these explosives are ignited it's over.
There is no second chance. We have to get off this mountain."

A seemingly peaceful Lenard continued to pray.

"What is this, some sort of death wish? You're talking suicide."

"Delford, the only way to be free from selfishness is to help
others."

"You're playing God! You can stay but I'm leaving."

"You ain't going anywhere Mr. Prophetic Voice. Now shut up
and watch these soldiers execute your dirty work. It's easy to see what
a coward you are when the pressure is on."

With Reenie by his side he rushed out of his tent and signaled to
his soldiers to listen up.

"Ruben, are you there?"

"Yes, Eli, what is your decision?"

"Those in position to ignite I command you to stop. This mission
is suspended. Reenie has been to Zion and has seen your families.
They are safe."

"She's with Lenard. You can't trust her."

Another soldier suspiciously shouted, "You have no power to
stop what our prophet has decreed. We must carry out his will."

Raising his hands he hollered back, "What purpose is served by
murdering innocent children? Hailstones are crushing our cities. God's

wrath will end when Jesus kills the followers of the Beast. I'm seeking another city illuminated by the glory of God, the Holy Jerusalem." 1

"Such heresy!" accused another. "We are the Israel of God!"

The division was obvious as several resumed wiring their explosives.

"Hold up!" ordered Eli. "I think it's time for each soldier to decide his own future."

As Lenard leaned forward for a better look the cult leader broke free, tackling him from behind.

A tense Ruben shouted, "Eli, what is your decision?"

Stepping away from the trees, his hands on his head, Lenard could hardly look their way. While holding a gun to his head the prophet smiled and waved to his men.

"Men from the Prophetic Voice I have come to lead you in your assignment. Continue wiring your timers."

"Delford Eiland is lying to you!" screamed Reenie. "Lenard brought him here against his will. When we arrived at Zion he was preparing to abandon you and your families!"

"Don't listen to this lying devil!"

"We have written proof! The families believing in Jesus agreed to write down their testimonies. These are letters of their salvation."

Carrying two leather bags, one over each shoulder, Jake Jamison popped up from his hiding place. After emptying the letters out on the ground he slowly backed away.

"No one move!" screeched Delford. "This is a trap."

As soldiers frantically rummaged through the huge pile of letters Lenard courageously made one last plea.

"The threats from this madman mean nothing. Anyone repenting of your sins and believing in Jesus can still be saved."

"Be silent!" hissed Anton. "You know, Reenie's mission was always doomed for failure!"

"Armageddon is almost here. Those of us who believe in Jesus will live on earth during the Millennium."

"Last warning," whispered the foul spirit.

"Give these children the same opportunity your children just received. Let us take hands..."

The reverberation froze everyone. His lifeless body lay in the dirt. As rain drops fell all eyes refocused upon his killer.

"Thus sayth the Lord, God Almighty has exposed the rebellion of Lenard Mayer. This blasphemer's fate was settled before he joined us."

"You're like Cain!" shrieked Reenie. "You murdered Lenard because his works are righteous and yours are evil. 2 Hear me; Lenard gave his life for ya'll to see what is of God and what is of Satan."

After cocking back the trigger the racist leader took aim.

Lunging to his left Eli pushed Reenie out of his line of fire.

A shot rang out cutting a crease of blood across his cheek.

From the ravine a soldier yelled, "The sniper is on the ledge just above the Beulah exit! Blow him up."

The next gunshot knocked the false prophet on his back. The hole in his chest was as big as a silver dollar.

The explosion scattered dirt a hundred feet in the air.

"No, Greg," begged Emma, "it's too dangerous."

He wasn't listening as he began crawling up the massive mound of dirt.

"In Jesus' name," proclaimed a valiant Eli, "I command these spirits of darkness to leave us. I cast Anton into the bottomless pit. I plead the blood of Jesus over every soldier here. Let us give up our weapons."

Suddenly a rain shower burst forth. Within this downpour one could see new converts holding up salvation letters praising the Lord.

"My sweetheart is born again," wept one soldier.

"My children are following Jesus."

"I want to live with God for eternity," confessed another.

A celebration erupted throughout the ravine. It was a sight to behold as thousands surrounded soldiers reading their letters.

Amidst such merriment Ruben watched his friend crawl through the mud. Her lips were barely moving when he reached her. Cradling her head in his hands their eyes met.

"Don't speak, Nate, just rest."

"Delford had to go. I took care of Doyle too."

"You're the sniper protecting our campers?"

"Once did a story on guns in America. The shooting lessons were the best part."

Greg could feel her pain. He knew what she was facing.

"Natalie, is there anything you want to say?"

In between breaths, she muttered, "Send my love to Tee, Jon too. Tell Ben his people were awesome. I never met her but I saw how God used Reenie. I guess we all had a love for children."

Shielding her eyes from the rain he could feel her tears touching his hands.

"It was nice knowing you, Greg."

As soon as her mud streaked face went limp her spirit left her body.

---

The air strikes over Israel were lighting up the night. Thousands of Kayin's troops, backed by artillery bombing, were breaking through the weak border resistance. The primary objective of this Jordanian militia was achieved in record time. His fully operational command post was just fifty miles north of Jerusalem. The Commander was also praising Allah for another miracle. Inside his tent the cuffed prisoner was thrown to the ground alongside the anxious teenager.

"Like a dog returning to its vomit?" his father taunted. "What are the chances of your Zionist hero being delivered into my hands? How can you continue to doubt the power of Allah?"

"Your men didn't capture him! He risked his life to rescue me."

"You're both insane."

Waiting to get eye contact, Aaron boldly confessed, "Fadi has twice the courage you have. Your rejection of him hasn't stopped his love for you. Soon the Word of God will appear. All following the Beast will be killed."

"I only follow Allah!"

"I want to ask forgiveness for your nephew's death."

"Mere words cannot bring him back."

"I also want to forgive you for murdering my father, 'Whoever hates his brother is a murderer, and you know that no murderer has eternal life abiding in him.'" 3

"I told him," Fadi openly confessed.

Sneering back, his father cursed, "Once a traitor always a traitor!"

"Your soldiers' flesh will dissolve when He comes. 4 Do you even care how many will die?"

"There will be no victor in this war. This is the end of the Middle East as we know it."

Tears running down his face, Fadi pleaded, "Father, physical death is not the end. There is still time for those who haven't worshipped Kayin."

Shockingly, he mumbled back, "Is Rafa still alive?"

"She is inside Jerusalem searching for my daughter."

"Why would she do such a reckless thing?"

Glancing at Aaron, then his father, the young man replied, "It's called the marriage supper of the Lamb. Jesus said, "'...I will no longer drink of the fruit of the vine until that day when I drink it new in the kingdom of God.'" 5

"What kingdom is Jesus referring to?"

"The marriage of the Lamb to His bride took place in heaven. The marriage supper will take place on earth. 6 The invited guests will be the believers living on a newly restored earth. This kingdom will be ruled by the Messiah from the House of God of Jacob."

"I now believe all religions contain some truth. Lakes, rivers, and oceans each have water. Just like all faiths flow through Allah."

"But what about a believing relationship with the Messiah? Jesus will soon reign over the nations for a thousand years."

"My son, such debate is fruitless. We all have regrets. Obviously, believing in some future kingdom can't affect what's happening now."

"Father, what you believe does matter!"

Untying their hands, he whispered, "Just leave while you can."

"Your eternal destiny rests on who you follow. Rafa and I have prayed for the salvation of Arabs as well as Jews. 'Blessed are those who do His commandments (teachings), that they may have the right to the tree of life, and may enter through the gates into the city.'" 7

"How does one partake of this tree of life?"

"Commander, the only way to be grafted into the tree of life and the Holy City is to believe in Jesus as your Lord and Savior."

Refusing to hide his tears he pleaded, "Father, do you believe Jesus is the Messiah to come?"

"I do."

"In Romans 9:5, the Christ is called the eternally blessed God. In Hebrews 1:8, the Son is called God by His Father. In Revelations 21:7, Jesus promises to be our God."

His voice cracking, the Jordanian officer suddenly broke down.

"I can't deny what I see. Jesus really can change a life."

"You mean you want to ask Jesus for forgiveness?"

Shaking his head he reached over and embraced his only son.

Their celebration was exhilarating. As intercessors prayed with soldiers to receive Jesus as their Savior, Jake, Emma, and Kurt assisted children in finding shelter. The Q Squad had successfully protected

Reenie Ann Tucker through the day of the Lord. She hadn't forgotten. Her mission would begin and end in prayer.

Over the loud chatter, he shouted, "Hey, Emma," "where's our Miracle Girl?"

"Last time I saw her, Greg, she was behind those pine trees."

Kneeling in the dirt, Reenie whispered, "Lord, I have no words to say how much I love You. Throughout my life Satan slandered You, mocked You, even tried over and over to make me reject You. The Devil wanted me in bondage rather than serving You. But You refused to give up on me. I was only able to do my Father's will cause of Your faithfulness."

They were watching from a distance. She was finally alone.

"Lord," she earnestly cried out, "I pray for those who have put their trust in You. May we remain faithful."

Crashing through the high brush the two boys charged their victim. Bent over she didn't want to look.

"The lord of the dead has sent us. Reenie Ann Tucker, Osiris will now consume your soul."

Emerging from the trees Greg blocked their path.

"You're both going down!" yelled Kurt from behind.

From their left, Emma called out, "Over here, boys."

"In the name of Jesus Christ, the Son of the Living God," commanded Greg, "we render you helpless. May His blood..."

"Nooooo!" they cursed. "Not the blood."

Falling to their knees they could only grovel in the mud. Osiris was nowhere to be found. Within seconds they lay still.

An ecstatic Jake wasted no time proclaiming, "Every knee shall bow!"

"Maranatha our Lord cometh," worshipped Emma.

Within the grasp of a big group hug Reenie thanked the Lord again. The members of the Rescue Squad had fulfilled their mission. The slender brunette had always dreamed of having a close friend. Someone she could always count on. Now she had four for all eternity.

# 39

## THE WORD OF GOD

"His eyes were like a flame of fire, and on His head were many crowns. He had a name written that no one knew except Himself. He was clothed with a robe dipped in blood, and His name is called The Word of God."
Revelation 19:12-13

The hailstones were no more. The rain was letting up. The converted soldiers were on their way back to their families. Most campers were praying for anyone who still could be saved. Huddled around a roaring fire were the Q and several staff from the Vineyard.

Opening his Bible Ruben read, "'Now I saw heaven opened, and behold, a white horse. And He who sat on him was called Faithful and True, and in righteousness He judges and makes war. His eyes were like a flame of fire, and on His head were many crowns. He had a name written that no one knew except Himself. He was clothed with a robe dipped in blood, and His name is called The Word of God. And the armies in heaven, clothed in fine linen, white and clean, followed Him on white horses. Now out of His mouth goes a sharp sword, that with it He should strike the nations. And He Himself will rule them with a rod of iron. He Himself treads the winepress of the fierceness and wrath of Almighty God. And He has on His robe and on His thigh a name written: King of Kings and Lord of Lords.'" [1]

Shaking his head a solemn Kurt confessed, "Jesus will soon kill everyone who worshipped the beast, his image or received his mark!"

There was nothing anyone could do. From the outskirts of Ram Allah both Watchmen watched the devastation of Mount Moriah. Massive flames were already reaching the Temple Mount.

"It's hard to watch, Aaron," wept the young Jordanian. "I don't understand. Zechariah prophesied the Lord will return to Zion and dwell in Jerusalem, the City of Truth God's Holy Mountain." 2

"It's His righteous judgment, Fadi. The armies of the Beast have overrun the entire nation of Israel. Not even Jerusalem will escape."

"Where did the prophets speak of such fire?"

"Isaiah prophesied, 'For behold, the Lord will come with fire and with His chariots, like a whirlwind, to render His anger with fury, And His rebuke with flames of fire.'" 3

"But why the Temple?"

"The Word and His angels will return any time now. After the supper of the great God is over our Lord will build the Temple which shall bear His glory for eternity." 4

The mass exodus was painful to watch. Aaron's announcement made no sense.

"Why leave now?" pleaded Fadi. "Are you sure this is from God?"

"Yes, with all my heart. When you and your father find Rafa tell her Johanna and I love her very much."

"We never would have been saved if the Lord didn't send you. You ran the race for my family as well as my people. Aaron, you're no respecter of persons. I'll never forget you."

The two brothers in Christ hugged.

"Oh yeah, your father was asking me about when Jesus will put all His enemies under his feet. Have him read I Corinthians 15:24-26. It says, 'Then comes the end, when He delivers the kingdom to God the Father, when He puts an end to all rule and all authority and power. For He must reign till He has put all enemies under His feet. The last enemy that will be destroyed is death.'" 5

"Doesn't this happen after the Millennium is over?"

"Yes, the King of Kings will rule the nations for a thousand years with a rod of iron. After the Millennium, Jesus will cast Satan into the lake of fire. Then the Son will conduct the white throne judgment. It will begin after the wicked are resurrected out of Hades. Jesus will judge their works before casting them all into the lake of fire. After this, the last enemy destroyed will be physical death. Then the Son of God will return His everlasting kingdom back to His Father."

"So when does Jesus receive the millennial kingdom?"

"Fadi, Gabriel once appeared to Mary and announced the birth of our Savior. The archangel said, 'He will be great, and will be called the Son of the Highest; and the Lord God will give Him the throne of His father David.' 6 After Jesus restores the earth and rebuilds the Temple the Son will return to heaven and stand before the Ancient of Days. This event is described in Daniel when the Ancient of Days gives His Son an everlasting kingdom."

"So God the Father is also called the Ancient of Days?"

"Yes, the Father will anoint His Son and grant Him the throne of David. Let me read it. 'I was watching in the night visions, And behold, One like the Son of Man, Coming with the clouds of heaven. He came to the Ancient of Days, And they brought Him near before Him. Then to Him was given dominion and glory and a kingdom, That all peoples, nations, and languages should serve Him. His dominion is an everlasting dominion, Which shall not pass away, And His kingdom the one Which shall not be destroyed.'" 7

It wasn't hard to see his sorrow.

"You okay, Fadi?"

"I was just consoling my father. Seeing so much death is overwhelming. Remember in the Book of Revelation where it says mankind will face the great wine press of the wrath of God Almighty?" 8

"Yes, the blood of those following the Beast will be splattered as high as horses' bridles."

"Rafa and I prayed for so many more to respond, if they could've just given Jesus a chance to show His everlasting love."

Glancing toward a burning Jerusalem, the ex-Israeli Commander regretfully replied, "He was just a prayer away."

"When will we see you again?"

"His reign over the nations will begin after Jesus returns with His bride inside the New Jerusalem. The Holy Spirit will help us find each other during the marriage supper of the Lamb. Be safe, Fadi."

"Goodbye, Watchman, because of your faith I now understand."

Before leaving a puzzled Aaron asked, "What do you mean?"

"Jesus' brother James once wrote, 'Thus also faith by itself, if it does not have works, is dead. But someone will say, "You have faith, and I have works." Show me your faith without your works, and I will show you my faith by my works.'" 9

The opening of heaven was a sight to behold. The white horse emerging had a Rider called Faithful and True. 10 His eyes were like fire. His head had many crowns. He had a name no one knew. 11 His robe was dipped in blood. Armies of angels dressed in fine linen were following on white horses. 12 Out of His mouth came a sharp sword to strike the nations with. A Christ rejecting earth was barely in sight.

The tanks were motionless; the shooting over. The planes lighting the sky mysteriously disappeared. From their hiding places the redeemed openly wept. The bloody carnage was indescribable. A vast multitude of soldiers, their flesh dissolving on their bones, lay dead. As prophesied they were consumed by the breath of His mouth. 13

"The Word of God and His angels have defeated Kayin's armies!" cried a teenager. "'And this shall be the plague with which the Lord will strike all the people who fought against Jerusalem: Their flesh shall dissolve while they stand on their feet, their eyes shall dissolve in their sockets, and their tongues shall dissolve in their mouths.'" 14

To the north, in Syria, birds were eating dead flesh. To the south, in Egypt, blood was flowing in the streets. To the east, in Jordan, bellows of smoke were covering her cities. Those persecuting the apple of His eye, the children of Israel, were dead. A sober reminder of the fierceness of Almighty God it would take months to bury their enemies. 15

Tears of regret suddenly exploded into joyful celebration. A multitude of redeemed Jews joined arms and started dancing in the streets. Yeshua had saved them from their enemies.

A born again Rabbi proclaimed, "'Behold, I will save My people from the land of the east And from the land of the west; I will bring them back, And they shall dwell in the midst of Jerusalem. They shall be My people And I will be their God, In truth and righteousness.'" 16

Johanna Glazer crawled inside the filthy underground chamber just before hundred pound hailstones demolished every country in the Middle East. She could hear their cheers in the streets as she headed toward Jerusalem. For now, all she could do was intercede. Her race was almost over.

# THE TEMPLE OF THE LORD

"Behold, the Man whose name is the BRANCH. From His place He shall
branch out, And He shall build the temple of the Lord."
Zechariah 6:13

They could somehow smell the brimstone. The intense heat was
already burning the lining of their lungs. Both were struggling to
breathe. The false prophet began by begging for mercy.

"You know my heart, Lord. I've always believed in You. Satan
threatened to kill me. No one deserves such pain."

The Beast was speechless. He knew everlasting fire was created
for the Devil and his angels. Coming into view the lake was enlarging
itself. They would become the first fruits of eternal damnation.

Each convulsed when they saw the flames. There was no hint of
defiance coming from their lips; just a pitiful groveling by two leaders
who deliberately deceived mankind. Both closed their eyes before
being cast alive into the lake of fire burning with brimstone. 2

A multitude of believers watched in awe. Right before their eyes
their beloved Jerusalem was being restored.

A young man joyfully proclaimed, "'Now it shall come to pass in
the latter days that the mountain of the Lord's house shall be
established on the top of the mountains, and shall be exalted above
the hills; and all nations shall flow to it.'" 3

The 144,000 had already reached the top of the Temple Mount. 4 It was time for the first fruits redeemed from Israel to proclaim the mighty works of God. The promise to restore Mount Zion to the highest peak in the world was always there. 5 The adoration of those believing in God's covenant with Abraham was beyond words.

A believer from the tribe of Judah proudly shared, "'Hear the word of the Lord, O nations, And declare it in the isles afar off, and say, He who scattered Israel will gather him, And keep him as a shepherd does his flock.' For the Lord has redeemed Jacob, and ransomed him from the hand of one stronger than he. Therefore they shall come and sing in the height of Mount Zion...'" 6

The prophets faithfully predicted it. A remnant from other nations was returning to Zion. Not in unbelief but with hands raised high in joyful praise of their Lord and Savior!

"This is about us!" announced an ecstatic teenager. "Let me read it, 'For though your people, O Israel, be as the sand of the sea, A remnant of them will return; The destruction decreed shall overflow with righteousness. For the Lord God of hosts will make a determined end (Armageddon) in the midst of all the land.'" 7

His discerning friend added, "Don't you see? We survived the day of the Lord! We are the remnant from Israel!"

The forty-five day countdown to the Feast of Dedication was underway. 8 The Lord began by supernaturally raising the Temple Mount above all nations. This was followed by the gathering of a Jewish remnant to the land previously promised to Abraham.

"We must not forget!" exhorted a grateful born again Rabbi to a crowd of avid listeners. 'And it shall come to pass in all the land," says the Lord, "That two-thirds in it shall be cut off and die, But one-third shall be left in it: I will bring the one-third through the fire, Will refine them as silver is refined, And test them as gold is tested. They will call on My name, And I will answer them. I will say, "This is My people'; And each one will say, "The Lord is my God.'" 9

Seeing the dead bodies of family and friends with the mark of the beast was heartbreaking. Nevertheless, their mourning had a higher purpose. Gentiles were arriving. During the Feast of Dedication, redeemed Gentiles will stand shoulder to shoulder with their Jewish brothers in Christ as the glory of God fills the Temple for the final time. The prophets spoke of it. Isaiah saw it.

"Look at them!" praised the thrilled Rabbi. "Yeshua is gathering believers from the nations! 'For by fire and by His sword The Lord will judge all flesh and the slain of the Lord shall be many...For I know their works and their thoughts. It shall be that I will gather all nations and tongues; and they shall come and see My glory.'" 10

His future reign over the nations always had a purpose. 11 The Lord was not only restoring; He was mending hearts.

For many arriving, it was a devastating feeling to see the tabernacle of David in ruins. Until they saw the Lord!

A captivated boy proclaimed in a loud voice, "'And with this the words of the prophets agree...After this I will return and will rebuild the tabernacle of David, which has fallen down, I will rebuild its ruins, and I will set it up; so that the rest of mankind may seek the LORD...Behold, the Man whose name is the BRANCH. From His place He shall branch out, And He shall build the temple of the Lord. Yes, He shall bear the glory, And shall sit and rule on His throne; So He shall be a priest on His throne, And the counsel of peace shall be between them both.'" 12

Ezekiel prophesied the area surrounding the mountaintop would be holy. 13 In the middle would be the Most Holy Place. 14 Followers of Christ standing shoulder to shoulder watched as the Temple of the Lord rose before their eyes.

A voice from above reverently declared, "He will be great, and will be called the Son of the Highest; and the Lord God will give Him the throne of His father David." 15

After the seventh bowl was poured out, the day of the Lord ended when the Word killed every follower of the Beast. 16 The mountain of the Lord's house was now the highest point on earth. 17 A redeemed remnant was joyfully returning to Jerusalem; the land promised the descendants of Abraham. 18 The Temple of the Lord was complete. Now the throne of David would be given to its rightful heir.

Angels reverently bowed as the Son returned in the clouds!

"...One like the Son of Man, coming with the clouds of heaven. He came to the Ancient of Days, and they brought Him near before

Him. Then to Him was given dominion and glory and a kingdom, that all peoples, nations, and languages should serve Him..." 19

Standing before the Ancient of Days the Son received dominion over a kingdom of peoples who will serve Him!

# FOR A THOUSAND YEARS

*"...And they lived and reigned with Christ for a thousand years."*
*Revelation 20:4*

His domain was icy cold. Swirling smoke exuded an atmosphere of death. His towering throne was made of pure stone. Satan was reading from the book of the dead. Bound in human flesh, this foul spirit loved the feel of it.

The angelic host had so much looked forward to this moment. With great anticipation a multitude in pure bright linen roared. An angel holding the key to the bottomless pit was descending. 1 It understood its task.

Hurling the book through stagnate grey smoke the prince of darkness cursed, "Enough!"

At the sounding of the seventh trumpet God stripped Satan of his power over the world. 2 He was now all alone. The rebellious angels who followed him to earth before the creation of man were awaiting his arrival.

After a radiant light enveloped his throne, the Devil defiantly howled, "What right do you have entering my domain?"

Not bothering to reply the warrior angel laid hold of the accuser of the brethren and bound him with a chain.

"I demand an answer! Is this not my kingdom?"

The key turning produced hideous demonic shrieks. Before casting him into the bottomless pit; the angel put a seal on Satan preventing him from deceiving anyone for a thousand years. 3

"You know this is just for a season! Someday I will deceive the nations from one corner of the earth to the other. I will gather them like the sand of the sea. We will surround the camp of the saints. 4

They will curse God. Those following me will once again pursue the darkness!"

Rising to the top of the bottomless pit a multitude of demons vainly spewed forth blasphemous threats no one could hear.

An animated Peter had just finished praying inside the eastern gate of the New Jerusalem. From behind, John and James caught him in a big bear hug. They cheered as Andrew, Phillip, Bartholomew, Matthew, Thomas, James, Thaddaeus, and Simon greeted them. 5 Moments later Matthias, the apostle who replaced Judas Iscariot, arrived completing the circle. 6

An angelic messenger made the announcement.

"'And I saw thrones, and they sat on them, and judgment was committed to them...Assuredly I say to you, that in the regeneration (Millennium), when the Son of Man sits on the throne of His glory, you who have followed Me will also sit on twelve thrones, judging the twelve tribes of Israel.'" 7

Gazing toward the Son seated upon His throne the apostles lifted their hands in praise. Their thrones were waiting. The pioneers of Christianity stepped forward one by one to receive the power to judge the twelve tribes of Israel.

Roads leading into Jerusalem were filled with bright lights. Carrying candles the redeemed were singing a psalm of praise. 8 The preparation for the return of the Lamb of God was a joy for all involved.

Within the Holy City, amidst a reverent hush, they were resurrected. Killed by the Beast for their witness of Jesus and the Word of God, these overcomers did not love their lives unto death. 9

One of the living creatures bowed before speaking.

"'Blessed and holy is he who has part in the first resurrection. Over such the second death has no power, but they shall be priests of God and of Christ, and shall reign with Him a thousand years.'" 10

The radiant Christ gave a loving glance as resurrected martyrs humbly approached their thrones. Magnificent shouts of affirmation rang out through the Tabernacle of God as they were seated. The marriage supper of the Lamb was ready. 11

---

An angel who poured out one of the seven bowls was given the honor to make the privileged broadcast.

"One and all come see the Lamb and His bride! 12 It is time for a new heaven to join itself to a new earth!"

Instantly the radiant city was moving. In all her majesty the Holy Jerusalem descended upon Mount Moriah.

An escorting angel acknowledged, "'...Behold, the tabernacle of God is with men, and He will dwell with them, and they shall be His people. God Himself will be with them and be their God. And God will wipe away every tear from their eyes; there shall be no more death, nor sorrow, nor crying. There shall be no more pain, for the former things have passed away.'" 13

Believers standing in her shadow erupted in praises unto God!

"It's the Holy Jerusalem; the great four square city!"

"The Lamb of God is returning with His Bride!"

"Could this be His Shekinah glory?"

"'And behold, the glory of the God of Israel came from the way of the east. His voice was like the sound of many waters; and the earth shone with His glory.'"14

Another read aloud, "'And the glory of the LORD came into the temple by way of the gate which faces toward the east. The Spirit lifted me up and brought me into the inner court; and behold, the glory of the LORD filled the temple.'"15

Those waving palm branches cried out, "Hosanna, in the highest, Hosanna, in the highest, Yeshua is the light of the world. 16 His glory is filling the Temple!"

A daughter of Zion proudly shared, "'And it shall come to pass in that day that the remnant of Israel, And such as have escaped of the house of Jacob, Will never again depend on him who defeated them, But will depend on the Lord, the Holy One of Israel, in truth. The remnant will return, the remnant of Jacob, To the Mighty God.'" 17

A holy hush stretched for as far as the eye could see. The glorious foursquare city was enveloping the Temple of the Lord.

His voice was like the sound of many waters.

"'...Behold, I make all things new...It is done. I am the Alpha and the Omega, the Beginning and the End. I will give of the fountain of the water of life freely to him who thirsts. He who overcomes shall inherit all things, and I will be his God and he shall be My son. But the cowardly, unbelieving, abominable, murderers, sexually immoral, sorcerers, idolaters, and all liars shall have their part in the lake which burns with fire and brimstone, which is the second death.'" [18]

One of the twenty-four elders bowed before requesting to speak.

"'...Her light was like a most precious stone, like a jasper stone, clear as crystal. Also she had a great and high wall with twelve gates, and twelve angels at the gates, and names written on them, which are the names of the twelve tribes of the children of Israel: three gates on the east, three gates on the north, three gates on the south, and three gates on the west. Now the wall of the city had twelve foundations, and on them were the names of the twelve apostles of the Lamb...'" [19]

Amidst such exhilaration a warrior angel was given the order to issue this final warning.

"In a thousand years Satan will appear a final time. Beware; his first rebellion took place in the Garden of Eden. His final rebellion, when mankind will once again embrace his lies, will occur outside the beloved city, Jerusalem." [20]

# THE HEALING OF THE NATIONS

"In the middle of its street, and on either side of the river, was the tree of life, which bore twelve fruits, each tree yielding its fruit every month. The leaves of the tree were for the healing of the nations."
Revelation 22:2

Within the Holy City is a crystal river. This water of life is flowing from the throne of God. 1 On each side is the tree of life. Its leaves will be used for the healing of the nations. 2

An angel stood and proclaimed a truth so many rejected.

"'And the Lord shall be King over all the earth. In that day it shall be "The Lord is one," And His name one.'" 3

There was no darkness within the New Jerusalem. The Lamb will be her light. 4 The glorified saints were praising God. His name was written on their foreheads. 5 Their reign with Him will last forever. 6

His rule over the nations was underway. Members from the Rescue Squad could hardly control their excitement.

"Do you really think so?" squealed Emma.

"Oh yeah!" predicted a giddy Kurt. "The Q was meant to be together for eternity! Someday it will happen."

"Have you seen anybody we know?"

"Not yet. Hey sis, remember when Greg asked us what one event we wanted to see on the first day of the Millennium?"

"Sure, we were all inside the Santino's cave."

"Well, how awesome was it watching the Lamb and His bride descending inside the New Jerusalem?"

"How can anyone describe the Holy City?" she beamed.

"Not me!"

"I remember your event. You could hardly wait to see the Devil cast into the bottomless pit! What a rush, huh?"

"Ask me in a thousand years! Having a front row seat when Satan is cast into the lake of fire has such a nice ring to it! "

"Many have entered the New Jerusalem. I've heard the thrones of the martyrs are breathtaking."

"Are you ready to catch a glimpse of our buddy?"

"Who do you mean, Kurt?"

"Yep, ole Delgado gave his life as a testimony of God's love."

"We get to see Carlos!" hollered Emma.

"I'd say the pain of martyrdom is well worth the price of admission. Nothing compares to this. Carlos is officially reigning on his own throne."

Weaving between believers celebrating was so much greater than he ever dreamed. In his mind he kept hearing, 'Eye has not seen, nor ear heard, nor have entered into the heart of man the things which God has prepared for those who love Him.' 7 Spotting them he called out after picking up the pace.

While Kurt was waving she took off running.  His hug would always be special.

"Wow, Em, you're looking a bit better since Armageddon."

"We really made it, Greg! Have you seen, Reenie?"

"Not yet."

"Trust me," reflected an out of breath Kurt, "our Miracle Girl would never miss our reunion."

"I wonder what Jake is doing right about now?"

"I know, Greg. Jake is searching for Jessie!"

"Bank on it, sis. The boy must be looking for his special someone. Gee, never thought the Q would ever be second place in JJ's life."

"I remember his prayer," cried a grateful Emma. "Jake got to see the earth restored like the Garden of Eden."

Turning around the three Watchmen joined a sea of overcomers gazing over a new earth; as far as the eye could see.

It was a special moment when the tall brunette waved near the enormous wall of jasper of the Holy City. Strolling arm in arm a mesmerized Judah and Hanna Lentz had no words.

Running up ahead, little Ruth shouted, "Hurry, Mom and Dad, can't you see her?"

Johanna Esther Glazer silently thanked the Lord for this precious family; descendents from the patriarch Abraham. A stranger in the city of David it was Ruth who rescued her. It was Hanna who not only loved her but was the first to believe in Yeshua. And it was Judah who shared the truth of the gospel with her infamous father, Matthias.

He was moving the best he could. Throughout his life, he was so misjudged. Even his best intentions were often misunderstood. Yet someone was always watching. The Lord had witnessed every trial, every heart break, and every hurt. The pain he suffered didn't matter now.

"Ben, Ben, we're here!"

Twanna's high-pitched shrill didn't bother him; not this time. Several saints from the Vineyard were also cheering. In their midst stood Ostenaco. The proud Cherokee Chief was waiting to thank the one affectionately called, Running Bear. The trials they endured together through the day of the Lord made this reunion extra special.

"I thank the Lord for every one of you," wept Ben.

"Isn't there someone you want to see?" suggested Twanna. "No one can miss his southern drawl! Even in his resurrected body."

"C'mon, girl, how fine is Cody looking in his new body?"

No one needed to point them out. The 144,000 from the twelve tribes of Israel had their Father's name on their foreheads. Surrounding them was the remnant from Azal. Divinely protected from His final wrath; they were praising Almighty God for His mercy.

Her search among the overcomers took a while before she found him. She could hear his familiar deep voice worshipping the Lord.

"I'm right behind you, Aaron."

He froze after hearing his name. Then he saw her smile.

"Glazer, I never doubted you'd make a great Watchman."

"Johanna and I thank the Lord for you, Miriam."

"So how was the race?"

"Better than I ever imagined."

After a warm embrace, she couldn't believe the change. Almost overnight the bitter soldier Matthias had become a man of God.

"We could feel your prayers. How was your intersession in Azal?"

"No doubt, the most intense time I ever had in the Lord."

"Honestly, there were times we wanted to give up. It was Holy Spirit who gave us the strength to run even faster."

Grinning from ear to ear she loved asking her next question.

"So, how much did the Holy Spirit achieve in twenty-five days?"

"I'll let Johanna tell you."

"We expected a lot from her, didn't we?"

"So did the Lord. She's a real warrior, Miriam. You were right; I learned so much from her. God's love really propelled her witness. As this dark world was passing away our Johanna became a shining light to those seeking salvation, both Jew and Gentile."

"Have you seen her?"

"Not yet."

"Can you tell me how many of your soldiers got saved?"

"A lot more than I expected."

"Oh ye of little faith!" she playfully whispered

Rushing toward them was Fadi and Rafa pulling their father along.

"Oh really," laughed Aaron, "If you only knew!"

# THE CITY OF MY GOD

"He who overcomes, I will make him a pillar in the temple of My God... I will write on him the name of My God and the name of the city of My God, the New Jerusalem, which comes down out of heaven from My God. And I will write on him My new name."
Revelation 3:12

The twelve gates of the magnificent city were open. All twelve apostles were seated on their thrones. The reigning bride of Christ, including those martyred by the Beast, were worshipping the Lord. 1

Even though she hadn't recognized anyone yet, she didn't feel alone. Walking through the western gate her first glimpse was priceless. The splendor was incredible. Each saint had His name and the New Jerusalem written on their foreheads. She could hardly wait for the day she would join them with her resurrection body.

All she could think of when she first saw the Lord was the night she was born again; a memory for eternity. It was all etched in her mind, the smelly loft, the dirty sleeping bags, even the noisy coffee maker.

Amidst their praises she scanned the multitude reigning with Christ. When their eyes met he smiled. He never looked so happy; so fulfilled. There was no need for words, no regrets, no what could have been. Tears of joy slid down her red cheeks as she covered her mouth with her hands. Reenie Ann Tucker silently thanked the Lord for the witness of Anthony Bret Santino. A believer who gave his life for those he loved. Not for power or prestige or for some sort of reward. Tragically in the end most never understood such a sacrifice.

Close to twenty-six hundred years ago, Isaiah prophesied of a new heaven and a new earth while standing on this very ground.

'For as the new heavens and the new earth which I will make shall remain before Me," says the Lord, So shall your descendants and your name remain. And it shall come to pass That from one New Moon to another, And from one Sabbath to another, All flesh shall come to worship before Me," says the Lord.' 2

Pastor Greg Hudson was silently reminiscing while members of the Q Squad were exchanging stories. He remembered the Ryan's big couch. Finding Lee's tape outlining the events taking place before, during, and after Christ's second coming. He thought he had missed being with the Lord forever. He had waited long enough. The pearl gate in front of him was open. There was nothing stopping him.

The Throne of God was dazzling. A joyful Jesus was sharing with His apostles. Amidst the marriage supper the pastor could feel the unity of the saints. The guests, those saved during the day of the Lord, were also celebrating the glory of His inheritance. 3

Somehow they knew he was coming. Their prayers had been divinely answered. Misty was seated between her mother Ivy and her brother Ethan. Clapping their hands above their heads; their joy was beyond words. Greg wept over the passage placed in his mind by the Holy Spirit.

"'For this reason I bow my knees to the Father of our Lord Jesus Christ, from whom the whole family in heaven and earth is named, that He would grant you, according to the riches of His glory, to be strengthened with might through His Spirit in the inner man, that Christ may dwell in your hearts through faith; that you, being rooted and grounded in love, may be able to comprehend with all the saints what is the width and length and depth and height—to know the love of Christ which passes knowledge; that you may be filled with all the fullness of God. Now to Him who is able to do exceedingly abundantly above all that we ask or think, according to the power that works in us, to Him be glory in the church by Christ Jesus to all generations, forever and ever. Amen.'" 4

## SATAN RELEASED

"Now when the thousand years have expired, Satan will be released from
his prison and will go out to deceive the nations which are in the four
corners of the earth, Gog and Magog, to gather them together to battle,
whose number is as the sand of the sea."
Revelation 20:7-8

He was a mere sixteen-years-old. Going solo this past year as a
witness of the final rebellion was his calling. It would be the hardest
thing he would ever do for the Lord.

"Hey, everybody, how is our Watchman doing today? Yesterday
he was stirring up the people big time."

The crowd surrounding the teenager was larger than normal.
Some knew his warning by heart. Others were just curious.

"He hasn't missed a day in months. I'm telling you these
millennium fanatics are out in force. Tomorrow, they believe a
demonic angel they call Satan will be released from some sort of
bottomless pit."

"Why release an evil angel?" mocked another.

"This Satan is somehow going to deceive the nations. Trust me;
this isn't a joke. This kid really believes this."

"Blah, blah, blah," laughed a visitor. "This past year I've heard
this fairytale over a hundred times. Careful, if you don't believe these
fanatics you're doomed to the lake of fire! Go ahead ask him. They
have an answer for everything."

"Hey, Watchman, why are so many entering the city of lights?"

The youngster could sense their deep hostility. When he first
preached Satan's rebellion against the nations, their joking was like a
mask. As the months dragged on their anger only grew bitter. His final

exhortation was in front of the eastern gate of the Holy City.

"'Blessed are those who do His commandments, that they may have the right to the tree of life, and may enter through the gates into the city.' 1 Tomorrow Christ's thousand year reign will end. Once Satan is released from his prison he will deceive the nations with his lies.

"What type of lies?"

"The nations will be deceived into surrounding the beloved city of the saints. Those who do will be devoured by fire sent by God. This is why all believers on earth are entering the New Jerusalem."

"Let me guess, if the Devil doesn't get us God will. Get a life; no one believes such nonsense. You obviously consider us second class citizens because we haven't visited the foursquare city."

"Only those in the Lamb's Book of Life can enter in."

"Where do you get this from anyway?"

The teenager calmly read, "'And the nations of those who are saved shall walk in its light, and the kings of the earth bring their glory and honor into it. Its gates shall not be shut at all by day (there shall be no night there). And they shall bring the glory and the honor of the nations into it. But there shall by no means enter it anything that defiles, or causes an abomination or a lie, but only those who are written in the Lamb's Book of Life.'" 2

"How does one know their name is written in such a book?"

"By believing in the death, burial, and resurrection, of Jesus!"

"Have you been inside?"

"I have. The Lord is reigning over the nations from the Temple on Mount Moriah. That's why I'm here. I'll pray with anyone choosing to believe in Jesus as their Lord and Savior. Anyone who does will receive eternal life! You will also be spared from the fire which will soon devour those following the Devil."

Over their howling laughter, another sarcastically asked, "Is this why you think you're so special? You freaks should be outlawed for using such fear tactics. Does anyone know this fanatic's name?"

"My name is David Glazer. The Gog and Magog battle is near."

"No joke, this kid really is a Glazer. His family tree can be traced back a thousand years to Aaron Glazer. Aaron was an Israeli freedom fighter during the Armageddon war. This propaganda has been passed down through his family for centuries. C'mon, prophet, you must know why we can't enter your Holy City?"

The teenager patiently waited for their full attention.

"'But outside are dogs and sorcerers and sexually immoral and murderers and idolaters, and whoever loves and practices a lie.'" 3

"Tell you what, Glazer, we'll all meet you here tomorrow and we'll see who practices a lie! You're just another self-righteous hypocrite incapable of seeing how many you hurt through such fear mongering."

"The White Throne judgment is for real!" countered David. "At this judgment all those not written in the Book of Life will be cast into the lake of fire. 4 This is the second death."

"You're confused! How many times can a man die?"

"Spiritual death is for eternity, 'Blessed and holy is he who has part in the first resurrection. Over such the second death has no power.'" 5

"None of us believe in your fairly tales about Satan, a lake of fire, or some phony resurrection. No one controls us; not even the One you say rules inside the foursquare city."

His reign over the nations would end within the hour. The slurs and cat calls from the unsaved outside the walls of the Holy City could be heard for miles. Saints were walking through the gates for the final time. Once inside the resurrected bride gave them a glorious welcome. For a brief moment the unsaved could hear them worshipping the Alpha and Omega, the Beginning and the End, the First and the Last. 6

His evil smirk reeked with revenge. Satan had methodically rehearsed his plan of attack over and over again. From the darkness of the bottomless pit he cursed several angels.

"Remove this chain at once!"

His exhortation was for the unsaved still on earth.

"Beware inhabitants of the nations; a battle is looming. Don't you have the right to do what's best for your family? Be honest, aren't you weary of the iron fist ruling your souls? I alone have the power to free you from such oppression. Once my army is gathered we shall conquer the beloved city."

Like the sand of sea, unregenerate mankind would once again

choose darkness over light. After surrounding the camp of the saints, this multitude received their final instructions from Satan. The fire raining down left no doubt. 7 No one was found alive amidst their charred bodies.

The grisly smell of brimstone was coming in waves. It wasn't long before he heard his name being cursed. Moving closer the foul spirit could see a line of light. Satan had no desire to step over this light. Yet when he tried to retreat, the Spirit of God only drew him closer. This wasn't the smoky bottomless pit he had just been released from. 8 Or even the dreaded weeping and gnashing of teeth of Hades. 9

An angel was waiting on him. His pronouncement would be final.

"One thousand years ago the two beasts were the first to be cast into the lake of fire. They refuse to believe you will be joining them in their eternal suffering. May it be as it is written." 10

Passing through the scorching orange flames Satan was allowed to see their spirits. The agony of the beast and his false prophet was beyond description. Their torment was before them, day and night for ever and ever! 11

## A GREAT WHITE THRONE

"Then I saw a great white throne and Him who sat on it, from whose face the earth and the heaven fled away. And there was found no place for them."
Revelation 20:11

The second resurrection unto eternal death was about to commence.

An angel between earth and heaven made it official.

"'The sea gave up the dead who were in it, and Death and Hades delivered up the dead who were in them. And they were judged, each one according to his works.'" 1

The resurrection of the wicked out of Hades was a sight to behold. The unsaved from the time of Adam until the final rebellion by Satan found themselves standing before the Son of God. From His great white throne Jesus watched as books containing the good works of the dead were opened. 2 The Book of Life was also opened. 3

"Where are we?" demanded an apostate minister. "This isn't heaven."

Not one person was found written in the Book of Life. Some were petrified; others just numb, while most vainly tried to defend themselves.

"This is a mistake!" begged a mother of four. "I never missed church, I tithed, and I never hurt anybody. I don't deserve this!"

They were all judged in a moment in time. Many blindly believed their good works would result in their salvation. Instead degrees of eternal punishment were being decreed.

A mega church pastor pleaded, "There were so many ways to believe. How was I to know? I implore your forgiveness, Lord."

"This is so bogus!" cursed a teenager. "Aren't You a loving God?"

"There is no such thing as eternal lake of fire!" challenged a pious theologian. "I refuse to believe this!"

The sheer depth of their deception was terrifying. Their beseeching for mercy never let up. The judgment by the Son of God was final. Everyone resurrected out of Hades was cast into the lake of fire. 4 A place of anguish where one's spirit never dies!

<hr />

The moment the wicked were cast into the lake of fire, Hades joined them. The enemies of the cross were no more. The last enemy, physical death, was also cast into the lake of fire. No one would ever die again!

'Then comes the end, when He delivers the kingdom to God the Father, when He puts an end to all rule and all authority and power. For He must reign till He has put all enemies under His feet. The last enemy that will be destroyed is death.' 5

Standing before the throne of God, the Son delivered His kingdom back to His Father, so God may be all and all. Surely, this event will be honored throughout eternity!

<hr />

Praying near the river of life she remembered. It took place in the first week of Christ's reign over the nations. Miriam was searching for her daughter. Her anticipation was obvious.

"Johanna, Johanna!"

Turning around the tall brunette rushed into her arms.

"Mama, I love you so much. Have you seen Daddy?"

"Sure have. We just had a long chat. I must say you two were quite a team. Honey, I have something I want to ask you."

"What is it, Mama?"

"When was the last time someone called you, Jessie?"

"Is it true? Have you really found the Q Squad?"

"Well sort of."

"What do you mean?"

"You'll have to find out for yourself."

Miraculously the Holy Spirit led her daughter to a sea of radiant faces fellowshipping near the western gate of the Holy Jerusalem. At first she didn't recognize the young man. After a long embrace, he grabbed her waist lifting her off the ground. Her smile never looked so good. It was like they were never separated.

"Jake, I've missed you so much!"

"I never let a day go by without praying for your safety."

"Have you seen anyone from the Q Squad?"

"Sure have. Greg, Emma, and Kurt are praising the Lord."

"What about Carlos?"

"He gave his life, Jess. He was numbered with the martyrs. He is reigning inside the Holy City. So tell me about your aunt and uncle?"

"The Lord saved them both. It's a pretty wild story."

"The Holy Spirit told me you wouldn't quit."

"You're such a blessing."

"Are you ready? The Q Squad is waiting on you."

"Where are they?"

"Have you seen the Lord?

"Not yet. I didn't want to go alone."

"You know, I actually saw someone who is very special to us. He's even wearing a crown."

"Who could it be?"

"Appleby looks mighty distinguished in his glorified body."

"Luuuke! Will you go with me to see him?"

Taking her hand he asked, "You know I found your letter in the Santino's cave. There was one thing you wrote I didn't quite understand."

"C'mon, Jamison, we've got all eternity to talk."

"Jess, couldn't you just tell me..."

Slipping her fingers over his lips she could only giggle.

"Honestly, JJ, some things never change."

# SCRIPTURE REFERENCES

Chapter 1
1. Rev. 15:1
2. Rev. 16:2
3. Dan. 12:10
4. Exod. 2:11-12
5. Exod. 3:13-14
6. Eph. 2:10
7. Zech. 14:16-19
8. Rev. 11:15
9. Rev. 14:14:1-4
10. Rev. 16:16; 19:11-21, Dan. 12:11
11. Dan. 12:12, Rev. 21:9-10
12. Zech. 6:12-13, Ezek. 43:2-5
13. Rev. 21:9-10
14. Rev. 19:7
15. Zech. 14:4-5

Chapter 2
1. Isa. 63:1-4
2. Isa. 35:8-10, 27:13
3. Rev. 11:11
4. Rev. 14:1-4
5. Zech. 14:4-5
6. Jn. 6:44
7. Isa. 62:6-7
8. Isa. 62:11-12
9. Rev. 11:18-19
10. Mat. 7:21-23
11. Mat. 24:45; 25:34

Chapter 3
1. II Pet. 1:10-11
2. Rev. 11:18
3. Rev. 19:17
4. Dan. 9:27; 12:11, Rev. 16:16; 19:17
5. Rev. 15:1; 16:1-21
6. Rev. 15:2-4
7. Rev. 11:19
8. Rev. 15:6
9. Rev. 15:7
10. Rev. 15:8

Chapter 4
1. Rev. 16:1
2. Rev. 16:2
3. I Thes. 5:2-3

4. Eph. 6:16
5. I Cor. 12:8
6. Mk. 10:15
7. Gen. 17:19-20
8. Mat. 8:11-12
9. Mat. 10:33
10. Mat. 28:18-19, I Jn. 5:7
11. Act. 4:12, Jn. 3:16; 18
12. Act. 1:7-11, Isa. 2:2-4
13. Zech. 13:8
14. Zech. 13:9
15. Joel 3:12-14
16. Rev. 7:1-8; 12:1-6
17. Rev. 10:1-7; 14:1, Isa. 63:1-3
18. Rev. 16:16
19. Rev. 19:13
20. Rev. 19:21

Chapter 5
1. Rev. 2:11
2. Dan. 9:27, Lk. 21:20, Ezek. 38:1-14
3. Mat. 24:21-31, Rev. 7:9-14
4. Rev. 8:7
5. Rev. 11:15
6. Rev. 15:1; 16:17-21
7. Zech. 12:3
8. Zech. 14:3-4
9. Zech. 14:12
10. Zech. 12:9
11. Isa. 2:11
12. Zech. 12:10
13. Rev. 21:9-10; 20:6
14. Zech. 14:9
15. Rev. 10:1-7
16. Jn. 20:19-22
17. Rev. 14:1-4
18. Zech. 14:4-5
19. Lev. 23:1-44
20. Isa. 10:20
21. Ezek. 43:1-5, Jn. 10:22, Dan. 12:12

Chapter 6
1. Jn. 17:5-6
2. Jn. 17:1-3
3. Jn. 1:10-14

4. Jn. 1:1; 14
5. Jn. 3:16-18
6. Rev. 9:20
7. Lk. 21:24, Rom. 11:25-27, Rev. 11:2-7
8. Rev. 10:7
9. Rom. 11:26, Isa 59:20-21
10. Rev. 12:11
11. Mat. 7:21
12. Rom. 5:1-6
13. Act. 2:38-40
14. Act. 2:41
15. Act. 10:44-47
16. Act. 11:17
17. Mat. 5:44

Chapter 7
1. Jn. 8:44
2. Rev. 20:4
3. Rev. 20:1
4. Rev. 16:13-14
5. Dan. 9:27; 12:11-12
6. Rev. 17:6
7. Rev. 18:13
8. Rev. 18:8
9. Isa. 2:2-3
10. Rev. 16:20
11. Ezek. 20:40, Mic. 4:1
12. Isa. 10:20-21
13. Isa. 10:21-23
14. Jer. 31:10-12
15. Isa 10:20-21
16. Isa. 66:16-19, Mic. 7:10-17
17. Isa. 66:18
18. Zech. 6:12, Dan. 12:11-12
19. Rev. 16:19
20. Zech. 6:12-13
21. Isa. 65:17-18a
22. Dan. 7:13-14
23. Lk. 1:32
24. Rom. 12:19
25. Rom. 6:8
26. Rom. 6:11

Chapter 8
1. Isa. 46:9-10
2. Gen. 49:10, Lk. 3:23-24
3. Mic. 5:2, Mat. 2:1

4. Isa. 40:3, Mat. 3:1-2
5. Isa. 53:5, Mat. 27:26
6. Psa. 41:9, Mat. 26:47-50
7. Psa. 22:6, Lk. 23:33
8. Isa. 53:5, Mat. 27:26
9. Zech. 11:12, Mat. 26:15
10. Isa. 50:6, Mat. 26:67
11. Isa. 53:7
12. Mat. 27:12-14
13. Psa. 22:16-18
14. Isa. 53:12
15. Mat. 27:38
16. I Jn. 1:10
17. Zep. 3:9
18. Isa. 66:8
19. Ezek. 35:3-5
20. Psa. 83:1-21, Zep. 3:10-12, Isa. 43:6
21. Ezek. 37:21
22. Rev. 16:19
23. Rev. 19:11-21; 11:18

Chapter 9
1. Rev 13:16-18; 14:9-12
2. I Cor. 12:14-18
3. I Cor. 12:26
4. I Cor. 12:25
5. Obad. 1:12-14
6. Obad. 1:15-16
7. Obad. 1:17-18
8. Jer. 49:17-18

Chapter 10
1. Rev. 16:3
2. Isa. 65:17-18a
3. Isa. 66:16, 18-19, Mic. 7:10, 16-17
4. Rev. 16:12-14
5. Isa. 14:12-17
6. Rev. 19:17-20
7. Rev. 20:10
8. Rev. 16:10
9. I Jn. 2:27
10. Rev. 22:1
11. Rev. 22:2
12. I Thes. 4:14-17, Mat. 24:30-31, Jn. 5:28
13. Rev. 21:9-10
14. Rev. 21:4

15. Rev. 21:5
16. Dan. 2:44
17. Rom. 11:25-27
18. Psa. 122:6
19. Isa. 2:3-4
20. Rev. 21:22
21. Rev. 22:3
22. Ezek. 43:1-7
23. Rev. 21:23-24
24. Zech. 14:6-7
25. Zech. 6:13
26. Ezek. 43:7, 9
27. Zech. 14:8-9
28. Rev. 22:2
29. Ezek.47:12
30. Rev. 21:4, Isa. 25:8
31. Rev. 21:27

Chapter 11
1. I Pet. 4:19
2. II Pet. 3:10
3. Ezek. 36:34-35
4. Ezek. 36:36
5. Rev. 12:5; 20:6
6. Rev. 21:9-10
7. I Thes. 5:4-7
8. Ezek. 37:21
9. Ezek. 36:25-26
10. Ezek. 4:3-6
11. Lev. 26:17-18
12. Ezek. 39:4, 7
13. Heb. 12:1-3
14. Jn. 15:13
15. Psa. 83:2-6
16. Gal. 4:29
17. Ezek. 35:3-5
18. Psa. 79:5-7

Chapter 12
1. Rev. 11:3
2. Rev. 11:7
3. Dan. 9:27; 12:11, Rev. 19:20
4. Rev. 19: 17-20
5. Dan. 12:12
6. Rev. 21:24-27
7. Jn. 13:7
8. Mat. 28:18-20
9. Mat. 21:42
10. Isa. 49:6

Chapter 13
1. Mat. 20:18-19
2. Jn. 1:11-12
3. Jn. 8:54-59
4. Jn. 14:54-59
5. II Pet. 3:9
6. Psa. 105:15
7. Lk. 4:24
8. Jam. 1:1
9. Isa. 20:24-25
10. Ezek. 37:26-28
11. Deut. 4:7-8
12. Jn. 6:65
13. Heb. 1:8-10
14. Zech. 14:12

Chapter 14
1. Rev. 19:8
2. Rev. 15:6
3. 1 Thes. 4:14
4. Rev. 21:3
5. Rev. 16:13
6. Rev. 3:21-22
7. II Thes. 3:13-14
8. Dan. 7:24
9. Heb. 11:8-10
10. Jn. 14:1-4
11. Heb. 12:22
12. Heb. 11:8-10
13. Heb. 11:13
14. Rev. 21:16
15. Gen. 12:1-3
16. Isa. 2:1-3

Chapter 15
1. Isa. 27:13
2. Isa. 66:19
3. Jn. 16:3
4. Rev. 19:17-18
5. Rom. 8:5-6
6. Mat. 24:30-39, Rev. 7:9-14
7. Rev. 16:14-16; 19:11-21
8. Rev. 19:20
9. Rev. 19:21
10. Rev. 21:9-10, Dan. 12:12
11. Rev. 6:1-17, Mat. 24:4-29
12. Mk. 13:33-36
13. Rev. 3:3

14. I Tim. 4:1
15. II Tim. 4:3-4


Chapter 16
1. Isa. 66:2
2. Isa. 62:6-7
3. Isa. 62:1-2
4. Act. 26:16-18
5. Mat. 24:21-31, 2 Thes. 2:1
6. Isa. 2:11
7. Dan. 12:11-12

Chapter 17
1. Rev. 16:4
2. Rev. 16:5-6
3. Rev. 16:7
4. Jn. 3:14-16
5. Jn. 1:11
6. Jn. 1:12
7. Rev. 11:15-17
8. Rev. 11:18
9. Rev. 16:9
10. Rev. 18:10
11. Rev. 17:16
12. Rev. 18:9
13. Rev. 18:20

Chapter 18
1. Rev. 3:8
2. Rev. 3:15-17
3. Col. 3:1-5
4. Jn. 1:14
5. Jn. 9:35-38
6. Rom. 9:4

Chapter 19
1. Jn. 1:14
2. Jn. 1:1
3. Rom. 12:14-15
4. Rev. 14:9-10
5. Rev. 14:11
6. Mat. 25:41
7. Jn. 15:6
8. II Thes. 1:9-10
9. Jn. 6:44, Mat. 13:41-43
10. Rev. 20:11-13
11. Rev. 16:8-9

12. Mat. 24:29, Rev. 6:12, Joel 2:30-31

Chapter 20
1. I Cor. 15:23
2. Mat. 24:21-31, I Thes. 4:14-17, II Thes. 2:1
3. I Cor. 15:51-52
4. Rev. 20:4
5. I Cor. 15:24-27
6. Isa. 52:7-10
7. Isa. 53:1

Chapter 21
1. Rev. 16:6
2. Rev. 16:5

Chapter 22
1. Rev. 16:9

Chapter 23
1. Jn. 3:16
2. Mk. 2:5
3. Mk. 2:9-11
4. Eph. 2:8

Chapter 24
1. Zep. 3:8
2. Act. 4:12
3. Jn. 2:19
4. Jn. 3:14-15
5. Mat. 18:20
6. Deut. 6:4
7. I Jn. 5:7
8. Mat. 28:19

Chapter 25
1. Dan. 11:43
2. Rev. 13:3-7
3. Rev. 20:1-3
4. Rev. 21:27
5. Rev. 16:10-11
6. Lk. 21:20-24, Joel 3:12-14

Chapter 26
1. Rev. 16:10
2. Rev. 16:11
3. Jer. 10:23-24

4. Prov. 20:24
5. Rev. 14:1-4
6. Jer. 10:25
7. Rev. 16:10
8. Jer. 31:6-7

Chapter 27
1. Isa. 27:13
2. Rev. 16:13
3. Rev. 16:14
4. Jn. 15:19
5. Rev. 14:10-11
6. Mat. 3:17
7. Jn. 1:36
8. Rev. 21:7; 22:13
9. Lk. 12:4-5
10. Rev. 20:11-15, Mat. 25:41

Chapter 28
1. Isa. 60:1-3
2. Isa. 2:2
3. Isa. 2:4
4. Mic. 4:1-2a
5. Isa. 66:18
6. Zech. 6:13
7. 1 Cor. 12:9
8. Rev. 15:3-4
9. Rev. 20:14
10. Jn. 5:22, 27, Act. 10:42
11. Mat. 25:31-32; 24:30-31
12. I Cor. 3:11-17
13. Mat. 24:51; 25:30; 13:42
14. Jn. 5:28-29
15. Rev. 13:15, 14:11
16. Isa. 14:12-17
17. I Jn. 2:11
18. I Jn. 2:22-24
19. I Jn. 3:7-8

Chapter 29
1. Rom. 10:1-3, 11:5
2. Rev. 10:7
3. Rom. 10:14

Chapter 30
1. Zech. 6:12
2. Zech. 6:13, Isa. 4:5, Ezek. 43:1-6
3. Rev. 21:24-27
4. Mat. 19:28

5. Mat. 19:29

Chapter 31
1. Rev. 16:12
2. I Cor. 12:1-8
3. Rev. 12:11
4. Rom. 11:11-14
5. Rom. 11:25-28
6. Rom. 11:1-5

Chapter 32
1. Mat. 21:28-32
2. Rev. 21:27
3. Gen. 2:10-14
4. Dan. 12:10
5. Rev. 20:8
6. Rev. 20:7
7. Rev. 20:9
8. Isa. 21:11b-12
9. I Tim. 4:1, Mat. 7:13-14
10. Col. 1:27-29

Chapter 33
1. II Tim. 3:7
2. Act. 3:19-21
3. Ezek. 39:14
4. Rev. 16:17-18

Chapter 34
1. Mat. 10:28
2. Rev. 2:27; 12:5
3. Rev. 19:21

Chapter 35
1. Rev. 16:17
2. Rev. 16:18-19
3. Dan. 12:11, Rev. 19:11-21
4. Rom. 10:9-11
5. Mat. 20:14-16

Chapter 36
1. Rev. 21:2-11
2. Rev. 18:2-3
3. Rev. 18:4-10
4. Rev. 18:21-24
5. Rev. 19:1-2

Chapter 37
1. Rev. 19:6-7

Paul Bortolazzo

2. Rev. 19:8
3. Rev. 19:9
4. Rev. 20:4
5. I Jn. 4:4
Chapter 38
1. Rev. 21:23
2. 1 Jn. 3:12
3. I Jn. 3:15
4. Zech. 14:12
5. Mk. 14:25
6. Rev. 19:9
7. Rev. 22:14

Chapter 39
1. Rev. 19:11-16
2. Zech. 8:3
3. Isa. 66:15
4. Zech. 6:12-13
5. I Cor. 15:24-26
6. Lk. 1:32
7. Dan. 7:13-14
8. Rev. 14:19-20
9. Jam. 2:17-18
10. Rev. 19:11
11. Rev. 19:12
12. Rev. 19:13-14
13. II Thes. 2:8
14. Rev. 19:15, Ezek. 39:12-13
15. Zech. 14:12
16. Zech. 8:7-8

Chapter 40
1. Mat. 25:41
2. Rev. 19:20
3. Isa. 2:2
4. Rev. 7:4; 14:1-4
5. Mic. 4:1
6. Jer. 31:10-12a
7. Isa. 10:22-23
8. Dan. 12:11-12
9. Zech. 13:8-9
10. Isa. 66:16, 18
11. Rev. 20:6, 12:5
12. Act. 15:15-16a, Zech. 6:12-13
13. Ezek. 43:12
14. Ezek. 45:2-3
15. Lk. 1:32
16. Rev. 19:11-21

17. Mic. 4:1, Isa. 4:2-6; 10:20-22
18. Isa. 27:12-13
19. Dan. 7:13-14a

Chapter 41
1. Rev. 20:1
2. Jn. 14:30, Rev. 11:15
3. Rev. 20:1-3
4. Rev. 20:7-9
5. Mk. 3:14-18
6. Mk. 3:19, Act. 1:25-26
7. Rev. 20:4a, Mat. 19:28
8 Psa. 13-118
9. Rev. 20:4; 12:11
10. Rev. 20:6
11. Rev. 19:7
12. Rev. 21:9-10
13. Rev. 21:3-4
14. Ezek. 43:2
15. Ezek. 43:4-5
16. Jn. 8:12
17. Isa. 10:20-21
18. Rev. 20:5-8
19. Rev. 21:11-14
20. Rev. 21:7-9

Chapter 42
1. Rev. 22:1
2. Rev. 22:2
3. Zech. 14:9
4. Rev. 22:5; 21:23
5. Rev. 22:4
6. Rev. 22:5
7. I Cor. 2:9

Chapter 43
1. Rev. 20:4
2. Isa. 66:22-23
3. Eph. 1:18
4. Eph. 3:14-21

Chapter 44
1. Rev. 22:14
2. Rev. 21:24-27
3. Rev. 22:15
4. Rev. 20:15
5. Rev. 20:6
6. Rev. 22:18

7. Rev. 20:9
8. Rev. 20:1-3, 9:2
9. Rev. 20:13, Mat. 13:41-42
10. Rev. 20:10
11. Rev. 14:10-11

Chapter 45
1. Rev. 20:13
2. Rev. 20:11
3. Rev. 20:12
4. Rev. 20:15
5. I Cor. 15:24-28

# AUTHOR PROFILE

Paul Bortolazzo is devoted to teaching God's truth concerning the coming of the Lord Jesus Christ. This ministry offers a variety of outreaches including 'Til Eternity Conferences, End Time Seminars, College and Youth Presentations, and Bible Prophecy classes. If you would like more information about this prophetic ministry, please contact us. It would be a privilege to work with you by helping bring an end-times presentation to your church or area.

**Paul Bortolazzo Ministries**
PO Box 241915
Montgomery, Alabama 36124-1915

email:bortjenny@juno.com

www.paulbortolazzo.com

Please check out my website. This site was created to help empower the saints to overcome in these last days. It contains my books, teachings, radio shows, and YouTube's on the coming of the Lord.

.

# 'TIL ETERNITY

## FACING THE CONSEQUENCES OF THE SECOND COMING

### By Paul Bortolazzo

A non-fiction, student-friendly, chronological listing of the 70 Events coming before, during, and after the Coming of the Lord.

In this late hour, the love for the world is at an all time high. False teachers are turning many Christians away from the truth. Church leaders are refusing to judge between the righteous and the wicked; between those serving God and those who aren't. Such compromise will usher in the greatest persecution believers will ever experience. The only way to overcome will be through obedience to the Holy Spirit (Rev. 3:21-22).

'Til Eternity highlights the events coming before, during, and after the Second Coming of Christ. We will begin with the next event on God's end time calendar. After studying the last seventy events in order you will discover:
- *What events will warn His Coming is near?*
- *Who are the teachers deceiving so many?*
- *Where will His Coming end?*
- *When will the Great Tribulation be shortened?*
- *Why will the Beast overcome so many saints?*

Purchase online at Amazon, Barnes & Noble, and the author's website, in paperback, Kindle and eBook. Visit www.paulbortolazzo.com for links, prices, and more details.